The Mulberry Bush

Laughton A. Parchment

PublishAmerica
Baltimore

ISBN: 1-60474-288-7
PUBLISHED BY PUBLISHAMERICA, LLLP
www.publishamerica.com
Baltimore

Printed in the United States of America

The
Mulberry Bush

Chapter 1
Birmingham, England, 1980

Karen entered the bedroom and stood looking at her Mother, sitting naked from the waist up, with two months old Michaela latched on to her engorged, left breast. She watched in fascination as she deftly breaks the baby's rhythm with a finger and moved her to the right breast.

She smiled, "Mom, David said that babies came…."

"Karen, we're not starting that again, are we? Never mind what David said. Don't you think your mother would know much more about babies than your fourteen-year-old cousin?"

"Yes Mom but…"

"But nothing darling, your mother knows best. Have you done your room?" Karen lowered her head dejectedly and turned away. "I'm just going to do it," she said politely.

Kim felt that Karen was not yet ready for the brand of liberated tuition her sister's children now took for granted.

Adrianne, her twin sister, was in the habit of turning up when it suited her. Sometimes alone, but more often it would be with her husband, Keith and their brood of five.

David was the eldest. Bonnie were twelve. Morris ten. May eight, and Dean was six years old. Throughout her pregnancy Kim had answered her daughter's questions, on her rapidly expanding stomach as, just putting on weight. "Lots of women do at certain times of their lives," she'd say, and Karen would pretend to accept this. Then her sister would visit with her precocious off springs, leaving Karen armed with a barrage of new questions.

How could any self-respecting mother share such intimate details with her children? Kim asked herself, and would frequently wonder if they were really twins, or even sisters? She would recall their father saying Adrianne wasn't his daughter and could now understand why. They could not have shared the same womb and be so incompatible.

They hadn't got a thing in common, and looked as if they came from different planets.

Kimbrely West was an astoundingly beautiful woman, with ice-blue eyes and luscious light-red hair. Gorgeous long legs, supporting a body fashioned to perfection, an outstanding woman who was a credit to her twenty nine years.

Adrianne carried her age like a heavy burden. She was born twelve minutes after Kim and it is said she looked ten years old on arrival.

She has a forest of delinquent black hair, Ghostly-white skin, loosely draped over a jumbled assortment of bones. A lean, hungry looking woman with a body that fell straight from her armpits, to her hips without a single defining curve or contour. She has cold, ravenous Grey-blue eyes, and the rampant sexuality of a bitch perpetually on heat. Adrianne believes children should be told everything, about love, life, sex, and reproduction, as soon as they're able to assimilate that knowledge, or have started asking those questions. Every question should be answered and explained with honesty, regardless how searching or intimate.

Kim wouldn't be surprised to learn that the children now sit on the end of the bed and watch their twice daily, lovemaking sessions. She once said sex was her only hobby.

"No wonder you're · always pregnant," Kim had joked but Adrianne was offended.

"Keith appreciates a good woman," she hissed coldly. "He knows a good thing when he feels it. Don't you know too much fat can harm you?" she added with a pointed glance at Kim's bust, then with a smirk her eyes dropped to her hips. Someone like you wouldn't do a thing for my Keith, he'd be lost with all that meat and wouldn't know what to do with it," she made a face.

"Are you saying there is something wrong with my body, or that Peter has no taste?" Kim calmly asked.

She forced a laugh. "Since we were kids you've had everything, all the love and affection. You married a man with his own House and a little money. All the things I wished I had, but the one thing I'm happy about is that you also got all the food, now look at you. Peter could do his back in trying to move you around in bed," she giggled. "As for his taste, all I'm saying is, he doesn't know what he's missing. Five minutes of me and he'd never touch you again. You've not got my experience. He's the only man you've had, what do you know about fixing a satisfied smile of sex on a man's face...?"

"Not nearly as much as you my little twin sister," Kim said with an expression of hostility. "but then you've been doing it since you were ten, and after five kids I expect Keith has to hang on to the bed to stop himself falling in. You are like an old car with too many previous owners. Worn out, smoking like a bush fire and badly needing rings. If Keith likes that kind of thing then it's only because he knows no better. As for Peter, he wouldn't touch you wearing a wet suit, surgical gloves, and a plastic prick."

Adrianne laughed. "And you can't take a joke. Can't you tell when I'm joking?" she asked.

Two can play that game, Kim thought. "Can't you tell when I am?"

God, I could strangle this woman, Kim murmured painfully.

Keith Turner was an ordinary, none-event of a man, whose specialty was drinking beer and sex. In whatever order they came. He was unable to assert himself or make the smallest decisions. He'd go to work and that was where his responsibility would end. He'd dump everything on Adrianne's slender shoulders and amble off to the Pub for another drink. Indifferently, he'd sit through the most heated argument between Bonnie and her mother as though he was deaf, but let there be the merest hint of a rumor that Adrianne was seen laughing with a man down the Road and he'd be beating her into a coma. That was the one thing that could bring him to life.

Kim didn't mind them visiting as often as they liked, she only wished the kids wouldn't fill Karen's head with their brand of garbage, and would love to put a stop to it. But there was no easy way to do that without causing trouble. Besides, the children weren't to blame.

However, something had to be done before they started giving Michaela the same treatment.

Peter wasn't of the same mind and had argued that she was too rigid and somewhat outdated in her thinking, citing his childhood and the value of having a liberated mother.

I know all about your mother and don't want that kind of thing repeated with my children, she would tell herself.

He would point to the fact that at nine he already knew the answers to much more than the meager questions Karen was asking, and that didn't make him precocious or maladjusted, but because of her ignorance Karen was easy meat for, idle gossip, sniggering innuendos and half truths. He didn't care for Adrianne, and detested her bawdy, indecent behavior as much as her anemic frame. Peter couldn't think of another person he detested with such intensity, but praise had to be given where it's due, and he applauded her liberated ideals. He felt she'd got it spot on, where the children's sexual awareness was concerned, and hadn't he hated the woman so much he'd have kissed her.

Peter West was a strikingly handsome man, with an easy contagious smile, a good husband and father, a man completely devoted to his family.

Although there were times Kim would wonder if he wasn't taking his love for Karen a little too far? She would question her motives and emotions, to see if they weren't colored by jealousy, but could find no such evidence.

Peter would be standing naked in the room, Karen would knock the door and he'd invite her in and she'd be the one reaching for the nearest garment, a towel, or anything handy to wrap around him. The times she'd asked him not to do it and had wondered what he was trying to achieve? She was allowed to walk in on him in the bathroom without restrictions, and this had begun to worry Kim and would ignite concerned stirring in her heart. There were other times when she felt he was stretching fatherly love beyond its natural bounds, and would pray history would not repeat itself, for the scars had barely healed. She would try to convince herself she was overreacting but couldn't subdue her fears and would hope it was all in her mind, as she watched six months old Michaela rapidly breaking into his heart and carving out a place for herself, with her toothless grin and light red hair.

Peter would stand silently admiring the child and thanking God for his good fortune. He'd wanted a boy and wasn't ashamed to admit he was disappointed when another girl arrived. But all that had been long forgotten, and now he wouldn't trade her for twin boys.

Kim said she wasn't bothered, but in truth had also wanted a boy, and had shared her thoughts with Adrianne who'd brought it back to Peter.

All this was quickly becoming ancient history, and his only regret was that his mother wasn't alive to see it all come together and share in their happiness. How he wished she was alive and had got to know Kim.

Thinking about her reminded him of something she'd said not long before she died. "Who said we can have it all? Who said we can have everything, or is entitled to more than our share? This could be all we were meant to have so let's be thankful."

Looking at his life at that moment he felt indecently close to having everything and he was thankful. He had his own House, without a mortgage, and over £30,000 in the Bank. Out on the drive was a brand new Ford Granada for which he'd simply written a check. Last April they spent four weeks taking in the Hawaiian Islands, and in the height of that euphoria, decided it was time for another addition to the family.

Karen was never meant to be an only child, but the mood was never right until now. One evening as they strolled along Waikiki beach on Oahu, Kim opened her bag and took out her four weeks supply of Pills. Together they punched them from the Cellophane cluster and ceremoniously threw them into the Sea.

"Do you realize we could be decimating this Island's fishing industry with our irresponsible behavior?" Peter joked. Kim laughed, and soon they were holding hands and racing back to the Hotel.

Their family was now complete and Peter could envisage nothing that could add to the fullness of their lives. Ever mindful things were not perfect, but this was all they desired. They weren't looking for perfection and didn't expect it. Utopia, if at all attainable would be too fickle, and transient. Much too finely tuned to be maintained without it frequently slipping off the rails and going wrong. Even so, he knew what they had didn't come with a forever guarantee, and could just as easily vanish with the next setting sun and be gone by dawn. There were no certainties in life, just hopes, dreams and ambitions. His home and family was the fulfillment of his dreams and ambitions.

Kim was the most deliciously perfect lady he knew, and he loved her with everything he had and in every way he could, but was still looking for new ways to show his love. She was his world and he was yet to meet the woman who could rival this Goddess for a place in his heart, his lust, or his most licentious imaginings. Including the multitude of ravishing ladies he'd come across on their Hawaiian jaunt.

Beyond Kim no other woman existed, for there had only ever been two women in the world. The first, and still the finest, was his mother. When she died Kim took her place in his life and now reigned supreme.

It had begun when Michaela was three weeks old, and since then she'd not missed a day. Karen would get out of bed each morning and go into the nursery to see if the baby was okay, and would spend some time with the smiling infant. She would express her joy at having a sister and not a brother.

"Boys got all the love and affection from their mothers. Had you been a boy I might soon grow to dislike, or even resent you when mom started showing you favors." She would explain that she'd seen it all happen with her cousins. The three boys were placed above the girls in everything, and Bonnie and May found it impossible to do anything right.

She was at their House one day when Dean snatched a Polo Mint from Bonnie and shoved it into his mouth. "There was no need for that, she was about to hand it to him," she stressed.

"Don't snatch," Bonnie said, and lightly smacked his hand. "The little six year old got so enraged that he spat the sweet at her and called her a fat bitch. The same words he'd heard David use. Bonnie dashed into the House to complain and angrily slammed the door behind her. Dean stood thinking for a few seconds, then quickly dropped his pants and peed on the steps, then told his mother Bonnie had locked him out of the house and he couldn't get to the toilet. Nostrils flared in anger she turned on Bonnie.

"What the hell did you expect him to do? How would you like to be locked out when you wanted to use the toilet?"

Bonnie stood looking helplessly at her mother, not daring to defend herself in case she really made her angry.

"And you are a fat bitch. A fat vindictive bitch, and you'll clean up that mess right now," she ordered.

As she went in Bonnie came down the steps, carefully avoiding the mess now dripping from the bottom step on to the paved path. She came up to Karen, standing just inside the gate.

"Aren't you glad you haven't got a brother?" she asked, as if soliciting sympathy.

Karen looked at her in silent empathy, unable to find the words to express her feelings. But if a dozen words had volunteered their services she would've remained silent, for fear of saying something against her brother and have her jump down her throat in his defense.

"Don't ever have one," she continued. "Believe me, they're not worth what comes out of my backside. Just pray your mother never gives birth to a boy—well at least you have no need to worry about that anymore, and you can be grateful you'll never have to suffer the same indignities as May and myself. And don't make the mistake of thinking things would be different in your house. Our mother's are twins and are more alike than you think. Why do you think they wanted a boy and were so disappointed when Michaela arrived? If they had got their prized son it wouldn't be long before they'd be standing around watching him, not just pissing all over himself when he feels neglected and wants attention, but all over you."

Karen would stand there relating these events and thanking heavens for little girls. She was besotted with the child and would marvel at how pleasant she was, gazing at the smiling child in wonder.

Why was she so good? Why did she hardly ever cry? Could it be she really had been made in heaven, and indeed was a gift from God as her mother had said?

No matter how wet or hungry she was she'd never cry, or show any signs of her discomfort, but would lie there silently. Then the instant someone walked in she'd flash her toothless grin, cooing like a contented Dove. Karen felt she was much too agreeable for her own good, for if she didn't cry how would they know she needed attention?

According to her mother, Karen cried incessantly from birth until she could talk.

"And why not?" she'd ask the silent child. "How could I get their attention otherwise? There was no other way to make them understand I wasn't happy with the times they were feeding, or changing me, and had to ring the alarm. That was the only way to reach them and communicate my discomfort. It was my only weapon until I could talk, then there was no longer any need for crying. Michaela, are you listening to me?" she softened her voice to a whisper and leaned into the Cot, rubbing nose with the child. "I'm ten years older and can tell you lots about mom and Dad, and as soon as you're old enough I will. You're still too young, but in the meantime you must let us know when things aren't right."

She would check her, and if she was wet, would pick her up and take her to her mother's room, then come back and get a clean Nappy, and the bag with her things. Kim would change her and take her into the bed and maybe give her a feed. Karen would take the dirty Nappy to the bathroom then come and join them in bed. Taking up the place her father vacated when he left for work. At weekends when he didn't work, all four would snuggle up together in the huge bed.

This routine only varied on the mornings Michaela was dry and didn't need attention. Then she'd stay with her, sometimes climbing into the Cot with her, and would be there when Kim came in.

Michaela was just what Karen had prayed for, a sister of her own, to even the score with her cousins. She would no longer feel left out and inadequate when they swung the conversation around to the advantages of having an elder brother, or sister, who'd protect, and even fight their battles if the need arose.

This was yet another subject she knew nothing about, and would be forced to listen in silence as the experts rambled on, but no more. She was now a fully paid up member of the club with her own contributions.

Michaela was like her very own toy and had completely dominated her conversations with her cousins, Classmates, and anyone who'd mistakenly lent her an ear. She was a long way from the days when she'd need to protect her little sister form the big bullies, but she could hardly wait, and no longer minded her cousins boasting about their experiences.

At times it was laughable to hear them talk, and she'd sit there wondering if they expected her to believe what she was hearing.

They had the innate ability to lie, cheat, steal, and fight each other. They would cut each other's throats for a packet of Crisps, and other trivial reasons, and if they couldn't find a reason they'd do it just the same. From their parents down, they were all the same. Except David, who was morally sound and didn't seem to belong among that bunch of rough and ready rouges.

Morris was only ten but he already had (A levels) in advanced thuggery and was rapidly on his way down a very bad road. He would pluck your eyeballs out while you were staring him in the face, then trade them back to you for money.

But no family, however bad, was completely without redeeming virtues and what she admires most was their uncanny ability to come together and close ranks when faced with outsiders. In the midst of their most violent battle they'd quickly zip together in a combined force if threatened by anyone from outside the family. It didn't matter who was wrong, they would stick together and hang the cost. She'd also noticed that her cousins were never wrong, or at fault when their parents came to administer justice. They would never be judged wrong regardless what they had done.

Like the time Morris asked this seven-year-old boy for a ride on his Bike and the boy refused. Morris got mad, punched the boy in the face and knocked him off the Bike, took it and rode off. But while Morris was busily putting the Bike through its paces, another child had gone to the boy's house and told his mother, and she was waiting when Morris returned.

The woman grabbed the Bike, snarling like an angry cat, and called Morris a few colorful names, then gathered her son and marched off to seek redress from his parents.

Unfortunately, May had got there first and told Adrianne everything. When the irate woman arrived, closely followed by the dozen, or so kids that was in the street at the time, Adrianne was waiting.

Before the woman could ring the bell the door swung open and she stood in the doorway in a defiant, legs-apart, right hand akimbo-stance, with Keith the wimp, backing her up from the rear and looking over her shoulder.

"What do you want?" Adrianne fired first.

"That blooming little bully of yours knocked my son off his bike and took it away and that is stealing, what are you going to do about it?"

"Where you there?" said Adrianne indignantly. "You're calling my son a thief, did you see any of this?" "No but I heard that…."

"You hold it right there, I don't care what you heard. I saw the whole thing from my living-room. Your son fell off his Bike and twisted the handlebar. Morris picked up the Bike and straightened it, then rode it around to see if it was alright. My son is neither a thief nor a bully, and next time you get the facts right before you come to my door," she said then slammed the door.

As the woman walked away, followed by the kids arguing among themselves, Adrianne rejoiced in another victory, and not a word of rebuke was issued to Morris.

The one time Karen had a dispute with another girl she had to stand quietly while her mother weighed the evidence in the girl's favor, and watch her walk away laughing. None of her cousins had to suffer that kind on injustice, despite their tendency to find trouble and invite it home. How she envied them at times. Then there were other occasions when she thanked God she wasn't born in that side of the family. Even David found it difficult, at times, to shake off the dirt that was attached to his roots, and had disappointed her, and shamed himself the last time they were invited to dinner.

It was not a simple matter catering for ten, but Kim had been planning it for days and had done them proud, with no thanks to Adrianne, and in spite of her.

They'd arrived an hour early and instead of offering her help, as Kim had hoped, Adrianne sat on Keith's lap watching TV. Kim bitterly needed the help but was determined not to ask her. Fortunately, Bonnie saw the need and briskly slipped on an apron and joined her in the Kitchen.

Kim was fuming, and wondered why she and her husband bothered to come if they'd rather be in bed?

It wasn't long after that they went missing, and a short time later Peter came down and whispered to Kim that they were in the bathroom working up an appetite.

The children, Kim thought, and her stomach turned with disgust. What if any of them needed to use the bathroom while they were selfishly using it as a cheap Motel?

Kim would've gone up and called time at that instant but Peter stopped her, his hand on her arm, gently restraining her. "I could be wrong," he said, trying to calm her. "I'm going by the sounds I heard coming from the bathroom but they could mean nothing, I could be wrong."

"Peter we both know what it means," she whispered through gritted teeth. She was so incensed she could've smashed a couple of plates....Theirs.

In spite of this the dinner had gone surprisingly well, and at Adrianne's request Kim had put some Bread on the table.

She'd felt somewhat peeved at this request but said nothing and hoped they hadn't noticed. She had spent most of the day in the Kitchen cooking her tail off, while she was in the bathroom fucking her arse off. Only to find she'd wasted her time and the woman just wanted Bread. Why didn't she say so earlier, they could've had a loaf each and it would've saved time. Well if she wants dripping with it she's out of luck, Kim thought as she put the bread on the plate.

The dinner was just winding down and there was one slice of bread left on the table. David reached for it, but Bonnie was quicker.

He called her a greedy fat Pig.

She laughed and silently mouthed a reply, which brought him angrily to his feet, threatening to stab her with his fork.

The laughter dropped from her face like a tear and she got to her feet, thrusting her chest across the table. Her budding young breast, excessively well defined beneath her tight tee shirt. "Yes Master David, you stab me. Come on David," she goaded him and stood waiting.

Kim and Peter looked at each other in mild amazement, unable to grasp what was being played out at their dining table. Was it real, or just a normal after dinner cabaret? Some game they normally played with Bread to perk up a sagging Dinner? Even so, the joke had gone far enough. They had brought it into her home and Kim didn't like it.

By this Bonnie had taken her seat again, but was still giving David the full measure of her rapier-sharp tongue, while David sat silently ignoring her.

There were six at the dining table, with the four younger children seated at a low table in the living-room.

Anxiously, Kim turned to see what they were making of the obscene act being played out by these two, but except for Karen, they all carried on eating as though bored with the familiar.

Kim looked purposely at her sister and brother-in-law, but they appeared indifferent.

At first she'd planned to sit back and let them get on with it, reminding herself, this was the family who hated outsiders butting in on their private wars. But as she seethed with rage her revulsion got the better of her and she had to act.

"Bonnie will you please shut up!" Kim barked at her. "You're not at home, so will you kindly behave like the young lady you're supposed to be? I will have no more of your atrocious behavior at my dining table." Kim got up and went into the kitchen.

"I noticed nobody said a word when David offered to stab me but..."

"Give it a rest Bonnie!" said her father, suddenly finding his voice.

Kim returned with a loaf of bread and put it on the table. "The way to get things in this house is simply by asking for it, not fighting," she said, her remark aimed at her sister.

Kim was never more ashamed and disappointed. Not so much in the kids as their parents, and her sister in particular. That was precisely the kind of thing she was trying to avoid with Karen. She had confused the children with adult ideas, and made them into a bunch of impudent brats. Then to sit there chewing her cud like the Cow she was, and did nothing was more despicable than what the kids had done. She'd kept glancing at

Peter, wondering what he was thinking of her family. He'd not said a word, but from the look on his face she could tell he was about ready to spit on the floor in disgust.

Chapter 2

One Sunday morning in late June, Karen went to the Baby's room and found her lying face down on top of the bedclothes. She'd first thought nothing of this, but as she lowered the side of the Cot and began checking her she became concerned. It was unusual for her to be asleep at this time of the morning, but more worrying were her lack of movement and the chill of her body. She tried to wake her but got no response and immediately panicked.

Sadly, her conditioning had said nothing about getting her parents, and as usual when the child needed attention she'd take her to their room.

Karen hurriedly swathed her in the blanket and picked her up, but as she lifted her out of the Cot the baby slipped from the blanket. There was a tussle as she tried to stop her falling, but she couldn't save her and the child hit the floor, head first.

With her young mind in turmoil, she stood clinging to the blanket as though it still held the child. She wanted to pick her up but couldn't move, her body paralyzed with fear, eyes staring blankly at the twisted body at her feet.

Her parents heard the thud of her body hitting the floor and came running, Kim shouting hysterically, then fell to her knees over the crumpled pink bundle that was her daughter, shouting at Peter to call the ambulance. She looked up at Karen. "What have you done?" she lamented eerily.

Karen was hanging there as though in a trance, without sound or movement.

Peter came in to find Kim knelt over Michaela's body, urgently trying to breathe life back into her, and mournfully pleading with her not to die, desperately coaxing her back to life.

Peter looked at the baby and a huge lump rose in his throat. He tried to swallow but couldn't shift it. Looking at her was like his mother's death all over again. Why did we allow her to take Michaela from the Cot in the first place? The thought ran through his head. "It's our fault," he heard himself say. "We are the guilty ones."

Suddenly, as though accepting the child was dead, Kim rose slowly on one knee and turned facing Karen. "You've killed her," she got to her feet. "She's dead, and you've killed her. Do you understand what you've done, she's dead?" she shrieked at her, with the tears filling her eyes and running down her face.

Still clutching the blanket she looked at her mother with sorrow and regret, then dropped the blanket and ran from the room.

When Peter got to her room she was sitting on the floor in the corner. He sat beside her and took her in his arms, then realized he was crying. "Your mother didn't mean what she said," he spoke softly. Her spasms of sobbing vibrating their bodies and drowning his words. "She was upset and said things she didn't mean. We know how much you loved Michaela and that you wouldn't hurt her. We love you very much and nothing can change that."

"But it was an accident," she said in a voice weakened by her sorrow. "Daddy I didn't mean to do it…"

"Darling we know that. It wasn't your fault, it could happen to anyone."

"Mom doesn't think so."

"Darling you're wrong, she's asked me to say she's sorry and didn't mean what she said."

The Detective was a short balding man in his mid forties, with heavy bags under his eyes, and a nose that showed signs of being damaged at some time, as though he was also dropped on his face as a child. The man fingered his crooked nose and looked at Kim with cold suspicious eyes. He glanced at the Cot, quickly judging the distance to the floor.

"And you're saying that is how the baby's neck got broken?" his tone studded with skepticism.

It had seemed so simple, nothing to it. Tell the truth exactly as it happened and it would be accepted. The truth is the last word and nothing comes after it. That's what they'd thought, but was rapidly learning the real truth.

"You weren't present when the child fell, how do you know what really happened?"

"Karen told us what happened," Kim answered.

"And how do you know it was the truth?"

"Because she wouldn't lie," Kim snapped.

The man took a couple of steps to his right and peered across the landing into Kim's bedroom. "That's your room?" he indicated with a jerk of his thumb.

She nodded.

"Did the child make any sound as she fell, a cry, groan, a whimper?"

"We heard no other sound but her body hitting the floor," said Peter.

"What made you so sure what you heard wasn't Karen tripping over something as she came into the room?" He glanced around the room and his eyes settled on a doll's pram near the Cot.

"At the time we didn't know what had happened….and yes, it could've been Karen stumbling as she came in, but it wasn't," Peter answered.

"What exactly did you see when you got here?"

Kim began repeating the story, but was interrupted as a couple of new faces walked into the room. The man, handsome and smartly dressed, about thirty, clean shaven and looking somewhat Greek. The woman was a pretty blonde of about twenty nine. She wore a plain white, loose fitting cotton dress. Her long blonde hair, raked back and pinned with a couple of combs and tied with a white ribbon. She wore no makeup except for a faint smear of rose pink lipstick. Her smile was a long statement of self-confidence and charm. She was so vibrant and alive that she seemed out of place in this house of death. Peter wondered who she was, and what was her business?

Over a dozen different characters had passed through his house in the past four hours, and he'd begun to lose interest in who they were, or what they did. But this lady was different, and stood out like a light in a darkened room. He looked her over as she came across the room. She caught his eyes and smiled, but his face remained passive, and he had the feeling he'd never smile again. First his mother, now his daughter, and right here in the same house.

The man broke off and joined the two newcomers in a huddled consultation. They were later introduced as Detective Daisy May Spencer, and Detective Andrew Howard.

Peter suddenly realized the gravity of it all, and the thing began to cut into his soul with an excruciating pain. Kim was so numb she couldn't feel a thing. They had lost a child under the most tragic circumstances. It was an accident and he felt a blind person could see that, so why were they being treated like prime suspects in a murder inquiry? What were they expecting to find? He asked himself as Kim led Detective Inspector Julian White downstairs to the living-room.

He was left in the nursery with the Greek, and the blonde lady was left with Karen.

Smiling broadly she introduced herself. "Just call me Daisy, I'd like us to be friends," she said, and sat on the chair at the foot of the bed, while Karen sat on the bed.

Daisy began with hobbies, then she talked about her Schools days and things she enjoyed doing at Karen's age. Gradually she steered her monologue around to Michaela and inquired what Karen thought of her, and what was she like? "Were you jealous of her? Did you resent her getting most of your mother's attention?" she came straight to the point.

Karen didn't answer and just continued staring blankly at the floor. "Don't you feel responsible for having caused the death of your sister?" Daisy turned up the heat. "I'm sorry and wished I had died instead," she turned her head and looked at the woman. "I love her and wouldn't hurt her."

"But that is just what you did," the pretty Detective reminded her.

"It was an accident," she said, showing the first signs of tears.

Daisy came and sat beside her on the bed and put an arm around her waist. She watched her wipe away the tears with her fingers.

"How often do you take the baby from her Cot?"

"When she needs changing."

"Did she need changing this morning?"

"I didn't get to check her."

"Then why were you taking her from the Cot?"

"Because she was cold."

"But you don't take her out for that reason, you just said you only take her out when she needs changing. Was this the first morning you noticed she was cold?"

"No," she shook her head.

"And what do you normally do when she's cold?"

"Pull the cover back over her, sometimes I get in the Cot with and warm her up."

"Then what was so different about this morning, why you felt this special need to move her?"

"She was much colder and didn't feel well."

"Why didn't you get your parents? You seem a bright intelligent young lady. Didn't you know it would be much safer to call your parents?"

"I didn't know that," she shook her head.

"Of course you're no more than a baby yourself, and wouldn't know how to handle an infant needing urgent attention."

"I'm not a baby, I am ten and a quarter and quite capable of taking care of her," she said recklessly.

"That's what you thought but the facts say different."

"But it was an accident. Anyone can have an accident," she said then sank into a shroud of remorse. Shoulders hunched, head bowed in self pity.

Daisy got up and walked slowly around the room, and carne to a stop in front of the TV, and Video. "You're a very lucky girl Karen. Ten years old—I mean ten and a quarter, and you've got your own room stacked to the ceiling with everything a young lady could wish for. Who buys you all this?"

"My Dad," she said proudly.

"He must love you very much?"

"Yes he does," she answered.

"I wish I had a dad like yours," she said with a smile then came back and sat beside her. "Do you know I had to share a room much smaller than this with two sisters until I was nearly eighteen?" she smiled. "I was born in North London and that's where we were living at the time. You couldn't imagine how horrible it was, having to share a room with those two. Having no privacy and no clothes I could call my own. Of course they were my clothes, I bought them with my own money, but that meant nothing to my two ugly sisters. They even took my underwear," she chuckled. "I thought that was bad but worst was to come. One night I went to a Disco in Camden Town and met this boy. He was my first boyfriend and was more precious than my own life. For four weeks we went out every night, and I'd began to lose some of my resentment for those two, now that I didn't have to spend so much time with them. Life was wonderful and worth living. The world was a beautiful place. Never been so happy since my sixteenth birthday and thought it would last forever. God!...Can you imagine how I felt on learning that my sister, Sue, was also sharing my Boyfriend? I asked him and he denied it, but three weeks later he finished with me, and six months after that she moved in with him. I was hurting but was glad to see the back of both of them.

Then just as my other sister, Joan was getting ready to move out, Suzanne started having trouble with Steve. It was the best news I'd had in years. It turned out that another girl had done to her just what she'd done to me. I went to my parents and told them Steve was kicking Sue out of his flat and asked them not to take her back. Joan had moved out by this and I had the room to myself for the first time, and didn't want to start sharing with her again. Mom said they'd have to take her in if she had nowhere to stay, but promised I wouldn't have to share with her again. I was overjoyed and began celebrating my independence, by getting a TV, a decent quilt, and some other little things....And of course some new clothes I could now call my own. As you can imagine, when they moved out most of my clothes went with them.

Everything went well for about two weeks, then one day I came home to find Suzanne was back and had been told to share with me. By then I'd learnt he'd dumped her because she was untidy. He said she was the most beautiful girl he'd ever seen, but she was also the most careless. And I knew just what he meant.

I was so angry at being let down I could easily have throttled Suzanne without a moment's regret…Karen, I could easily have killed my sister, and that wasn't because I didn't love her, I loved both my sisters, and still do. But until you've had to share a room with the likes of those two you wouldn't understand. They would test the love of a saint.

I was the only one paying for room and board, they never gave mom a Penny, and they made my life hell. I was driven to such drastic measures as hiding my clothes, Shoes, Perfume, Towels, and my washcloth. And if I didn't take a pair of knickers to work in my bag I wouldn't have a clean pair when I got home. There were that many dirty knickers in the room the place smelt like a hen house. I have never known those two to wash a single piece of clothing. They would wait until mom was doing the washing and would put them in with hers.

In the meantime they'd wear a pair of knickers until it stank to high hell, then would douse themselves with my perfume. I'm surprised Flies didn't follow them around, and even more astonished Steve had put up with her for so long.

I stood glaring at Sue and she glared back defiantly. That night I lay awake, unable to sleep, with my sister spread right across the bed, thinking she hasn't changed in the least and never will. I thought about Joan, and it occurred to me that her boyfriend could soon be kicking her out also. I wasn't prepared to start that all over again and decided they could have it to themselves. The next day I bought a copy of the London evening Standard and began looking for a flat.

As I thumbed through the pages I saw this add for the metropolitan Police. Before that I'd never given the police a thought, but I knew my parents would hate the idea and I thought it would be a good way to get back at them. It also meant I'd get to leave home." she laughed. "I'd planned to stay for two years then move on, and here I am ten years later with no hope of leaving. Karen I'm trying to point out just how lucky you are to have parents who love you so much. If I had parents like yours there is nothing I wouldn't do for them. Nothing! I would lie, and might even steal if they asked me to, and no one could blame you if you did the same.

But I'd like to think we're friends and that you'd tell me the truth." Daisy lightly stroked the back of Karen's hand with one finger. "Are you sure you've told everything as it happened?" she asked.

"Yes I have," she said, sounding tired and harassed.

"Do your parents get on? Do they quarrel, have arguments?"

"I have never heard them argue of quarrel."

"Do you ever get smacked?"

"Yes," she answered, and fed the question back to her. "Did your parents smack you?"

Daisy shifted around and adjusted her seating, "Unfortunately my parents didn't seem to like me very much and preferred Joan and Sue. Consequently I'd get beaten for the most trivial reasons, and that went on right up to my fifteenth birthday. How often do you get smacked?"

"When I'm naughty."

"How often are you naughty, once a week, twice maybe?"

"No," she said.

"When were you last smacked?"

She thought for a little while then said it was about a month ago. She was late home from School and hadn't done her chores.

"Who did the beating?"

"My mother."

"Is it always your mother who does it?"

"Yes."

"Hasn't your dad ever smacked you?"

"Never," she shook her head.

"Don't you resent your mother hitting you?"

"If I've done wrong I deserve to be punished, and besides, it's for my own good," she said. Daisy laughed.

"Who told you that?"

"My mother," she sighed wearily.

"And you believe her?" Daisy inquired. "Don't tell me you believe that being beaten does you good and make you a better person? If that was so I'd be the best person alive. Instead it only made my backside sore but was no deterrent."

"Maybe you didn't care, but I do. I don't get smacked for the same thing twice. Once I know it is wrong I don't do it. My dad says I'm the prettiest and best behaved girl in the world. My dad loves me," her voice filled with admiration.

"Doesn't your mother love you?"

"They both love me but my dad loves me more."

"How does he show this love? Does he touch you? Holding, kissing?"

"Yes, and he tells me he loves me everyday."

"How does he touch you?"

Karen was puzzled. "I don't know what you mean," she looked at her expectantly.

"Let's get back to Michaela for a while," Daisy suggested.

Kim had barely taken her seat when the man asked. "Do you like children Mrs. West?"

She looked at him disparagingly, and said it was a very stupid question to ask someone who had two children.

"Are you planning to have more children?"

"No!"

"Why not, wouldn't you like to replace Michaela?"

"I can tell you haven't got children, or you wouldn't make it sound as if I could just pop out and pick up another child. Every baby is someone special and can never be replaced. If I had another ten children Michaela would still be dead."

"Why did you get sterilized after just two children?"

"That is my private business and has nothing to do with you or your investigations," she said bitterly.

He looked straight at her, "Why did you resort to such a draconian method of family planning at such a young age?"

"What are you suggesting? That I should've waited until I was forty, and had ten children? Pity I hadn't met you earlier, your advice could have been invaluable," she stared at him with contempt.

"You are a very hostile person and I'm wondering why?" he said accusingly.

"Because I've just lost the child I've been wanting for nine years and you're sitting here asking me damn fool questions. Well I have neither respect nor time for you, and you can do what you like," she got up and walked out.

The Postmortem later revealed that Michaela died from, Sudden Infant Death syndrome, Cot-Death, and was already dead when Karen tried to pick her up. The fall and resulting broken neck had occurred: after she died. The Coroner decided there was no need for an inquest, and the family was exonerated.

Karen however, refused to accept this and persisted with the belief she was responsible for her sister's death. Her new friend Daisy, was among those trying to make her understand and accept the truth, but she could not be appeased.

Losing her sister was like having both arms chopped off at the elbows and this was something she couldn't handle. How she died was unimportant. It was the fact she was dead and she'd now have to face each day without her. She was her child, her sister, Playmate, and a friend. The best friend she ever had. Who would she teach the facts of life the way David had taught her?

It was as if an evil force had taken over her mind and body. Driving her like a possessed being towards the single goal of righting the wrong she'd done. She was convinced what she felt in her heart was right, and that others were only being magnanimous to make her believe that everything was fine, while still blaming her.

During the days her parents would say one thing, and at nights she'd hear them shouting at each other, belying all the good things they'd said. Night after night her mother would sob her heart out, with her father doing his best to console her with words of love. One night he promised they'd have more children. Her mother screamed at him. "Have you forgotten I can't have children? I've been sterilized for God sake."

Her father calmly explained that the operation could be reversed, and when she felt up to it they could see the Doctor and get his advice.

"Peter I'm in no mood to think about that, and doubt if I'll ever be. In any case it would serve no purpose. I don't want another Baby, I want Michaela, but I can't have her because she is dead."

Kim could see no reason for her death, and weeks of counseling couldn't justify her tragic loss and didn't stop her walking along the street peering at every baby she saw, wondering why they were alive and hers had died? Not able to understand why she was behaving in this weird manner. It was no consolation to be told that everyday five babies died of Cot Death in England, and no one knew the reason. This only heightened her problem, and sent her walking into Karen's room at nights to see if she was still alive, wishing she had done the same for Michaela, and blaming herself for not having thought of it sooner. They said it wasn't her fault but how do they know? How can they be so sure about something they don't understand? It could've been the way she'd fed her, or put her to sleep? And where were all the experts before her baby died? She hadn't seen one, but now they were everywhere tossing out suggestions and recommendations. What good is it now, didn't they know Michaela was dead? Perhaps she should've taken her into her bedroom, or into the bed with her? Maybe they weren't meant to have another child. Or it's something that runs in Peter's family? His mother also died in bed without a reason.

There were a thousand if's and maybe's, but in all this there was one thing of which she was positive. Michaela should not have died like this. Not in England in 1980. Not in this age.

Kim had no wish to spend the rest of her productive years bloated out of proportion, spitting out one baby after another, like her sister had done. And the prospect of spending the next fifteen or twenty years on the pill didn't excite her. During her pregnancy they'd discussed it and after much hesitation Peter finally agreed.

Karen had already heard from her cousins that her mother couldn't have any more children, and although not wholly dismissing it, had handled the news with some skepticism' until now.

Suddenly she was pushing herself, head first into an instant maturity that wasn't compatible with her mind, body, or experience. The once close, and idealistic family was soon fragmented. Shattered like a priceless piece of porcelain exploding on a concrete floor.

Karen now believed the key to their happiness was another baby—regardless what her mother said—and this couldn't come about without her help, and began diverting her energies towards solving the problem.

Two months later she'd arrived at the answer and started preparing the ground for the plan she was about to hatch. For the next three weeks she discretely assessed her School friends and all other acquaintances, in a diligent search for the right candidate. Each was carefully scrutinized and evaluated, then rapidly rejected. She needed someone who could be trusted with a secret of the magnitude she was fermenting, and most of those would've shouted it across the Classroom, or to the first person they saw coming up the other side of the street. It appeared there weren't too many kids of her age, adult enough to lend themselves to her plan with the maturity of mind it demanded. At least not among those she knew. Karen thought about it for another week, and was about to write off the whole thing as just another silly childish dream when the name David just presented itself. Why not? There couldn't be a more suitable person. David would meet all her requirements. He was also the person who'd taught her all she knew, while her mother was telling her Michaela was a gift from God in heaven. David would know what to do and how to do it. And if he wasn't sure about the details he could always ask his mother, she had no secrets from her children. Why wasn't her mother more like Aunt Adrianne? Twins are supposed to be alike, why weren't they?

As she rehearsed her approach to David, doubts began creeping into her head, throwing her plan into confusion. All at once she wasn't so sure of herself, and wondered if David could really be trusted, and what seemed a grand scheme now looked Jaded and impossible. As she tried to put the pieces together she realized how much of the puzzle was still missing, and wondered if she had the maturity to fix it and make it work? How would he react as she unfurled the thing in front of him? What made her so sure he could indeed be trusted? He was as tough and resilient as old shoe leather. Too much so, for someone of his tender years, which could well be a cover for the wimp he was, and at heart was really a mother's boy. Her parents were also tough and resolute, but were now cracking up under the strain of Michaela's death. If they could fall apart, why not David?

What if he was so repulsed by her suggestion that he took it straight to his mother? Who would then take it back to her sister.

She could almost see the rejoicing smile on Aunt Adrianne's face as she pointed out that her little angel wasn't so pure after all, in spite of wrapping her in cotton wool to protect her from the dirty facts of life. Your daughter has a darker, more sinister, and perverted mind than any of my so-called precocious brood, and you have the nerve to issue your warnings about what will become of my children if I insist on filling their heads with sex, her Aunt would say. It was your monsters that filled her head with it, her mother would retort. And so it would go on until her mother probably lost her temper and slapped Aunt Adrianne's face. Her aunt would then call her all the dirty names she could think of.

A month after Michaela was born they had a quarrel and Adrianne called her. "A prim, tight-arsed, frigid Mule, who thought she was better than everyone else because she had a little money. But don't kid yourself sister because you're only half a woman now. You could never perform in bed and now you can no longer produce, so what good are you?" Then she breezed out swearing never to set foot in her house, or speak to her again. The next day she was back as though nothing had happened, and they were as thick as rice pudding and twice as sweet. It wasn't safe to come between them, and even Peter had learned to keep his distance when they had a disagreement. If he saw them cutting each others throats with long knives, he'd retreat to a safe distance until it was over. Anyone foolish enough to get in their way would be pulverized, as they shifted their combined frustrations to the unfortunate intruder.

The first time Peter heard them arguing he was so shocked, he blundered straight in and Kim had to put him right.

He'd come home and found them having a vicious argument in the Kitchen, and had got between them and ordered Adrianne out of the house.

"She's my sister, you can't do that," Kim turned on him. "This is something you don't understand."

Peter was struck dumb with incredulity, and for a long moment he couldn't speak. When he finally found his voice, he began with a stutter. "How…how can you defend her after the names she just called you? If she wasn't your sister I'd have killed her, nobody talks to you like that and gets away with it. Not in my presence." He turned to Adrianne. "They put your mouth at the wrong end, didn't they? That gap in your face isn't your mouth, it's your arse-hole."

Adrianne chuckled with amusement.

"Peter I'm quite capable of handling things without your help," Kim said dryly.

"Well, I think it's time to leave," said Adrianne turning through the door. She strolled calmly into the living-room, picked up her bag and left.

"What the hell was all that about?" Peter demanded.

Kim smiled. "There are things I have to explain, and I think the bedroom is the best place to do it." She took his hand and led him out the door and up the stairs. At the top of the stairs she looked in on Karen, she was still asleep.

"Kim I don't understand you," he said, sulking.

"And we can't have that I want you to understand me completely," she answered. Then lay on the bed and brought him down beside her. "Do you know, I believe Adrianne and I began fighting before we were born? I think we had our first battle in the womb, and that must have been when I got her number. Since then I've been running rings around her. I know her more intimately than her husband, and I can handle anything she throws at me. Adrianne has two burning passions in life, and she couldn't live without either of them. The first is sex, and the other is fighting with me. She gets a kind of sexual gratification from calling me names, and her whole face seems to light up. She suffers from a weird sort of ailment. It's a cross between inferiority, and envy, and I like to accommodate her when I can. She said I got the best of everything since we were born, and that I tend to treat her like a poor relation… She was given a very raw deal as a child and I felt the pain with her, But as for me treating her badly— well that's all in her mind. She thinks I'm superior and there are times when she's downright subservient, and insecure."

"That is no reason for you to stand around and let her abuse you, Jesus Christ, she has a mouth like an open drain," he snorted.

She kissed him. "Darling I can be ten times worse than Adrianne and she knows it. I just don't choose to be. She is no match for me, I just like to indulge her because it makes her happy," she kissed him again. "The next time you hear us debating, please get out of the way and leave us alone. Go as far as you can, so you don't have to hear me at my worst, or you may never want to kiss these lips again."

"Can you get that filthy?"

"Can't we all?" she grinned" Adding. "Adrianne and I have the kind of love for each other that even I don't understand. All I know is that I love her very much, and would do anything for her, although there are times when I'd find it very easy to hate her."

"She's a very easy woman to hate," Peter agreed. "I could hate her without trying."

"Adrianne…." she'd begun but he covered her mouth with his hand.

"Let's forget your sister for now," he said. "She wasn't the only reason we came up here."

"I did have something else in mind but it's too late now. Karen will wake any minute," she said.

"We'll see about that," he said lifting her dress somewhat hurriedly.

Karen didn't want to be the cause of more trouble, not after Michaela. This thing with David would have to be handled much more delicately than she'd first thought.

What was now taking place between her parents didn't allow her the luxury of time, to think and be sure. If she was to save their marriage and return sanity to their home, she'd have to act now before they tore each other apart.

All at once her mother had lost some of her finest qualities. Her patience and calm was now a thing of the past, and she'd now taken to shouting at her father for no reason. Then in an effort to be heard he'd shout back at her and a small war would follow. There was no time to lose, but before she could make her move she had to be sure of David.

Chapter 3

About this same time Daisy paid Karen her second visit, and as they talked she decided to throw the pretty Detective a few questions, to see if she might play a part in the show she was currently putting together. After careful scrutiny she assessed that the woman could become the key to her entire plan, and if she was agreeable, then David would be out of it.

Karen waited for a suitable pause in the conversation then inquired if she was married.

"I'm much too busy for that," she said with a smile. "Since joining the force I've not had time, and besides, some people think I'm already married to my work."

"Have you got a boyfriend?" Karen followed through with the next question.

"Not really, but I'm seeing someone at the moment," she smiled.

"Is he a policeman?"

"No, he's not with the Police."

"And he's not your boyfriend?" She pressed for more details.

"He's just a friend at the moment, a good friend."

"Do you love him?"

Daisy suddenly realized the questions were not being thrown at random but put together with a sound objective, and she was being expertly grilled by this ten year old. She exhaled heavily. "I like him a lot but I'm not sure about love at this time." she finally answered.

"What is the difference between a good friend, and a Boyfriend?" The child inquired.

"Which of us is the detective?" Daisy asked, a broad smile on her face and her silver-blue eyes, sparkling with intrigue. "You would make a good Detective. Have you thought about that?"

"Not if it stops me getting married and having children." The child informed her.

"It does not mean I will not get married and have children," said Daisy defensively. "I'm only 30 and still have lots of time for that."

"Mom is twenty nine and she has two—well she had two children, and her twin sister has five. You haven't even got a boyfriend. All you have is a good friend. Can a good friend give you a baby? I know boyfriends and husbands can but I'm not sure about a good friend."

Shortly after she'd interviewed Karen that first day her father had questioned her, and she had related every word Daisy had uttered. He suggested she ignored everything she had said about her family. Informing her that Police was trained to use this kind of deception to gain someone's confidence and get them talking about themselves, to break down their resistance. Karen was very disappointed at being deceived by this lady she so badly wanted to be her friend. But as her father had said, she was only doing her job. Now she had her own job to do. Daisy looked at her hard and long, her face without visible expression.

"Can they?" said Karen breaking into the calm like a pebble in a still pond, sending a ripple of emotion through Daisy's body.

"What are you doing to me?" She asked, her face creased into a puzzled smile. "Friends are expected to be honest with each other, so let's be honest and tell me precisely what you want."

"I only want to know if your good friend can give you a baby?" She said innocently.

"If we have sex without protection he could give me a baby, but we have not had sex because I'm still not too sure about him. Men can be extremely nice until they get you in bed then they change, but why all the questions about babies?" Daisy asked.

"I was only thinking that if you had a baby then I'd have another friend," Karen explained.

"I would think another friend would be the last thing you needed, with your five cousins."

"But I'm talking about a baby. My youngest cousin is six. He's a rotter, and he thinks he's a man. Do you know?" she lowered her voice to a whisper and drew closer. "He swears. He swore at me and I told him he could be arrested for that. He just laughed. Can you arrest him for swearing?" she inquired. Daisy laughed. "I'm afraid not. We haven't got a cell that could hold him. He's too young and would squeeze through the bars," she joked.

"Pity," she said disdainfully. "I think some time in jail would show him what it's like to be a man."

Except for the sweet erotic smell of her perfume that lingered in the living-room for hours after she'd left, Peter hadn't thought much of her first visit. She was a dedicated Police Officer, who'd come to show his daughter the human side of the Police force and he hadn't expected to see her again. That is why this second visit had him worried. He'd have to talk with her and try to find out just what her game was. An innocent friendship was fine, but this was not innocent. She was a Police woman and her kind was in the habit of making other people's business their business. What was she trying to make of the fact that he loved his daughter? Why was she interested in how, and where he touched his daughter? He didn't know what to make of her, but the thought that she might be snooping around to see if Karen was being abused, was one of many notions that crossed his mind. He was so unnerved by it all that when she emerged from the living-room he was conveniently standing in the hall by the door. Just to be sure he didn't miss her.

Jesus Christ! He exclaimed silently, as she emerged and he saw the real woman for the first time. Who cares what your motives are? Something inside him was saying. You can walk into my house any time you like. He'd not seen her when she arrived, and stood there wishing he had. She wore a tight fitting black dress with a low neck, showing just enough cleavage to be challenging. From what he could make out she was wearing nothing beneath the dress. But was ready to accept he might be wrong, but had found it more exciting to foster that belief and had clung to it, as her hypnotic perfume kept hitting him in the head like an incessant left hook from a prize-fighter. For a long wasted moment he hung there searching for the right words, wondering if he shouldn't explain his presence at the door, in case she think he'd been listening? Finally he mumbled something about wanting to speak to her. She flashed a puzzled smile then turned and went back into the living-room, as Karen came out.

He offered her a drink. She didn't want one, adding that his wife had already offered.

"Are you on duty Miss Spencer?" he quickly asked.

"My name is Daisy," she said, explaining it was her day off.

"And I'm Peter, Peter Philip West," he grinned.

She sat silently appraising him and detecting certain uneasiness as he spoke.

"You are an exquisitely beautiful lady, and that dress is....like something straight out of my most erotic dreams," he said trying to conjure up a picture with his hands.

"Thanks for the compliment, and I think I know what you mean. You don't have to draw me a diagram," she smiled sincerely.

"I hope that dress isn't standard Police issue, for I can see innocent men throwing themselves at your feet begging to be arrested." She freshen her smile. "What about you Peter? Are you one of those men?"

He massaged the back of his neck confusedly. "Daisy you've got me so perplexed I don't know if I want to crawl across the room on my knees and lick your feet, or throw you out of this house and tell you not to come back. I don't know what to make of you. You've done your job and the case is closed..."

She sat listening attentively, her eyes fixed on him. "Why are you still seeing my daughter?" She attempted to speak...

"Please let me finish," he said gently asserting himself. "You are the most desirable woman I've met in a very long time. You are simply bubbling over with charm. Bursting at your cleavage with elegance, and I'm curious. I can't understand why you should be spending your priceless free time in such a mundane fashion."

"Are you describing your daughter as being prosaic? Are you saying she's not of enough value, or importance to merit a visit from me? Just who do you think I am? Or let me put it another way. What do you think I want from her? Why do you think I'm here?"

"That's the question I'd like you to answer, and I don't want to be misunderstood, nor do I want to pin the wrong labels on you. Daisy, I was twenty before I had my first close encounter with the Police, and that only came about when I bought my first car. That incident did nothing to endear me to the Police. I—in common with lots of others—see the police as the people you call when you need them, and at all other times they should be kept out of our affairs and our homes, and out of our lives. This has nothing to do with you personally, for I could not ask for a finer woman than you. It has to do with the badge you wear."

"Because I'm a police Officer I have no right to a normal friendly relationship with your daughter, is that right?" she questioned.

"I'm not saying that."

"Then what are you saying Peter?"

"Daisy it's a question of trust. If you are coming here out of genuine friendship then you are welcome here as often as you like. If you have other reasons then I'm asking you not to come back," he said gravely.

"I don't know what grisly notions you've got lodged in your head, but I can assure you that my visits are out of sincere affection for Karen. I can offer no further proof than my word. If you feel you cannot accept that then I'll leave your house and never trouble you again," she said with quiet resignation.

"Daisy I'm not asking for a signed confession of intent. All I need is your word."

"And you've got it Peter."

"Great!" he exclaimed. "One other thing," he smiled mischievously. "That story you told Karen about your family. How much of it is true?"

"Mr. Peter West," she said throwing her shoulders back haughtily. "I'm not in the habit of telling lies to little girls. Every word is true."

"Incredible!" he said.

"What do you find so amazing?"

"The bit about your sisters, I find it hard to believe that someone like you could have ugly sisters," he lied, too embarrassed to ask if she still carries her knickers around in her bag. He was now positive she wasn't wearing any.

"I didn't mean they were physically ugly, they were far more attractive than I was. It was their habits that I found ugly and repugnant. But let's forget my sisters and talk about you. Are you always this trusting, or is it an act?"

"It's no act," he grinned assuredly. "That trust is all we have. Daisy, I do not want the Police, I only want the woman, and would like you to leave your job at the door before you come in. However, that is impossible so I have to take you on trust, and my trust is implicit. I'd like to think that if you walk into this house and saw a hundred stolen TV sets, and two hundred Video Recorders, you'd turn a blind eye. That is how much I trust you." He searched her face for signs of surprise or shock, but her expression didn't change.

"Peter, if you were trying to shock me it hasn't worked," she asserted confidently. "You are not a thief, but if you were, I'd have to do my job."

"And how far would you go to do that job?"

"As far as I need to, and whatever I have to."

"What about friendship? Doesn't that count for anything in your line of work? Would you put away a man you're living with because you learned he was a thief?"

"Without losing a moment's sleep," she said simply. "That is my job and I cannot pretend otherwise. A thief is a thief, even when he's the man in my life."

"Well," he lifted his arms resignedly. "If I'm to be taken away one day it might as well be you."

"You're playing silly games with me and I don't know why?"

"It's no game…You'll see," he said mysteriously.

Chapter 4

Karen sat in the centre of the bed scrutinizing David as he moved aimlessly around the room looking at everything, and nothing in particular.

"What do you think of women who snatch other people's babies?" she asked.

"What do you mean?" he asked, Face wrinkled in a puzzled frown.

"Do you think they should be put in jail, or given help and forgiveness or shot on sight?"

"Shot on sight," he said, anger in his tone. "After a woman has carried her child for nine months and bore the pain of giving birth, she does not deserve the added pain of having that child stolen. Anyone who did that should be stoned in the street, then shot and hanged, just to be sure they were dead."

Karen's heart skipped a beat. "Don't you have any sympathy for such a person? Don't you think there could be a good reason for doing it?"

"For stealing a mother's baby?" David questioned. His face twisted with disgust. "What's got into you Karen? My sympathy would be with the parents….The victims."

"I understand, but couldn't you just lend your heart to that person…."

"No, I wouldn't trust her with my heart," he interrupted.

She grinned. "Come on Dave let's be serious…"

"But I am serious."

"Would you recommend the same punishment for me?—Don't tell

me you wouldn't understand if I did it, after knowing what I've been through?"

"That would be even more repulsive, and as much as I love you I'd gladly shoot you myself. You, above everyone else, should be able to understand what that mother would be going through," he stressed.

"I couldn't do it if my mind is right, but there was a moment shortly after Michaela died when I could easily have taken someone's baby. There is a stage when the mind goes off the rail and one drops into a pit of depression from which some women never escape. Others see snatching as the only solution and have no scruples about taking it." She proclaimed pompously.

David laughed. "How could all this wisdom be coming from someone who, not so long ago, believed babies were sent from heaven and delivered to the mother on the doorstep? That is Daisy talking there, isn't it? What has she been telling you? Doesn't she know you're only ten?"

"Ten and a quarter," she corrected him. I am a Ten and a quarter year old woman. I have everything a woman has. I may not be fully grown but I'm still a woman." She climbed down from the bed and faced him, shoulders drawn back, stretching herself up to her full height. Stifling his laughter he gazed down at the spectacle in front of him.

"And is this Dwarf planning to go out and steal a baby to replace Michaela?"

With her clenched fist she hit him hard in the stomach. "Who are you calling a Dwarf?" She said shaping up to hit him again.

"No more," he said holding up one hand in surrender, while holding his stomach with the other. "You hit hard for a...little person," he gulped a lung-full of air. "How about answering my question?" he said, wisely stepping back out of range.

"I could be," she calmly said.

"What's wrong with you, are you lame in the head?" he growled. She smiled disarmingly. "Don't you think I'm woman enough to handle that?"

"You're joking?" he nervously inquired. Her face narrowed as the smile vanished and she became somber. "My mother can't have children anymore, and that baby has to be replaced. How would you handle that problem?"

"You're talking as though it's your business."

"It is my business David. The problem is mine."

"It is none of your business. That is your parent's problem and you have no right to be taking it on. Why don't you get on with being a child and stop pretending to be something else? Do you think she'd thank you for turning up with someone's baby? Here Mom, I've just stolen this one for you. Sorry it's black but I couldn't find a white one."

"Stop making jokes and answer my question," she said irritably.

"How would you handle things?"

"I'll tell you again my short cousin who thinks she's a woman. Leave it alone. You have not got a problem....Well apart from being deaf. That is an adult affair, they don't need your help, keep out of it Karen."

"But I was the one who killed the baby and it's my duty to replace her, don't you understand David? You have to help me. Please," she pleaded ruefully.

"Let me explain something," he said drawing confidentially close to her. She tilted her head, expecting a secret of some kind, but instead he blew hard down her right ear. She jerked her head back, more in surprise than discomfort.

"Maybe that has cleared your hearing so let me repeat something for you. You did not kill Michaela. She died from Cot-Death. Karen, your sister died from Cot-Death and you were not responsible for her death. You may have dropped her on her head but she was already dead."

She stood prodding her ear with her little finger. "You shouldn't have done that David, I think I've gone deaf."

"You were born deaf," he laughed. Wishing the whole thing was a joke that could be laughed off and forgotten. He sat on the floor and leaned against the bed. He beckoned and she joined him. Her back against the bed and her legs stretched out on the floor."Karen I'd hate to lose you," he said dolefully. "But the way you're going I just might. Kidnapping is a crime and you could never get away with it. You could be put in a home and your mother would have no one left. Instead of helping her you'd make things a thousand times worse. Would you like to be taken away from this beautiful home and be put in a place where you may have to share a room with ten other girls? Some of these homes are not fit for pigs." He turned admiring the room. "This is a beautiful room and you don't know how lucky you are…"

"Hold on a moment," she said. "not you as well? I've heard all that before from Daisy. Why is everyone so obsessed with this room? What's so great about it? It's just another room," and I suppose he'll be telling me how he has to share a room much smaller than this with two brothers, and how they wear his clothes and use his makeup.

"Karen you'll never know until you lose it. You've got this room to yourself and I have to share one the same size with two brothers."

There! I knew it was corning. Go on David. Tell me how they wear you clothes and use your perfume and never take a wash."You've got your own TV and Video."

Never mind about that David. Tell me about Dean wetting the bed and stinking out the room.

"We share two single beds pushed together in a room that is as cold as a Polo Bear's Backside."

A Polo Bear's backside. That is a good one David I must remember that one, she chuckled inside.

"Don't take your good fortune for granted, you are a very lucky girl," he said.

"We have got a problem and if I can't solve it then none of this means anything to me," she told him straight.

"That is because you have no idea what it would be like in a home."

"Nor have you David. You've not been in one so how do you know?"

"I live in one," he retorted impatiently. "In fact it's worse than a home, It's a madhouse and I often wish I could escape."

"What would you do in my place David?" she said getting back to the matter in hand. Explaining, she was only ten years old and couldn't be expected to have all the answers.

"And at fourteen you think I should have those answers?"

"Well you know so much more than I do, and must have some ideas on the best approach."

"What do you really want from me?" he asked.

"I want you to give me some ideas on the best ways of replacing the baby. Just tell me what comes into your head, there must be something there I can use."

"The only thing I can think of is adoption. Your parents will have to adopt a child."

She shook her head vigorously. "Mom won't have that. Dad suggested it but she refused even to discuss it."

"That's tough, for there is no other way," he said finally.

"But there is," she countered. "There is still another way."

David picked himself from the floor and walked across the room to the chair and sat down. "I'm all ears dear cousin, enlighten me please," he sarcastically intoned.

"I have read somewhere that women who can't have children can pay other women to do the job. How much do you know about that?"

"Nothing, except what I've read in the Newspapers," he said with a distinct lack of interest.

"So you are aware that it goes on and is a possibility?"

"Certainly, all you have to do is find a woman who's prepared to rent her body for the right amount of money and you've got your problems licked."

"It's not just money. There are women who will do it for love."

"And you'll find those a lot more difficult to come by," he said.

"But not impossible. Do you agree?"

"That's true," he said indulgently. "It could be very easy for some handsome man who knew where to look, but for a ten year old child...impossible."

"That is where you come in David—And by the way, I'm ten and quarter—you being a man would be more likely to know such women."

"Where would I meet such a woman, in school maybe? And by the way. I have noticed that when it suits your purpose you are only ten-Do you think one of my teachers might lend herself to something like that? They are the only women I know. But let's suppose we find someone who was willing, what would you do next?"

"My mom says a lady can adjust her age whenever it suits her, and when we find that woman my next move will be to tell my Dad so he can make her pregnant," she proudly disclosed.

"All of a sudden you've adjusted your age to about five," he laughed. Maybe you'd care to tell me what your mother would be doing while her husband is committing adultery with this woman and making her pregnant? Your father would have to be a complete idiot to go for that, and what if he did and your mother decided to divorce him for adultery?

"I didn't mean that he'd actually…well…you know, do it with her. There is another way, isn't there? You know, where the man gives some of his thing and it's put into the woman by a Doctor."

"Where do you get all this stuff? Who've you been mixing with? Karen, you've began to worry me, and I'm dreading what you'll suggest next. So now all you have to do is find the right woman, then get some of your father's thing while he's asleep—Or why not ask him for it. That shouldn't be too difficult. You might get more than you bargain for but what the hell? Nothing ventured."

"Be serious David this is no joke. I've just been thinking and we really couldn't use just any woman. She would have to be someone we know something about. David?" she said, hesitating diffidently. "Do you think your mother would do it?"

"You are a scheming…" he paused, searching for the right word. "That's what you had in mind from the beginning. All that talk about snatching babies was merely a trial run."

"David you have to admit there is no one more suitable, and it would work. I am sure if we put it to your mother she would agree."

"You can deal me out of that," he said angrily.

"I don't want you to be a part of it," she said in her most placating voice. "All I need from you is an opinion on how she might take it. I'll approach her myself. You know her better than anyone. You must know how she'd take it." David felt a sudden distaste. "Does my mother strike you as being some kind of a loose woman, a whore Maybe?" he said accusingly. "How would you like it if I suggested your mother was a whore?" She shrugged. "It wouldn't matter to me because I know she isn't and neither is yours. You're forgetting she's my Aunt, my own flesh and blood." She tried to stretch out the conversation but soon realized that David was no longer interested. The subject was closed.

Three months after Michaela's death, Kim was still not eating or sleeping properly and had lost a stone in weight. She was suffering bouts of severe headaches, and depression and would spend her days sitting in Michaela's room staring at the empty cot. Because of this, and her habit of wandering into the street to look at other women and their babies, Peter felt it was not safe to leave her in the house alone. He had been advised by his doctor that she should be admitted to hospital where she could be properly cared for, but he had grave doubts about this. He had no intention of sticking her into some institution where she might wind up being drugged up to the eyeballs. It was not a question of money, for he could afford the best, but what was the best? Peter decided that keeping her at home under supervision was the better move, and after talking it over with Adrianne she agreed to take on the role of day nurse, brushing aside his offer of payment. It turned out to be the most arduous task she'd ever undertaken. Raising five children had produced some trying moments, but nothing to rival this babysitting role. Bonnie was an impossibly difficult child, who would demand constant attention and would cry her brains out if she woke and there was no one with her. But even with her peculiar habits she'd go off to sleep during the day. Not so this baby, who hardly seem to blink, and would move around the house, her lifeless blue eyes staring into space. She had to be assiduously monitored to stop her walking out the front door, or trying to make a cup of tea and scalding herself. This meant she had to be followed around the house all day. Fortunately, within a week of Adrianne taking over she started showing some improvements and was taking her medication without assistance. Her sleeping had also improved, and that deep depression was on the retreat, but her continuing weight-loss remained a problem. Peter was more than concerned, he was worried sick about her rapidly shrinking state. He would come in from work and take her in his arms and could swear she'd lost another five pounds in those eight hours. The thinner she got, the more she looked like Adrianne and he found that same resentment he had for Adrianne was strangely manifesting itself against Kim. Peter had met Adrianne shortly after meeting Kim and had taken an instant dislike to her from that first moment. Over the years he'd not looked at her long enough to see, much less read, the signals she'd been throwing him. Now trapped in his house each day he could not avoid her, and suddenly she was coming at him like bullets from a 9 millimeter gun. One evening he came home to find Karen and her mother in the living-room. Kim said Adrianne was upstairs getting dressed. This was unusual. Normally she'd be ready and waiting for him to take her home.

As he climbed the stairs he could hear her in the bathroom and wondered what she was doing, but thought nothing more of it and his thoughts had wondered back to Kim. But as he got to the top of the stairs, the bathroom door opened and out she came, naked and dripping wet, a seductive grin splitting her face. She explained that she'd forgotten to get a towel before she went in. He looked on in astonishment and near revulsion, as she opened the airing cupboard and took out a towel then went back into the bathroom, leaving the door open.

"Adrianne you should be more careful," he said sardonically. "We can't have you becoming ill as well." He pulled the door shut.

This was toward the end of her first week, and for the following two weeks of her stay she was relentless. Then after failing to tempt and arouse his passion she finally came right out with it. She'd waited until the very end of her stay, and as he was driving her home on the last day, she turned to him as he was pulling up outside her house.

"Peter I know Kim isn't up to anything right now and I know what you men are like, but there is no need to go short. Just pick up the phone and call me and I'll be there in ten minutes," she looked into his eyes, her right hand gently handling her breast through her clothes. "If Keith picks up the phone tell him Kim wants me, I'll understand. I will do anything for my sister, including keeping her husband from going astray."

"Thanks Adrianne I'll bear that in mind if I find I'm going short," he said, not wanting to offend her. He thought of all the gorgeous creatures that'd made him similar offers over the years and had to laugh out loud as he drove away. He appreciated what she'd done for them and didn't quite know how he'd thank her, but if this was her price it was too high. He wasn't paying. When I feel the need to stick my prick into a bag of bones I'll go dig in the cemetery. He told himself.

One night he woke in a cold sweat, fresh from another of those re-occurring nightmares he'd been having of late. These had begun about nine months earlier when he'd first dreamt he was in bed with Adrianne. A week later he had another, and could not understand why he should have such dreams about a woman whose body he found so repulsive, and had never given a sexual thought in his waking hours. He would look at her bony arms and legs, her near skeletal frame, and wonder what could any man see in such a woman? There was a time when he'd asked himself. Why, with so many desirable women on this earth should men turn to their own kind for their sexual pleasures? He would lay deeply embedded inside Kimberly's body, savoring the electrifying pleasures of her body, and the gentle rotation of her hips. Drinking of her breasts, damning such men to the fires of hell. But having seen Adrianne in the flesh he was rapidly adjusting his thinking, and now believes that if she was the measure of all women He'd seriously think about turning to men. Adrianne was just a cheap excuse for not fucking a man. It wasn't only her repulsive body, but her whole persona and her base vulgarity. The first time he heard that her husband regularly beats her he'd expressed real sympathy for the man, and could understand what he was suffering.

He had mentioned the first two dreams to Kim and they'd joked about it, but when they began in rapid succession and with a heavy sexual flavor he decided not to share these in case he was accused of having lustful intentions toward her sister. Kim was not normally a jealous person but details of what he'd been getting up to with her sister, right there in bed next to her would unnerve any woman. She might think that after listening to her boasting about her sensuality and sexual ability for so long he was probably itching to try her out.

Peter would look back to happier times and find it hard to accept that their lives could've changed so drastically. They had gone to bed the happiest family in the city, and woke to find everything had changed, and three months later they were at each other's throats. Kimberly had been the gentlest, most even tempered woman there was. Her words were carefully measured and weighed before they were dispatched, less they should cause offence or misunderstanding, but these days she was so touchy and bitter he had to wonder if she was the same person. He knew the loss of a baby under such circumstances was enough to change a saint into something evil: Just the same he could not understand why her aggression was aimed at him when he was suffering just as much and was no more to blame. But it seemed her frustrations had to be vented and he was the most likely candidate.

One Saturday afternoon he was in the living-room watching football when the phone rang. He'd ignored it for the first half a dozen rings, hoping Kim would take it upstairs but she was in another of her moods and couldn't be bothered. Finally he gave in and picked it up. "Hi Peter, it's Daisy," she breathed softly. The sweetest voice he'd heard in days. "You're just the person I need to speak to, I'm glad you called," he said, unable to hide his extreme pleasure.

"Why, what's wrong?" she said frivolously.

"Nothing is wrong I'm just longing to hear your voice again," he said gleefully.

"Is that all?" she said indifferently.

His heart sank. "Are you off today?" He said foolishly, unable to think of a single thing to say to her.

She said she was at work but would be off tomorrow and would like to drop in to see Karen.

"You are most welcome, what time were you thinking of?" he asked, the excitement back in his voice.

"You tell me what time will be most convenient for you."

He was silent for a short spell then suggested 3pm. "Yes, 3 o'clock would be the best time for us. How does that suit you?"

"That time will suit me nicely," she answered.

"Good, we look forward to seeing you then." He was about to hang up.

"Peter!" she said, catching him the instant before he did. "Before you go, could I speak to Karen?" She inquired.

"I'll call her," he said resting the phone on the table. He stood silently counting. At twenty he picked up the phone. "Daisy, I'm afraid she can't come to the phone, she's having a bath but I'll tell her you called," he'd said, but before the phone was back in it's cradle he had began to resent the person he had suddenly become. He slowly released the phone and slouched into the chair, a perplexed grin on his face. "What's going on?" He asked himself. "What am I doing? I'm in love with my wife and shouldn't be doing this. Kim is still the only woman I've ever needed since my mother died, so why am I doing this?"

Daisy was a remarkable woman but she was not the best. He'd had much greater temptation placed in front of him and had turned his nose up and walked away, telling himself he could derive more sexual gratification from cleaning his wife's shoes. So why was he sitting there salivating over this dish? What was so different about this one? Why was he twitching like a drug addict for a fix of this lady? Perhaps it was Kim's fault, for suddenly becoming a bit of a bitch? He thought in a sudden capricious change of opinion. Kim had been the breath of his life and she still held that place in his heart, but her suffering had changed her into someone he hardly knew, so why not? Why shouldn't he claim this slice of harmless pleasure? Where was the harm in sharing a moment of light relief with a pretty woman who could lift his heart and soul back to the heights he once shared with Kim? Since this thing began he'd forgotten how to smile and his face was fixed in a frown. He had smiled more at their last meeting than he'd done in the past three months, Where was the harm in reveling in this piece of heaven? Reminding himself of a time when this woman could not have held a light for his Kimberly, but most of all he needed her for himself. After so many years his ego was now demanding to be fed, and she was ego vitamins of the finest quality.

Chapter 5

Peter checked the ground ahead as he rehearsed his moves, putting together a piece of deception that could have been spawned by the Devil—himself. Could he carry it off? He wondered. It was so grossly out of character and so alien to his thinking that he'd began to question his sanity. He looked at all the things that could go wrong, long before she walked into his house, and even then it could explode in his face. Having learned of his deception she could get up and walk out. The other thing that kept chewing away at his nerves was her status. The woman she was. She was not a love-sick female who'd walk in with her eyes closed, but a woman who was a trained observer. She was trained to look for things that did not belong and could well spot the frayed edges of his plan, long before he got into his act. How would she take to him blatantly deceiving her? Deception was a crime, and her job was to investigate crime. Not that he thought she'd throw him up against the wall and frisk him, then pull a pair of handcuffs from her knickers, or wherever she kept them on her days off, and shackle his hands behind his back. In fact he might even derive some kind of erotic pleasure from that. He was more concerned about what she'd think of him. Would it affect his standing or destroy his credibility? He had to keep her sweet and foster her best thoughts of him, not to have them devalued and cheapened by his duplicity.

He picked up the phone and called Adrianne and inquired if it was alright for them to drop in tomorrow afternoon. Explaining, they'd have an early lunch and come over about 1.30pm. He hung up and dialed again.

This time he called a friend, a guy named Ian Batten, with whom he worked. Later he went upstairs and told Kimberly they'd be spending tomorrow afternoon with Adrianne. That Sunday afternoon he called Ian at 1.15pm. just before they left the house.

At 2.30 they were gathered in the living-room watching TV when the phone rang. Adrianne picked it up and said it was someone for Peter.

"It's too noisy in here," she said unplugging the phone. "You can take it out in the hall." Peter followed her out the door. A moment later he came back and announced that he'd have to go out for a while but would be back soon. Karen was curious and wanted to know why he had to leave? He said Ian's car had broken down and he had to go help him. At 2.55pm the doorbell rang and he opened the door. She was casually attired in tight blue jeans, white blouse and white open backed flat shoes. The, late September sun, gleaming in her lustrous ash blonde hair. And that perfume. How would he clear her sweet smelling scent from the house before Kim came back? He stood wondering as she came in. She was a disgustingly attractive woman, and it stood out in whatever she wore. Eroticism just poured from her most simple gestures. In the living-room she sat on the sofa and he took the chair across from her. Again he offered her a drink but she wasn't interested.

"Daisy you're a gorgeous lady," he said regarding her with unashamed lust. "I'm so glad you're here." a note of admiration in his voice. "Karen has been talking about you again and It's only fair to warn you that I have an unfair advantage."

"Where is she?" Daisy inquired. "I'm surprised she isn't already here. Didn't you tell her I was corning?" a suspicious look in her eyes.

"No," he said hesitantly. I…I'm afraid she doesn't know you're here."

"Would you mind if I spoke to her?" she asked.

"She's not here," he said with a lame grin of pure guilt.

"And I take it your wife is not here either and we are alone?"

"Daisy, I have not been honest with you and I'm ashamed of myself. It's a cheap trick and I should not have treated you this way…"

"Ok, you've got me here and I expect you've got a detailed plan. In that case would you mind telling me what comes next? You see, I would like to know exactly why I'm here?"

"You came to see Karen," he said without sincerity.

"That is what I thought but it would seem you have different plans for me," she looked at him in a long scrutinizing gaze, as though trying to work her way into his head to take a look at this great plan. It wasn't that she was worried. Curiosity was more what she felt. This was obviously a seduction scenario and she was intrigued by his methods. At their last meeting she'd carefully analyzed him and he came out more like a sheep than a wolf. He would quite possibly make a clumsy grab for her if he could summon the courage, but was the type that could be frozen out, by simply throwing her body into a petrified state. The ice treatment would soon cool his passion, and without fail, his kind normally back away and apologize for their behavior. This was the kind of man that responds to a battle. Fight him off and he could kill. The sheep are the worst of the lot, but they mostly stick to one woman because of the pain of rejection. They take it very personally.

Peter felt a warm stream of pleasure coursing through his body as he realized she wasn't going to walk out on him.

"Let me explain," he offered copiously. "My wife is the finest woman I've known, but since our baby died she's changed. I am not blaming her for those changes but I can't help resenting them and what she's slowly becoming. What we now have is only half a marriage. In spite of that I am not looking for an affair with you. All I want from you is companionship and someone with whom I can share lighthearted conversations, someone to listen. My needs are the same as my daughter's, and I'm asking for some of the same pleasures you bring to her, nothing more. And if I step out of line you could always arrest me," he laughingly suggested. She smiled uneasily. "Right now I'm more concerned about your neighbors, and what your wife will think when she finds out we've been here alone."

"Don't be concerned with that," he said brushing her fears aside. "Let me deal with that. Let's talk about your boyfriend. How is he?"

"I haven't got one," she said dismissively.

He shot her a cynical glance. "That might do for a ten year old but I'm an adult and I know better," he said grinning with conceit.

"What do you know?" she said dryly.

"I happen to know that those overused words…We are just good friends…is always a very thin covering for the real thing."

"And what in your opinion is the real thing Peter?"

"Would you like me to spell it out?"

"By all means Peter, we're both adults," she settled herself in the seat and gently pushed a few recalcitrant blonde hairs back into place behind her right ear.

"I think you're sleeping with this guy," he speculated wildly.

"I slept with my sisters for many years and can find nothing sinister in just sleeping with someone. Isn't that the kind of thing that good friends would do? Wouldn't you share a bed with a man who was a good friend? Wouldn't you share a bed with your sister?"

"That is not what I meant."

"What did you mean Peter?"

"Come on Daisy, you know what I meant."

"But I don't know what you mean Peter?"

"I'm talking about sex," he said. "And I believe you're having sex with that good friend of yours."

"I didn't think you'd ever get it out, you seem reluctant to use the word sex. Are you embarrassed by the word?" a taunting smile on her face.

"The word doesn't bother me. I love it too much for that."

"Which do you love; the word or the act?" mischief in her tone.

"I love both the word and the act. How about you, do you like sex?"

"There's nothing better," she said with a warm smile and a breathy seductive tone. "I love it, naked bodies coming together. I know of no greater pleasure in this life, I thrive on it."

"No wonder you look so well. It's plain you're getting plenty of what you like from that good friend," he said with a festive smile.

"Looks can be deceiving," she frowned wrinkling her brow. "I am not having sex with him, and as a matter of interest I have not had sex with anyone for the past three years. "

With a fixed smile of incredulity, he assessed her carefully but said nothing.

"Did that surprise you?" She asked.

"I'm astounded," he shook his head, grinning fatuously. "I thought a woman like you would spend most of your day beating men off with your truncheon. Don't you like men?" He said as another thought entered his head. Or do you prefer little girls?

"I detect an accusation in you tone and that is almost an insult to my sexuality," Daisy met his skeptical gaze head on. "Peter I can assure you I'm all woman," she chuckled. "I expect you're wondering what I want with your daughter?"

"The thought hadn't entered my head to question your sexuality, or cast doubt on your gender. Daisy you're the most sensual woman I've known." She felt a compulsion to wipe the doubts from his mind and confided that just over three years ago she broke up with a man, and was still living with that bitter memory. "Since then I've become cynical and wary of men. Tell me Peter," she rapidly moved on. "Did you have many girlfriends?"

"Not really," he said still contemplating those three celibate years. It seemed impossible from where he sat. The woman was sex itself, and she was doing things to him that no other woman, except Kim had managed.

"How many of those can you remember, or is worth remembering?"

"I married the only girlfriend I ever had," he answered.

She looked at him as though he'd just landed from another planet and was dripping with green slime. "Are you saying Kimberly is the only woman you've ever had?"

"She is the first and only woman with whom I've had sex," he said with a measure of uncertainty. Not knowing whether to be proud or ashamed of the fact.

"A truly honest and virtuous man," she said in a monotone of irrepressible admiration. "You are a dying breed and there are not many left."

"I'm not unique, I'm not even exceptional. There has to be lots of men around who haven't met another woman that could distract them from their charming wives," he scoffed.

"But you are the exception Peter. Since the age of 13 I have not met a man who wouldn't have screwed me up against the nearest wall if given half a chance. And the married ones are the worst. They are always trying to prove something." She crossed her legs loosely, her shoe hanging from her toes. "Are you uncomfortable with women?" she asked. He looked puzzled. "I don't think so," he answered lamely.

"Aren't you sure Peter? Are you relaxed at this moment?"

"Very much so," he responded with an assumed confidence.

"You seem a little restless and uncomfortable to me. Do I make you uneasy?"

"No." He was concise.

"I have noticed that men are sometimes intimidated by my presence. They tend to doubt themselves. Are you a shy person Peter?"

"Daisy, I'm neither shy nor intimidated by you in any way," he said, then got up and strolled assuredly over to where she sat. He lifted her head and planted a long lingering kiss on her lips. "How is that for shy?" he asked. "Does that seem like a man who's afraid of you?" Then before she could reply he kissed her again.

After a long moment she aborted the kiss and looked at her watch.

"It's a quarter to four," she said. "I must go."

He was surprised. "Are you running away because I kissed you?" he asked, beaming a smile of satisfaction. "Now who's afraid?" He dared her to stay. She smiled at him.

"I'm leaving because it's time I left. Peter I would be a very silly person, and would get myself into all kinds of trouble if I couldn't tell when it's time to go." She got to her feet and slowly his hands encircled her and they were kissing for real. Bodies jammed tightly against each other. Once again she broke off, and breathing harshly she pushed him away and picked up her bag from the floor.

"Not so fast." He held her hand. "Why the sudden rush to get away from me?"

"I am trained to spot trouble and Peter, you are trouble."

"I need your number," he said, both arms around her, literally holding her back from the door. Her cast iron composure began to fritter away by a single kiss, leaving her fighting to protect her honor like an innocent young girl. She gave him her number. He hurriedly jotted it down and followed her to the door, unable to comprehend the speed at which things were now moving.

Karen had waited a full month just to be sure David had not mentioned their discussion. He had indeed run true to form and things were looking good.

"My mother is very ill," she said…. going straight into her sales pitch. "She has been losing a lot of weight, but more, than that I think she's began to lose her mind. She goes into Michaela's Room, and stands over the cot talking to her as if she was still there. She claims my father has not touched her in months and I know that's a lie…"

"How do you know that?" he asked.

"I've seen them!" she bristled, "with my own eyes."

"You actually saw them?" David inquired.

"Yes!" she said impatiently. "Two, three, half a dozen times a day my father would take her in his arms and tell her how much he loves her. Every time she cries he'd go to her and she'd be in his arms, and that is much more than he'd done for Michaela. How can she say he's not touched her when she knows it isn't true, and that I have seen them together?" For a short while he was tempted to explain things to her but changed his mind. Her innocence was pure and refreshing, and he felt it would be nothing short of sin to destroy something so rare. Sadly, that day was on its way, and as he'd already done enough harm to her in that department he saw no need to add to his crimes. He was astonished at the thought that his eight year old sister was far more enlightened and would have known the score. He dragged his thoughts back to the matter in hand. "Alright your mother has a problem but what has that to do with me?" he rasped impatiently.

"It has to do with both of us, you and me, you giving me a baby. You're a man and I'm a woman, you can make me pregnant. My mother would then have the baby and the problem would be solved. What do you say?"

"I'd say you're the one that's going out of your mind and not your mother. You are absolutely out of your ten year old mind. You are a sick child and I refuse to have anything to do with you or any of your wild schemes."

"But you promise to think about it and give it your full attention," she reminded him.

"I have thought about it and the answer is no, and if I had another two years to think about it the answer would still be no. You are ten years old, what makes you think you could become pregnant?"

"I'm ten and half and I know I'm ready."

"What are you ready for Karen?"

"Whatever it takes to make me pregnant...And why do you keep reminding me of my age David? It can't be for my benefit, so it must be to remind yourself that you're not dealing with a 16 year old. I am much nicer and more grown up than that stupid girlfriend you have so what are you complaining about? I bet you wouldn't have to be asked twice to give Petra James what she wanted?"

"She is not my girlfriend, I don't even like her."

"That's not how she tells it, and what about that night in this very room?"

"I keep telling you there was no such night," he protested.

"Anyway, you promised to think about it and you've gone back on your word, you can't be trusted," she began to cry. "You promised," she cried.

David was concerned in case his mother heard her crying. "Stop crying, my mother will hear you," he coaxed her.

"I don't care," she wailed.

"You should if you know what's good for both of us." He covered her mouth with his hand. "How would we explain this if my mother should walk in now?"

She jerked his hand away. "I don't care," she repeated, and quickly turned up the volume.

"Alright I'll do it," he relented.

"You will?" she inquired in disbelief.

"I said so, didn't I?" He barked angrily.

She stopped crying and began to dry her eyes.

"Take off your dress and your knickers," he ordered. She gazed at him more incredulous than before, a petrified look in her eyes.

"Don't just stand there staring at me like an idiot I said take off your dress and your knickers, are you deaf?" his face in a fixed grimace.

"What for?" She asked, in a tiny panic-stricken voice that barely carried.

"You want a baby, don't you?"

She licked her lips nervously, but offered no reply. "Well you want this baby or don't you?"

"Yes but we can't do it now."

"Why 'not?'"

"We have to wait until it get's dark, adults only do it in the dark." Eyes wide with fear she added. "I can't take my clothes in front of you cause you'd look at me."

"Alright I'll leave the room."

"No!" She said frenetically. "what if one of your brothers came in and saw me?"

"They are all out except for my mother, and she will not come up here unless she hears something suspicious. Karen you're wasting my time. I want to see what I'm doing and don't intend doing it in the dark. You either take off your clothes in the next five minutes or we forget it. Let me help you," he offered, and reached out for her.

"No!" she said tucking her dress between her legs and locking her knees together. "I can't. I can't do it now."

"So you don't want the baby?"

"Yes, but when it gets dark, you can come over to my house and we'll do it," she offered without conviction.

"If you can't do it in the light you're not ready for it, so make up your mind. Are you ready or not?"

"Can't I think about it?" She said.

"You are clean out of time." His discordant words sent a chill through her. "You have had weeks to think about it. All that time you kept dancing me around with tales of snatching babies, and surrogate motherhood, this was where you were heading. You knew all along that you wanted me to make you pregnant, and should have thought it out before now...I am a woman, you said. I have everything a woman has. So where did that woman go? How is it that all I can see is a sniveling, frightened little child with her dress tied to her body as though there was a mouse loose in the room?" She moved lethargically across the room and sat in the chair. On the floor next to her was a huge Teddy Bear. She picked up the huge toy and embraced it. David smiled triumphantly to himself. He called her bluff and she fell apart like a broken toy. He had her right where he wanted her. Maybe now she'd get off his back? Still, he felt some guilt for what he'd done to her. He'd felt real sympathy as he watched her secure her dress. A look in her eyes as if she was about to wet herself, and if she did it was her own fault. She brought it on herself. He looked at her, the Teddy Bear almost obscured her from view.

"Those tears were a pretty neat trick," he said.

"Are you angry with me for crying?" she asked.

"Why should I? You are in training to be a woman and I expect you have to start somewhere. Someone has to be your first victim. Tears are a very effective weapon my mother has used it many times on my father."

"I don't understand what you're saying," she frowned irritably.

"Oh, I suppose tears come naturally to a woman?"

"You're not making sense David I don't know what you're talking about," she said in consummate innocence.

"Okay, let's talk about sex, a subject you know even less about. Let me enlighten you. First if all, to get a baby we need to have sex, and to do that you need to get undressed. Until you're ready for that we have nothing to talk about."

"David Turner," she said with a pretentious air. "I am not asking you for sex, from what you tell me it's not much fun anyway. I only want to be made Pregnant, and was hoping there was another way we could do it."

"I don't want to know about it, or any further ideas you may have in mind. I've had enough of your childish games," he said quietly.

She shrugged indifferently. "If you don't want to help me I can always find someone else. There are boys around who'd be willing to do it," she smiled.

How true, he told himself. There were too many lads around who'd jump at such an opportunity, and would be allover her before the words were out of her mouth, and there was one living next door. Jason Bennett. He was the same age as David but where the subject of women was concerned Jason was ten years older.

David had thought he was well versed on all things sexual. Thanks to his liberated mother, he'd learned much about the man's role, and the functions of the female anatomy. To supplement her teachings she'd bought him two books on the subject, which he read studiously. David knew all there was to know about the theory of sex and what to do when the time came, but the time had not yet come.

Yet in spite of not having read a single book, or anything else Jason could teach him things about women even his own mother didn't know.

They would sit for hours while Jason enthralled him with the details of his exploits with women. One of these women was said to be twenty-years old, and David found this a little hard to digest. A sudden concern for Karen's welfare flashed through his mind and he knew he had to stop her making that offer to anyone else. It didn't matter what he had to promise her. She was naive enough to try it, and desperate enough to go through with it. He had shown her up for the child she was and she was hurting in such a way that she was ready to go out and show him she was not afraid.

What had possessed her? He wondered as he watched her playing happily with the Teddy Bear. She was a gorgeous child and he'd been proud to say they were cousins. She wasn't just family. She was a friend, and was the kind of person he'd have chosen as a friend even if she wasn't family. Not like his two sisters. None of whom he'd have chosen.

If only Karen knew what she was asking of him? He reflected their discussions. He'd been waiting a long time to put some of what he'd learnt into practice, and had been kicking around some ideas of how to go about it, but couldn't decide on how to make the first move.

What would he say to this person? What words would he use, and where would he find the courage to get those words out for the first time, without stuttering or mumbling?…Without his shyness and lack of experience grabbing him by the throat and choking off the words before he got them out? Perhaps he could walk up to the girl and ask. Can we have sex, or can we make love? What if she was so sheltered that she didn't know what he meant? Would he need to be more explicit? He saw that as being very unlikely, but felt he had to be prepared. He hoped held never have to use that dreaded word to a girl, for fear of biting his tongue in the process. But if that was the language of love then he'd have to do it somehow. David realized for the first time how inadequate his mother's teaching had been. The approach was the most vital part of his education and the first thing he should've been taught. How to meet girls, should have been the first thing, and next how to ask for sex. What was he doing with this vast store of superfluous knowledge when all he needed was the basics? It didn't matter a bean how much he knew about the mechanics of a woman's body, without the approach he had nothing and was going nowhere, because everything follows on from that.

So why wasn't there a single word about this in any of the books he'd read? Perhaps, both his mother and those pseudo-intellectuals were of the same mistaken belief that it would come naturally at the right moment? In his mind this was the right moment, so why wasn't it coming? His definition of that moment was anytime he was ready for sex, and he was ready. In truth he'd been ready a year now and had been trying to get it right in his head before making the move.

If he dared move before he knew what to say he'd be doomed to failure and ridicule, and this was his worst nightmare. He'd heard girls talking in very derisive fashion about boys who'd not lived up to their expectation. Soon the entire school would know that David Turner didn't know how to ask for it. Next it would be all over Lozells and he'd be forced to leave home to avoid the shame. Now here was this sweet child begging him to take it. Here was his chance to slay that confounded Goliath and he stood there prevaricating like an harassed politician. This was a golden chance to begin his carnal journey with someone much less versed than he was. One he could twist around his lack of experience and she'd go away thinking he was a genius. Best of all she'd keep her mouth shut. Would he ever be so favored again? If only she knew what she was asking, or the size of this temptation she was pushing at him? But how could she? He had taught her all she knew, but what the hell did he know? The child would've been shocked out of her pants to learn that he'd never done it, or knew how to ask for it. He was so fired up and anxious to get over this first hurdle that had she removed her knickers and faced him, there was no telling what he might have done to her. Even with it being the furthest thing from his mind. He had no intention of doing such things to her. She was his cousin and her loved him endlessly, and would have hated himself for the rest of his days if he succumbed. Only a short time earlier he'd gone to Jason, inquiring how he'd gone about getting girls for the first time. This time Jason told him about another woman, and this one was twenty five years old. The advice he got was the best he'd received and was the plan to which he was still holding firm.

Jason said he'd gone off girls his own age from the time Cathy Taylor led him into thinking she was ready for the real thing. Then after taking her into the Gym and sticking his fingers inside her knickers, she began screaming. After he took his hand away and stepped back she was still hollering. For that he got a caining from the Headmaster and another from his mother. "Then the bitch went and told her brother a pack of lies and he damn near broke my nose one night as I walked home along Lozells Road. Can you imagine how I felt taking all that beating for a dirty crotch I never got?"

"I can imagine how you felt," David was sympathetic.

"Although, knowing what I do now I can't blame her for screaming. It could've been my fault," Jason acknowledged, and mused with a wan smile. "I was so anxious, I pulled her in and shut the door then went straight for the meat. I didn't know any better and was so excited that I could easily have injured her with my nails."

"Didn't you speak to her after that?" David inquired.

"I didn't go near her after that. Bloody hell!" he exclaimed. "I was afraid she'd scream again. Besides, that beating from her brother had put me right off the bitch."

Chapter 6

Jason told him about a story he'd heard when he was twelve years old. It was about a 35 year old mother of three who'd taken her twelve-year-old babysitter to bed. She'd got away with it for about nine months until the day the boy had a disagreement with his mother, and in a temper, told his sister he was leaving home to live with the woman and her husband because they didn't handle him like a child. He suddenly strayed from the story. "Little girls are not nice," he said shaking his head disdainfully. "When they grow up they're okay, but until then they are dirty scheming brats."

I know exactly who you're talking about but I didn't think you knew my sister that well, David smilingly thought. Jason continued. "The girl conned her brother and got him to tell her the whole story, then took it straight to their parents. Stay away from girls your own age, try to find someone older. A woman in her twenties would be best," he asserted confidently. He explained that she would be more patient and tolerant. Such a woman would have enough experience for both of them, and wouldn't expect him to know a lot. In fact she'd like it much better if he was as green as a cucumber and never been touched.

"You could always lie about that, and play the fool. That's easy," he said, laughingly. "and she'd be willing to teach you all she knew. They love the sense of achievement and the satisfaction that goes with having something no other woman has had, or ever will. She was the first and nothing can change that. David, these women are more easily available than you think. I've had three, and each time I was a virgin," He laughed childishly. David sat mesmerized by his courage and audacity.

David had no great love for Jason but he couldn't help admiring the boy. He was a number of things that David detested, but there were others where his admiration bordered perilously close to envy. He would've swopped both his sisters for a little of Jason's guile and prowess with women, but there was nothing else about the boy that inspired him.

Jason had an intense aversion to school, the teachers, the entire establishment, and the discipline that went with it. He would spend his days walking the Streets and on the rare occasions he turned up in school he'd be so disruptive that the teachers deemed it a blessing when he was absent.

One teacher who came in for some strong attention was Joan Meredith. She was a delicately enchanting, twenty-five-year-old, not long out of training College. Unfortunately Jason took a liking to her and gave her his special attention. Joan came from Frome in Somerset, and had brought with her a rich West Country accent, which the kids loved to mimic, even as they addressed her. She was a pretty woman with short blonde hair. Flat, somewhat underdeveloped breasts, a slim waist and fine generous hips. An unassuming and over indulgent lady, who would smile luxuriously as they mocked her phrasing and intonation. Joan had no right in that vocation, not in this age. Three decades back she might just have carried it off, but as it stood she couldn't lift it, and she couldn't carve it where it sat. She was the classic example of someone taking a wrong turning and winding up at the wrong place, at a bad moment. She was fresh meat. Prime and tender, just the way they liked it and within a month of her arriving the kids had began to eat her alive, as she stood there smiling sweetly.

Joan should have gone in for something where her beauty and temperament would have been an asset, a job dealing with people who would appreciate her fine qualities, and grace her with the respect and gratitude due to such an outstanding lady. A profession that did not demand constant assertiveness. A quality she did not possesses in abundance. She'd have been better suited for almost anything, but standing in front of a gaggle of obnoxious children, trying to enlighten and mould them against their will, into responsible citizens. Children who were quick to spot her inadequacies, noting that she tended to wobble under pressure, and kept her teetering on the very edge of her endurance. She was completely wasted on that bunch of protesting delinquents. Tossing her in their midst was like feeding best Caviar to a herd of pigs.

She was a lady of priceless serenity and impeccable taste. Never wearing the same outfit twice inside a fortnight, which some of the girls considered a good reason for resentment. One day she gave the class a lecture on their lack of personal hygiene. Giving special attention to the girls and highlighting their special problem. Pointing out that there was a special time when they had to be exceptionally vigilant, something they were clearly not taking on board. Stressing that this could lead to some embarrassing moments, especially in a mixed gathering such as a classroom.

"To spell it out for you so there can be no misunderstanding, you need to wash more often. At least once a day. If you can't wash the whole body then do the vital areas, and I don't expect you need to be told where those are." The boys were rocking about in their seats with laughter and derisive comments. Jason looked across knowingly at Cathy Taylor.

"You boys have no reason to gloat," said Joan gravely. "Because that advice is also aimed at you. Soon you'll start forming relationships, and no girl with pride in herself would get close to you if you smell of last week's perspiration—"

"Jason has already started a relationship miss," shouted one boy from the back of the class.

"I have no desire to share that kind of information, thank you very much Andrew," she said crisply. "What Jason does after school is his parents concern."

"But he does it during school hours miss."

"Shut up Andy you're only jealous," Jason barked angrily.

"Me jealous?" The boy spat vindictively. "I don't want to be a play thing for someone eight years older than me." David was taken by surprise, and knew for the first time, that what he'd shared with Jason was not a secret but was in fact public knowledge.

Jason looked at Miss Meredith and saw a look on her face he could not decipher. Her eyes fixed on him, but seem to be looking straight through him as she tried to assimilate what she'd just heard, trying to assess its authenticity. For a rare moment Jason was trapped like a frightened Rabbit and didn't know which way to turn. "My mother does the washing in our house Miss," he suddenly said without rhyme or reason.

"Don't change the subject Jason," cried one of the girls.

"I wasn't," Jason argued vehemently. "Miss was talking about washing…"

"And we were talking about babysitting. Boys who spends more time with the mother than the child he's supposed to be sitting," she retorted.

"You will all shut up!" Joan shouted brusquely. "I don't want to hear another word on the subject."

"Do you mean washing or babysitting, Miss?" the girl inquired to a burst of laughter.

"Both!" said Joan, trying to inject an element of calm.

After that the thing wouldn't let her rest and she wished it hadn't been brought to her attention, or that it could be flushed from her mind and forgotten. Instead it hung there heavily on her mind, reminding her that it was her duty to, at least, try and save the boy from himself. Someone had to do it for he was incapable of rational judgment or knowing what was best for him. The woman was also breaking the law and should be put away before she does further harm to the lad, and keep her away from others who might get caught up in her web of obscenity. Something had to be done but first, Joan had to be sure it wasn't a prank they normally played on new teachers. For that reason there was no point asking the kids for the truth. Their credibility was now suspect and she could not believe anything they might say. For the rest of the morning she wrestled with this thing that kept fouling her mind, trying to get an angle on the truth. Then just before lunch the answer strolled into her classroom…Victor Rush… Victor was Jason's teacher before she took over. At lunch she had a talk with Victor and was strongly advised to pretend she hadn't heard and leave it alone. "Forget it Joan, the boy isn't worth saving," he said bitterly. She was horrified. "How can you say that he's somebody's child and it's our duty as teachers…."

"Forget everything they taught you in college," he said shoveling a load of coleslaw into his mouth, then dragging a tissue across his lips to mop up the spillage. "They spend all that time training us to teach children, then the minute we were ready they brought us here to the Radcliffe Road Menagerie, and threw us in a cage of wild animals. This is not a school, It's a Zoo, and you don't walk into a Zoo and start reaching out affectionately to the animals. You don't go around poking your hands into cages until you know the kind of animal you're dealing with. You could lose your hands, or any other part of your anatomy you treat with such base disregard. Joan you're about to lose your head over something that is quite the norm around these parts. We've been deceived, we don't belong here. You upset one of those kids and he'll punch you on the nose, and don't think they won't do it because you're a woman. You'll forgive my language," he said apologetically. "But that boy, Bennett, would just as soon fuck you as fight you, and the girls are even worse. I wouldn't have the nerve to repeat some of the things those budding whores have done to me. I have gone home and opened my briefcase to find a used sanitary pad. One morning I opened my draw and found a pair of tiny red knickers with a note attached. Guess who fancies you and isn't wearing any? Don't wear your heart where they can get to it or they'll break it," he said finally then closed his cutlery along with his mouth. He sat back, his tongue rolling vigorously over his teeth and around his mouth as he cleaned up, sucking his teeth noisily. Joan was disgusted, and sat picking at her food thinking. You are the animal Victor Rush, not those kids. And whatever they are you are probably responsible. You're not fit to handle cockroaches. She looked at him. "Victor I think you're wrong," she said decisively. She watched him, her eyes grave with concern. More for him than the children. At least they had open minds, his was clogged up with fear and intolerance. "I think those children will respond if we touch them with love and some decent human emotions. I sense that they're crying out for a little understanding and a lot of love. There is nothing wrong with an adolescent girl liking you, I was the same at that age. And that boy could be going with that woman because of the affection that's otherwise missing from his life."

"The-boy is going with that woman because he's a filthy degenerate bastard. Dear Joan," he smiled commiseration. "You are much too young, too pretty and much too idealistic for this place, and you're heading for a broken heart." He got up and pushed his chair back, excused himself from the table and walked away. She'd learnt that Jason was not only seeing the woman—who was unemployed and had a boyfriend her own age—in the evenings and at weekends, but had began spending school hours with her. Joan looked at her plate of food with regret, as she tried to digest the information that was now lying heavily on her chest and had wiped out her appetite. She pushed the plate away gloomily and got to her feet. She was going out the door of the staff canteen when a feeling of resentment and heart thumping animosity swarmed over her like a sheet of fire. "Damn you Victor Rush. Damn you. I will not let you depress, or defeat me. Those children are not lost and I will prove you wrong," she said talking loudly to herself as she headed back to her class.

For the next twenty minutes she sat at her desk marking some papers and plotting the way ahead. By the time class re-assembled she'd got it finely tuned and was quite pleased with herself. Having carefully looked at Jason's case she decided that a little wise counseling would be the best way forward. There was no profit in blindly barging in and getting the woman arrested and earning the boy's resentment and hostility. She would calmly point out the dangers of his involvement with this much older woman, and get him to see reason. Tomorrow evening, she promised herself. I'll keep him after class and have my first talk with him.

For the next three days Jason was not in school and her well prepared talk had to be postponed. Then much to her surprise, when she arrived on Friday Morning there he was sitting high on the back of his chair, with his feet resting on the desk. As she walked in—as though it was a mark of respect—he lowered his feet to the seat of the chair.

"Mr. Bennett," she said addressing him with her most ebullient smile. "I see you've honored us once again with your presence. It's good to have you back, are you better now?" she added artfully.

"It was my mom," he said. "but she's much better now and she said I could come today." The entire class erupted in a burst of cynical laughter. Joan lowered her head in stifled amusement.

"And what was wrong with your mother?" She humored him.

"She was sick miss."

"I know, you've already implied that. What I want to know is the kind of illness. What did the doctor say?"

"We didn't get the Doctor Miss."

"Oh, it was that kind of illness?" She said, promising herself she'd talk to him that evening.

She took a couple of books from her bag and placed them on the desk, and put her bag under the desk, then turned and opened the blackboard. She stared at the board, her eyes blinking rapidly in disbelief. She read it again, then once more. Yes it was meant for her, it was in her name. What had she done to deserve this? Hadn't she been nice to them? She read it again.

MISS MERIDITH HAS A FAT ARSE AND NO TITS, BUT I'D GIVE MY RIGHT BALLS TO RIDE HER. BAREBACK, OR WITH A SADDLE. AND TO CHECK HOW OFTEN SHE WASHES THE PARTS WE CAN'T SEE.

Saddle was school slang for french-letter.

This was downright complimentary compared to what other teachers had to endure daily, but for Joan it was the ultimate insult. She could not believe he'd done this to her, what harm had she done him. With her body tremulous with rage and the name of the culprit pounding in her brains, she turned and marched over to where Jason languished. "'This is your dirty work, isn't it?" she accused him. Astonished laughter rippled through the classroom, at her glaring error.

"Jason didn't do it." Someone said, but Joan was too affronted to hear, or care. In her mind everything pointed to him being the offender. Wasn't he in the habit of standing behind her making rude gestures? Wasn't he guilty of sleeping with a twenty-two-year old woman, and was now thinking he could do the same to her? Then there was Victor Rush's words ringing in her head. That boy Bennett would just as soon fuck you as fight you.

With this evidence he'd been summarily tried and condemned. Guilty, guilty, guilty on all counts.

"Miss I didn't—" He'd began, as her right hand swept upward and met his face with a resounding crack—that echoed around the room and could be heard above the residue of laughter that had lingered in the air— cutting the words off in his throat.

"And you're also a liar," she said, spewing her frustrations. The class fell into a deathly silence as they waited for Jason to physically take her apart. They had watched him lay into Victor Rush for calling him a stupid git, he didn't take this kind of thing from anyone.

It was with astonishment and disbelief that they watched him slide from the back of the chair onto the seat. His eyes fixed on her and his face in a confused and pitiful half-smile. She glaring back at him as if trying to decide if another blow would finally alleviate the pain she still felt inside. Wiping away the tears from her eyes she turned and walked remorsefully back to her desk, already repenting her silly mistake. She had been tested and found wanting.

How could she let a childish prank get that far, and lose her head, along with whatever little respect they might have had left for her? Where were all her good intentions now? What will Victor think when he hears this? Then horror-struck, she suddenly remembered Jason couldn't read, and Joan wished she could die and go straight to hell.

A feeling of clemency for this inexperienced young woman was rapidly replacing any anger Jason felt toward her. He felt she had not struck out for what she thought he'd done, but had been chosen to pay for all the pain and discomfort they'd caused her since she had arrived. Joan stood by her desk. The class, hushed and waiting for her imminent address, then she seem to quail, as though her nerves had deserted her. She raised her hands, as if asking to be excused, or it could have been in surrender, and walked out the door. Before the door had closed behind her a heated and untidy debate began, with almost everyone clamoring for the sinner to own up. Jason didn't care one way or the other. Where he was concerned the matter was closed and he hoped Joan felt the same way. His mother was the only other woman who could've gotten away with that. She had made an enormous error, but the odd thing was that he found himself liking her even more.

Jason was rapidly learning that sex and aggression were first cousins and members of the same family. Or perhaps it was the fact she was capable of mistakes like everyone else. Whatever it was the lady had warmed his heart and school was about to become a pleasure after all.

As this was going on his head Cathy Taylor went to the blackboard and wiped it clean, then admitted she'd done it and was sorry Jason got blamed, but she had to bring the—Butter wouldn't melt in her mouth—bitch down from her high horse.

God, she's still making me pay for putting my finger inside her. He was thinking, as she came toward him smiling. "Jason I'm really sorry," she said oozing sincerity. "I didn't think you'd get blamed."

"Don't worry about it," he smiled. "No harm done. Sit down I have a question for you." His smile broadened. And as she sat next to him he knew that school was going to be a great place from here on.

Chapter 7

Peter lay in bed watching Kim as she got dressed, thinking about the woman she was. Wildly speculating that her beauty could have been one of Mother Nature's mistakes she was now hurriedly putting right. He had always thought Adrianne was the freak, and that nature must have meant her to look exactly like Kim, but the process had gone horribly wrong somewhere. Now he was forced to adjust his thinking for it seemed Kim was the mistake. He didn't know what the real reasons were for her state of mind or body, but he suspected it was not just Michaela's death. Her death had been the catalyst but now they were in the realms of things supernatural. The woman he'd known was changing into someone he didn't care for and couldn't possibly love. How could he? When he had spent so much of his life idolizing the woman she was and detesting the one she wasn't. Thanking God for handing him the better end of the deal. Now he was being robbed of everything. The Gods were not satisfied with merely taking Michaela and was back playing one of life's most evil games. Kim had lost everything, including her disposition, which was now a parody of her sister. Then there was her tendency to sink into deep depression for days at a time. She was the innocent victim of a cruel conspiracy, and deserved his undivided love and affection. But having to sit at the receiving end of her most irritating mood-swings had begun to rattle his nerves and exhaust his patience. Filling a corner of his mind with an invasive doubt, a feeling he'd never before experienced. Thoughts that would question the depth of his love for her, and challenge its very existence. Defining the nature of what he'd felt for her as pure licentious lust. A salacious craving for a body that was no longer desirable. True love was much more resilient, and would've easily weathered such adversity and be bouncing back for more, not shamelessly withering away at the first sign of drought.

But he was truly in love with her, he reassured himself. He had always loved her. How could he not love her when she was the air he breathed, the breath of life. Without her there was nothing but darkness. She was all he'd ever needed, and a dozen forsaken friends would gladly testify to that. Of course he loved her, he battled with his conscience. Telling himself it would all pass as soon as her condition improved.

What if she didn't improve? A conflicting voice sounded off in another part of his brains. What if she kept on sinking into that vortex of pain and misery, addicted to sleeping pills and tranquilizers? What if she became a drug popping zombie, existing from one handful of tablets to the next with nothing in between? He felt anger at the thought of losing her, as though she was already dead. Almost that same feeling he'd experienced when his mother died, robbed cheated. Angry at losing someone he'd loved beyond words, emotion, beyond thought or deed, beyond Kimberly, Karen, or himself. Beyond any measure of love that had ever been thought of, devised, or had ever been expressed.

A large part of his heart had died with his mother on that day, robbing Kimberly of the full measure of love that should have been hers but had no longer existed. Kim wasn't dead, and the woman he'd loved was still alive within her somewhere, but where? How could fate suddenly change the rules and alter the game beyond his comprehension and expect him, as though by some miracle, to understand and accept the rules of this new game, and continue playing as if nothing had changed? When his entire world had fallen crumbling around his heels, and his pretty wife was vanishing faster than a magician's dove? How could this be fair? They had taken a lovebird and were trying to replace her with a squawking Crow, as if he was so damn stupid that he wouldn't notice. Well he had noticed, and was fucking angry at being played for a fool. He hoped that whichever God was watching over him could see that he was trying to hang on to his love for her and trying to make sense of the evil that was tearing them apart. The only trouble was, she had precious little left that he could wrap his love around. And the speed at which she was changing, very soon there would be nothing left, except memories. Exciting memories of bath-times and bedtimes. Times that were filled with nature's most rapturous gift. A time when bedtime did not mean night time, but could be ten minutes before Karen was due home from school, or five minutes after she'd got home. It was anytime the mood was right. It could be a stolen few moments in the midst of preparing the Sunday dinner, and it very often was. It seemed the smell of food being prepared had that effect on him. The profuse salivation and hunger it induced did not, as in other men, emanate from his stomach, but from somewhere lower down his anatomy.

There would be times when nothing was going right in the kitchen. Those days when it would seem someone had put a curse on her, and she couldn't turn her back on a kettle of water or it would burn. The beef was tough and putting up such a fight it seemed dinner would not be ready before midnight, and she had no stock for the gravy. She would reach for a cup and her clumsy fingers would knock it to the floor. Or one of those times just before her period, with her breasts aching, or that lingering promise of a headache at the back of her head. A slight pulsating charge that never becomes a real headache and would be gone the instant her period began. She could be up to her elbows in sweaty rubber gloves, and up to her tits in a sink-full of dirty dishes. A chore she hates with a passion. Wishing she could throw the bloody lot out the window and start using disposables. She may be a little tired, hot and sticky, and the last thing she'd want would be this man pushing at her. The next instant she'd turn and there he'd be, standing in the doorway with that dirty sexual smile on his face and she would always respond, Regardless of her mood. She would gently lower the fires and shed her apron, then assign Karen to watch the pots as she followed him upstairs. In the bedroom he'd slowly undress her, then lick the smell of food from her body before making love to her.

Although, he didn't always get it wrong. He had got to know that the first five days after her periods were her most receptive. In fact that erotic phase normally starts with her period, and she'd have liked nothing better than for Peter to do his thing twice a day right through her periods. But he had some inordinately outdated and puritanical thoughts on the matter and had refused to touch her during that time. Stifling all her requests with a tedious recital of excuses and speculative pronouncements on why it shouldn't be done.

It wasn't healthy…Or he might hurt her…He may get hurt. He could contract a disease… It was immoral and disgusting. Filthy and degrading to the woman…Messy and indecent. And the one she likes best of all that always breaks her up in laughter. "Because she may become pregnant and give birth to an albino, because of her loss of blood. Sometimes he'd dry up and refuse to discuss it. Other times he'd fly into a rage. One day after a heated discussion he blurted out that his mother had told him. A man should have enough respect for his wife to leave her alone at that most improper time. If he has no respect for himself, at least he should have some for his wife, and only a man with the morals of a swine would stoop so low."

She believes this to be the real reason, and since that day. Which was about a year after they got married, she has not raised the subject again.

However, to be sure he didn't also miss the rest of her good days she had taken to leaving him little signs so he could see she was clean, and would know the coast was clear. This had become necessary because of his, almost paranoid refusal to touch her menstrual blood. It was as though it would mark him for life and his mother would know what he'd been doing. Once she did start as they were making love and he almost fainted when he got up and saw the speck of blood.

"Kim I'm very sorry," he said in a dolefully pathetic manner, then raced off to the bathroom. After that she decided it wasn't worth risking it and losing him to a heart attack. So she gave it some thought and finally came up with a gem of an idea, in which she used one of Karen's discarded dolls. This Doll now lives on top of the headboard and has two dresses. One in red, the other in green. Two days before the start of her period the doll is dressed in red, and the moment it ends the doll goes green. This was only for Peter's guidance and had no bearing on her sexual mode. Not that he cared. If she was green it meant yes, and she never once rejected him. The prime reason being her undying love for him, and also because of a promise she made him two days after his mother died. At the time he was so depressed she was in danger of losing him to a severe attack of bereavement, and saw for the first time the full extent of that love he had for his mother. How much she'd meant to him, and his dependence on her, and that need he still had for her. It was only after reflecting on the events of that day, it occurred to her that she should have been offended by his undivided loyalty and devotion to his mother. Kim felt she had good reason, for these were not shared emotions but were devoted solely to his mother. By this time They'd been married a year and nine months, and Karen was eighteen months old. Yet the only roles she was allowed to share were those his mother could not fill. Such as sex, and even there she had doubts.

He would consult her on everything, down to the color of his underwear. And she had sent detailed washing instructions on how she'd done them, and the method Kim should adopt to get them white again. Kim felt as though she was an outsider. Like an uninvited stranger who'd turned up to find this poor man had lost his dearly beloved wife. Kim felt that his mother had been his first, and only true wife. So who was she? What had she been doing in this man's life for the past two years? She tried to define her role over that period and it came out. Whore and mother. Fortunately, she was first in line, and was about to make an application for that now vacant role as his wife.

"Peter I know how much you loved her but she's gone and you're left with a wife and daughter who loves you very much. I love you Peter with all my heart, and I know you'll never love me as much as you loved her, but I'm not asking for that much, I'd be setting you an impossible task. Just love me as much as you can, when you can. Whatever is left in your heart I'll take. The sadness, the grief and the pain. The sorrow and the emptiness. Give me what is left in your heart, I ask for no more. In return I'll give you only the best of me. I promise to fill your heart and your life with a love you've never known. I will never reject, refuse, or turn my back on your needs," She'd pledged.

Kim had remained true and is yet to break a single promise she had made that day. She was as close to perfection as any woman could be, and their love was even closer to that elusive and deceptive excellence.

Now he wasn't sure what he'd been carrying for her all this time was really love. It had the look, smell, taste, and it felt like love, but was it love? Or simply the attraction and fascination a lecherous man feels for a good cheap reliable strumpet with an open smile at both ends? In four months things had changed so dramatically that there were no longer any daytime activity, and he's began to dread the fall of darkness, because it brought him closer to that painful moment he'd have to climb into bed beside her. Painful, because although his feelings had changed, hers was still riding high, and may even have been heightened by their adversity. She would demand that he did his duty to her, and if not to her, then to their marriage. Making what he considered to be unreasonable claims, at a time when sex was the last thing on his mind. All he wanted was sleep, for in his slumber there was always the hope he'd dream of erotic and exciting times past. But in recent months sleep had become a brief and infrequent visitor, and while Kim's sedative-induced snores echoed around the room. He'd lay there trying to look into their future, to see where they were heading and how much life they had left together, or looking back into the past. Trying to discover the point at which it all went wrong. Perhaps it had gone bad from the moment they met? Could it be that they should only have remained friends, and his mistake was in marrying the wrong woman owing to his abysmal lack of experience? Hadn't his formative years been so sheltered, might things have turned out differently? With experience, might he have known the difference between love and blinding obsession?

Peter had only known two girls before meeting Kim and both girls had rejected him within a month. Dropped and kicked him aside in favor of boys that were more like men. Boys who knew the first moves and was ready to make them, without being coaxed, or led like a dissenting child. The experience had taught him that there were more to girls than gossip, make-up and giggling. These two must have studied men in school and had acquired their degrees on the subject. They knew more about men than he did, and expected more than he had, or knew how to give. They were nothing like the silly mindless creatures he was led to believe by his friends. And was exactly the type his mother had described in her many warning.

They were pushy and overbearing. Odious and obscene in the extreme. Especially in the deplorable language they'd use, just for the hell of it. Peter was appalled by this behavior, and decided that his mother was right in advising him against taking up with girls. He now saw the wisdom in her words, and they were no more eager to dump him, than he was to get away and save himself. Secure in the safe sanctuary of his mother's possessive love. Patricia West had known nothing of her son's brief encounters with the deadly and repulsive sex. He'd made sure of that. And the speed at which they'd died also aided his cloak of secrecy. He felt guilty and responsible for not heeding her warning. Like a delinquent child who was told not to touch, and had disobeyed and got his finger burnt.

Peter was an only child, whose father had died in very tragic circumstances when he was eight years old. For years his mother had kept the truth from him by handing out the story that his father had died of a heart attack. This was very near to the truth, for the knife had indeed been plunged into his heart. His heart had been attacked. It wasn't until he was twenty, and just a year before her death, that she told him the truth.

Philip and Patricia West were married in 1948. Two years later Peter was born. A child Philip did not want. It had been agreed they wouldn't have children, and Pat was prepared to forsake an ambition she'd cherished since childhood. An ambition to marry and have two children, a boy and a girl. This was a dream she was quite happy to relinquish in favor of a husband who was loving and loyal, but within a month of the wedding a pattern had emerged that was to be the template for the rest of his life, right up to the moment he died.

All of a sudden she was no longer a young bride, but an old married woman, sitting alone each night awaiting the return of her husband. It was clear that he was getting plenty of what he wanted and Patricia, decided it was time she got something for herself.

For the next few months they had numerous arguments and debates, at which she'd plead with him to be allowed to have a baby. She would introduce one reason after another, only to have them scorned by a man who thought he knew what was good for her. One day in anger, and blinding despair she asked him. "What would it matter anyway? Philip you're hardly ever home and wouldn't have to see the child." After that she saw no point in trying to reason with him, and began a process of skillfully doctoring a selected number of his French letters… She was three months pregnant before she broke the news to him. Philip could not understand what had gone wrong, and castigated himself for his carelessness. One day he called her into the bathroom, and she watched as he shoved one of his prized sperm-collectors on the cold water tap and began filling it. He looked at her. "How do you suppose that got there?" he said pointing at the thin spray of water squirting from the end of it. She shrugged innocently. "I don't know, they must have been defective when you bought them." She'd said, but could've kicked herself in the head for making that silly mistake and getting caught.

He smiled, threw the rubber in the bowl and flushed the toilet, then stood looking at her, nodding his head ominously.

Philip West was an avid womanizer, but she'd been forbidden from having even a passing acquaintance with men, and that included their neighbors and friends. He was so jealous and possessive that he'd been known to rummage through her dirty clothes, checking for signs of indiscretion. The only piece of humiliation he'd not yet adopted, was to check her at the door as she went out, and check her again as she came back.

He didn't mind her having women friends and had positively encouraged it. This she thought was his way of compensating for his unreasonable jealousy. Until the day she came home and caught him on the stairs with this woman. There they were as she opened the door. His trousers and underpants around his ankles, and the woman's lime-green knickers lying on the carpet where he'd dropped them. The hurriedly discarded knickers were one of his trademarks. It turned out that the woman had come to the door selling carpets. How he'd converted her from selling to giving herself to him, spread eagled on the stairs, still wearing her dress and shoes. With a knee jammed against each wall, was something she couldn't understand. And could only Justify with the belief that women were all tramps and couldn't wait to spread their legs for the first smiling man they spot. Otherwise, how would he have made it with so many women? His chat was pathetic, and his performance would have been none existent if he couldn't take his lips to bed. It was only after that escapade on the stairs that she learnt, to her astonishment, that he'd already shafted most of her friends.

In spite of his moral destitution, he had loved her with all his heart, and was devoted to her in his own special way. Still, there were times she'd wonder if he truly understood the meaning of love, and would loathe, and despise him with such intensity that she'd happily have taken a knife to his prick and chop the damn thing off. Secure in the knowledge that she'd never miss it. Reasoning that she could not miss something she'd seen so infrequently, and had had even less. Especially when he began bringing women back from the Pub and would do them in her living-room, on her sheepskin Rug, thinking she was asleep. Not once did she confront him in the dozen, or more times he'd done it, and he died thinking she never knew. However, someone had to account for this, and she found it easier to lay that blame Squarely at the repulsive crotch of those women who had so willingly given themselves to him. It was they who made him what he was, and she vowed never to make friends, or form any close and trusting relationship with another woman.

One evening as she sat waiting on him to come home from work, worrying herself that his dinner was drying out in the oven, the doorbell rang. The two young Policemen had tried to break the news as gently as they knew how, but there was no way to soften the blow.

Her husband had been caught in bed with another man's wife and had been stabbed through the heart. He died instantly. The woman had managed to reach the accident Hospital but was dead on arrival. Pat had sat in a cataleptic trance in the corner of the sofa and wet herself, thoroughly soaking the cushion beneath her. She felt faint, but the shame of these two young men finding out she'd just piss her knickers, drove a shaft of steel through her spine and kept her sitting erect, and proud. Although inside, her whole system had died.

Pat was devastated, and for the next four weeks, survived on tranquilizers, and would have given up, but for the demands of an eight year boy to whom she was devoted.

After that she dedicated the rest of her life to the task of turning

Peter against women. Without going into details she'd told the child that women had caused the death of his father, and he'd end up the same way if he didn't keep away from them. The insidious litany against the evil of women was vehemently maintained with an added vengeance right up to the time of her death. Day, after day he'd hear the same recital, that women were never satisfied, and spent their time prancing from one man to the next, and he could not expect fidelity from any woman, for they'd climb into bed with another man the moment his back was turned. She said they had dirty, disgusting habits, but would not expand beyond her warnings that he'd find out, to his dismay, if he ever got involved.

Peter could not remember much about his father or the time he died, and each time he asked his mother about his death, she'd fill in the blank spaces in his young mind with what she considered to be the relevant details. About a year after he died, and just around the time of his ninth birthday, he'd come home from school informing her that it was possible to get him another Daddy, and requesting that she did. On inquiring how she would go about it, and why? He explained that lots of his friends had lost their fathers and have had them replaced. Some even had two daddies, he informed her excitedly. She immediately deposited the potato she was peeling into the sink and angled her body to face him, her right hip resting heavily against the sink, as she looked back at him over her left shoulder.

"And where do you suggest I look for this daddy you so badly need?" She laughingly indulged him. He shrugged. "I don't know," he said, then graciously threw in a few choice suggestions. "Pubs, clubs, dances, or even the Supermarket."

"Do you mean I can walk into Sainsbury's and pick one off the shelf, the way I do a can of beans? What price are they?" She placed the knife in the sink and faced him square. This was too good to miss. Arms folded high on her chest, a quizzical smile on her face. The boy looked at her with a surprised frown, as if he'd just encountered an idiot. "Mom they're not on the shelf!" He said patronizingly. "They're walking around like everyone else, doing their shopping."

"And I suppose I simply go up to the one of my choice and ask him if he'd like to be a Daddy to my little boy? Is that how it's done?" She humored him.

"I-I don't know how it's done Mom," he stuttered helplessly.

"Peter, you are the one who suggested this, and when you make a suggestion it should, at least, be constructive. Didn't your friends say how they got their Daddies?"

"No," he shook his head, innocently.

"So let me get this right," she said speaking softly. "You would like your thirty five year old widowed mother, who is still in mourning for her husband, to shed her dreary colors and get into something bright and glittery and hit the dance halls in search of that father you so badly need?"

"But he wouldn't be just for me, he'd be for you as well," he said.

"What makes you think I need another man?"

"But you must do," he asserted confidently. "You said you missed Daddy a lot, and you missed him mostly at nights. Well my new Daddy would sleep with you, and you wouldn't be lonely anymore."

Good God, she thought. My nine year old son is a pimp, and he's ready to prostitute his mother so he can have a father. "Darling your father is dead and can never be replaced," she said with a motherly reassuring calm. "I am thirty five years old and I'm much too long in the tooth to go chasing men in Supermarkets, Dance halls, or any other place, even if I had the desire or the inclination. Your father is dead and you'll have to learn to live with his memory just as I have." Her lame reasoning did not impress him and he wasn't accepting it.

"But why mom? You're not too old. They say you're a very sexy lady with great Boobs and you're here going to waste when any man would love to take you on. Stewart's Mom is not as pretty as you, and she's old. At least forty, and he has two Daddies. He's got two of everything. His real Dad buys one, then his other Dad buys him a bigger one. It isn't fair, when you're prettier than all the other Moms put together," he expressed his displeasure.

Pat was glad she hadn't shut him up as she was tempted to do when he mentioned the word Boobs, for she would not have known what was being said about her, and what was on his mind. She was somewhat peeved that they had been saying these things to her son, but in her heart could not but feel flattered, for what she'd heard could be taken as a complement. Although she wished they had left her Boobs out of it. The idea of nine and ten year old kids sitting in school discussing her tits was a little disturbing. "Which of your friends were talking about me?" She casually inquired.

"James Bolan," he answered.

"Isn't that the boy whose father is in Prison?" she asked.

"Yes, his mother has got a boyfriend, and it was him James heard telling her you had a great pair of Boobs, and a sweet arse," he frowned, staring at her. "What's an arse Mom?" he asked.

She hesitated a long moment, her mind kicking around thoughts of how to explain this without it sounding cheap and crude. She met his gaze with a warm smile. "It's a very unflattering way of referring to someone's bottom."

The boy smiled. "He's right Mom, you have got a nice arse…"

"Peter!" She menaced him with voice and eyes. "That is not a nice word and you shouldn't use it," she said coldly. As the thought ripped through her head that the little blighter was going to be just like his father. Normal well adjusted nine year olds do not go around looking at women's bottom. They are not interested in that sort of thing at that age.

"But it's true Mom," he insisted

What do you know about that kind of thing? She almost asked, but held her tongue, for fear he might tell her. "That is beside the point, and don't let me hear you use that word again."

Peter had kept up his request for a new Daddy until he was eleven, when he suddenly stopped, and began telling her to forget what he'd been saying, he no longer wanted a Dad. He told her they could do better by themselves, and didn't want any strangers coming between them. Pat questioned his change of heart but could get nothing out of him, which didn't really matter. He had finally come to see things her way, and the reasons were not important. All of a sudden he was the man around the house, taking on all the things he felt a man should. Cheerful, caring, loving and attentive. He couldn't do too much for her, and would even help with the dishes. A chore he'd always despised. Without being asked he'd take out the garbage, weed the garden, help clean the house, and along with his own shoes, he'd clean hers. And now when they watched TV he'd be sitting right next to her, no longer across the room in his own chair. Some evenings they would go to the park, other times it would be the swimming bath, and when the time allowed, it would be the Cinema. It didn't take long to work out what was happening, as he desperately worked to fill the role of any man she may have been considering. Peter made sure there was no longer a vacancy, and was bold enough to let her know he was now the man of the house. What he wouldn't say, was what had brought about the changes, but Pat knew something had shoved him into it, for he now appeared almost petrified at the thought of a man coming into their lives. One day as she talked to one of the other mothers in the Street it came out that James Bolan had tried to stop a fight between his mother and her boyfriend was knocked unconscious. He was off school for three days. The boyfriend had been arrested, but wasn't charged. She claimed her son had accidentally hit his head against the table and James was forced to back up her story. Peter had learnt, the hard way, that a new man in their lives wasn't worth the trouble. From then on it seemed no one else mattered as they grew closer, and lived only for each other.

Chapter 8

It was wrong and Peter could feel it. He knew he was in big trouble. His affliction had diligently worked its way into his system and took over without warning, possessing him like a terminal illness. He was rapidly losing the battle but could do nothing to save himself. He'd thought he could stroll in and out again without being affected, emerging on the other side with a refreshing and innocent friendship, nothing more. He had no need for more. That was the shrinking hope on which his conscious mind had fed, but down where it mattered he'd needed Daisy from the moment he saw her. She had reached out and touched him in a way no one had before. With Kim it was gentle and soothing, but with Daisy it was like a stab at his heart with a cattle prod, sending a thousand electrical charges surging through his body. One kiss and he was ready to forsake the woman who loved him, as rapidly as he'd deserted Michaela's memories.

For the past three days he'd thought of nothing but the time they'd spent together on Sunday. The way she sat, spoke, smiled and looked at him. That barely perceptible, residue of a north London accent that lingers in her intonation and phrasing. The way her silver-blue eyes seem to look straight through to his soul, leaving him thinking this was a woman from whom he could have no secrets. It was as though she could look into his eyes and read his mind. He picked up the phone and dialed. It was answered on the fourth ring, he'd been counting, as he'd done the first time two days earlier, when it rang thirty two times before he gave up. Yesterday it was twenty five times.

"Hello?" said the familiar voice.

"Hi Daisy, it's Peter," he said, a very pleasing tone in his voice. "How are you?"

"I'm fine, just a little busy, that's all."

"I know, it's three days now I've been trying to reach you."

"Can't understand, I haven't been that busy. What times did you call?"

"Tuesday at l0.30am."

"I was at work then. I am a working girl and can't afford to be home at that time of the day," she said frivolously.

"What about 6.30pm. Wednesday?"

"I was taking a bath." she said. Explaining she'd just got into the bath when the phone rang.

"And just now?"

"I was in the bath again."

"Did I drag you naked to the phone, or are you dressed?"

"Sort of. I'm wrapped in a dressing gown."

He breathed heavily down the phone.

"Not too much of that," she joked. "I had to interview a man only last week who makes a habit of that" she giggled.

"Is the dressing gown all you're wearing?"

"I've also got a towel around my hair."

"You are standing there wearing a dressing gown and a towel?"

"I'm not standing, I'm sitting," she informed him.

"This has really begun to affect my breathing, and I'll probably have another asthmatic attack."

"I didn't know you were asthmatic."

"I'm not but you've began to have that effect on me."

"When did this start?"

"The second time we kissed." He chuckled. "But it seems I wasn't alone. That kiss had a strange effect on you. Did I make you nervous Daisy?" He teased.

"Ha! Ha!" She sniggered.

"You may well laugh Miss Spencer, but you tore out of this room on Sunday as if I was chasing you with a loaded gun. Then I couldn't reach you for three days and had to wonder if you were trying to avoid me."

She was silent, except for a long thoughtful sigh.

"Daisy?"

"Hmm?"

"Speak to me," he coaxed. "Tell me what you're thinking."

"Peter," she hesitated briefly. "No man has ever done what you did to me and I didn't think it was possible. I must have appeared silly, but I didn't care, I had to get out. I needed time to think but couldn't get hold of my brains with you so close to me. Yes I unashamedly ran away from you and I'm glad I did."

"Daisy, you were the one who lit that fire under me, remember? By subtly, daring me to make a move. Do you always start things you can't finish?"

"Peter I never start things I can't finish," she said with quiet confidence. "That was merely a tactical withdrawal. You are a man who'd not looked at another woman with an impure thought since you met your wife, and I was curious. The next thing I knew you'd wrapped yourself around me like you had a dozen arms, and was looking at me with the nicest impure-dirty-thoughts I have ever seen in a man's eyes. We both know what would've happened if I'd spent another ten minutes in that room, and I wasn't ready for you Peter. In case you don't know. What you were brandishing was more dangerous than a loaded pistol." She pointedly added

"I wouldn't use it against you Daisy," he joked. "It may look aggressive but It's really very friendly."

"That's what I was afraid of. Anger I can deal with, but that kind of friendship I don't handle too well, especially in my present state."

"And what state is that?" he innocently inquired.

"Work that out yourself," she answered cryptically.

He grinned, having finally deciphered her message. "Are you getting ready to go out?" he asked.

"No, I like to take a bath once a day whether I need it or not," she said laughingly. "No Peter, I'm staying in again tonight.

"Your Boyfriend is coming over?" He questioned. She let out a sigh. "We've been over that, and I've told you there is no such person."

"Your good friend, Is he coming over?"

"I go to his place when I feel like it but,"

"When you feel like what?" He impatiently interrupted her.

"Visiting," she said emphatically. "We are talking about visiting, nothing more. I was trying to say, I visit him but he never comes here."

"Daisy I want to see you, can I come over?" he politely requested. She was silent for a long time. "Daisy May, are you still there?"

"Hmm-Hmm, I'm still here. I'm thinking about it. The trouble is that I'd love to see you but don't think I *should,* not tonight."

"Why not tonight, there might never be a better time?"

"I'm troubled….By your home. Your wife, and your daughter. I truly do care for your little girl and would hate myself if I disrupted your lives."

"It was because of that tragedy in our lives why we met, and there had to be a divine purpose to our meeting. Daisy, we did not meet by chance, this was meant to be."

"What about the problems you'd have if we got too close?"

"Don't you think it's already too late to worry about that?"

"It's not too late Peter. Not if we stop right where we are and not let this thing go any further."

"And what do you think would happen the next time you visit here? Don't you think it's best that we meet at your place?" She slipped into another bout of thoughtful silence, which he decided was to his advantage. "I'm coming over, what's the address?" He said with an assumed dominance.

"I don't think I should," she was saying, but in the next breath gave him the address.

"Edgbaston. That's only about three miles away. I'll be there in 30 minutes, and don't get dressed up for me, I like what you're wearing at this moment."

"Peter, I'm still not happy with this arrangement," she voiced her concern.

"What part of it is making you twitch?" he asked.

"I'm not twitching, just a little nervous and uneasy about you coming over."

"Baby I'm a pussycat. How could I unnerve a girl like you?"

"Pussycats are the worst. They start by rubbing themselves up against your legs. Next they're on your lap. Then before you know it they have crawled into your brains, and your bed. And what kind of a girl do you think I am, Mr. Peter West?"

"Self-confident, and arrestingly beautiful."

"Don't come the sarcasm with me," she said lightly. "You've seen a sample of my self-confidence, and probably know I'm scared stiff at this moment."

"But why Daisy, what's the reason for that?"

"It is a combination of many things. Three years abstention, and the little matter that you're another woman's husband. How is that for a start?" she questioned.

"What if I promised not to handle government's property without due respect? Then if I step out of line you could always caution me," he suggested.

"The only government property here are my Handcuff," she said dryly.

"Whose property are you?" He persisted.

"Nobody owns me, I'm my own woman. I am my own private Property."

"What do you think of men who try to handle your private property?"

"That depends on who they are, and how they're handling it."

"How do you like it handled?"

"With love and care, proceeding slowly and attentively. Stopping in all the little places of interest, before moving on slowly, with due care and attention. I dislike men who are always in a hurry. They miss all the beauty spots and invariably runs out of gas long before the tour even get's going. Tell me. What kind of man are you? Bearing in mind that whatever you say is being taken down and will be used against you later."

"You've got nothing to take down, they're already down," he laughed.

"What makes you so sure I haven't been getting dressed ?"

"I would have detected something," he speculated.

"Only if I was slipping into caste Iron knickers, maybe?" She cynically offered.

"Or stainless steel chastity belt," he contributed, quickly adding. "If you own one of those you'd better get into them, for that is the only way you will keep me away from that delectable body tonight."

"How about bolting my door this instant, and not opening it again until morning? I would be a very silly girl to let you into my apartment after all that."

"Then I' b be waiting outside your door when you come out in the morning, and that could make you late for work. I'm at my very best in the mornings."

"It would be such a shame for you. I'm at my worst in the mornings when I have to get up for work. Meet me in bed and I'll slip your discs and send you home on crutches. Meet me at the door first thing in the morning and you'd think you had seen a ghost.""That is quite a threat coming from an officer of the law, Detective Spencer."

"That is not a threat, it's a promise."

"I just remembered a previous engagement for this evening," he joked.

She laughed. "What must you think of me talking like this? Even in jest."

"I hope you're not climbing down, I like you where you are," he said hopefully.

"Heaven alone knows what's got into me," she said sounding apologetic. "I expect it's because we're on the phone. I wouldn't have the nerve to say such things to your face."

"Stop it Daisy, you're disappointing the hell out of me. Don't tell me I won't see the person you are now, or that you're not planning to honor your promises? Are you a welcher?"

"No I'm English," she answered.

"And a comedian," he parried. "I'll see you in half an hour."

"Oh no," she said. Explaining that he'd said that fifteen minutes ago, and now only have half that time left.

"I'll be there in fourteen minutes," he said. She put the phone down and sat thinking about Peter's concerned interest in her friend. Michael had now outlived his function and was no longer an asset. He had become a liability and had to be laid to rest before he messed up the show.

Chapter 9

Michael Saddler began losing his hair in his early twenties, and at thirty three, was almost completely bald, except for a thin line of hair skirting the back of his head, from one temple to the next. He may have been a handsome devil, and a real lady killer in his younger days but on this day he didn't add up to much and Daisy could've done without his attentions.

She was standing at the Estee Lauder counter in Lewis's when he came up and ask her out to dinner. Daisy stood holding the Lipstick she had chosen, letting her eyes wander around, looking at all the pretty women and wondering, why me? Of all these lovely women, why did he choose to annoy me? It was the most vulgar and flagrant pick-up she'd ever suffered. This man had not even granted her the honesty and respect he'd give to a cheap strumpet. To come out and ask for what he really wanted. He certainly wanted to stuff her with something but it wasn't food.

"I'll take it," she said, handing the lipstick to the assistant. She turned facing the man with the ill-fitting hairpiece. "Do I look starved or hungry to you?" She spat poisonously. "Do I look like someone who could do with a good meal? Surely you've been following me around and staring at my backside long enough to know the lack of food is not one of my failings?"

He grinned. "You don't look at all hungry, in fact-"

"Good, go look for someone who is hungry and stop annoying me," she calmly requested.

"Forgive me, I know I'm making an ass of myself but you are the most delightful lady I've ever met, and would like to take you out and buy you something. Flowers, a drink, a meal, anything," he was saying as she walked away. For the rest of that day she was left with a painful conscience for having put him down so crudely. He wasn't the first man that had tried to pick her up and he wouldn't be the last. They could be a damn nuisance at times, but there were times she actually enjoyed the attention, and life wouldn't be the same if they didn't try. She'd have to start handling it better, she promised.

A week later as she walked up New Street someone tapped her on the shoulder. She turned and was greeted by that same amiable smile, and ill-fitting hairpiece.

"What have you got against a man who wears a rug?" He asked, his face straight and without emotion.

"Absolutely nothing," she said. "In fact I hadn't noticed, but since you've brought it up, I prefer a man to leave the rug where it belongs on the floor."

"That can easily be arranged," he said, backing away in front of her. Then without warning he lifted the thing from his head and held it aloft like a much prized scalp, before dumping it on the pavement in front of her. She came to an abrupt halt. Not knowing whether to step on it, kick it, or walk around it, while he stood grinning, arms outstretched as if soliciting her applause oblivious of the attention he was attracting. This man is insane, the thought came to her and she found herself silently mouthing the words. She gazed at the thing at her feet. This is not a rug, it's a fitted carpet, she silently mouthed another critical observation. Hands to her mouth, holding back the laughter, she hurriedly stepped over the thing and walked on. Forcing a path through the circle of onlookers now gathered, thinking it was someone's pet that had been run over. Ten yards up the road he caught up with her and the thing was back on his head, but the wrong way round.

"Are you a curse of some kind?" she asked, a lame smile on her face. "Did someone send you to haunt me?"

Michael Saddler turned out to be the most naturally funny person she'd known. He was incapable of a solemn thought. His whole life was laughter, and the world was one big joke. He could extract a laugh from the ugliest event, and would probably see the funny side of his right leg falling off in the street. It was odd, but the very quality that had attracted her was now driving a stake into the heart of them having anymore than a laughing acquaintance. Michael was just a big joke. Even his first attempt at kissing her was preceded by a joke and was reduced to howls of laughter when his rug slipped over his face as their lips were about to meet, and they never did kiss. Michael had shown a distinct lack of interest in her as a woman, in spite of having pursued her with such tenacity. Not that this bothered her unduly. It was so refreshing to have a man take her out to dinner, and could go back to his place without him demanding payment for the food form up her dress. It was just that her inquiring mind would not let her rest until she'd solved the mystery that was Michael Saddler. From the moment she saw him he'd come across as being effeminate. He'd entered the store behind her in the basement and had followed her up the escalator to the ground floor. She didn't see him again until she came out of the lift on the 2nd floor. None of this seemed unusual as it was normal to keep meeting the same people as one moved throughout the store. She took the stairs to the third floor, thinking she'd left him behind but he'd got there ahead of her. She still thought nothing of it.

It was when he turned up at the next counter, in cosmetics, that she realized he had been following her, and the notion that he may be queer didn't seem so real anymore. Now it was back on her mind and she was noting all the things that didn't add up, like trying to scuttle any conversation that strayed on to sex. His walk and gestures were much too ladylike, and there could only be one reason. One night as they got back to his place after the Theatre, she came straight out with it. "Michael, are you Homosexual?"

For a long time he just stood looking at her, his face in a troubled frown. Then he slowly smiled. "I should have known better than to try and con a Detective Constable," he said with a sigh of relief.

"It didn't need a Detective to notice that. You had no more interest in my body than a Jew for a side of roast Pork," she told him. "What I don't understand is why you bothered? Why walk into the Butchers to look around when you're strictly vegetarian and never touch meat? Why did you come after me with such ferocity? I still feel ashamed of myself for the way I treated you in Lewis's, yet you kept coming at me. Why?" Michael came across the room and took her hands, brought them to his lips and kissed them. "Sweet Daisy," he said looking into her eyes with deep sincerity. "It's a long story and I hope you won't be angry with me when I tell you."

She suddenly had a strange uneasiness in her stomach, as though he was no longer the same person. Here was this queer holding her hands and staring into her eyes.

"Let's sit this is going to take a little time." He led her to the sofa and they sat down.

Michael had started out a normal red-blooded heterosexual, with an addiction to women that bordered on fanaticism. He loved women. Fat, thin, black, brown, enormous women, or tiny ones. Rabid lesbians or by-sexual. If a green woman with two heads and three horns had suddenly appeared in his local Pub one night, Michael Saddler would probably be the first man to bed her. In his pursuit of women he'd go anywhere and do anything. At age twenty four he was bagging two or three women a week regularly, and at twenty five he tried marriage. Two years later she walked out crying infidelity. Taking their twelve-month-old son with her. He was never to see them again. Michael was broken in two with one half screwing everything he could find, and the other drinking itself silly. Two weeks after she left him he was fired for being drunk, at work. One night while looking for a quiet place to die, he wandered into a small homely Pub In Digbeth, close to Birmingham City centre, called The Happy Tangerine Man, and was sitting at the bar for a full five minutes before he noticed there wasn't a single woman in the place, not even a barmaid. Any other man would have bolted from the place covering his rear with both hands, but not Michael Saddler. The man was so sure of himself and his rampant sexuality that even in this nest of rear-end-jumpers he was unperturbed.

He left an hour later, thinking they weren't as odious as he'd thought. No one had waylaid him in the toilet, or tried to talk him into bed. He'd had a normal chat with a man, a little older than himself whose name was George, he was married with two young children. George had quickly assessed he was not Homosexual and had wandered in by mistake. Michael told him he was simply looking for a quiet place to die, then went on to unload his martial pains on the man and found him an ardent listener. When he'd finished, George sympathized and said he had a deal that could be beneficial to both their interests. Michael felt his hackles rising with indignation, and resentment. George saw the scowling look of disgust on his face and assured him it had nothing to do with what he was obviously thinking. Having convinced him of his good intentions, he asked if they could meet the following night and Michael agreed. The next night they met as planned and after a few drinks George invited him back to his house. Michael chewed it over for a little time then accepted.

Daisy delicately pulled her hand away form his and sat, arms folded, legs crossed in frowning disbelief as the story unfurled. Thinking there must be insanity in his family for this man was touched to the bone.

George lived in Oakhurst Road, Hall Green, fifteen minutes away. He got into his Red BMW, and Michael in his clapped out, rust colored Morris Marina, followed him out of town, through Digbeth and over the Camp Hill Flyover, and up Stratford Road. He hadn't got far when a strange uneasiness shot through his guts his body quivered, and he felt an urgent need to pee. Questions were being raised in his head for which he could find no answers, and his bowels were screaming for immediate attention. A chronic fear like he'd never experienced washed him and his hands sweated. He pictured himself arriving at this man's house and a dozen queers jumping on him all at once. He had just passed the Warwick Road exit and cursed himself rotten for not taking that Road to freedom, but decided to take the next on the left, which was Weatheroak Road. There was a right turn before that, Fulham Road, but he couldn't take a chance on a right turn because George would see him turning off. The Road was quite busy and he'd have to wait there in the middle of the Road indicating his intention for George to see.

Michael had just gone past the Mermaid Pub on the left when the Police pulled him in for a defective rear light. He was never so happy to see the police in his life. At this point it didn't matter how he got shot of the man and this way was as good as any. He got out and looked up ahead but could not see the B M W and assumed the man wanted nothing to do with the Police. His heart-rate was back to normal and he no longer wanted to pee himself. Calmly he stood at the back of the car trying to convince the two Officers the light had only gone wrong earlier that night. Suddenly George appeared. "What's the trouble Michael?" He addressed him as though they were the best of friends and had known each other for years.

"Hello Mr. James," said one of the officers. They began talking and it came out that George had a break-in at his house three weeks earlier and these were the officers who'd investigated. Michael was let off and told to get his light fixed. After that he saw no harm in continuing his journey.

Michael could not believe his eyes when George pulled in through the gates and he saw the house. It was a modern six bedroom house standing in three acres of magnificently landscaped garden. As he drove up to the garage the doors opened, to reveal two other cars inside. A Rolls Royce Silver Shadow, and a Mercedes Benz 450 SL Sports.

He rolled the BMW in next to the Benz, got out and closed the door. Michael sat wondering, what could this man want with me, trying to work out what he was getting himself into. George beckoned and pointed to a spot to park his car. He swung the car around in one turn and parked facing the gates, just in case he had to leave in a hurry. As they walked to the front door George lightly mentioned he'd like him to meet his wife, then he'd show him around the house, and after a drink they'd discuss business.

They entered the house and walked into a huge Gold carpeted hall. From the centre of the hall the stairs rose, and in a gentle turn to the left, curved its way to the first floor. A resplendent crystal chandelier dazzled from the high ceiling as they crossed the hall, then entered the spacious living-room to the right. A stunningly attractive woman wearing a close fitting light summer dress, rose like a vision from a large leather armchair to greet them. They were introduced. After a moment of strained and uneasy conversation, she offered him a drink, and he gladly accepted, said he'd have a whisky. George didn't say much. He just sat quietly sipping Courvoisier Brandy while Marcia got on with the job of straightening out the wrinkles in Michael's mind. After two generous Whiskies and fifteen minutes of looking at this great lady, he was beginning to feel he'd known her for years, and when George suggested she showed him around the house he almost sprang to his feet before she did.

Without hesitation she got to her feet, wearing her finest smile and led him through the Patio doors outside. As she closed the doors she flicked a switch, illuminating the underwater lights in the huge swimming pool. They walked slowly around the pool, and she inquired about his hobbies and the things he enjoyed. Michael immediately moved swimming to the top of his list. They came back into the house through the changing room area, where they had a small gym and a sauna, emerging in the hall directly behind the stairs. Upstairs she showed him around the entire floor, except the children's room, and finally her bedroom. She led him to a chair and he sat down. She sat in a slightly larger version of his chair on the other side of the bed. She smiled at him from across the bed. "Do you know why you're here Michael?" she asked, fiddling with her gold earrings.

"George has promised to discuss that with me later," he said."But at this moment I have no idea, I'm in the dark."

"You know my husband is gay?" she said, gazing straight at him.

"Yes," he nodded.

"Well as for sex my husband has no further use for me," she smiled. "Are things getting clearer now?" The picture was still a little hazy, but it was rapidly getting clearer and he liked what he could see. Michael turned his head and quickly scanned the sumptuous surroundings. The smell, taste, and the feel of money was everywhere, together with the fact he'd been wanting the woman since she'd rolled her delightful tail over to the bar and got him that first drink. He had sat admiring her exquisite body, thinking isn't it marvelous the things one can buy with money? His eyes had not left her delicious rear as he followed her up the stairs and around the rooms.

"What are you offering me? I need to know precisely what I'm being offered. I need you to spell it out for me, please."

"We are looking for a good sound steady relationship, not a one night stand. My husband is having his needs seen to, and I am looking for a man to take care of mine. I understand your marriage has recently broken up. I'm sorry about that, but it also makes you the perfect candidate, for I'd prefer someone without further ties. You are here tonight so I can look you over and see how much you are worth. If you can match my expectations you're in. Do you accept what I'm offering?" She sat back in the chair looking at him expectantly.

"Before I can accept I need to know what I'll be getting out of it," He said, surprising himself with his audacity. She stood up and did a twirl then faced him. "You'll have me whenever you want, don't you think I'm worth it?" She went on without waiting for his response. "You'll also have the run of the house and its amenities. You can come and go as you please, and you get to use my car, the Benz, providing I don't need it. I take two holidays a year. Winter and summer, and you'll be expected to accompany me. It won't cost you a penny, my husband will pay for everything. What do you say?"

"Just one more question," he said, eyes tracking her hungrily as she moved aimlessly around the room. She was a piece of God's most enchanting creation, in which he must have personally taken a hand. She came toward him, commenting that he was a very cautious person and she couldn't blame him. Then sauntered pass his chair to the window behind him that looked out over the pool. He twisted around to watch her. That walk was pure sex, and her body spoke the language fluently. Her aimless rambling ended as she came and propped her behind on the arm of his chair.

"You had a question," she prompted him. But his query had got lost in the commotion now taking over his mind. He looked up at her wearing a foolish grin, thinking, why am I asking these damn foolish questions when all she wants is a simple yes, so we can dive into bed? But what if she isn't telling the truth? He had to know precisely what he was getting into, there just had to be another handle, it was too good to be real. He was in hell doing penance for his crimes against his wife and child. Suddenly he was plucked out of the fire and brought to heaven and had one of the masters finest angels thrown at his feet. This was the stuff that dreams are made of and he'd be a fool if he didn't question it. How did he know she wasn't recruiting him for George, that he wasn't being suckered into a web of homosexuality? Michael quickly marshaled his fragmented composure. Reminding himself he was not an inept teenager, but a man of the world who'd had more women than he could remember, and after all she was just another woman.

She was saying something about George being the nicest man she'd known when he remembered his question.

"Your last child is only a year old, how did George turn against you so suddenly? What made him reject you?" He wanted to know.

She got up and walked the six paces to the bed and sat facing him.

"George was Gay when we met. I was twenty one, naive, and full of my own self-importance and foolishly thought I could change him. He was merely experimenting, as he put it, and I was confident that my wanton sexuality could alter his thinking. I was convinced he could not have had a real woman, at least not one with my glowing abilities. God, I was such a young fool," she exploded with embarrassed laughter. "I thought I could change the world with this miraculous thing I had inside my panties and honestly believed I could've been a roving ambassador, traveling the world and bringing peace to troubled nations by taking down my pants and showing those men it would be more rewarding to make love than war. So you can see George and his minor indulgence was going to be no problem for me. I was Catherine the Great. Cleopatra, and Helen Of troy. I was the reincarnation of all the great women this world had known, and best of all I was Marcia Rowena Green, the only woman in a world inhabited by inexperienced girls. A woman no man could resist...Well—things didn't quite work out," she said grossly understating the facts. "In spite of all that, we had a sound marriage with a healthy and vigorous sex life which lasted five wonderful years. Twelve months ago he watched me giving birth, and as the baby's head appeared I could see George's face turning green. Then as the head popped out, so did George's dinner. He stood vomiting his guts out and had to be helped from the room. He told me later that he had no idea what a woman had to go through to give birth, and the sight of my womanhood stretched beyond endurance, had wiped him clean of any sexual desire, or affection for that part of my body. I'd heard it does affect some men, that they were never the same afterwards, but didn't believe it. Over the past nine months I've tried just about everything, but George is not interested and I have to accept that he's now a dedicated homosexual. I was then faced with the choice of going without sex or having a cheap affair, neither of which I liked. After some long debates we arrived at this solution, and three weeks ago George put it into action for the first time." She explained that the break-in George had talked about wasn't strictly true.

He was driving home one night when he saw a man struggling to push a car away from the traffic lights, so he got out and helped him push it to the side of the road. It turned out the car was out of gas. George offered to take the man to the Gas station, and he accepted, but as they drove off George made some excuse about having to get home in a hurry but would come back with him to see about his car. The man agreed and they traded names. His was James.

"I was in the living-room when they came in. He was good looking and decently dressed, somewhere in his mid twenties I quickly assessed. George then left us and came upstairs, but within a minute, and before I'd offered him a drink the phone rang and I went into the hall to answer it. When I got back the patio doors were open and James, or whatever his name, was gone and so was my bag with £100 cash, check book, and credit cards. The Police were called and fortunately they caught him the same night. The car had no tax or Insurance and was not registered in his name."

She looked Michael straight in the eyes. "You are the first person we've had here since, and I hope we can trust you," she said with a sudden solemnity. He got up and slowly walked across to where she sat and stood towering above her.

"Marcia, you've got a deal," he said stretching forth his hand. She gently took his hand." I hope we can do better than a handshake," she said scrutinizing him thoroughly. "Yes, I'm sure of it." She bounced across the floor and locked the door. Fleetingly, she came back to where he stood. "It's the kids," she said. "They tend to wander."

A month later Michael got shot of his car and was using hers, when he did manage to tear himself away from the house. He had a rigorous program of sex, swimming, sauna, some gentle weight training and more sex. This went on throughout the summer of 1972. In December of that year they went to Malta for fourteen days, leaving the kids at home with a Nanny.

In August of the following year they had a party for about two hundred guests. At 2am Marcia went up to bed, he followed and they got into bed, giving her the usual nightcap, staying with her until she fell asleep. He then got dressed and went back to the party. By 4am all the guests had left, leaving just George and himself trying to drink the place dry. By 5am Michael was in a cataleptic state. At midday he woke in one of the bedrooms to find Marcia standing over him inquiring if he was alright? He told her he was fine, but the strange discomfort he felt had nothing to do with the drinks he'd consumed, and was sure George had been poking around in his business.

At first he wanted to kill the man, to tear the bastard apart with his bare hands. He wasn't sure what he'd done and it might not have been the full measure, but the man had inserted something inside him and he was as sore as hell, in both sense of the word.

He was still there wondering how best to handle things and had decided there was no point in cutting his throat to save his arse. Suddenly she came back, got undressed and crawled in beside him. He quickly realized how much he'd stand to lose by making a fuss. Along with shafting her, night and day, she was handing him £30 a week of George's money, and he was using her car to pull a number of women that wouldn't normally give him a second glance.

About a week later George came right out with it and Michael said no. George threatened to move him out and bring someone else in, and within an hour Michael had caved in like a wet paper bag. Soon he was taking care of both their sexual needs, while keeping Marcia in the dark. He was amazed how readily he'd taken to something he had hated so poisonously.

Throughout that brilliant summer of 1976, he and Marcia rarely left the pool, except to make love. Some evenings he and George would go out under the guise of having a drink but would wind up in some Hotel room.

In October that year George's business went belly up and he lost everything. The house was sold and they moved into a council house in Redditch, but shortly after that Marcia left him, and Michael never saw her again. He'd kept in touch with George for the next two years but lost touch with him when he moved from Redditch at the end of 1978.

One day he was talking to his present friend about George and commented that he could not go off women the way George had. His friend said he had, and told Michael he was only kidding himself and wagered £100 he could not have sex with a woman within the next six months. Michael picked up the challenge.

"That was three months ago, since then I've failed four times in the past two months, but didn't think too much of it. They were just some tired looking specimen I picked up in pubs that did nothing for me. I was sure that with the right lady I could do it, and walked around town looking for the prettiest woman I could find. That was where you came in," he said toying with the ring on his middle finger. "I spotted you going down the underpass near Rackhams and followed you into Lewis's."

Daisy was incensed. "Was that all I meant to you, a bet, research fodder? Just another specimen in a skirt to test how queer you were?" She voiced her distaste at being used like a laboratory animal.

"Daisy I'm sorry about all this and that is why I've told you everything. You have a right to know the truth and I couldn't lie to you because of the respect I have for you. I was not motivated by the money, but the challenge. It was something I just could not ignore. Like sitting in that pub when I knew better, or accepting George's invitation, then letting him have me for that first time. My whole life consists of a series of challenges and reckless behavior." He said, trying to justify his actions.

"Where would it get us if you'd passed your test, what would we have?" she asked.

"Not much I suppose."

"Not much?" She questioned. "You're being too polite Michael. The truth is much more brutal, in fact we wouldn't have shit."

Daisy left his apartment that night and never returned. When they met she'd told him she was living with someone and could not give him her address or phone number, and he'd accepted this without question. She had found it very helpful to say she had a man, whether she had one or not. This put her in control of the situation while she assessed the person at hand and decided what to do with him. Peter had been carefully looked over and she knew precisely what she wanted to do with him. From here on her mystery friend no longer existed.

Chapter 10

It was exactly 6.45pm when Peter drove into the small parking bay in front of the large white Georgian house on Portland Road. This was a three story building converted into three flats. The ground floor was occupied by two female students, Daisy was on the first floor, and the top floor was vacant.

Peter covered the linoleum clad steps two at a time, but as he neared the top he cut the pace to a more sedate, one step at-a-time. At the top of the stairs he turned left. To his right the stairs carried on to the second floor. Three paces along he was at the door of flat two. He knocked, and the door swung open almost immediately. She stood in front of him wearing a pair of pink lycra slacks, no shoes, a little white t-shirt that left her midriff bare. Long blonde hair, streaming down her back.

He remembered thinking, Kimberly, in her better days was much more attractive, only she'd never mastered the sale of her sexuality the way this woman had. Kim had not learnt how to set her stalls and was a confusion of latent promises. She was shy and reserved, and always seem to be holding back, saving herself, as though, for another day which never came.

With Daisy it was all for today and to hell with tomorrow. She was holding nothing in reserve. It was all there. Sparsely packaged and being handed to him like a gift on his birthday.

Hungrily, he studied her delicious body. His lips rapidly drying as he drew quick bursts of air through open mouth. She smiled. "Aren't you coming in Peter?" Silently he stepped inside as though in a dream and watched her close the door, then slowly took her in his arms in a long luscious embrace.

"Hello Daisy," he whispered in her ear. "You are an exceptional lady and I can't believe l am standing here with you in my arms. I can't believe my luck." She adopted a benign frown.

"But Peter, less than half an hour ago you made out that our meeting was sanctioned by the Gods. How can you now say it's luck?"

He kissed her lightly. "Daisy l am all confusion and contradictions. My mind is running way ahead of me and is already in your bedroom, before I can make sense I'll have to catch up with it…So can we go to your bedroom now?—Just—just to catch up with my mind, you understand?"

"Original," she commented. "tame, but creative. I love a man who can create even without his mind. It seem I am in for one hell of a time when you get your mind back, and I can't wait. The bedroom is through there," she indicated with a jerk of the head. "I'll wait here." She chuckled. He felt the spasms of suppressed laughter rippling through her body.

"Oh no," he shook his head. I'm not letting you out of my arms, when I get back you might not be here."

"Where could I go dressed like this?" She asked. "I don't know," he said. "but where do dreams go when you're suddenly shaken from your sleep? Daisy you're a living dream and I will not be shaken from your embrace." They kissed again. Tenderly, Lips barely coming together like the touch of a feather…Then all at once they were locked together with passions exploding. Their hips suggestively docked, without motion. She was a rare delicacy, he told himself as he savored a kiss that was like no other.

With that enthralling kiss she'd honored every promise she'd made. She was more woman than he'd ever imagined. But how could he have hung his dreams beyond the ultimate woman? How could he have thought of her before she'd existed in his mind? Right up to that moment he thought he'd already married that woman. Kim was the epitome of feminine sexuality, the Zenith. Beyond her nothing existed but a dark dank void. He'd thanked God daily for his impossibly good fortune in finding the perfect woman even before he'd truly started looking.

Kimberly.... Kimberly, he silently repeated her name as Daisy worked magic with her lips on his neck, both cheeks, and tickled just inside both ears with an expert tongue, sending his body into a wild erotic shiver. He wondered if any woman, one leg, one tit, and a nervous tic in her one good eye, might not have seemed the perfect woman in his desperation to sever that close suffocating bond with his mother? At the time he wasn't conscious of that burning need to escape, but it must have been there in his subconscious, fighting for his attention and waiting for the right moment. He had been granted no time to make what was his most important decision. No time to compare, and weigh her qualities against others. Instead he was obliged to grab the first one at the head of the line and make for the door in a mad dash to escape. Then having got out and tasted what he thought was utopia, proceeded to harass himself into believing he had indeed arrived and there was no place left to go. That was what he'd thought, and all he was capable of thinking. He was now thinking clearly, and could see his decisions were based on ignorance, further clouded by myopia.

They held hands and he stood back admiring her body with disbelieving eyes. "Phew," he blew heavily through pouted lips. "Daisy you're all I expected and much more."

"Are you always this easily impressed?"

"It's not that I am easily pacified, but I've only been here a moment and already my back feels peculiar," he joked.

"Oh no," she said, her head hung low. "Those things I said on the phone. It isn't fair, you can't throw them back at me now. Jesus, I hope you didn't take them to heart. I am a bit of a tease, as you'll discover when you get to know me better." she shuffled out of her promises.

"It wasn't so much what you said on the phone, or at any other time. It was the promises you made with your body. The ones you've been making since I first saw you. The ones you made as you opened the door and the one you're making now."

"How do you know I'm not teasing? That it isn't a part of my act?"

"I can tell an act when I see one, and what you said as you came out of the living-room that day with Karen was not an act. Nor what you were saying as you sat there on Sunday."

"Peter I hope my body hasn't been making you promises I can't keep, and don't intend trying to honor."

"Now you're teasing."

"Don't be too sure. I'm in the habit of making far more promises than I can keep."

"Like promising you wouldn't get dressed?"

"Peter West, I did not promise. I simply remained silent and you assumed I'd agreed," she said with a smile. "Anyway, I'm hardly dressed. You couldn't call what I'm wearing street clothes, and I wouldn't dare open my door like this for anyone but you. I put this on for you, and to give us a little more time." She propelled herself back into his arms and kissed him. "To talk and lust after each other's body. Peter it's been three years but I wasn't going to let you walk in through that door and straight into my body. If I hadn't put something between you and my body we'd be rolling on the floor right now and that would be much too quick for me. I meant what I said Peter. I want to be handled gently.

I want your hands, and every other part of you to become intimately acquainted with my body. I like to be touched and I want you to touch me everywhere. We're in no hurry so let's not rush."

Once again Peter stood in speechless wonder, meditating his good fortune and asking himself how could any man be so lucky?

"Can I offer you a drink," she suddenly said, shattering his thoughts. "Coffee, Tea, or some lemonade? No spirits for you tonight, you'll be driving later." she stepped back, turned and walked through the archway into the dining room. The sudden capricious change of mood from steaming passion to casual acquaintance was startling, and left him thinking she might just be teasing him. She was like no other woman, and by his thinking, only existed in the movies, and between the pages of raunchy romantic novels. Women didn't look like this. They didn't feel this way. They didn't lock themselves in your embrace, talking eroticism and sending the blood rushing around your body like a swollen stream in a thunderstorm. Women did not talk lasciviously. They simply climbed out of their knickers and reclined gracefully and did it. They didn't talk about the things they liked, and how they liked it. They didn't tell men how to handle their bodies, and direct them to their most interesting places. They didn't need to, men knew it all. Men knew what was good for them and they took what was handed out with gratitude and without question. Women have always known their place, and that place was beneath the man. Kimberly was the personification of all women and he knew women intimately. What kind of woman is this now riveting herself to his heart, sapping and subjugating his will? While gently, and with the dexterity of a heart surgeon, cutting his wife loose to drift with the tide? He could feel her tearing Kim away from his heart, like a boat being wrenched from it's mooring in a storm but was helpless, and could neither resist his own impending enthrallment, nor go to the aid of his unfortunate wife. God, she was enchanting.

"Coffee with two sugars Please," he said, adding. "It's just as well you're not offering me alcohol for I'm already intoxicated by you."

"That kind of insobriety meets with my full approval," she said turning to look at him before going through the door into the kitchen. "Come and talk to me Peter, you gorgeous man," she called out from the kitchen. "Tell me about yourself, your job, and what you like doing with your spare time. I want to know everything about you."

He stood at the kitchen door watching her as she filled the kettle. He'd been here so many times before, only in a different place and with a different woman. "There isn't much about me that's interesting," he said.

"You let me be the judge of that," she retorted. "You are one of the most interesting men I've known. A man who can think without his mind is worth knowing." They laughed.

"As for my job," he said, laughter in his voice. "I am a Junior Foreman at Alpha Castings in Oldbury."

"What exactly does a Junior Foreman do?" she asked.

"As little as possible," he joked.

"I believe that Peter, you look the type," she grinned.

"I work on the shop floor, doing a job along with the men. I'm not one of these office Foreman who rarely gets out among the men and has no idea what's going on. As for my spare time, from here on I want to spend them with you," he said.

"Flatterer!"

"How about your job?" he asked. "Now, that is a very interesting job."

"It isn't half as interesting as you think. Police work is mostly routine with the occasional interesting interlude. We spend lots of time waiting around for things to happen, and hoping they never do."

Peter kept his eyes fastened on her as she talked and moved around the kitchen, every movement seem designed to excite him. She was a tease. A bitch of a tease. He wanted to take her right there up against the sink, in Kimberly's favorite position. Get his hands on those slacks and pull them down and stuff himself inside her. This was his way. He had no time for magical mystery tours. All that could come later, but right now all he wanted was to shaft her. Not to handle her body. All those things could come when his body wasn't so caste iron rigid and wasn't causing him such discomfort. He could almost feel her euphoria as she watched him wanting her, knowing the game was being played by her rules, when she was ready, and not before. She would give when she was ready and would not be taken a moment sooner. For the first time in his life the woman was at the controls and he was the disgruntled, but subservient passenger.

"Daisy May, you've got the sweetest arse I've ever seen," he said disrupting her running account of Police work.

She suddenly stopped what she was doing and turned to him in surprise. "You learn fast Peter West," she gushed, her face glowing with pleasure, her voice lilting with passion. "I like a man to say what's on his mind, using the right words." She came over and put her arms around him. "If you don't know the language you can't communicate. If there is anything you like about me. My tits, Pussy, the way I fuck, I want you to tell me in plain adult words. That kind of talk I like," she said in an erotic whisper, then kissed him, she was full of surprises. All at once he wasn't so sure of himself and had began wondering if she'd really let him fuck her, and when'? He was coming apart and wasn't sure how much more he could take.

She talked a better sex than any man he'd known. Tearing his stereotyped presumptions that this was exclusively a masculine indulgence to shreds. She could talk but what else? Each time she began it would bring her to the torrid edge of excitement. Her voice would mellow and her eyes would take on dream-like qualities, but it would all lack reality. Like a bad actress putting on a second rate performance. How could a woman, who'd not made love for so long, and wanted that loving as much as she was pretending, be so cavalier? How could she hold herself in check with his stiffness jammed in her crotch? Was she just a clever voyeur, someone who got her pleasures from talking dirty? She had him weighed up from the start as good candidate for her purpose, whatever that was. He wasn't surprised she hadn't been cocked in three years. No other man would stand for this eccentric shit.

As they stood locked together a thought crept into his head that she was not a nice lady. She was precisely the kind of woman his mother had warned him against all those years ago. Vulgar, dirty and disgusting. Every lewd word represented her signature on the label his mother had stuck on her kind. "Cheap whore." But how should a man feel with a whore locked in his arms and her tongue probing his tonsils? If this was evil, then he was evil. If this was the kind of woman that led men down the slippery road to degradation, they can make room for one more in that great hotbed of debauchery and shame, for Peter West was on his way. Daisy was carrying a number of genes that belong strictly to the devil and his crowd, but she was an angel and her body was heaven. If she caught him on the right day he'd gladly do wrong for her. But right now he had to know just how far she would go for him.

As she worked her tongue around his mouth, he worked his hands down her body and over her firm behind, moving his open hands smoothly over each globular cheek, slowly moving one hand up to her waist and down inside her clothes. Soon he had both hands inside the flimsy garment caressing her nakedness. His mind ticking over erratically as he nervously contemplated his next move.

With a mixture of uncertainty and apprehension, he worked one hand around the side toward the front, then realized that with their bodies locked together he had no place to go. It was then he saw for the first time how inexperienced and unprepared he was for a woman like this. Brandishing his ineptitude like a flag of truce, with his conviction sagging, he blundered on feeling like a cart-horse that had challenged a thoroughbred three year old mare and was about to be defeated. Suddenly his mother's disapproving face flashed in front of him and faded, with Kim's face appearing an instant later. Guilt, fidelity, excitement and fear.

Fear of what he was doing and what he'd become was churning out a cocktail of disaster inside his head. He should be home with his sick wife, not here doing this, his conscience struck him like a bolt of lightening and brought his roving hand to a stop. Then as he hovered there, riddled with indecision she gently arched her hips and spread her legs. This rapidly brought him back to life and his hand was moving again. His fingers working their way through a forest of thick pubic hair, finally arriving at her wetness and as he touched her she broke from the kiss, gave him a wistful look and backed away.

"Not before coffee," she smilingly smacked her lips. "Let's have coffee first."

He stood behind her as she made the coffee, salaciously circling his hips against her bottom, his hands caressing her soft breasts.

By the time they finished coffee he was ready to explode from wanting her, but were now aware of his limitations and was prepared to play by her rules. He thought he knew it all, and maybe he did, in his own league but this lady was in a different class.

As she closed the bedroom door behind them she removed her T-shirt and threw it at him. Catching him unaware. He held the warm garment to his face then brought it to his lips and kissed it. His eyes fastened on her body in open admiration. She helped him out of his shirt then removed his shoes and socks and got on the bed, lying on her back. Her left leg raised and bent at the knee, her foot resting flat on the bed. Still wearing his trousers he followed her lead and got on the bed beside her. He kissed her once, then shuffled down her body, his lips falling naturally on her right breast. His right hand caressing her body and working its way down.

"I was thinking that you haven't told me a thing about yourself," she said. "Like what turns you on in bed, and what doesn't. What would you like most? What are your dreams? What would you like to do to a woman but have never done, or would like a woman to do for you? Let me make your dreams come true tonight Peter. And don't be modest, you can't shock me. As for myself I've always got men to do what I want and there is nothing I can think of that I haven't had. What's your desire Peter?"

He made no response except to change breasts. She moaned softly as he drew her nipple into his mouth, and began a slow undulating rhythm with her hips.

"You haven't told me what you like," she issued a breathless whisper. He came up for air. "I'm thinking about, it," he said then went back to the breast. His right hand moving inexorably down her body until two fingers gently entered her. Once again she suddenly aborted his mission just as he'd docked. Deftly she slipped out from under him and worked him on to his back, then climbed on top. "I'll find out for myself what you like," she said working her way down his body with kisses. He lay there quietly resenting the woman for what she was doing to him. She was the most fascinating, yet the most exasperating person he'd known. When will she stop playing games and let me fuck her? He angrily asked himself.

It seemed like an hour had passed before she unzipped his trousers and took out his cock, just as he was wondering if she'd ever get around to it? Lovingly she worked it in her hands then between her lips, glancing at his face, constantly gauging his reactions. All of a sudden his dick faded as if it had been chopped off at the root. She looked at him questioningly but said nothing.

He stared back into her eyes but Daisy was no longer there. It was his mother, her long Brown hair falling over her disapproving face, and those eyes, full of disgust and dark with anger. He blinked and Daisy was back. She hurriedly unbuckled his trousers and pulled them down. She had not planned on getting them off this quickly but things had changed and it was now an emergency. The man was dying of carnal arrest and needed oral resuscitation. Daisy tried every trick in her vast repertoire, but half an hour later—tired, despondent, and somewhat bedraggled. Her long blonde hair bunched on his stomach in an untidy mass, like golden seaweed washed up on the shore—she picked up her head and dejectedly admitted to herself she'd lost him. The man had died right there in her hands and she couldn't save him. God, she could've cried, and might have had she thought it would've helped. She needed him this night like it was her last. She hungered for the thrill of him exploding inside her. Releasing her years of pent up emotions and desires and to unload those stagnant and frustrating dreams. But it was not to be, for nothing could breathe life back into this dead, not even Christ himself. In her desperation she'd summon his assistance but to no avail. It would seem he was not in the business of raising the dead anymore. A sign of the times, she mused, trying to extract a moment of light relief from what was the most tragic event of her recent life.

The night was not a complete loss thanks to Daisy's efforts and dedication, and in the event had taught Peter some new tricks but, with his ego deflated he was not in the right frame of mind for more of her games, believing that she was partly responsible, and would have sat moping but she insisted he put it out of his mind and got on with other things.

"There is more than one way to skin a Rabbit," she told him. "It is much easier with a knife, but when you're without one you have to use what you've got, and you have almost everything I need."

It was no consolation to be told he was not the first man who'd suffered a deflation, or the first one she'd known, and that lots of other men had to deal with the same thing on a more frequent basis. What did he care about other men or what they suffered, this was the end of his world.

At the door, she kissed him half a dozen times and assured him that nothing had changed, and she didn't want him walking out feeling embarrassed and sorry for himself and not get in touch. "Call me tomorrow," she insisted.

"Daisy, you do believe me when I say this has never happened to me before?" He said for the fourth time in as many minutes.

"Peter I believe you, stop worrying. You are fortunate, some men have to live with that problem all their lives," she consoled him. "You've had an unfortunate experience which may not even be your fault. Maybe I'm to blame for holding you back and allowing your frustrations to get the better of you? Next time I'll be waiting naked behind this door and we won't loose another moment, it'll all work out, you'll see. Peter, you're a fine, very normal virile man, there is nothing wrong with you that we can't put right next time. You are down and I know how you must feel, if I were in your place I'd feel the same…"

"But you're not in my place and you only think you know. It's different when you're faced with it and the strange emotions come rushing to the surface. Daisy, I've disappointed you, and disgraced myself and my masculinity. Jesus, just look at you, you're the most desirable woman I've known. I came here to fuck you and had believed there was nothing on earth that could stop me fucking you tonight. I stood in that kitchen wanting you so badly my balls ached, and after all that….The worst of it is that I'm in love with you…God I wish you were someone else. Some woman I could leave tonight and never meet again. I want to go out there and walk under a bus so I never have to look you in the eyes again," he said painfully.

"Oh Peter, don't be silly," she smiled disarmingly, took his hand and led him back to the sofa and gently guided him down in the seat.

"You sit there I want to talk with you," she said coldly. "Peter, I want no more of that kind of talk from you or I'll be very angry." She knelt on the floor between his legs, her arms around him. "Stop it Peter. I can't take anymore of your stupid talk it's hurting me. Don't you care about my feelings? Can't you see I'm also feeling your pain…?"

"I'm sorry," he quickly apologized and wrapped his arms around her. "I have been extremely thoughtless, please forgive me."

"Peter, I have a confession to make and I hope you won't walk out thinking I've been a calculating bitch for it matters a great deal what you think of me…"

"That is also my problem, I worry like hell about you and what you'll think of me after…." Her kiss brought his ramblings to an abrupt end, and as she took his breath away, she unzipped his trousers and took his problem in hand, then sat back on her heels. She kissed it lightly… "Peter I've been in love with you since the first moment I saw you. I walked into that room and my heart caved in and gave up the battle it's been raging against men. Since that moment I've wanted nothing but to get my hands on you and I finally have. Now to hear you say you're in love with me has made me the happiest woman in this world. All that matters now is this love we share. This," she kissed him softly. "Is very important but isn't everything, and heaven forbid, but if it never came back to life and you have to do me with your fist, or a vibrator, for the rest of our days I'd go on loving you just the same." her face expressing love and sincerity. He slouched back in the seat looking at her. His face draped in disappointment and condolence for his dead member.

"Peter I used your daughter to get to you. I used her to get back into your house to see you, and what I told her about my family was my way of sending you a message. To let you know who I was. Why I joined the Police, and where I was from. I knew you'd ask her what we talked about and that she'd tell you everything. That doesn't mean I don't care for her. I love you both and wish she was my child. Our Daughter," she kissed him gently then drew him violently into her mouth.

This was an exceptional lady, the thought again burned itself into his head. She was no Kimberly and it seemed she was setting out to prove it. Don't stop, he was telling himself, not having the nerve to say it out loud, but she did stop.

"Peter I want you, I want all of you. I want you to myself, and want you to leave your wife for me. If there is anything about me you don't like just say and I'll change it, especially my job. I'll do whatever you want and I can give you children. As many as you desire, and I can be six times the woman your wife will ever be, in or out of bed…"

"Daisy you're messing up my head," he covered his face in mild confusion. "What are you doing to me? I love you Daisy, and I need you in my life but I can't leave Kim."

"Why not, you said it wasn't much of a marriage."

"That may be but I can't walk out on her, she needs me, and what about Karen, where would she fit into all this?"

"She would come with us."

"That would kill her," he said grimly. "If we took Kim's only child away she would die."

"Alright, she can keep her, we can have our own children," she offered.

He shook his head in despair. "What a night you've chosen to hit me with these decisions? Daisy my brain is in as big a mess as my dick at this moment and I can't concentrate," he said quietly.

"Don't try to think about it now, we've got time. Just remember I'll be here waiting for you. Whenever you're both ready," she squeezed him pointedly. "I'll be right here." She gently returned him to his trousers and zipped him up. "Do you know?" She said getting to her feet in a slow meditative mode, her blue eyes narrowed in thought. "I think your problem is guilt. Thoughts of your wife and how good she has been to you are throwing up subconscious barriers in your head."

"Don't tell me you're also a shrink?" He smilingly retorted.

"There is no end to me Peter. You would be surprised at what I am, or could be for you. I'll get that woman out of your head. I will shift her because I plan to take her place, and if I can't evict her I don't deserve you. Call me tomorrow," she said. "I'll be home at 4 o'clock, and will be here until eight. I'll be waiting for your call."

"I will," he promised.

Back at the door she was having, doubts. "Peter I hate you leaving like this, why not stay a little longer?"

"That would achieve nothing and could only make a bad situation worse," he declined her offer.

"Not necessarily," she said, explaining that she had an idea and would love to try it.

"No!" He threw up his hands in fear. "No, I couldn't put you through another disappointment and I couldn't face it."

It was 10pm. when he got into his car and aimlessly drove away telling himself he should've stayed. Desperately wanting to get back to the place he'd just left his heart and what was left of him. Daisy-May-Spencer, was the air in his lungs and the blood coursing through his veins. She was the beat of his heart and the one thought in his head. He was back in her flat retracing his steps and reviewing the whole scene. Cutting out the mistakes and successfully doing to her, in his mind, what he couldn't do in reality. Then as her erotic vibrations filtered through his head the life began returning to his body and he wanted to go back. Convinced in his mind he could correct his mistakes tonight and wouldn't have to sleep on them. What sleep? He briskly corrected his thoughts. Reminding himself that with this thing resting on his mind he'd probably never sleep again. Half an hour later and six miles away, he pulled up at the side of the road somewhere in West Bromwich, with his member in a rage.

"If only he'd taken her up on that final offer," he said, almost shouting at himself. "Why did I leave when there was no hurry to get home?" But what if he went back and failed again? What excuse would he have this time? Five minutes later he was still there with this rampant problem, wondering what to do with it? Home to his wife, or back to Daisy? Suddenly he got the answer. He started the engine and swung the car around in a sweeping u-turn, bumping over the curb in the process. Twelve minutes later he arrived home and went straight to bed. That night he made love to his wife for the first time in two months. Kimberly would have died had she known who he was really shafting during those three sessions that night. By morning his self-esteem was mended and his doubts were being laid to rest. That day Kim was happier than at any time in the past four months. Once he couldn't get enough of her and wouldn't leave her for a moment. Always touching, pinching, stroking, kissing, nothing got in his way. He could unhook her Bra through a thick jumper in three seconds. Now he claims he can't get to her because she wears too much clothes. Since her illness she has not worn a Bra around the house and he hasn't noticed. He had changed so drastically that if she was to put her breasts near his mouth he'd probably be sick with revulsion.

I'm not the woman I was four months ago, but why is he punishing me for something he has admitted wasn't my fault? She thought about the time shortly after his mother's death, when, but for her love and devotion he'd have killed himself. He'd have gone into that same bedroom, lay down on that bed and put his lights out forever. She wondered if he could really have forgotten those days, and if he hadn't then where was his conscience? She swears he's already forgotten they had a Daughter named Michaela, whose death had started it all. His only concern, seem to be with the state of her once beautiful body and his own selfish loss. To think she once worried that Karen would grow up with a warped mind, from constantly catching him with his hands, either up her dress or down her blouse. Over the past four months she'd thought all that was dead, and after last night's adventure she was even more confused. He was back on the breast in a mean and hungry fashion, as if he was discovering her body for the first time, and that was the trouble. He was a totally different man. He did things he'd never done before and lifted her to heights of sexual pleasure and satisfaction she never thought possible. Where did he learn these things? He was the most honorable man alive. She smiled with delight as she reflected their meeting and the unequaled joy of that unforgettable moment.

Chapter 11

Adrianne had been married a year and Uncle Bertram was still teasing her about the pretty one being left on the shelf. He would sit looking at her, shaking his head in simulated astonishment. "Kim you're the prettiest girl in town, but it's a crying shame no one wants a Pretty girl these days," he'd say, and her mother would also join the light hearted banter at times. In fact every close friend and family had derided her at some time. All, except her father. She was his favorite and visions of her leaving home would send his heart into series of palpitations. He disliked Adrianne, and would say she wasn't his daughter. He'd point to a pretty Redhead, Kristen McDonald, who lived on Granton Road, not far from Beilby Road in Stirchley, where they lived. Kristen was born in Selly Oak Hospital at about the same time they were born.

"That's my daughter!" He'd say in mild agitation. "That is your real twin. Those incompetent bastards made a mistake and gave us the wrong baby. I don't know who Adrianne's real parents are but I'm ready to bet her mother is a cheap trollop from the deprived end of Moseley, or Balsal Heath. That woman on Granton Road could never be her mother, which means there is another woman involved and it's a three way balls-up. Look at Adrianne," He'd said two days after she got married. "She was born on her back with gaping thighs and a cushion beneath her arse, and since that day has not managed to get off her back or closed her legs. That's no way to get a husband. If that boy had any sense he wouldn't a touched her with a borrowed prick. You don't listen to them," he'd say to

Kim. "There is a man out there waiting for you, a good man, someone professional with something inside his head, who is not only looking for sex. They don't come along every day so you may have to wait, but he'll be worth waiting for. I want only the best for you because you're the best."

Kim didn't want to shatter his illusions and kept her conflicting opinions to herself, but would wonder what made him think she was in the market for a man? Thinking that when she took a man it would be for love and not because his oversized brains were sticking out the side of his head. She would look at the neighborhood and would break up in laughter. What would this great professional man be doing in her neck of the woods? Her father had said he'd come and sweep her off her feet, so he could be a professional Road-Sweeper.

One evening she went for a drink with a couple of girls from work and wound up in the Mulberry Bush. This was a large modern Pub on the ground floor of the Rotunda on St. Martins Circus in the Bull Ring.

Five years later on the night of November 21st 1974, an I.R.A Bomb blew the place apart killing nine people. The name has since been changed a couple of times and now it's known as The Bar St. Martins.

Kim and her friends arrived and walked up to the Bar, with the other two girls ahead of her. As they waited to be served she curiously turned to scan the room and their eyes met. He was standing directly behind her, no more than an arm's length away staring into her eyes. To this day she cannot remember a word he'd said, or her response. All she knows of their meeting was what she'd been told by Peter and her friends.

"What would you like to drink Kim?" Her friend had asked.

"Beer," she responded fatuously.

"Beer?" said the astonished girl. "Kim you don't drink beer."

"Beer," she repeated.

They bought her a Babycham, but it could've been vinegar for all she cared. Later that night she told her friends she was going to marry him. The next day she told her mother.

"Your father won't like it," she warned her.

"That's too bad," the love-struck girl said happily. "Him and his dreams…Peter is the greatest man I'm ever going to meet, men don't come any better. He is six feet tall with the body of an athlete. His hair is dark brown, his eyes kind of greenish blue and he has a smile more lethal than a Baseball Bat, with rows of pearly white teeth. "

"That's just as well," said her mother cautiously. "That smile will come in handy when he meets your father."

"He is disgustingly handsome," she went on.

"That won't win any prize with your father. You know what he's like. He hasn't got a penny to his name and has been living off the state for the past five years, yet he manage to look down on everyone else from his perch on the ground."

Kim didn't give a hoot what he thought. Peter was the man for her and there was nothing more to be said. Holding hands they would walk in Kings Heath Park in that winter of 1969 and it would be like the middle of summer. She would watch him with glowing admiration as he moved ahead of her, then turning to draw her attention to some specific point he was trying to make. Gesturing with his hands and body as he planned their lives right there in the park. He was the gift she'd always wanted but hadn't dared to hope for, a gift of eternal love. Peter was beautiful, dynamic, and handsome. The whole world was glowing with a new magnificence and he had made it so. He had opened her eyes to so much she'd not noticed before. The wind in her hair, the grass, trees standing bare, as though waiting to be clothed with snowy white. Like some young virgin awaiting her adornment on the morning of her wedding. Everything was wonderful, joyful, exciting. Peter was love itself. The most caring and affectionate person she'd known.

When she told her father the first question he asked was, "What does he do?" When told he worked in a foundry he hung his head in despair and shame. As though he'd just heard his mother was a whore and he was the son of her first client.

"A fucking powder Monkey!" He angrily exclaimed. "I expected much better from her. I worked in foundry for one day, and at the end of that day I was blacker than a nigger's balls. Soot and black shit was everywhere, even up my arse. I packed it in."

"And where are you working now?" She calmly asked.

"Don't give me that shit," he rasped. "You know I can't get a job anywhere."

"Well at least that young man is working, he's doing a job and will be able to maintain his wife if she gets pregnant or have to stop working for any other reason. You can't criticize him for that."

"Don't make me laugh?" He snorted. "That isn't a job it's a prison sentence…. I wish you would go out and get yourself a prison sentence like that if only to get your nose out of my crotch for a change, you idle sod. She said to herself.

….He's only nineteen years old, he's got no fucking ambition. I'd rather not work than do that."

"Yes dear," she said ungraciously and without interest.

Peter was put on the staff soon after Karen was born and was now attending most of the company's functions. Including Christmas and Easter, this added up to about six functions a year. Mostly dinner-dance. The first one Kim attended left her so sick with jealousy she felt as though her heart would explode. Every time she looked around there was a woman smiling at her husband and he was smiling back. Next he was dancing with them, laughing and chatting so intimately, she was sure this was more than a normal working relationship. On the way home he told her she'd have to pick up her self-confidence and dust it off for she'd left it dragging on the floor all night.

"Those are people with whom I work, that's all, they mean nothing more to me," he calmly explained. "The fact some of them happen to be very gorgeous ladies alters nothing. They are no different from the other tools I use to do my job and as women, they mean as much to me as a broken shovel. Don't belittle yourself by descending to petty jealousy. I love you and want no other woman."

It had taken three years to lift her confidence to the height where she trusted him completely and had no fear of other women. Peter was indeed one in a million. But all those women were just a parade of boring pedestrians, compared to the class of ladies to which he was exposed on that memorable · Hawaiian trip. Peter could have taken his pick from a dozen exquisitely desirable ladies. Women much younger and more attractive than herself, and she'd watched him turn up his nose at women, lesser men would've committed murder for. If there was only one man on this earth who could be trusted implicitly, that man was Peter Philip West. Husband and father par excellence. Now everything had changed and she was beginning to have real doubts.

At 5pm. the phone rang and Daisy' quickly picked it up. "Hi Peter," she said in a rash but correct assumption.

Taken by surprise, he was silent for a moment, "You seem to possess psychic abilities Daisy," he remarked, a pleasing tone in his voice.

"You did promise you'd call, that made it very easy," she said.

"How are you?" She inquired.

"I'm fine now," he said. "much better for hearing your voice."

"That's a nice thing to say to a love-struck girl, and thanks for the flowers they are gorgeous…Peter, I wish you were here with me now, I need you this very moment. Would you like to know what I'm doing right now?"

"How are you dressed?" He questioned.

"I'm not," she answered.

"I don't want to know," he laughed nervously.

"Coward!"

"I'm at work and such thoughts don't go well with a man who has to handle machinery."

"Peter, can you get away and come over I need you now."

Just stop what you're doing and get dressed and you'll be alright, he said to himself. "Daisy I'd love to but I can't," he told her.

"Is there someone there with you?" she asked.

"Yes, I share an office with a colleague."

"So you are an office foreman after all? You gave me the impression you were too macho for that."

"Well I am the macho type….but of course you know all about…."

"Don't start that Peter, don't you dare. This is a new day," she firmly smacked his wrist.

"I expect you're right, it doesn't help to dwell on the past."

"What time will you finish work? "Five fifteen, but I have to take a shower and will leave here at 5.30," he explained.

"Why don't you leave early and take a shower here?" She offered.

"You wouldn't like it," he laughed. "I defy you to recognize me before I've taken a shower. That's how black I am."

"Very intriguing, it would be the closest I've got to having a Blackman."

"Do you want one?"

"Not really, but eight years ago I almost did."

"What stopped you?"

"Silly reservations. Wish I had though, then I'd find out for myself whether it's truly magic or just another myth. I'll see you in about half an hour then?" She quickly changed the subject. "What I have for you will keep until then."

"I'll see you at 5.40…. Daisy, I love you. I love you very much."

"And I love you too…" she hesitated. "what must that person with you be thinking at this moment"? "He's left, we're alone now," he answered brightly.

At 5.35 he knocked the door and it swung open as if by remote. He stepped inside and looked behind the door. She stood smiling, and just as she'd promised the smile was all she was wearing. He hurriedly shut the door, unable to hide the pleasure in his eyes and his voice but managed to keep his face impassive. "You are a remarkable woman and full of pleasant surprises."

"Just a loving girl who can't wait to have her man wrapped around her, and we are going straight to bed… Unless you'd like a drink first?" She added.

"Coffee," he requested.

"You can wait in the bedroom," she said, "but don't get undressed I'll do that myself."

The instant she touched him he died in her hand and she was suddenly more concerned for his pride and self-esteem than she was for her own impending loss. He would've known long before she did but found herself wondering how she'd break the sad news to him, and what it would do to the paper-thin ego of this ultra sensitive man? She felt a searing empathy, guilt, and responsibility. As though she was at fault and was the cause. Peter was saying nothing, but didn't need to. It was all there on his face, written in the scarlet hue of embarrassment. She had to say something. She kissed him. "Darling this doesn't bother me too much but I know it's killing you and I don't want to put you through another of these. Peter we need more time, we'll need to spend a night together, can you manage it? Could you get away for a whole night?"

"Maybe, but I think getting away for a whole weekend would be easier," he said. "That will be much better than one night and would give us all the time we need, but how would you manage it?"

"Every so often one of us is sent on a weekend course. I could tell Kim I have to do a course, she knows the routine and would accept it without question. I leave Friday afternoon and return Sunday night, or Monday morning."

"Peter, that's brilliant," she said with unbearable excitement. I think we've got our problem solved. How soon can you go on one of these?"

"Whenever you say," he answered quietly. "I only need to give Kim a few days notice."

"Great!" she exclaimed. "I'll be off Saturday and Sunday next week....Damn!" She remembered. "We can't my period is due then... Unless you don't mind?"

"I do mind," he said fixing her a rancid look. "I want you clean."

"Leave it to me, I'll get the time within the next 4 weeks," her face lit up with a new exuberance as she began making plans inside her head. "We'll lock that door on Friday evening and throw the key away until Monday morning. I promise we'll open the door on that Monday Morning with our troubles behind us. That's if we haven't got it licked before, and if we have I'll still be holding you to that weekend," she said hopefully.

"Absolutely," he concurred.

"In the meantime I think we should carry on as normal and see what comes up," she said. He laughed. "What comes up," he echoed her poignant words. "I know what I'd like to come up," he said wishfully.

"I wonder what made me say that?"

"Wishful thinking laced with desperation," he offered. "And who could blame you?"

Peter had gone home and given Kim the business as he'd done the night before. And as on that occasion she'd felt something was wrong but was afraid she'd shake the thing apart by questioning his benevolence. She noticed his daytime behavior had not changed and he was still avoiding her. The real Peter West had not returned. Just this shadow that would crawl into bed after dark and behave as though he was carrying a grudge for her body, and would throw her around like rag-doll. Suddenly he'd become this great Acrobat putting his assistant through her paces for a new act, but as she'd been throughout their lives. She was right there for him. She took it all and came right back for more. Showing him she'd only lost a little weight, but nothing more. She was all there and not yet dead. He would exhaust himself, then turn his back and go off to sleep as if she wasn't there. Then just before dawn he'd be entering her again even before she was awake. No kissing, caressing, touching, holding, no love, just raw sex. She would lay there wondering if the man doing these things to her was really Peter, for she never saw him, and can't recall him speaking to her. He would come home about midnight and come straight to the bedroom, undress in the dark, then take her through some of the most delightful sexual acrobatics imaginable. Then he'd be gone before dawn. So it was on the third, fourth, fifth, and sixth time he failed.

In just under four weeks he had a dozen failures, and each time he'd walk away from Daisy's arms, shame-faced and despondent but would be hanging like a prized Stallion by the time he got home, ready to prove to himself that he was still a man. Peter was unaccustomed to failure and couldn't handle it. In eleven years with Kim he'd not failed her. Not once, and the first time he stepped outside his marriage he fell flat. He had run out of excuses and didn't know what to say anymore, and she must be thinking he was no good. The thought nagged him. How could she think otherwise when this was all she knew? How did she really feel about him, deep down where she hungered? Not the stream of altruistic niceties she fed him, but what she told herself. And what was she telling her friends? Was he being ridiculed and laughed at, and how soon would they start laughing to his face?

As the empty weeks dragged on he began to dread facing her, but couldn't stay away from her. On the days he didn't visit her they'd be on the phone, and would spend hours at a time listening to her as she gave an erotic commentary on what she was doing to herself. They would do it all by phone. Sadly, she'd noticed a new despondency and an increasing lack of confidence had crept into his behavior and his conversations. He implied their planned weekend was a waste of time and suggested they called it off. He then proposed giving things a rest for a month. No phone calls, nothing. At the end they could see how they felt and go on from there.

"Not on your bloody life, Peter West!" She spat her disdain.

"How could I live for a whole month without, seeing, or hearing from you, are you sure you're in love with me?"

"Daisy, if I loved you any more I'd be arrested for there' is a law against that. I need you every minute of the day and can't stop myself thinking of you. Daisy, I have no desire to drop out of your life because I'm not sure I could survive without you. But I'd rather take a chance on a month than lose you completely."

"What's this about losing me? Is there something going on I don't know about?" She questioned.

"I'm scared out of my mind that if I don't shape up you'll walk out in frustration and feel that time could be near. I couldn't blame you for wanting a real man."

"But darling you are a real man. Men do not come any better, believe me. There is more man in you than anyone I've known, and if we care to be honest, we have to admit that sex is the least important of all virtues. That's if we can truly call it a virtue. In a normal relationship we spend less time doing it than almost anything you care to mention. Think about Peter," she coaxed him. "We can do everything except the one thing, and how much time does that take? I have had men who've lasted less than fifteen seconds and have left me tearing my hair out with frustration. And they walk around calling themselves men, and telling their friends how good they are in bed. If they are men then you are Superman, because you have yet to leave me frustrated. I need you inside me, I want to feel you there, but in the meantime I'll take what you have to give without complaint, you are still the best deal in town. I love you for who you are, not what's inside your trousers. We've got a minor situation on our hands which will soon be put right, and if I fail to do that on our weekend then I'm not the woman I'm supposed to be."

Four days later he told Kim he had to do a course, and at 5pm. that Friday he packed his bag and called a cab. At 5.30 Daisy let him into the apartment, securely locking and bolting the door behind him. "You're all mine for two days and three nights," she enthused. "What should we do first?" She said with breathless glee.

"First you stash my bag out of my sight until Monday morning." He wrapped his arms around her, crushing her to his body. "Next I kiss your lips," he kissed her lightly. "Then I kiss your Breasts," he opened her robe and kissed both nipples. "Then…"

"Then I'm afraid you'll have to stop right there," she smiled. "Your best girl is in a bit of a mess at the moment."

"What do you mean?" His heart shuddered and almost stopped. She's menstruating and I'm locked in with her for three nights, he thought. "What kind of mess are you in?" She kissed him, rapaciously drawing his tongue into her mouth, but he quickly aborted the kiss. "What kind of a mess?" he repeated, his face in a festering scowl.

"Nothing that a hot bath couldn't fix," she ran her fingers through his hair. "After you left me last night I could still feel your lips on my body and could smell you all over me. You were everywhere and I was in no hurry to wash you down the drain and I just went to bed with you. This morning I woke late and had to drag on my clothes and dash out…"

"You're trying to tell me you're not clean in places?" He butted in, interrupting her flow. She grinned with embarrassment as she went into a long explanation about not being able to take a bath before, for she was expecting him earlier and didn't want him to come while, she was in the bath, and was waiting until he arrived so they could bath together.

He waited until she'd completely dried up and stood looking at him expectantly.

"I don't believe it," he said cynically.

"What don't you believe?" She giggled self-consciously.

"That you could be so embarrassed by such an insignificant matter," he smilingly indulged her a moment longer.

"It's not a small matter. No self-respecting woman wants to go around smelling like rotting fish, and if she has to put up with it for a little time, then she will but the last thing she'd want is for the man she loves and respects to suffer it also."

He studied her eyes, the shadow of his cynical grin still on his face. "I would think a competent Detective like you could come up with a more convincing story," he said. "Would you accept a tale like that from a suspect?"

She made a face. "I don't know what you mean."

"Yes you do. No matter how late you got up you could have taken a wash. You could've done it in thirty seconds, I have seen it done many times."

"I don't want to know about your wife's private habits, or to be taught feminine hygiene by her examples," she said, without rancor or maliciousness.

Impatiently he shoved her statement aside and went on. "And at any time after you got home you could have gone to the bathroom and left the door open so you could listen for the bell and got on with it. Maybe you'd care to tell me the real reason you're standing here like this?"

"I've just told you Peter."

"And I have told you no periods or unwashed genitals. You asked me what I liked and I told you. I also told you the things I didn't like. Why are you offering me something you've described as rotting fish at the start of what is to be our most glorious weekend?"

She unwrapped herself form his arms, exhaling heavily with frustration and disappointment. "Peter, why are you so paranoid? Jesus, one would think I'm asking you to eat your lunch out of it." She moved to the chair and slumped into it in exasperation. "Peter, there is sound reasoning to this, don't question it, please? I know what I'm doing."

"And what are you doing? Trying to stir and awaken the animal deep within me? Trying to arouse me with your personal aroma? As with food, they say the smell can sometimes be more exhilarating than the taste, but that is one smell I, don't need."

"How can you be so sure you don't need it, or that it won't work for you?"

"I know it will not work because I do not intend trying it," he flashed her a look of defiance and near anger.

"Peter, you're spoiling everything I've worked so hard to accomplish."

He moved lamely to the sofa and sat facing her. His feet stretched out and crossed at the ankles. "Daisy, some things I like and others I don't. I love you but I could quickly go off you if you were the kind of woman who didn't wash too often. That is how strongly I feel."

She draped her right leg over the arm of the chair, her robe gaping, displaying her blondness. "None of this is coincidence or accidental," she said with a soft serenity. "This weekend was diligently put together and is not about some dirty sluttish bitch that refuses to wash herself. It is about a woman who's prepared to prostitute her decency and integrity for the man she loves. I am not the kind of woman who drags herself around in an unwashed state, and in four weeks you may have noticed that. I'm prepared to try anything I think will work, regardless how bizarre it may seem. I have three nights to wake the sleeping Dragon and have locked away my pride, self-respect, and shame. I have a task to perform and I will not let vanity stand in my way, but I must have your help. We are supposed to be fighting this thing together you can't just drop it in my lap and walk away. You also have to make an effort and that mean dumping your pride and making sacrifices. Don't fight me, fight with me, let's work together."

Peter languished in the chair not hearing much of what was said. His eyes fastened on her matted blondness, as she overtly tried to coax the life back into him. She was an outstanding woman, and this was yet another part of her plan, he told himself, as his eyes drank in this rare delicacy of a woman. She was attacking from every angle. "You've got to give me a free hand," she gestured with her hands. "I can't work in shackles, neither can I work with you while you're hiding behind your principles. Surrender those hang-ups just for tonight and take this small step for us."

"What if I make the great sacrifice and it doesn't work?" he asked.

"You will have lost nothing in trying. There are no guarantees but we owe it to ourselves to try."

"No," he shook his head."

She sighed. "Alright Peter, I give up, we'll do it your way," she said softly. "Will you join me in the bath, or is that also against your high ideals? Sitting in my contaminated water," she asked.

He smiled. "I'll come and wash you," he offered.

What kind of a weekend will this be? She pondered the difficulties she already faced. He's so tightly screwed up I may never be able to work him loose in a year. God knows how I'll do it in two days. She picked up his bag and led him into the bedroom, and as she put the bag inside the closet he started to undress. When she swung around he was naked. This is another thing she couldn't understand. He wasn't shy or embarrassed by his, or her nudity, and was totally happy walking around her apartment naked. He was always ready and willing and would try anything. He was the most uninhibited man she'd known, yet he was so puritanically wound up about menstruation and feminine hygiene. He was the first man she'd known who didn't accept a woman's natural odors. She'd known men who did not care for it, and men who literally craved it, but had not met one who detested it with such corrosive contempt. This was another enigma to be filed away on the man to be decoded at a later date.

He came towards her, carefully studying her expression. "I hope you're not annoyed with me," he gently peeled the robe from her body and tossed it behind him on the bed.

"Why should I be mad with you? We've all got strong principles to which we have to adhere. You are simply being true to yours," she smiled. He stood back admiring her body for a long time. He liked his lips and swallowed hard. "Have I told you you're the most gorgeous lady in this City?"

"Not today, you haven't."

"You should be told three times a day, everyday," he said 'brightly.

Standing outside the bath Peter soaped the cloth and began washing her, as he would a child. He carefully did her face, taking care not to wet the towel wrapped around her hair. He washed her entire body from the side of the bath, refusing her invitation to get in with her. By eight o'clock they were stretched out naked on the floor in front of the fire drinking Champagne. Peter picked up the phone and called Kim to say he'd arrived safely, and was having a drink with a friend before turning in. He spoke to Karen for a moment, said he'd call again tomorrow and said goodnight. With his head resting on Daisy's stomach as he spoke, he could not afford a protracted conversation. It wouldn't do to show her the kind of liar he could be, knowing they might live together one day. Earlier Daisy had asked about his mother as she tried to unravel the knots in his head, throwing him a string of searching questions.

"Why didn't she take another man after your father died?" she'd asked.

"She didn't need one," he postured at first, but soon smiled warmly as he began to talk about the lady Patricia. She was still his most favored lady.

When he'd finished Daisy was stretched out on her back in thought. He looked at her and suddenly realized this setting was exactly the same as the night he'd proposed to Kim. They had just made love on the floor of his friend's living-room and Kim was on her back, looking at the ceiling, wearing a fixed smile of contentment.

The door had rattled, and she sat bolt upright. Picked up her knickers and pulled them on. "Don't be so edgy, it's only the wind," he soothed her jagged nerves, his hand affectionately stroking her thigh. "Peter I wish we had a place of our own. I can't help being jumpy, thinking your friend could walk in on us at any moment." Slowly she relaxed and reclined again but her smile had gone.

He'd lain there thinking about what she'd said and all at once he sat up. "Kim will you marry me?" And without a moment's hesitation she sat up. "Yes Peter I will marry you." Without another word they slowly reclined and he rolled over on top of her, pulled her pants askew and slithered into her.

Later as she talked about making Adrianne her chief Bridesmaid, he learned for the first time they were twins. She remarked that Adrianne was not the nicest sister in the world but she was stuck with her, and had said nothing more. However, the story was already well known that Adrianne, although recently married, was very free with her favors. She had given birth to her first child at fifteen, and at sixteen she was christened, THE PADDY FIELD, because she was mostly flat, and always wet. At seventeen she got pregnant again and Keith was forced to marry her, in spite of protesting the child was not his. Her third child was born in 1970. The same year Karen was born. The fourth, two years later when she was twenty one, and the fifth when she was twenty three.

Daisy had known just what she wanted and thought she knew how to get it, but he turned out to be a maze of complexity and her plans had to be rapidly altered. Her new strategy was to let him take charge and make his moves in his own time, and at his own pace when he felt comfortable. She was now so clean, she sparkled. He had made sure of it and had done it all himself so now he could have no objections to touching her. She would stay close, making herself available. Showing how much she needed him and how eager she was to please him. The entire weekend could gravitate into disaster if she pushed, or led him into another spate of disappointments. Hitting his ego so hard that he may decide to pick up his bag and walk out.

She had spent the past ten minutes going over his failures and a definite pattern had emerged. He'd entered her apartment that first evening with an enormous erection, and had maintained it right up to the moment it faded in bed. She was positive about this, for she hardly took her eyes off it in all that time. After three years without a man it was the kind of thing a girl would notice. It was only when she flipped him over and climbed on top that he faded. This had her thinking it was her dominance that had put him out of action. Then the moment he died she took over completely, demoralizing his fragile male ego beyond repair. Since then she had been in the driving seat and he was no more than a visiting tourist on a mystery tour, with no idea where he was being led. There she was again, even before he'd got into the apartment, nagging him into doing something that was abhorrent and distastefully against his nature. It was time she let him lead the way. This night was his to do whatever he liked and if he ran out of ideas she had a number of tricks that would surprise and delight the hell out of him. At the moment he needed no help from her, and between kisses, were whispering the most obscene things in her ears, moving from one end of her body to the next, covering her body with hot, passionate kisses, sending her into tingling ecstasy.

All at once she shivered with erotic excitement as the first drops of chilled Champagne trickled on to her back, just between her shoulder blades and slowly ran down her spine, to be met by his eager tongue lapping it up just before it sank into her cleft, sending her body into the wildest convulsions. Soon he was turning her over, so delicately. As if she was asleep and he was trying not to wake her. Then he was drinking from her navel and licking her dry. Slowly he drew his tongue up her body to her breasts, dealing with both nipples before moving on to her lips. As they kissed her thighs came apart and he slid comfortably between them.

"Daisy you are a delicious lady and you enhance the taste of best Champagne," he whispered. "I want you for breakfast in the morning, no coffee or toast, just you. I could live for a very long time on nothing but you," he breathed.

She could feel his maleness lying soft against her and began slowly rotating her hips, grinding her body against his softness. Inviting, tempting, teasing him into action. How nice it would be at this moment, she was thinking. And as if he'd read her mind, he lifted his head from her breast, and on his face was a marked look of disappointment and an air of silent apology.

"Peter I have never been happier than I am at this moment, nor have I been so much in love with a man. I want you Peter." Her gyrating hips signing her name to the promise her entire body was making. "I want to live with you, and want to be with you for the rest of my life. Leave her and move in with me. I can make you happier than you've ever been…"

He kissed her. "One thing at a time," he said. "Let's climb one mountain at a time."

At 8 o'clock next morning the radio announced that a Mr. Richard Mills, a prominent Birmingham Solicitor had been arrested as he tried to board a plane at Heathrow for the U.S.A. and had been charged with embezzlement and extortion.

"I don't believe it," she said looking at him with a fixed gaze. "I know him very well, who'd have thought he was a crook?"

"How do you know he is a crook?" He asked, pointing out that he'd only been arrested and had not been tried. "Peter we don't simply arrest people in the street on such a charge with out intensive investigation."

"Which sometimes goes horribly wrong and innocent people get convicted and put in prison," he said gravely.

"You sound like a man with an axe to grind?" She responded.

"Not and Axe," he grinned. "but the most succulently delightful woman I've known."

"And you will," she kissed him, a huge grin on her face. "You will. Oh, I've got to go," she said with breathless urgency, and clambered over him, collecting two of his marauding fingers as she did so. She gasped with delight and her grin became a grand smile. "Do that again Mr. West and I'll be forced to arrest you for a most disgusting and delightful assault on my person. No doubt you'd claim wrongful Arrest?" she said going out the door.

"I would deserve to be arrested, for impersonating a man if nothing else," he said loudly to himself.

Suffused with a feeling of acute redundancy, and an overwhelming and crushing sense of inadequacy, his thoughts drifted back over the past to his mother, and those early days. Could she have done something to him? Planted some hypnotic suggestion in his subconscious to stop him emulating his father? She had to be involved somewhere for him to be seeing her face at that crucial moment and no other time. But if that was so why didn't she stop him going with Kim? She had tried everything to stop him marrying Kim, and why didn't it work the first time he made love to her? Perhaps she'd planted a suggestion that he could have only one woman and would stay faithful to her always? "Naw," he scoffed. "She knew nothing about such things, and if she did, would not have done that to me," he said, in a wild assumption.

Chapter 12

Still deep in thought he pulled back the sheet and uncovered his sagging manhood. He raised himself and sat with it in his hands, a look of irrepressible sorrow on his face, a feeling not unlike bereavement. It was the same sense of loss and emptiness he'd felt as he touched his mother's dead body, and again that morning as he held Michaela in his arms. Once again he was hit by the same melancholia as he held this dead piece of his anatomy.

"What are you doing to me, what are you trying to tell me?" he said with so much sadness he was almost in tears. "You can talk to me, you are my best friend. What are you trying to say, that I shouldn't be cheating on my wife? That I shouldn't be wanting this woman, shouldn't be locked away in her apartment while my wife thinks I'm at work, what lessons are you trying to teach me by making a right cunt out a me? What the fuck does all this mean? I know that I could get out of this bed, go home and be fucking the arse off Kim in less than half an hour, and give her a repeat performance thirty minutes later and you'd still be rearing to go. So why aren't you rearing now? Speak to me. Twitch if you understand me. He stroked it lightly with one finger, up and down its full length. "We have come a long way together," he said in a near whisper. "thirty years and one woman. Don't you think it's time we tried another one? We have seen nothing of life and this can't be the way it was meant to be. I need this woman and I'm entitled to her, I have a right to her. So please. For Daisy's sake, and mine, stop sulking and get on with the fucking job you were bolted to my body to do. All you've ever had to do are two little jobs, and that is the trouble with you, you've had it too good. Everything else is hanging on the outside in the cold, wind, rain and all manner of shit. They all have a thousand different jobs to do and none have ever let me down. All you have to do is piss and fuck. It is not your job to choose my women. Because you're wrapped up, cosseted and privileged you think you're king of the castle and can do as you like. We came into this world together and will be going out together. I'll be in a right shit if I allow you to expire before me, and I'll be fucked if I'm going to let 'you chose my women now that I know you've got no fucking taste whatsoever. If you can look at a woman like Daisy and not feel, or see anything, then you were blind before you withered and died…."

Daisy returned, pushed the door open with her foot and came in with two cups of coffee. She looked at him and her heart leapt so violently the cups rattled in their saucers.

"Calm yourself girl," she spoke softly. "relax, no need to get silly with excitement."

Gently placing the cups on the bedside table as she spoke silently to herself, afraid to address him in case she broke the spell, not daring to take her eyes from his body in case that too broke the spell. Peter made no attempt to speak, he just sat holding this thing in his right fist, smiling up at her as though he couldn't quite believe it himself.

Pandering to his paranoia, she'd gone to the bathroom and taken a wash and was regretting it painfully. All that soap and water had left her as dry as the Sahara and there would be no time to play around until she was ready, but she wasn't going to lose him again. Calmly, she stuck two fingers into her mouth, saturating them with saliva, and quickly got on the bed, hovering above him for a mere instant before lowering her body in a squat and gently impaling herself.

"Jesus Christ!" She sighed as he settled inside her. "Peter you are huge….Jesus…how long have you been sitting here like this, couldn't you call me?" She said, but before he could answer she was kissing him.

It was 3pm. when they got up, and by then he was sure Kim would never return to that sacred place she once held in his heart. The only question now was when he'd leave her? Daisy May Spencer had to be the most accomplished lover ever, and she was his. Nothing, or no one else mattered.

Monday morning he left her apartment and went straight to work. He called her at lunch, and by 5.30 pm he was back in her apartment, making love to her on the living-room floor without bothering to take off his jacket. "We have a lot of catching up to do," he'd said.

For the rest of that week he was in her apartment every night, and Kim was right back in the Dog house. This might not have bothered her too much, but he was now staying out most of the night and wouldn't get home before two, or three in the morning.

Since the day they met Peter had slowly dropped most of his friends and didn't go out after work, except for the time before his mother died when he visited her daily. Since then his pattern had remained the same. Now he was coming in at these wild hours, telling her he was out with friends. She tried telling herself nothing was wrong but knew it was self-delusion; He was having an affair and she didn't need to see him with the woman to know that. She tried discussing it but he simply laughed, saying it was all in her mind, and would try to explain by offering more excuses, about frustration, and a need to get out of the house and all its sad memories. First it was his mother, then Michaela. Now she was getting thinner each day and seem to be drawing closer to death's door. A mere shadow of what she was, a living ghost looking for a place to haunt. He was quick to point out that until she got back to being the woman he'd loved, he wasn't sure what kind of life they'd have, or if they would have one.

Kim was more anguished than at any time since Michaela's death. Along with losing her baby she barely had a husband. Once he would grudgingly give in to her demands for sex but now he just ignores her without the usual pretence of being asleep, or claims of exhaustion. There wasn't a single aspect of their lives that had not been touched by the tragedy, and Karen was the latest casualty. She was no longer that sweet innocent adorable child. The brief suspicion of murder was all it took to twist her mind beyond reason, and she blamed herself for that, having been the one who first pointed the accusing finger at her. Now she was slowly losing another daughter. If only she could take back those words.

Daisy didn't call at the house anymore, and had resorted to phoning Karen. With things as they were she was a touch uneasy sitting within a whisper of his wife, pretending she was there just to see Karen. In addition, they could not keep away from each other's body and knew it would not be long before Kim walked in and found him with his fingers, or something else inside her.

Peter sat looking around the bedroom, letting his thoughts drift back to happier times. So much had changed since those enchanting days with his mother, but he could close his eyes and recall the room exactly as it was when he was sixteen years old. He could remember one very interesting conversation they had one evening as he sat on the end of the bed watching her brush her hair. For work she'd wear it pinned up and clipped into place with a series of combs, and sometimes it would be tied with a single ribbon, to match either her dress or shoes. In the evenings she'd let it loose, and with a little shake of her head a cascade of, shimmering golden brown hair, would fall about her shoulders. At times she'd let him take out the pins and he'd have the enthralling pleasure of watching this exquisite show at close quarters. She was the prettiest woman he'd ever seen.

As he sat watching her this warm sunny evening, a light refreshing breeze gently ruffled the curtain through the open window. The wallpaper was pink rosebud on a blue background, with flecks of gold. The Carpet was a thick shagpile in plain Ivory. He could still remember the luxuriant feel of the carpet as he sat caressing its thick pile with his toes. The dressing table had been backed on to the window for as far back as he could remember, but after having the room decorated she had it moved sideways-on and backed against the wall, to let more light into the room.

As she brushed her hair she paused and leaned forward, peering into the mirror, fingering a spot to the right of her nose. "I must be getting old," she remarked. "Every day a new blemish appears on my skin. The time is drawing close when you'll be dragging me screaming out of my house and committing me to a home for the aged and infirm, so you can bring in your women."

Peter fell back on the bed in wild laughter.

"You can laugh but that day may be closer than you think," she peered at her reflection, inspecting her face for further signs of aging.

He sat up. "Why are you talking like this Pat? What's got into you?"

"I've just told you. One day you'll kick me out…."

"Pat I'm trying to be serious," he said irritably.

She turned facing him. "So am I son. So am I, and I know a lot more than you," she said with the pseudo concern of a mischief-maker. "I have to be realistic and face facts. There will come a day when you won't want this old woman hanging around your neck any longer and will shake me loose. When I'm seventy you'll be forty four, a comparatively young man. Why would you want to remain tied to me when you could be out living life? Having a good time with someone your own age, or half your age?" she smiled cryptically.

"Mom, don't talk silly," he said showing he was no longer amused. "I don't know what they've been saying to you at work but I wish they would shut up."

"No one said anything to me at work," she said innocently.

"Then where did this depressing subject come from, and why? Mom you're still a young woman, and very beautiful. I love you now, and will love you just the same fifty years from now. Pat I'm not saying this because you're my mother or to flatter you but because it's the truth. I've been sitting here thinking that if I was ever to get married she'd have to be a woman just like you."

"So you are planning to get married," she said triumphantly.

He exhaled heavily. "Mom, will you please listen?"

"All right I'm listening," she humored him.

"I was saying, it would have to be a woman just like you, but as I'm not sure I'll find someone like you, I don't think I'll ever get married and is destined to spend the rest of my life here with you." He touched her hair. "Mom, we'll be together a long time and there will be no other home for you. Do you think I'd put you in a home and leave strangers to look after you?" His lips curled in scorn. "You think I'd let a bunch of impatient strangers ill-treat and abuse you, have them drag you in and out of the bath like a lump of dead meat? Look what happened to Mrs. Douglas. She was only seventy one but she died a week after being put into that home. Mom I hope I don't die before you, but if I do I'm hoping you'll come shortly after me. I don't want you getting old and helpless without me here to look after you. I'll take good care of you, devoting my whole life to you. Caring for you as you've done for me since the day I was born. I hope we have each other to the very end."

She'd sat quietly with her face turned toward the window as he spoke and was still in the same position moments after he'd finished.

"Pat?" He spoke softly, touching her shoulder. She turned, eyes glazed with the first beads of tears filtering through her lower lashes. She wasn't crying because of the nice things he'd said, although they had touched her more deeply than anything he'd said before. It was the sheer innocence of the child. Naivety laced with ignorance and an over simplified expectation. She took his hand and squeezed it tightly, feeling a sense of responsibility for having instilled and encouraged his rose-colored outlook.

"I love you Mom," he got to his feet and standing behind her, wrapped his arms around her in a tight embrace.

"You are the best son a mother could have," she looked at his reflection in the mirror. "You've got a heart of gold and I love you. I am flattered that you care so much for me, but there are things we have to discuss, important things. It's my turn to talk and I want you to sit and listen.

"Go on I'm listening," he festively intoned.

"I can't talk while you're standing there squeezing the breath out of me," she shook him loose. "Sit down!" He reclaimed his position on the end of the bed. She pointed out that it was quite natural for a boy to be in love with his mother and wanted to marry someone just like her, it happens all the time but they usually grow out of it, and so would he. "There are no women just like me," she said emphatically. "We are all different and you'll have to accept that and make your choice based on love, and not beauty."

He seemed confused. "I don't understand, I thought you wanted me here with you always. Instead you're trying to pawn me off on some ugly woman?"

She smiled. "I'm not trying to get rid of you, it would be nice having you here always."

"So what's the problem?"

"The problem is what I want and what I'll get will be two different things. I happen to know that one day you'll walk out and find a girl and start talking marriage, which is exactly as it should be."

"Pat you are wrong. There will never be any other girl for me but you. I won't ever leave you….you are all I need."

"Peter I'm not all you need," her voice chilled with concern. "You are soon to have needs that I will never fill. Things of which you have no knowledge at this time but will soon begin to discover. There will be times in your life when I'll be of no use to you and would be the last woman you want around. I have managed to fill your life so far and have done the best I could. Now you're at a stage when your needs are rapidly changing and very soon you'll start looking outwards. This is nature's law, and it's in the nature of man to obey this law. You are soon to be a man and there is nothing you or I or anyone else can do to alter the course you must take. The tide will be too strong and will sweep you away before you know what hits you."

"And what form will this miracle take?" He gestured. "This thing that will come in and drag me out, how will I know when it arrives, this thing that will fulfill needs I'm yet to have?" He grinned facetiously.

"It'll come to you in the shape of a girl and when she arrives you'll know about it. All your questions will be answered, including those you've not asked."

"It seems that girl will be the answer to all my prayers," he chortled. "Prayers I've not yet said, but I still don't understand. I thought it was I who had to go out and look for this girl, and was the one who decided whether we got together or not? So what chance will she have when I've already decided I don't want her?"

"You're only sixteen years old and right now you think you know what you want. Such decisions are not yet yours to make, and even when that day comes you'll think you're in control but you'll be wrong. No man is ever in control where a woman is concerned. Your father wasn't looking for marriage, he was after something else, and when he got it he couldn't leave it alone. Men like to think they're in charge of a woman's body and like to believe in their mastery and prowess. Your father wasn't ready for marriage and wasn't suited to it, but I had no way of knowing that. I was in love with him and he never stood a chance. Don't be so sure of yourself Peter. A woman can slice your heart open with a mere smile and walk straight in. You have a lot to learn about life, and women in particular."

"Maybe Dad wasn't in love with you," he thoughtfully offered.

"He was in love with me, I'm sure of that. He loved me with everything he had, he just didn't have enough of anything, and was exceptionally deficient in fidelity...Still, he wasn't all bad and I could not have loved him more."

Peter hung there like a wet rag trying to fathom this woman who was suddenly behaving like a total stranger. This was a side of her he'd not seen before. All his life she'd been poisoning his mind against women and now the poison had worked it's way into his system she was feeding him something else. For years she'd sold herself as the only woman who could love him and be true to him. The only woman he could trust. Why was she now trying so hard to prepare his mind for this mystery woman he was yet to meet? A woman who didn't exist, and if she did it wouldn't matter for his heart had already been taken. He had a woman, he told himself.

"Patricia," he said her name with a soft sigh. "I'm even in love with your name. Pat...Patricia...You were right Pat. Calling you by your first name has brought us so much closer. It has removed the wall between us and made you so much more..." he wavered, diligently searching for the right words. "so much more approachable. It took away my mother and gave me you. A woman I could give the kind of love a man gives to a woman and not that of a boy to his mother. Pat I don't think you understood what I was trying to say earlier..." Eyes quizzically narrowed she stared at him, a germ of light seeping into her darkened mind for the first time, and awakening her senses.

"I was trying to say I'm in love with you," he said. "All those things you described, this woman who walks in and steals my heart. She isn't someone who'd be waiting up the road for me, she is already here. All those things you talked about I now feel for you. Pat, you are that woman and I have no need for another. Not now or anywhere in the future.

"But Peter, you don't understand…"

"Pat I do understand. I understand more clearly than you think. I know what it means to be in love with a woman, I know what lovers are and I know what they do, and how 'they feel for each other. Pat we've been lovers for years and have done all those things."

"Peter we have not been lovers, what are you talking about child? We have a great mother and son relationship, don't confuse it with something you know nothing about. There is a difference, and when you are experienced you'll be able to make that distinction."

"You think I'm still a child but you're wrong, I know all about love and sex," he sounded hurt.

"Sex, what do you know, have you experienced sex?" She realized her words were corning out more bitter than intended, and reigned in her anger. It wasn't meant for him but was directed at herself for making such a mess of the boy's mind.

"Just what you've told me and what I've read in those books downstairs," he answered fretfully.

"What I've told you is only a very small part of a long story, and scanning through medical journals is yet another tiny part of that story." Her tone now lightened and sweetened with a smile. "A true knowledge of sex will come with experience. When you find your first girlfriend it will all begin, and come together. I am your mother and cannot be your lover, the two do not go together,"…Dear father above, how could I have got it so wrong and made such hash of things? She castigated herself. All I wanted was a normal well adjusted son who loved me, not fall in love with me, a son who'd grow up a credit to himself and his mother, and make a good husband, and father to his children.

Peter watched her brushing her hair with a strange detachment. Looking more confused than at any other time in her life. She seemed lost and irresolute, as though she was having trouble believing her own words. He thought about stretching the conversation but changed his mind. She may be perplexed but she still had her wits about her. He'd learnt from an early age he could not defeat her with words. She could take his winning argument, wrap it in confusion and throw it back at him like a poisoned dart.

"But I didn't say that," he'd defend.

"What did you say?" She'd smile. "What exactly did you say?" He'd begin again, but would soon be so muddled that he'd repeat just what she'd accused him of saying. She'd then laugh as if to say, you're not yet ready for me son. He decided the way to win this battle was by deed. He would show how much he loved her and she'd understand he was no longer a child and wanted no other woman. She would come to know he was a man, and the kind of man that kept his word and stood by the woman he loved. He wanted her and no one else, and would sooner die than look at another. This he'd told himself as he sat admiring her that evening.

At the time held recently left school and was filling time before College with a job at Daley's Restaurant in the City, not far from where, she worked. Some mornings they'd plan the dinner together and he'd have it ready by the time she got home. Other times held get it started, run the vacuum cleaner through the living and dining rooms, tidy up a bit, then hop on a bus and meet her at work and they would walk home together. Then while she was taking her bath he would finish the dinner and have it on the table when she came down. His hours were 10am. to 3pm. and this left him lots of time to charm her with his love and obsequious devotion. Some days he'd turn up at 3.30 and would sit waiting in her office until 6.o'clock. One day he arrived at 3.45 but soon disappeared, and didn't return until 5.30. Two days later he did the same thing, explaining that he'd gone for a walk around the City. This didn't seem right and instantly triggered her suspicion. She couldn't think why he'd want to lie, and would have to look into it. She also enjoyed his company immensely, and had enjoyed popping back to the office every so often for a chat… On the third occasion this happened she followed him, not quite knowing why she was following her son like a jealous wife, but there was this compulsion to know what he was up to and she couldn't explain it. She felt like a nosey interfering bitch, hands covering her face and dodging behind customers each time he looked around.

She followed him down the stairs to the floor below and tracked him all the way through fancy goods and into kitchen utensils. She saw him approach this young woman, who obviously knew him quite well, from the width of her smile. She knew the girl, her name was, Cindy Davies, a nineteen year old recently transferred from furniture to kitchenware.

She kept wondering where they'd met, as they laughed and chatted like old friends. He said something which made her giggle and she held his fore arm for an instant, a harmless gesture. Just someone touching a friend in a festive mood, but Pat felt her blood pressure surged, and a chronic possessiveness instinctively saturated her body and soul. Face flushed and tight with a peculiar discomfort in her stomach, she wheeled around and marched broodingly back to her department.

He returned at 5,45pm, and told her he'd gone to the Palisades, New Street Station, The Bullring. And so he continued reading out the names of all these places, but she'd lost interest and had stopped listening.

Men! She said to herself. They start learning to lie from the cradle. They stand in front of you wetting their nappies at one end while lying from the other.

The next day she went down to Kitchen Ware and inspected a kettle as if she was planning to make a purchase, and rapidly steered the conversation around to Peter. "I see you've met my son," she said with simulated glee.

The girl stared at her somewhat bewildered.

"Peter," she said excitedly. "That tall dark haired young man you were talking with yesterday."

"Oh!" She said. "I didn't know he was your son?"

"A fine boy," Pat said. "They grow up so fast, you wouldn't think he was only fifteen, would you?"

The pretty brunette suddenly gasped with surprise. "He told me he was eighteen," she said.

"Oh God, what have I done?" Pat exclaimed. "He'll hate me for this, I had no idea," she said making all the noises of regret and atonement.

"Don't worry about it I won't say a word," The girl promised. "I liked him," she added. "I liked him a lot, but I didn't know. I'm glad you told me before I did something silly."

"How did you meet?" Pat asked.

"We met last week at the Cliff Richard Concert. He was there without a ticket and I had two because my friend was ill and couldn't make it. He said he was 18 and I believed him.".…Fifteen is against the law, she reminded herself. Cindy Davies charged with molesting a minor. She saw the imaginary headlines. Pat couldn't tell what had transpired but he never went for another walk, and had shown no signs of rejection. She couldn't have meant much, she thought in trying to justify what she'd done.

As Peter got more competent he became wildly adventurous and had partially taken over the cooking. Planning the meals and going out of his way to provide her special favorites, like grilled Rock Salmon and his own brand of Lobster Supreme. On her 42nd birthday he arranged a surprise dinner.

That evening she came home to find a dazzling bouquet of Carnation and white Roses with a charming card that simply said. "To Patricia—from Peter." He later spent ten minutes going through her Wardrobes and finally took out a slinky black velvet dress he'd help her choose three months earlier, and was yet to wear.

"There!" He said laying it gently on the bed.

She made a disapproving face. "Black! Why Black?" She politely inquired.

"Because I feel in a black mood tonight," he cheerfully answered.

"But Peter, do you Know what it means to be in a black mood? It means you're depressed and…."

"I Know what you think it means," he said sharply. "But a black mood isn't necessarily a bad thing. What about Black people? Would you say their moods are all bad? They also say the devil has a black heart. But then I also hear you can't get into hell on a Saturday night because of all the people coming down from heaven to have a good time."

"Where did you get that?" She laughed heartily.

"Tonight I want you to be the devil's lady," he grinned roguishly.

Isn't it like a man not to care how I feel? He wanted black to match his mood so black it had to be. And what about my mood, didn't that count?

"Peter, have you forgotten I have to lose a little weight before I can comfortably get into this dress?" She tried a little subterfuge but Peter wouldn't hear of it.

"You get dressed and if it doesn't fit I'll let you know. I want you looking your best tonight and until you do we're not leaving this house," he said projecting a new and disturbing dominance.

She didn't care for his strident tone, but with silent reluctance, she acceded. She could see no other way. An argument now would've spoilt the night beyond repair.

At eight o'clock the living-room door swung open and she appeared looking like someone from the front page of Vogue. She was stunning. Long brown hair shimmering like threads of dark gold, soothingly, harmonizing with the rich ebony of her dress. Peter was bewitched by her splendor. He got to his feet and ambled across the room as though in a dream and kissed her, his lips pressing hard against hers, his tongue darting into her mouth.

This can't be, he's my son, she kept reminding herself. He can't be kissing me like this. Oh dear God, what have I created?

All at once he pulled away and his head sagged to the floor... "I-I-I'm sorry mom, I'm sorry, I don't know what made me do it. I didn't mean to." he frantically repented, his voice creaking with emotion.

She placed a hand under his chin and picked up his head. "I see nothing wrong with a son giving his mother a sloppy wet kiss on her birthday, do you?" She tried to lift the heavy burden of guilt from his shoulders.

"You didn't mind?" he 'sounded surprised.

"Of course I didn't mind. Only next time don't make it so sloppy. And I suppose that meant the dress is alright?" She added dryly.

"Yes Mom it's beautiful and you look great," his voice exploding with delight.

"I'm glad the devil approves," she said liltingly.

Just then a horn sounded outside. "The taxi is here," he said heading for the door.

"You've got lipstick on your face, just open the door and ask him to wait. You have to clean up your face and I have to repair my lips," She headed up the stairs battling her dilemma. She'd spent years sowing the seeds without giving a thought to the crop, or how she'd reap it. Now the ripened fruit was standing there demanding to be harvested. She had no wish to encourage him, neither could she reject him, and could see some difficult times ahead as he became more enamored with her as a woman. He no longer saw her through the eyes of a child but was seeing her with the appraising, and approving eyes of a man. She may even have to start locking her door at night, the crazy thought crept into her head as she sat doing her lips.

Chapter 13

Before getting into the taxi he whispered. "Mom you're stunning, and I'm filled with pride going out with you and to be seen with you." Pat had asked where they were going but Peter wouldn't say, and she was hoping to hear when he told the driver, but it seems he already knew the destination.

"Aren't you telling him where we're going?" She said when they were half way up the road.

"No," he said smiling mysteriously.

She drew closer and linked her arm with his. "Darling, where are we going?" She whispered. And how can you afford all this, flowers, Taxi...?"

"You worry too much," he told her. "Can't a fellow take his best girl out for her birthday?"

"Yes but..."

"But nothing, it's a surprise," he said flatly.

Throughout the five minute journey he kept glancing at her in disbelief. Wondering if she could have made a mistake with her age, for she looked closer to twenty two, than forty two. He wished the entire City could see him stepping out with this exquisite lady.

As they arrived at the Restaurant the manager met them at the door and discretely inquired if there had been a change of plans?

"Why?" Peter asked.

"Because we've made all the arrangements for your mother and wasn't told about anyone else," the man said in a quiet dignified, but slightly ruffled tone.

"But this is my mother!" He proudly proclaimed. "Mom, this is my Boss, Mr. Hammond, This is my mother, Mrs. Patricia West."

To her profound delight it had taken several minutes to convince the man she was indeed Peter's mother.

Peter sat looking at her across the table with desire in his heart and a flame in his soul. In his head was a feeling of disgust for wanting her the way he did. Something had begun inside him, the moment he'd seen her in that dress, and was rapidly taking him over. At the same time someone else was competing with him for her attention and he didn't like it. Mr. Hammond was a man he admired immensely but the man had began to annoy him, and as he hovered attentively around the table a streak of pernicious resentment grew inside him and Peter lost his smile to a brooding face.

Pat read his face and she knew that very soon he'd become restless, agitated and would try to bring the evening to a close. It had been the loveliest birthday she could remember and was not about to have it spoilt. She leaned across the table and took his hands. "Peter I'm your lady, yours alone. Don't worry about him he could never come between us, no one can." she smiled sweetly.

She knew this was his way of showing how much he cared, and as nice as it was, she'd told herself it was the final flickering flame from the dying embers of childhood love that had raged within his heart for her. Like the final flame that spurts out when a fire had been doused. She knew that some time between now and his 18th birthday she'd begin to see marked changes in him as he shed the mantle of childish desires and adopted the role of a man. She knew that one day he would indeed find a girl and start talking marriage. All this she'd long accepted, her one desire was that when the day came he would not leave home, but would chose to bring his wife back into their home. It was his home and nothing could be more natural than for him to bring up his kids right there in the house in which he was brought up. This was her fervent hope.

As Peter continued enchanting her with an ever increasing passion she was slowly being sold on the notion that he could be different, and could conceivably be true in his preaching.

He was now taking her out at least once a week. A play at the Alex, a concert at the town Hall, or a night at the Rep, or the movies. He had even managed to take her into a Pub and bought her a drink. The first time she'd been inside a Pub in twelve years. She was worried sick as she stood in the crowded pub thinking any minute the Police would arrive and arrest her son for drinking in a public house at his age. She quickly swallowed the brandy. "Come on we're leaving, you're not supposed to be, here," she said.

"Pat you worry too much, I don't look sixteen," he said.

"I don't care," she said locking arms with him and marching him out.

Over the next few months Peter had skillfully banished her doubts and worked his way around all her sound rational arguments. She wanted to believe he was the exception to nature's stringent rules and needed to believe, for without this she had nothing except that shrinking hope he would move his wife in. The emptiness she'd seen in looking ahead to a time when he'd no longer be there for her was something she could not face, and as he continued to enthrall her. Once impossible dreams began to seem a reality, and the thought of having another woman—not only sharing him but—taking him over completely and exclusively, and right there in her own home was worse than torture. No one to embrace her at the end of a hard day and tell, her how much he loved her, and remind her she was still the most attractive woman in town. Now she'd be reduced to watching another woman take her place as the most important person in his life. She found that the only way to wipe this horror from her mind was to believe he'd never leave her or take another woman. Then when the time came for College and he realized the closest placing would put him out of Birmingham, and meant he'd have to leave home for the first time, he refused to go. Said he was not leaving her and would wait until a place was available in Birmingham. Pat hated the thought of a separation as much as he did but had to shelve her own feelings and make the sacrifice for the sake of his career. Peter had always wanted to become a Chef, with his own restaurants, and Pat would've sooner died of loneliness than stand in his way. Sadly Peter didn't see it that way. His mind was set as though cast in concrete, and he wasn't leaving home. She threw everything she could find, including tears but nothing worked.

He was not going to college until something came up closer to home where he could get home at the end of each day. One day as she pleaded with him not to throw his life away waiting for something that may never come, he suddenly got angry and accused her of wanting to get rid of him because she had other plans. Finally she gave up and left him in peace.

By this time, she was so well primed that she was now firing automatically. His determined stand had said it all, and as far as she was concerned there was no longer any need to sell her his devotion she was now busy selling it to herself with the tenacity of an insurance salesman. Talking herself into believing that if he could pass up his golden opportunity for a career he'd so desperately wanted to stay by her side then nothing else could come between them. Forgetting this was just a repeat performance of his first day at kindergarten, when he'd clung to her crying his heart out, he didn't want to go. Except for the tears and the tantrum, and the fact that he now stood facing her, this was no better. In truth this was much more disturbing, for he was nearly seventeen years old and was still clinging to his mother's dress, refusing to be parted form her.

"Peter was the most conforming and obedient child a mother could have," she'd said, when he was fourteen, and was so worried he'd grow up to be a gutless yes-man, who would not stand up for himself, and would be used as a virtual piss-pot by women, that she'd asked if he never felt like defying her, standing up to her and saying what he felt? He'd explained that he'd always showed exactly what he felt, and that was love and obedience, and a desire to please her always. It wasn't because he was afraid or intimidated, but because he loved her so much.

One day, about a year later, he waltzed into the shop on the corner of their street and saw her talking to a man. He stood for some time glaring at the man and as she tried to introduce them he stormed off in a huff. The moment she arrived home he demanded to know who he was, and what did he want? She promptly slapped his face, reminding him he was the child, and if he'd wanted to know he should have behaved like the civilized person she'd brought him up to be, and not walked out like an ill mannered pig. The perversity was that she had reveled in this behavior and things were moving along the route she'd long chosen. He was brought up to be dependent on her for his very thoughts.

Pat had never needed a babysitter, Peter was too precious to be exposed to that kind of influence and had done it all herself. Except for school, and the brief period before his father died, he was not accessible to any other doctrine but hers. He was inordinately possessive and suffused with jealousy, but this was as planned. The broth had not gone bad, that was exactly the way she'd seasoned it, rich and slightly pungent. This offensive behavior was a part of the agreed price for what she was getting in return and she was quite happy to live with it.

Peter was laid off from his job shortly after his 17th birthday, and Pat suggested he took a job at the place 'his father worked. This was meant to be a mere pause, before College but he was never to leave again.

Chapter 14

After his unhappy experience with the first two girls, Peter began to adjust to the sense and sound reasoning of his mother, and was slowly being converted to the premise that all women had been created with a major design fault, and his own mother was a classic example. She'd begged him to stand up for what he believed and show his steel, and when he did she hit him. This experience left him thinking that no woman really knew what she wanted. He'd thought she was perfect but she had the same glaring deficiency as all the others she'd so vehemently derided. This had been his belief until the night he strolled idly into the Mulberry Bush and met the perfect woman. This time he had no fear of his mother knowing and had literally ran home to break the news that he'd found the one girl that was different.

Peter entered the house floating on a cloud of fermenting desire, and a frenzy of excitement. He bubbled over with an effervescence she'd not seen in her little boy before. With a broad grin and the breathless intoxication of one who'd just experienced his first orgasm he brandished word like love, exciting, enchanting. He said she was the most refined girl he'd ever seen, she was magnificent.

His mother sat with a thinly veiled expression of hostility, sick to her stomach with the disappointment of his betrayal, as he raged on about it being the happiest day of his life. But it was the part about marrying her one day that goaded her into the response she'd been battling to contain.

Suddenly she exploded. "You fool! You pathetic innocent idiot. Haven't you taken in anything over the past eleven years?"

"Mom, she's different and you'll see when you meet her…"

"Don't you bring her into my house I don't want to meet her!" she spat through gritted teeth."

"But Pat…"

"Don't you dare call me Pat I'm your mother, not some filthy trollop you picked up on the street," she hissed.

"But Mom all women are not the same, Kimberly is different."

"Don't be a fool, you know nothing about women and even less about this—girl you just picked up. Think son, think. I'm on your side," she said, her tone altered to a measured calm. "I've been on your side since the day I screamed myself silly and gave birth to you. I stood up for you against your father and since those days I've been right beside you all the way. Darling, do you think I'd do or say anything to hurt you? All I've ever wanted is what's best for you, and this is the kind of disaster I've devoted my life to avoid. You don't know what you're saying, this girl is no different from any other."

"How can you say that when you haven't met her and don't know her?"

"And I suppose you know everything about her in the little time you've known her?"

"Not everything, but enough."

"How much is enough—just what do you know about her? Peter, how long have you known her?" she demanded. He didn't answer. "When did you meet her?" she barked, her abrasive tones suddenly returned.

Peter's shoulders sagged and his head fell. "We met earlier this evening," he said in a tiny voice.

She burst into a loud synthetic laughter that died as rapidly as it had begun. "This is not a joke but if didn't laugh I'd cry, and I don't want to start crying again, I've had enough of that with your father. Right now you're in danger of breaking my heart and trampling it to death, with your innocence and stupidity. Peter, how can you be so blindly in love with someone you've known a few hours? You know nothing about love and what you're feeling has nothing to do with love."

"What about the love we share, isn't that real?" he asked.

"What we have is good, pure and perfect, so much different from anything you could feel for her."

"But it isn't," he disagreed. "I feel the same love for her I have for you."

She shook her head. "Son you're wrong, what we have is different. What you're feeling for that person isn't love but lust, sex, perverted bodily cravings. Your heart is being ruled by the filthy thoughts in your head. I bet she was dressed in some vulgar little skirt that barely covered her backside and wearing no knickers? Son, if you let your body succumb to those depraved longings you will find yourself in big trouble. You don't know how to protect yourself, what if she isn't clean and gives you something? What would you do then, come running to me I suppose? Peter you're not ready for any of this, you have so much to learn. So much I have not yet taught you."

"Mom I know everything I need right now, the rest can come later."

"After you've made her pregnant?" she bristled. "nothing gives a truer meaning to love than telling a man you're pregnant. Suddenly his love has died and all he wants is to get his trousers on and run like a dose of salts. Don't wait for that Peter, turn back before it's too late. Even if your lust survives that hurdle, the sound of babies screaming in your ears day and night will finish you off." She took a shallow breath. "Get through that and you will find your troubles are not yet over, for the first time she leaves her blood-soaked sanitary towel on the bathroom floor your so-called love will die screaming and you'll come running back to me. I know son, it will not be easy living out there with such a woman after coming out of a home like this. Soon you'd begin to see her filthy habits, like not washing her hands after using the toilet, then preparing your food.... Like washing herself and her knickers in the kitchen sink, and drying her private parts with your best tea-towel. Or not bothering to wash at all and bringing her foul smelling body to bed. You understand what I'm saying to you Son? I am not making this up as I go along or dramatizing it to scare you. Some of those things I've witnessed many times at work."

Peter sat grinning openly, as though to say. Pull the other one Mom. He threw up his hands. "I don't believe you," he said, unable to hold a straight face and chuckling. "You are desperately trying to put me off Kimberly and I can see that."

"Are you calling me a liar?" She said, face rancid with distaste.

"No I'm not, just that, you'd say anything to stop me getting close to Kim. Mom I know what you're doing and it won't work. You're using my fears and misgivings against me, along with some others you've tossed in for dramatic effect," he laughed. "You've gone back into my childhood, haven't you? It's those days all over again. If you don't eat your dinner you'll be like Kenny down the road, unable to walk and have to be pushed around in a wheelchair. If you don't behave I'll put you outside and the darkness will get you....Oh, and the one about black men coming to cut my heart out. Mom I'm nineteen years old, I've grown up now. Parts of what you've said is scaring the devil out of me, and I'm deeply concerned. I dread having to face those faults in any woman of mine but I'll deal with it, if and when it comes. It may affect me but will not defeat me. I'm ready for anything they care to throw at me. In fact it doesn't matter at this point because I have no plans to leave home. I'll be here with you for a long time, and I hope you'll come to accept Kimberly because I'm not losing her. I love her and want her in my life for all times," he postured.

She poured scorn on his brave words. "I can't believe I've spent all those years trying to put you right only to discover you're no better than your father, and your first sniff of a sour crotch has turned your head the same way. Come to your senses, you don't know how she feels about you or if she cares at all. How do you know she hasn't got another man, or a couple of kids at home waiting for you to adopt?"

As she went on he dropped out of the conversation, reverting to silence as was his way throughout his life. The moment she swung into one of her incantations, he'd play the sweet, silent, subservient child, too reverent and polite to talk back, regardless how strong the urge to put her right. He'd learned to lock himself away from her words while pretending to be listening attentively.

Looking back he could see he'd been mistaken, for with his tacit approval had created a despot who couldn't understand why this feeble brainwashed peasant, whom she'd washed, fed and clothed—Given a good home and a taste of the good life—was suddenly revolting?

The trouble wasn't in what he'd said, but that he'd dared to have an opinion and had voiced it. Her pernicious anger, had taken him by surprise and left him so perplexed he wanted to cry. He was never more shocked than the moment she slapped him down for calling her Pat. Since he was nine years he'd been allowed to call her by her first name, providing they were alone. She had suggested, and had actively encouraged it, saying it would bring down that matriarchal barrier, and bring them closer to being real friends, and he could converse with her on equal terms. The choice was his, whether he called her Pat or Patricia, it didn't matter, and for years it didn't. Now all of a sudden it did, and he was wondering why? She was like an angry fish-woman caught with her fat fingers on the scale, using words that had not passed her lips before, simply to defend her bigotry and speculative opinions. Arguments to which he'd given no credence, and was opposed, but had gone along with her out of respect and the erroneous belief that it couldn't hurt and would keep her sweet.

She'd had enough pain in her life and he felt duty bound to play the part she'd written for him and had spent all those years rehearsing him to perfection. He could see she'd been diligently grooming him for a life that excluded all other women, but wasn't concerned. He had spent some time formulating his own counter plan. He would have all the girlfriends he needed when he was ready, like any other young man of his age. Except he'd keep this side of his life from her while maintaining the facade of that celibate monk-like existence she'd carved out for him. This he thought was the just thing considering his objections to her having a man. This plan, although flawed with garish imperfections, might still have worked, hadn't he stumbled on the gorgeous Kimberly Stevens, who had torn his plan to pieces.

Two weeks after meeting Kimberly he'd not managed to talk his mother around to using her name, and she was still being addressed as that girl, at best, and other times she was, that bitch. Meeting her was something Pat would not accommodate under any circumstance. Peter threatened to bring her home whether she approved or not, and for a moment she was caught without an answer. He'd ignored her rantings, and hysterical jealousy and had defiantly stood his ground through the full force of her bluster. This ranged from not letting the girl into the house, to letting her in and showing her she was not welcomed, by not speaking to her. And if this failed then she'd give it to her in plain English. Peter regarded this with suitable indifference, until she threatened to go out and bring back the first willing man she could find, of any color.

"There you go again trying to menace me with the black man," he let out a simulated sigh of boredom, but inside his guts were knotted up at the thought of a black man wrapped around his lady Patricia.

"I said nothing about a black man," she protested.

"You didn't need to, you implied it. Well, it's your body you can give it to who you like."

"I'm glad you don't mind," she smiled, and it was as if he just realized what she was talking about. "You won't find it so easy at your age," he said, thinking if she wasn't his mother and he didn't love her so much he'd really show her.

"There is nothing wrong with my body," her indignation overflowing. "I have taken care of myself and look as good, or better than most women of forty five. My body is exactly as it was when I was thirty-five, and you are responsible for every piece of clothing I've bought since you were thirteen years old. Like an old woman you've nagged, coaxed, and bullied me into looking my best every time I've left this house, even for short periods. Except for my underwear, you've inspected and approved everything I wore, and if you didn't like it, or decide it didn't suit me, I wasn't allowed to wear it. Whatever I've become you're partly responsible so don't start backing out now, as though it was all a mistake. I did it all to please you. Whatever made you happy I did it without question. Twice a day you've told me how well I look," she frowned. "have you been lying to me all this time Peter?"

"I have never lied to you about your looks from the time I was nine years old, and you are truly the prettiest woman I've ever met. It was true then and it's true now. You are an enchanting lady Patricia, and you've earned the respect and admiration of everyone and I'm proud of you and want the whole world to know you're my mother," a pleasing tone in his voice.

"And if you bring that girl into this house some of the men in this town are going to know a lot more than that about me, and they could well lose that respect they have for me. I've been saving it a long time, I have lots of it and still know how to use it."

He pretended not to hear.

"I mean it," she said. "I meant every word."

"You're disgusting," he said under his breath. She picked up her head. "What did you say?"

"I said whatever you think you have you'd better hang on to it and don't start dishing it out while I'm still around. The day you do that to me I'll pack my things and leave and never speak to you again."

"I see there is one rule for you and another for me. You can bring your slutty women here but I have to take my friends elsewhere?"

"What you want to do is out of revenge, it's cheap and vindictive. You, my own mother?"

"What's wrong with me? What makes it any more cheap and degrading than what you want?"

"What do you think I want?" he asked. "You're talking about bringing men here for sex. I only want to bring my girlfriend home to meet you. That's all."

"And you're expecting me to believe that?" she sneered. "me, the woman who gave birth to you and know you better than anyone else?"

She told him he was only using that excuse to get her into the house for other reasons, which would soon become clear if she was stupid enough to allow it.

"Pat, you've got sex on the brains," he said nastily, and turned his face away in irritation.

"Don't tar me with your brush, you're the one with sex on your mind. I am not the one with a lamb to be slaughtered and searching for a place to do it."

"And it's that belief that makes you want to go out and get some of the same?"

"Why not, I'm human too, and haven't had sex for eleven years. There is nothing wrong or immoral in a lonely widow wanting a little male companionship. I'd say it was positively indecent to have left it so long. I wasn't made with caste iron desires or repressed sexuality, and could repel or strangle every emotion that might give birth to a longing for sexual fulfillment. You may have mistakenly thought so because of the way I always seem to cope, but in truth I really didn't manage it all that well. In your presence I'd put on my best disguise, but in bed at nights I'd shake hands with the devil and accept his invitation and gladly warm my naked, hungry body around the fires of hell, and would wish to God I didn't have to return to this selfish lonely world. I have the same burning desires and longings. I am no less a woman than any other, and a damn sight more than most. Why should I be more capable of suppressing my needs than you or anyone else? Since the day you were born I've lived only for you. Your father had his women and I had you. When he died I devoted my life to you, and that was the reason I did not seek a life for myself. I gave up my own life for you, and to sit there and make out I have no right to basic human needs, is like saying I should've grabbed my piece of life when I had the chance. But when did I have that opportunity? Throughout those years your needs were always greater than mine and you came first. There were nights when I'd lay in bed chewing my pillow ragged with frustration from wanting a man, but each time I thought about filling my needs, I'd think of him coming in here and laying his hands on you. Then there was that incident with James Bolan when his mother's boyfriend knocked him unconscious, and that sealed my fate."

Peter was awash with guilt and compassion for this woman who'd sacrificed so much of herself in his name. If it was possible to love her more his heart would've been cramming in that love as he sat there. He wanted to express his thanks and eternal gratitude, but where would he find the words?

"Haven't you got anything to say?" she asked, her face hopeful.

He crossed the room and sat beside her, his arms draped around her body, pulling her close in a crushing embrace. "Don't ever doubt that I love you Pat," he whispered. "I care for you more than there are words to express my feelings, and love you more than there are ways to show it. Nothing can change that or come between the love we share."

"Not even that girl?" she said softly.

"Not even my love for her," he replied.

"How can you say that when she's already between us? Look at the trouble she is making. Two weeks and she has us fighting already. We will never have a stable relationship with her competing with me for your love," she said softly.

"Pat, there is no competition, there shouldn't be. You once said you could not be my mother and my lover, for the two things did not go together. Well nothing has changed, they still do not go together. You are my mother and she is my lover. There is no conflict of interest except that you're trying to create. Pat, you're messing up my head with these double signals. Since I was fifteen you've been flashing me red and green and now I'm completely bemused. At sixteen, I wanted you so much I thought my heart would explode. That night of your 42nd birthday, Pat, I wanted you. I will never again need another woman the way I needed you that night. I needed you to be the first woman in my life and wanted you to teach me sex. I came to your room and ask if I could stay with you. "No go back to your room," you said. I would've slept on the floor, or on the end of the bed at your feet, or on the chair, anywhere to be near you that night. I couldn't understand you. Two weeks earlier I'd found a girl I liked and you went and told her I was only fifteen and she would have nothing to do with me after that. You didn't want me but you wouldn't let me have someone else. You rejected me, said I was a child and knew nothing of love or sex. Well I'm about to learn and Kim is one girl you won't drive away so easily, so you can put it out of your mind. I promise she will not come between us and things will not chance." he said assuredly.

She unwrapped his arms from about her and sat back looking blankly across the room. "Things have already changed and I can see the day when I'll be alone in this house," she scanned the room slowly. "This place will become my prison and you my jailer. Visiting when it suits you and not caring if I live or die from one brief visit to the next, while vetting all my visitors and banning men. I'll be here suffering while you're out there feeding your dirty cravings. That will be a high price to pay for not letting my son have sex with me when he was sixteen years old. I think you went out and picked up that bitch just to punish me, you don't love her and you never will, and I'm warning you. Get rid of her or I'm going out and get myself a man," she said with a vengeance.

"Not while I'm alive dear Mother," he grinned, but his eyes took no part in this and stared at her with a chilling promise. "You think I'd sit on my tail watching while some man move in here and start beating you?"

"Don't give me that, it's not the beating you're bothered about. It's the sex, admit it Peter. The thought of me giving your body to another man after rejecting you, because it's your body, isn't it Peter? You own me, don't you? All right, anything you say. Tell me Peter…. Do you still want to have sex with me?" she said with a grand smile, "right here Peter, right now!"

He impatiently shoved the question aside and went on. "I made a promise to myself at age eleven and it still holds strong." With tears filling his eyes he'd sworn he'd kill any man who laid a hand on her. "Any man hitting you would pay for that mistake with his life and it wouldn't matter why he did it, even if you were giving it to another man. It's your body to do as you feel, and not his to batter like a lump of steak being tenderized. There are no reasons that could justify an attack on you," he wiped away tears with his wrist.

During the course of the long stillness that followed she glanced at him and saw the same fifteen year old boy who'd demanded an explanation that day. After slapping his face she'd gone to his room and found him in tears. He apologized for being rude and showing her up, but said he'd do it all again because he was now the man in her life and there would be no other. She'd had no intention of explaining her actions and thought it would do her no harm to make him jealous, but he seemed so helpless and vulnerable she felt obliged to placate him and quickly made up a story about the man being someone from work she'd met by chance. In truth, the man had been after her for nearly a year and was the first man she'd met who could've meant something if she was free. Pat had thought his father was the most possessive man, ever, but this boy could give him lessons in domination. About that same time she'd began noticing distinct changes, that said he'd began to see her as a woman and not just as his mother. But he could not separate the two as his adolescence, which was at the roots of his dilemma, brought more confused emotions to the fore.

She took him in her arms. "Peter I appreciate all that you've said, but do you realize that with those words you've sentenced your mother to a life of eternal celibacy? With that kind of threat hanging over any man who hits me I couldn't risk it, you'd go to prison and I'd lose you. You'd come in and see me with a black eye and without bothering to find out whether I'd walked into a door or a left hook, you'd start killing. I would love to believe you didn't mean it and would never do anything so silly, but no matter what you say from here on those words will live in my mind forever. Don't you realize there are no perfect relationships, and there will be disagreements?"

"You can argue without coming to blows."

"Look who's talking," she winced with belated fear. "I slapped your face that day out of a crushing fear you were about to hit me. I had never seen you in such a state and I was petrified. I stood there telling myself, Patricia, he's your son, not your father or husband, you can't let him do this to you. Any second now he'll hit you and once it starts you'll never stop it. To this day I believe that hadn't I hit first and brought you to your senses you would've struck me...Son, would you really have done it?" she asked.

"I don't know," he' said confusedly. "It was a long time ago and I can't remember, anyway that was different, it's not the same with me."

She tore herself from his arms and glared at him. "So you have a divine right to hit me? Who gave you that right? That is precisely the point I'm trying to make, in the heat of the moment these things happen. It may interest you to know your father wasn't above hitting me, and could crawl among the sickest, most depraved wife-beaters and not look out of place. I am not a china doll and do not need the kind of protection you're offering. In fact it would be no help at all. Tell me who would protect me after you've killed the first man and is sent to prison?"

"If you didn't learn to stay away form men by then you wouldn't deserve help," he said, an eerie quality in his voice.

"Women don't go off men forever because one inadequate specimen lost an argument and resorted to his fist. A woman's need for love and sex isn't knocked out of her the first time she stops an angry fist with her face."

"You are my mother and should be above all that kind of thing," his supercilious nose in the air as he reproached her.

"What kind of thing are you talking about, sex, Is that what you mean?" she asked.

"That is exactly what I'm talking about Mother," he patronized her.

"Peter, I missed your father so much I wanted to leap into the grave with him…" she was saying, but he'd heard it all before and had suddenly lost interest. She sat calling after him as he went out the door.

Chapter 15

In the silence of his room Peter reviewed his thoughts and wondered if he hadn't been demanding too much of her? She was making the same demands but in his mind, felt she had a right, for she wasn't the one who'd broken their unspoken agreement to live just for each other. Somewhere back over the years they'd both arrived at the same decision, and without voicing it their thoughts and desires had converged. A pact drawn up and signed as though through some process of thought transference which neither party had the temerity, or need to ratify verbally, yet was more sacred than a contract of marriage. And except for sex' it was a kind of marriage, one that satisfied both their needs. For years he'd had no problem with this for it was all he knew and the stuff on which he'd been weaned and brought up to expect, but it had lost it's flavor and had become unpalatable, and suddenly he couldn't live with it anymore.

This began shortly after his father died when she requested he brought all his problems to her. Explaining that his father would normally take on most of this role but as he was no longer around she would play both parts. From those early days he'd began to see her, not as his mother, but as a loving and benevolent big sister, and above all, a friend. A caring altruistic pal with whom he shared everything. All his diffidence and childish reserve was briskly wiped away by her liberated stand, and there was nothing they couldn't discuss. Everything that troubled, amazed, confused, pained or gave him the slightest discomfort, were brought to her to be translated. She didn't always have the answers but what she didn't know she'd find out, and had never left a question unanswered.

Since he was one year old she'd been taking him into the bath with her. This had continued until he was seven years old, when his father said the boy was getting too old for that kind of thing and she was ordered to stop it. Reluctantly, she conformed, accusing him of being narrow-minded and indecent. Sadly, he'd not lived and soon she was picking up where she'd left off. This went on until he was eleven when he decided he was now the man of the house and started taking his new role into the bath. Suddenly, the bath wasn't big enough for two and it was time she got out. Along with telling her she had a nice arse, she'd began to wonder just what kind of little monster she'd created? And would have been happy to get out of the bathroom and let the little man get on with it by himself, but was afraid the sudden rejection might have an adverse effect, unraveling years of diligent teachings, and began bathing him from the side of the bath, explaining that he was now a big lad and the bath wasn't big enough for two. At this time the female form held few mysteries for him and hardly any secrets. He knew what sex was all about and the basics of the female reproductive cycle. Peter had found this subject intensely fascinating and would question her incessantly, but would avoid the deadly topic of menstruation like it was the plague. Refusing to listen and would suddenly lose interest the moment she touched on periods and would walk away.

A year earlier he'd barged into the bathroom and found her with one leg propped on the toilet as she changed Tampons. For a few seconds he'd stood frozen to the spot like a petrified ghost, face ashen with fear. His first thought was that she'd injured herself and was bleeding to death. He wanted to help her, to ask if she was alright but couldn't speak and a debilitating tremor took over his stomach, and his heart leapt into his mouth, and he took flight into his room and shut the door, ignoring her calls and requests to come back. When she entered his room he scrutinized her with deep concern, his eyes darting all over her. Face, hands, body, and especially her legs.

"Didn't you hear me calling, why didn't you come back?" she calmly asked. "I only wanted to explain things to you. We have no secrets and that is something I've wanted to discuss with you for a long time."

He sat there, silently staring at her. She flashed a reassuring smile, "Darling what did you think, you looked so worried?"

"Are you alright Mom?" he finally spoke, his breathing harsh and labored, as if he'd been holding his breath.

"I'm fine son, never better," she said cheerfully.

"But you were bleeding and I thought you were dying?" He blurted.

"You thought your mother was dying and you didn't try to help her, why didn't you come to my aid?" she smilingly asked.

"I hate blood I don't like it," he said tightly.

Pat explained what it was all about. Pointing out that the woman he married would have to go through the same thing.

He cringed in horror, his lips drooped in scorn. "Why do women have to go through that, can't the doctors do something to make them better?" he demanded to know.

She said it was not an illness and was a natural process. "I won't ever marry a woman like that," he said with a disparaging tone and posture.

"You'll grow out of it," Pat said with an air of certainty. "You'll have a better understanding of life as you get older."

His thought flashed back to the bathroom and he could see the blood. "No, I won't," he told her. "I'11 never have a woman like that."

A few nights later she heard him stumbling about upstairs and went up to investigate. When she got to his room his books were strewn around the floor along with bits of torn paper. A pernicious bolt of anger took hold of her and she felt like hitting him. She glared at him sitting on the floor among the carnage, wishing his father was alive to administer the sound thrashing he deserved.

"Peter I paid good money for those books, don't expect me to replace them when you throw them around like waste paper. What is the meaning of this?" she growled irritably.

"I can't do it" he said petulantly. "It's too hard I can't do it."

"Are you talking about your homework?" her tone slightly softer. "Yes Mom I've tried but it won't work, I can't do it."

"Don't keep saying you can't do it," she rasped. "You can do it I know that." She got down on her knees and started collecting the books, he quickly joined in. "Peter you do not throw your books away because the work is too difficult. A man does not throw his tools away because the work is too hard, and I cannot walk out of my job because the customers are proving difficult. Whatever task we take on we have to see it through to success, we can't just give up." Together they gathered the books and stacked them in a neat pile on his little table.

"I will help you defeat this thing and show you how to master most of the difficulties you'll face throughout your life," she slipped her arm lovingly around his shoulders. He grinned broadly, and expeditiously opened a book and handed it to her. She took the book and snapped it shut, shaking her head, face in a dissenting scowl. "Not like that," she said. "That is not the way. This is your work and you have to deal with it by yourself."

He was puzzled. "But you said you'd help me?" he demanded.

"That is the worst kind of help I could give you, in fact it would be no help at all. How will you manage tomorrow or the day after, when you're stuck with another problem and I'm not around? The problem is not in the book, it's in your head. I see nothing in any of these books that you can't master, given the desire, the will, and determination. You've told yourself it can't be done too many times and you've began to believe it. If you defeat yourself before you start the task what chance have you got of success? It can be done…"

"But I tried—"

"You didn't try hard enough. You can do it. Instead of telling yourself you can't, just say I can do it. Keep repeating those words to yourself and they'll repair your self-confidence and change your life."

"But why should I tell myself I can when I know I can't?" he said.

"Peter you don't know that you can't you haven't tried. It's just as easy to be positive, why be negative? You want to give up without a fight and I won't let you. The day your father died I thought my world had come to an end, but a week later I realized it was worse than that. I was left to bring you up alone in a house with a heavy mortgage and some pressing bills. The £1,000 he'd left went on funeral expenses and I hadn't got a penny to my name. What would've happened if I had sat around saying I can't do it? I made it work because I had the motivation. You were the reason I had to make it work, it wasn't easy but I did it, and if you want to do it badly enough you will do it."

She opened the book, and at the front she wrote in bold letters. It can be done, and I, Peter Philip West will do it. There is a way and I will find it. There is no such thing as failure, just people who've given up. As long as I'm in there pitching I have not failed. Failure is but a stop on the long road to success and I will not stop at failure. I will never be defeated by that imposter.

She handed the book to him. "From today and for the rest of your life I want you to repeat these words to yourself twice a day, everyday. So you'll be ready and in the right mind to deal with the task ahead. Don't even think failure, cultivate success and no matter what comes out you'll feel better for having given it everything you've got. Don't look for easy options. When you go after success it's alright to come home without it, but it's not acceptable to come home with failure," she took his hands, clasping them warmly. "It's within you son. It's all there inside your head. Everything you'll ever desire is already within you. You have the choice, it's yours to make. To be rich or poor, to succeed or fail, you alone can decide that. You have to cultivate that desire to win within yourself. I could order you to do your homework and get you to sit down to it, but without that motivation to do it successfully I'd simply be wasting my time. It is up to you."

They were so close, and she was so much a part of him, he could feel her presence in everything he did, and even as he contemplated sex with Kim he felt guilty, as though he was beholden to his mother to stay faithful. It was as if he was planning some heinous and unforgivable evil against her and his conscience would not let him be. The more assiduously he worked on his plan, the more contrite he became. She had been so many things to him that he could not see a time in the future when held not need her. There would always be a special place in his life for her, and as chronically as he needed Kim he'd sooner dump her than alienate his Mother, and would've done so with an indecent haste if he'd thought there was the slightest danger of that. She didn't want a man and if she got one he doubt if she'd know what to do with him. They both knew what time it was and her time had long past. Now she was merely firing blanks over his head to try and rake his guilt to the surface. Knowing his insane possessiveness would not stand for her taking a man and would sooner drop Kim than have her drop her knickers. It seemed she knew him more intimately than he'd imagined. She was his mother, and that is where the line should've been drawn, as in most normal families, but instead had grown into something weird, now sitting on this precarious perch. "What are we?" The question he had asked himself a thousand times. Mother and son, or simply man and woman? He loved the woman with such intensity that the mere breath of an idle thought, of another man embracing her, would affect his breathing, increase his heart rate and leave him sweating in a fit of ineffable jealousy. If she took a man to her bed he'd never forgive her, but would love her with the same passion. That was the extent of his obsession, and it was for this reason he had to break loose.

Since Kim appeared she'd become openly attentive and their feelings had heightened, drawing them even closer. He now dreads to think what may be waiting up ahead and lurking behind their next embrace. It wasn't fair on her but was worse from his side. He'd had no sex life and it was his turn. She'd had some and at least, could dwell on memories of her past glories, or she could return to the devil's fire and warm her naked body some more. There was nothing wrong with that, he reasoned. He'd resorted to it a number of times. Just the same, he'd rather not have heard about his mother's naked masturbating sessions. He laughed. The devil's fire indeed.

Peter's need to get Kim into the house had become more desperate as his mother became more strident and vehement in her objections. For the next seven days things progressed as normal, but beneath that thin veneer of sobriety he was a bubbling cauldron of strategy and duplicity.

He would rise each morning at 6.30, and about 6.55 would wake his mother with her first cup of tea, and would sit talking with her a little while, before leaving for work about 7.00.

At 8.30 she would leave the house and take her normal leisurely walk to work in the City, where she managed the furniture department at Ragland's Of New Street.

As senior assistant she was never late in ten years, and in the past three years, since her promotion and added responsibility, she was more determined to keep her record clean, and set an example for her subordinates.

Her hours were 9 to 6 daily, and 9 to 1 on Saturdays. One Monday morning as they talked Peter suggested doing the dinner that evening, and asked if she had any special requests.

"Surprise me," she said. "Darling you know the things I like, give me a surprise."

He promised it would be ready and on the table by 6.30 after her bath.

On arriving home each day she would go straight to the bathroom and take a bath. Personal hygiene was something she'd been injecting into his system since he could talk. For years he'd seen her washing herself twice a day until he was addicted to the belief that this was the norm, the only standard by which a woman should be judged, and anything less was slovenly.

She said washing her hands wasn't good enough after mixing it all day with people who were either not keen on general cleanliness, or had a distinct aversion to it. And this didn't only apply to the customers, but also some of her colleagues, whom she felt wasn't fit to be chopped up for dog meat. She would cringe at the thought of what she could be dragging into her home each day, and would dump everything she'd worn into the wash before getting into the bath, to be sure she didn't have to handle them again before wash day.

Peter assured her he could manage, adding it had all been worked out and finely tuned. He'd run her bath and have it waiting at 6.15, and the dinner would be on the table when she came down.

That morning she left for work with a bounce in her stride like a new spring lamb. It wasn't the first he'd plan something like this but each time she was more pleasantly surprised and it would take on new meaning for her, especially this time. Since meeting that girl he'd been drifting away from her, and she could feel the draft of an increasing void the young trollop was opening between them. Oddly enough, over the past week or ten days he's not mentioned her name and she'd not phoned, nor had he gone out to meet her. This was most unusual and she'd deduced that something was wrong. Maybe it was a fight and they weren't speaking, or she'd finished with him? It would be just what he deserved. This piece of wishful thinking pleased her, for it would show him the inherent dangers of not heeding her prophecies. Sadly, this possibility had to be dismissed for there was nothing in his behavior to endorse this. Peter had a way of sulking at such times—a regrettable trait he inherited form his father—but there was none of this and there could only be two reasons. Either a deceptive move to soften her up and catch her off guard, which didn't bear thinking about, or her more favored assumption, that he'd, finished with the girl and this was his way of saying sorry for the pain he'd caused her. If he had finished with her then he had no apologies to make and the matter was closed, and everything was forgiven.

At work that morning, the time was dragging like a two legged donkey, and was the longest morning she'd experienced since the day of his birth.

She had passed the latter portion of the morning dealing with a complaint, and had listened with silent attention as the irate couple demanded their money back. Occasionally she'd nod her agreement but not interrupting or passing any comment, until they'd finally talked the fire out of their guts and began repeating themselves, as they tried to extend an exhausted theme.

"You are absolutely right and I completely agree with you," she said earnestly. "We have been all the things you said, and what's more we do not deserve a forth chance to get it wrong again. You've been more patient than I would. I can only say that if this matter had been brought to my notice earlier it would've been suitably resolved long ago, and I can promise, if you leave it in my hands I'll have it cleared up today. However, if you want your money back I will see that a check is made out and sent off within the next two hours, or if you're still in town at 2 p.m. you come back and get your money. Having said that, I am asking you to give me one chance to get it right. I am glad you brought this mess to my notice so it can be cleared up, we can't afford to lose valued customers. We'll go outside and you can point out the bed to me and I'll personally see that it goes on the van today and be at your house before teatime. Failing that you have my permission to come back here and kick my backside around this office until you're satisfied, then I'll personally give you your money. What do you say?"

The man smiled. "I hope that will not be necessary," he said.

"So do I," his wife joined in. "Your feet are not what they use to be," she joked.

Half an hour later she went down to the loading bay and had the bed loaded on an empty van to ensure there were no further foul-ups.

Patricia would normally have lunch in the canteen but because Peter was planning something special that evening she decided to have sandwiches.

Her office was a tiny cubicle in a grudging little space, it seem they could ill afford, situated in the middle of the department, between bedroom, and dining furniture. Inside she barely had room for a desk, chair, and a single filing cabinet. Having a door with her name was an added treat and a privilege. Not for the name but the door, which she could close and have a little privacy from prying customers and marauding colleagues. At least they'd be obliged to knock and not barge in, as was the case with other door-less offices on other floors.

Lately she'd found that Peter was the only one with whom she could relax and relate. She'd always been a very private person, but of late was feeling a growing need for even more seclusion and saw others as strangers and outsiders who should be kept at bay.

At one o'clock she made a drink and sat down to lunch at her desk. The sandwiches were good, Peter had done her proud, he had truly gone out of his way to please her today and had outdone himself. One was Cheese ham and Tomatoes, the other was grated Lettuce and Celery, with a pinch of white pepper, and a slight promise of Salad Dressing. She wondered if he'd had the same for himself, knowing his penchant for giving her the best and having what's left.

All this care and attention, the loving touches he'd thoughtfully put into preparing her lunch was overwhelming proof he'd finished with the girl and she was once again his best girl. She smiled, her very soul in rapture and her heart pounded with jubilation. The pretender to her throne was dead and the threat to her rein was no more. Yet as this festive thought was working its way through her mind she felt a sudden premonition of danger, and a disturbing uneasiness washed over her and a ball of sickness rose from her stomach up to her throat. At the same time a gripping pain shot through her guts, wrenching her insides apart. Fear rose within her as she fought for breath, clinging to where her stomach use to be, but it was no longer there, it was now in her throat and rushing up into her mouth and spewing out over the desk before she could move.

Trying to hold back the flow with her hands, she pushed the chair back, and dropping to her knees, she emptied her hands, and her stomach into the wastepaper bin.

As the contents of her stomach splashed into the bin she was thinking how fortunate she was to have a door, and had barely stopped heaving when an assistant knocked the door, walked in, and for what seemed like a lifetime, stood staring at her.

"For God sake Jackie, will you shut the door?" she said in a frenzy of impatience.

"Could it be your sandwiches?" the girl offered after Pat's explanation, "maybe they'd gone off, there's a lot of food poisoning going around."

"I don't think it's my sandwiches I made them myself this morning," she reasoned, but the girl had sown the seeds of doubts in her mind and she was busy telling herself Peter wouldn't do that to her. Not my Peter, he loves me.

Jackie offered to go with her to the hospital but Pat declined, said she was feeling much better. The girl insisted, so to placate her she agreed to visit First aid, on the ground floor.

Before she got to the room she'd made a complete recovery and would not have bothered but for this solicitous underling now supporting her left forearm and elbow.

She cleaned up her office and left for home an hour later, her clothes in a mess and needing a bath. Three minutes into her walk a slight pain shot through her lower body and for a short time she thought about taking a Cab, but decided the walk would help cleanse her mind of obscene thoughts. What possessed her to think that Peter would do that? And if he'd tried to poison her she wouldn't be alive now with the quantity she'd swallowed. She focused her thoughts on all the things that could have caused it. Maybe Peter was having the same trouble and was already home in bed, she hoped he was all right. She would hate having to face life without him. She lightened her steps as though in haste. Not to get home faster, but like an Aircraft in imminent danger that sheds its fuel, she was depleting nervous energy so she'd be too exhausted for all but restful sleep. She would take a long relaxing bath, then sleep for two hours, then get up and make the dinner, giving Peter a surprise instead. As she neared the house, visions of the first cup of tea that morning flashed through her disturbed thoughts and she tried to banish the wild speculative ramblings. My son did not try to kill me," she told herself, speaking at full volume as if to bully her mind into accepting it, then immediately repeating the words. This time with the calm deliberation of an hypnotist implanting a suggestion in the sub-conscious mind. Repeating it time and again, only to realize that once a disturbed thought has been engaged it doesn't take lightly to being pushed aside, and like the dripping tap that can not be silenced, continues to nag one to distraction.

An indescribable calm came over her as she entered the house and she was back in control of her thoughts, as though the stupid business had been picked clean from her brains. And she was back to that state of elation she'd enjoyed that morning. She climbed the stairs thinking about the bath she'd take then flaking out on the bed, but her mind suddenly dived back into confusion when she saw her bedroom door open. She distinctly remembered closing it before she left, and Peter's door which she left open, was now closed. This could mean he was home and was in the kitchen or had gone back out, but as she neared the door she heard sounds, voices coming from his room.

Burglars, she thought. Peter was not home, it wasn't him. The nagging pain in her stomach reminded her of its occupancy, as she berated herself for not having intruder alarms fitted. Something she'd considered a hundred times but had kept putting off. Tomorrow she was going out and get someone to do it, she wasn't leaving it a day later. She swore to herself.

From where she stood—trembling—she could just see the end of her bed and a part of the dressing table, and it seemed nothing had been disturbed in her room. Stealthily, she crept closer to his door, her ears cocked, trying to pick up, and identify the sounds.

In spite of a debilitating fear that had now began to affect her bladder, she was not going to summon the Police or dash out into the Street and scream she was being robbed, only to find she'd made a silly mistake.

She clamped her ears to the door and listened, but for a long time she heard nothing. Then she heard the faint murmurings of a voice. Peter's voice, but who was he talking to? The person was either not answering or doing so in a whisper. She squeezed her ear against the door and listened but could hear no other voice, he was the only one speaking, saying something about love. She heard him babble something about—Oh God…and suddenly it hit her like a bullet in the brain…"He hasn't? He couldn't? Please God let me be wrong, and all this be an innocent misunderstanding. She prayed, but in her guts she knew it was no mistake, and that he'd brought the bitch into her house and was….. With her heart racing she exploded into the room, almost ripping the door from its hinges and stood staring at the two naked bodies on the bed, as the door hit the wall and swung back, hitting her somewhere around the right shoulder and upper arm, jolting her sideways and forcing her to adjust her balance. She hung there as though in a trance, without feelings and impervious to pain. All except that now exploding in her heart and taking over her head.

"He's fucking her," she could hear the words softly issuing from her lips but couldn't hold them back. "My Peter, is fucking that girl, but he can't he doesn't know how, I haven't shown him, not yet. It's her, that whore, she's shown him, and in my own house." The pain inside her head began growing into a screaming cacophony of her own voice and she felt the pain as he tore his way out of her. "It's a boy…. A gorgeous little boy," the smiling midwife announced.

It took six stitches to repair the damage he'd done to me that day. Eleven days later his father tore me apart and I had to be stitched up again. Since then I'd been constantly ripped apart some time or another, by one or the other but never as savagely and as painfully as this. How could you do this to me Peter, you know I could never do it to you. I could never be unfaithful to you, how could you betray me like this, her eyes tracking him as he got off the girl and pulled the sheet over her naked body. Distraught, and hurting as if she'd been stabbed in the heart, she watched him as he moved unhurriedly to the chair, picked up his underpants and pulled them on, then his trousers. He came toward her, arms outstretched as if to guide her from the room.

"Don't touch me," she screamed hysterically. "You thought I was dead, didn't you? You didn't bother to make sure, you moved her in straight away." She looked at Kim with distaste. "So this is your piece of strumpet, you finally brought her home, and this is the dinner you were coming home early to prepare? I asked you to surprise me but wasn't expecting anything like this."

"Mom I wasn't expecting you home until 6.15," he said pitifully.

"Don't lie to me Peter, you weren't expecting me home tonight or any other night and had no intention of cooking anything."

Peter adopted his silent posture as she talked it out of her system, in any case he had no excuse, what could he say? "You've disappointed me I didn't expect this from you," she said, close to tears but managing to hold it back. After your father I wasn't expecting anymore of this. You have plunged a knife into my heart and I swear if you don't get this tramp out of my house in five minutes I'll be taking a knife to her just as you did to me." she turned trippingly out of the room.

Chapter 16

When he waltzed into her room a minute later she was waiting and before he could close the door she hit him across the face. Eyes tightly closed he stood and took it without flinching.

"You dirty deceitful swine, how could you do this to me, I would sooner commit suicide than do it to you," she hissed poisonously.

He closed the door and leaned against it, his face crimson with the tracks of her four fingers. A spot of blood appeared on his lower lip, the stone form her ring must have caught him. He drew the lip into his mouth and cleaned it up, standing with a foolish grin across his face as she came back at him.

"I did not devote my entire life to you for this, my God is this the way you repay me?" she slapped him again, this took the grin off his face.

"That's enough!" he said angrily. "Do that again and I'll..." he hesitated.

"You'll what?" she demanded. "What will you do, hit me?" she slapped him again, so hard his teeth rattled. "Go on Peter, hit me, Please, hit your mother," she goaded. "You tried to poison me and that didn't work so why not hit me with your fist, that might kill me?"

"Pat, have you gone crazy, have you lost your mind?" he said with real anxiety. "What's this about me trying to poison you?"

"My sandwiches, you put something in my sandwiches..."

"Of course I did, cheese ham tomatoes celery...."

She hit him again. "Don't try to make a fool of me you know damn well what I'm talking about, you tried to kill me."

He raised a hand to his face and gently massaged both cheeks. "Pat why are you hitting me, can't we discuss things like adults? You hit me for the first time when I was fifteen, and now four years later you're doing it again, why?"

"That was my mistake. Had I done it while you were a child there would be no need to be doing it now. You'd have known your place and wouldn't be using my house as a brothel. You brought her here to show her your manhood, but I will show her how much of a child you are."

"Pat, I'm a grown man, accept it and loosen your hold on me."

"You're not a man, you only think you are, stop fooling yourself child. Because you've found another use for that thing in your trousers does not make you a man. Because you can pull it out and shove it into some stinking slut, does not make you a man. The measure of a man is responsibility, duty, loyalty, honesty and respect. The respect he commands and that which he gives to others. Reverence for his mother, or if he thinks she doesn't merit it then at least show some for himself. I didn't want you to grow up watching me climbing in and out of bed with men fucking me from all direction and sacrificed my life out of respect for you, and not so I could watch as a dirty tramp waltz into my house and fuck you."

He stared at her in disgust and disbelief.

"Yes Peter you heard me right. I said fuck not tickle. Fuck," she rasped. "I did not sow the seed and lavish it with my love just to stand by and watch someone else reap the crop."

"Mom, you have to let me go you can't hold me any longer. I'm nineteen years old and have to find my own way," he said in a small voice.

"All right Peter," she nodded. "Perhaps the time has come to let you do as you like but you're not doing it in my house. I know what's good for me, and when you start putting things in my food and bringing women into the house it's time to get out of your way or get trampled and don't deny you put something in my lunch. As I began eating I started vomiting and was so sick I thought it was death coming to claim me."

"At this point I should be slapping your face," he said, an injured smile on his face. "Mom I love you so much that I wonder if there'll be enough love or anything else, left inside me for that unfortunate girl next door? How could you believe I'd hurt you like that and for what reason? What in this world could induce me?"

"Not what, who?" she offered.

"You mean Kimberly?"

She nodded.

"A dozen Kimberly's couldn't make me do that to you and you know that. Pat, you know I didn't try to hurt you, and you should be ashamed of yourself for thinking that," he rebuked her.

"What was I to think? On the way home I'd convinced myself it was just a bug I'd picked up, then walked in and found you in bed with her, and the big picture of you trying to put me away so you could move her in came together in front of me. I warned you what would happen if you brought her into this house, and you said you'd rather see me dead than with another man. Well Peter, you have just shoved a dagger into my heart and at this moment I wish I was dead. How could you do this to me? A blind person could see you didn't simply bring her here on a passionate impulse, but after careful planning. The only thing that doesn't fit is the dinner, I can't see why you brought that into your plans but I know it's also a part of your wicked deception...Oh! It makes me so mad." she turned and walked away in anger. "I want her out of this house now, get her out!" she shook her head furiously.

"Pat," he said following her halfway across the room and putting his arms around her. She stood rigid, frozen like a block of ice, arms hanging tightly at her side. Her eyes a piercing blue flame.

"She's already in the house, why not come and meet her?" he smiled. "We'll never get a better chance."

"Are you deaf, out of your mind, or don't you understand English?" She tried to break loose but he held on, and her face suddenly curled into something evil. "Get your filthy hands off me!" she pushed him violently back. "Have the decency to wash your hands before you touch me, and I don't want to meet her, get her out of my house now."

He smiled. "You keep saying your house, aren't you forgetting this is also my house, that we both live here?"

"She doesn't."

"She's my guest, I invited her."

"Without my consent."

"But I tried 'and you didn't want to know."

"And didn't I say you were only looking for a place to stuff her? How could you expect me to sanction that? What do you think happens to respect when this kind of thing is brought into your home? The second you brought her in through the door our respect for each other went down the toilet, as a result I'm talking to you like you were dirt on my shoe, and using words that degrade my dignity and fouls my self-respect. That is what you've brought into this house. We've lived here alone for eleven years, and in all that time I've never made a move without considering your feelings and opinions, and as you got older I took to consulting you. To this day I'm guided by your wishes and desires, and if you don't like it, I don't do it, no matter how much I want to. Love and devotion has to run both ways or it dies. We live here together and have to consider each other's feelings, good God Peter, just ask yourself how you'd like to come home and find me naked in bed with a man? And you don't have to give me an answer. That is a question to be answered in your own mind. Ask yourself, and keep repeating it each time you get the urge to bring her back into this house. Just imagine me lying on my back with my legs in the air, giving it…"

"Stop it!" he barked, "You shut your mouth," he menaced her in a whispered voice.

"Can't take it, can you? Even the mere thought of it makes you sick," she grinned.

"I'd never forgive you, because it's not the same, it's different with a man. Pat, I'd hate you if you did that to me." he said solemnly.

"Yes Peter you are a man I can see that now. That kind of cockeyed justification could only come from a man. That's the same tune your father use to sing." she forced a smile. "In all that wonderful love you have for me, isn't there any forgiveness?" she asked.

"Not for that," he snapped.

"It may interest you to know I've already forgiven you and could never hate you no matter what you did. I haven't got it in me to hate the only person I've truly loved, and that puts you above my parents and your father." She stood scrutinizing him with a benign look, her eyes traveling over the top half of his naked body and settling on his face. "No woman will ever love you as I do, or could give you the kind of love I can, and would love to give you. I gave birth to you, you are a part of me and I'm part of you. I am closer to you than you realize, and I know what you feel and when you feel it. That is something we'll never change. I'm here for you and need no one else, you're all that matters to me. . . . Get dressed and get her out of the house," she finally said, and watched him strolled away.

Pat could've strangled him for walking away as though nothing had happened, and without a word of apology, or any sign of remorse. A posture, a look in his eyes or on his face that said sorry, or by using one of the many silent ways he had of showing he was wrong. Why were men so unfeeling and insensitive, have they really got hearts?

She heard them go down the stairs and as the front door slammed she fell across the bed in tears.

Although not in tears, Peter was equally sick. It would've been bad enough to find out a week later but to walk in and see it taking place was something she didn't deserve. He cursed his rotten luck. Of all the days she could've come home sick it had to be this day, squandering all his meticulous plans. Perhaps it would've been better if Kim had stuck to the afternoon plan?

Kim worked for a firm of solicitors, Roe and Steadman, in Temple Street, and that particular day had been chosen because it suited her. He would've preferred Saturday morning but she couldn't make it on a Saturday, so it had to be 3.pm that Monday. The only other problem was that his mother would sometimes, come home early on a Monday, not often, but it has happened and he couldn't risk it. It would be just his luck that she'd chose to be early this day, and this was where the dinner came into the plans.

Telling her he was preparing a special treat for her would ensure she'd not be early. It would have to be something close to death that would bring her home early. She'd have preferred walking the streets until the appointed time than spoil his surprise.

Peter had planned to leave work at 2.pm and be home long before Kim arrived, they'd spend an hour in bed, then he'd take her into town to catch the 45 bus on John Brights Street, which would take her home. Next he'd pop into Lewis's and pick up some King Prawns, Rice, a packet of Curry and a bottle of Sparkling wine. It would take about an hour to prepare the meal, everything would be ready by 5.45pm.

This was the plan, but as he was about to leave that morning Kim rang to say there had been a change of plans. Her Boss had called to say he'd be needing her in the afternoon and could she take the time in the morning?

As he hung up the phone his mother had shouted down inquiring who'd called, he said it was a wrong number. Peter could have shot himself for being found out, and felt he also deserved to be hanged for what he'd done to her, but in spite of this he was determined not to prostrate himself at her feet begging forgiveness in an apologetic stupor, whimpering promises never to do it again. He may have gone over the top in projecting his image of iron but felt it was better this way than have her thinking she'd reared a wimp who couldn't even pretend to be a man. He had to make the break from her and it had to be done without wavering. He had to stand up to her, in spite of being wrong, and lock his heart, mind, and conscience out of her reach, to stop her crawling back to that place in his heart and taking over again. Kim came into his life and had saved him from a fate worse than insanity. She'd rescued him from the daily battles with himself and his fugitive integrity. Engagements of will, valiantly fought but with the knowledge that he had no hope of winning. Try as he may he could make no sense of his real role. It could not be reasonably defined with anything that came close to satisfaction, and all the time there was this unspoken allegiance drawing them inexorably closer. Knowing that in the name of morality and decency they couldn't be any closer without diving into the deep end of degradation. He was caught at the centre of a swirling vortex, exhausted and unable to help himself. Sick from his vain struggles and slowly being engulfed, as he surrendered himself to the hope that when he arrived he'd find he'd misjudged her, and such dreaded thoughts were equally abhorrent to her. Time and again he'd been tempted to take things to their imminent conclusion so he could be proven wrong, and finally lay that burden down. But it was her tacit approval and general indifference to their frequent encounters that was most disconcerting. There were things that told him she was simply waiting on him to make the ultimate move. After all, she'd engineered and unreservedly executed all the others. This led him to believe she was expecting more of him than he'd given. Yet he could no more blame her than he could the midwife who'd delivered him, for like birth it was inevitable. It just had to come out, and whatever she had inside he was instrumental in putting it there. He was neither coerced nor bullied and had gratefully given himself up to her for their treacherous walk along life's most forbidden path. Eyes wide open they'd strolled arm in arm, knowing the slightest slip could mean doom. He'd reveled in the love and affection she'd lavished on him, and had consumed it with a ravenous possessiveness, while displaying his childish indignation and jealousy at the mere idea of someone coming between them and tapping into that priceless love. He inspected his own conscience and had to accept responsibility for what she'd become, for he was the senior partner and the one who made the decision. She may have been standing up front making out she knew the song but he was the one feeding her the words from behind. How could she be any different when he never gave her a chance? From the age of eleven he'd been standing over her dictating and directing her life and he was the only male she was exposed to. How could he spend all that time tenaciously guarding her like a doting husband without her reacting?

A week later, Pat had another attack of the mysterious complaint that had brought her home from work. It was a Sunday night and she was alone. Being alone was the new state of things to which she'd been desperately trying to adjust since Peter discovered sex. She was watching TV when it struck, and as, she reeled from the pain his name just issued from her lips.

"Oh Peter," she said, and as quickly as it came it was gone, as though it had never visited. No nausea or headache, nothing except a feeling of contentment, a strangely calming and relaxed aura. A sudden intense calm seem to permeate her body.

Later that night, she told Peter about the pain, but said nothing about it's bewildering after effect. He suggested seeing the Doctor and offered to make the appointment but she declined, saying she wanted to watch it for a while. She felt if they were all like the last one then she had nothing to worry about and might even be glad of them. Two nights later she had another visitation while waiting up for him. It was exactly 12.30am. At 1 am. she could wait no longer, she bolted the door and went to bed. He came home at 2.am and woke her up to open the door, wanting to know why she'd locked him out, but she didn't answer. She quietly turned and went back upstairs to bed.

The following morning they had one of their most violent rows and he threatened to marry Kim and move out if she didn't stop treating him like a child, refusing to accept her explanation that she was afraid of being in the house alone, and wouldn't get to sleep if she didn't secure the door before going to bed.

She pleaded with him, begging him to be reasonable and try to understand he was all she had left in the world. Finally in a bid to win back her place in his life she dropped her objections to meeting Kimberly. When this didn't work she capitulated further, by offering him the freedom of the house, to bring Kim home anytime he liked, night or day, whether she was home or not. Peter promised to think about it but never gave it a second thought, knowing the kind of sacrifice she'd be making and the severe emotional pain she'd suffer. This was like an insanely jealous wife consenting to her husband bringing home another woman, and he loved her too much to torture her like this. Reasoning that if she couldn't see Kim, then it wouldn't hurt so much. In the meantime he'd continued telling her he was evaluating her offer, while spending all the time he could with Kim, but as he was no more welcomed at her house than she was in his, their more private moments were at the discretion of his friend.

He was seeing her about four or five times a week and Pat was having three attacks a week. Soon he was no longer surprised by this and could almost predict them. By this they were no longer a concern and he saw them as an irritating nuisance. To her they were a kind of relief, but from what, she couldn't say. Since her first encounter they had brought no pain or sickness and now after some thirty visits could no longer be described as an attack, more a constriction of the body, something akin to the sensation of a good sneeze.

At first Peter was very concerned about these mysterious visitations that would only occur when she was alone, and equally confused by her obdurate refusal to see the doctor. This made him suspicious and set him thinking she was simply faking it to get his attention away from Kim. Everything pointed to this, for she never had them while he was in the house with her or during the day, except the first time. Things would be fine while they were in the house together, then he'd leave at 8 o'clock to meet Kim and would return three hours later to hear she'd had another.

He carefully retraced his movements over the past ten weeks and found that every time she had one of these he was with Kim, never while he was at work, out alone or with other friends, only when he was with Kim. Why only at this time and how would she know they were together? Because she was so insanely jealous he didn't always let her know they were meeting, and would tell her he was going out with friends, but it wouldn't matter who he'd claim to be with, she could still sort out the times he was with Kim and would get herself fixed up with yet another. One night he went out to meet Kim at the Mulberry Bush but she didn't turn up so he went to the pictures alone. When he got home she was fine, although she knew he had gone out to meet Kim. How did she know unless she'd followed him, but she hadn't left the house. For some time he did wonder if she was having him followed but this seemed even more implausible. The whole business was stranger than fiction and had began to unnerve him, for without leaving the house she seem to know everything he and Kim was up to.

One night he decided to run a test and told her he was going out with Kim. They met at 8 o'clock in the Mulberry Bush—this had become their favorite haunt since the night they'd met there—they'd spent two hours in the Pub then he took her home on the bus. Getting home himself at about 11.pm. She was sitting up watching TV when he came in.

He sat beside her, kissed her on the cheek and she took his hand in hers. "Had a good time son?" she inquired with real interest.

"Just a few drinks in the Pub, nothing special," he said, but by this he knew she was Okay or she'd have said as he walked in, but he had to ask. She said she was fine, no problem. The following night he said he was going out with a friend but in fact was meeting Kim. He got home at 11.30

and before he'd closed the living-room door she was telling him about her latest encounter, and suddenly it was all coming together in his mind.

He instructed her to make a note of the exact time of any further attack.

"But why?" she questioned.

"No special reason, just curious."

A week later he began comparing his own detailed records with hers, and ten days later the mystery was solved.

For a whole day he'd sat going over the details looking for another answer. Any answer. One that was not so conclusive, anything but the one facing him. How could he believe this and continue to think himself sane? He checked it from every angle, circumstance and reason. It was impossible and could never be, but there it was staring back at him, challenging his sanity. There was no one with whom he could share this and not be marked down as slightly imperfect, damaged stock or raving lunatic. Except his mother, and she was the one person he could not tell that everyone of her little visitors had dropped in at the precise date and time he'd made love to Kim, and exactly at his moment of climax.

From the first day, when her reactions were so hostile that it made her sick and brought her home from work, she'd been tuning into his sexual vibrations. Not the entire act, just his moment of intense excitement. He was mysteriously transmitting these electrical charges of the mind directly to her and she was picking them up and was vicariously sharing his orgasms. That day as he had sex for the first time, he felt the ecstatic pressures building up from deep within and thought his body was locked in a vice and being squeezed dry. Then as he rose higher into this rapturous aura, now totally engulfing him he clamped his teeth on Kim's nipple and somewhere in his mind he was screaming his mother's name. He felt this had no special significance because he'd always called her name in times of pain, stress, fear or intense excitement. This began when he was nine years old, and had woken one night from a bad dream calling her name.

She'd rushed into his room to find him sitting up in bed crying. He told her his father had held his head under the water and tried to kill him. She picked him up in her arms and embraced him, he felt safe against her nice warm body. She took him into her bed and he'd slept with her that night.

When he broke the news he was marrying Kim, he saw his mother's complexion change to a deathly white and thought she'd pass out. She was standing at the dining table arranging dried flowers in a vase. Slowly she drew a chair and eased herself daintily into it, and there followed a long painful silence. He wanted to say something to break the spell but nothing that came to mind seemed right. He hung there like a wet rag dripping with guilt as he watched her demolish a sprig of chrysanthemum by crushing it in her fist. She picked up her head and he saw the pain in her eyes.

"Why must you hurt me like this, what have I done to you? Peter, I wished you'd died at birth," she said, then got up and brushed passed him and scampered out into the living-room and swept out the door. Next her footsteps were bounding up the stairs, then the house vibrated as she slammed her bedroom door. He threw up his hands in despair and lifting his face toward the heavens. he first pleaded for God's help then quickly got angry and demanded it. "If you are really there, dear God, why don't you do something? Am I expected to handle this alone? Tell me what to do. You show me another way and I'll take it, and I don't care what it involves. Point me in the right direction and I'll go. I don't want to hurt her but what choice have I? Your son has never asked for anything before, but is now pleading for your help, begging for your guidance.

His mother had been a keen advocate of leaving things in the hands of God and letting him deal with it. He'd not given this much thought before, but now he found himself hoping she was up there praying for both their deliverance.

A little later he pushed the door open and walked in. She was sitting on the bed in a mood of consummate hopelessness. He closed the door, sauntered across the room and sat beside her. She made no movement but for the displacement of her body as the bed sank under his weight, rolling her toward him and forcing her to adjust her position. They sat staring silently at the floor, their thighs gently touching.

"Pat, you didn't mean what you said, did you.… about me dying at birth?"

"Don't you call me Pat I'm your mother," she said dryly and without malice.

He laughed. "Patricia, do you realize how childish this is? You allow me to play with your toys while things are going well, but the minute I step out of line and upset you things change and you snatch them back. "Call me Pat," you said, "I'm not only your mother I'm also your friend," are you saying we're no longer friends?"

"I'm sorry for what I said, it was all very childish and I didn't mean any of it, but it's not easy to sit back and watch the destruction of your life without fighting back. To watch everything you've worked for. Hopes, dreams, and desires being gathered to be flushed away like used toilet paper. That is what you're doing to me by marrying this girl. Peter it'll be a death sentence for me. Much worse than when your father died, because I had you but with you gone who will I have? What will I do without you, how will I live? You are more of a man than your father ever was and I need you, please don't leave me," she appealed, with tears in her eyes.

Her words scampering through his head, reminding him of things she'd said about his father. What exactly did she mean by, he was more man than his father? She'd said, he couldn't leave women alone but he was all mouth, nothing more. Then he remembered the morning she'd walked in on him in the bathroom and he finally understood.

He was standing naked, quietly reliving the best moments of the night before with his manhood pointing accusingly at the mirror when the door opened and she glided in, looked at him, and her eyes almost jumped from their sockets. "My God!" she exclaimed, hands to her mouth. "You are three times the size of your father." Then she strode boldly over and stood directly in front of him looking at it.

He wanted to run and hide himself but couldn't move, as she seems to hold him with her eyes. It had been an open house all his life and they'd been walking in on each other since the beginning of time. It was routine and meant nothing. They looked at each other and didn't see, there was nothing to see, and it had all been taken for granted. But this was different, for she was seeing him in action for the first time. Raging rampant anger, and she was loving it.

"This is all that girl's doing, isn't it?" she slowly lifted her head and looked him in the eyes, with the same lustful hunger he'd seen in Kim. Her fingers twitching like a nervous gunfighter. Chest heaving as the breath rushed in and out of her lungs. He'd not seen her in such a nervous and agitated state before and was rigid with fear, thinking any second she'd reach out and take hold of it. He'd almost certainly die on the spot, but what if he didn't drop dead at that point? Would he manage to resist her, or would he finally succumb, taking his mother right there on the floor? He kept looking in her eyes, reading her mind and wishing she'd go away, hoping his cock would die, willing it to fade so she'd go away. Still she stood there with that pathetic longing in her eyes. He wanted to move but she was in control of his mind and he couldn't break the spell she was casting. The next move would be hers.

"It's that girl," she said. No more. a question but a definitive statement. Then she smiled as only she could. A smile that spoke a thousand words of love. "Put it away," she said. "Put it away before someone trips over it," Then she turned brushing hard against it with her left hip and went out the door mumbling. "I don't believe it. I do not believe it."

Nor could he believe that she'd dragged him so close to the edge then let him go when it was all there in her eyes. She wanted him. His mother wanted him. After that he could all but see her in bed at nights chewing her pillows ragged, thinking about him out there giving it to Kim, and as if that wasn't bad enough he now wanted to marry her and move out. A feeling of sadness washed over him like a dark shadow. "I love you Pat." The words seem to escape from his heart and spilled from his lips. "I love you more than any man should love his own mother, and I hate myself for hurting you. If there was a way to avoid all this suffering I'd take it, Pat, you know I would," he wiped tears from his eyes with his fingers.

"I don't know that Peter," her voice creaking with pain. "there is a very simple way out. Don't marry her."

He shook his head. "I can't do that."

"But why?"

"Pat you know why I must marry her, we both know why."

"You don't have to marry her to get that and I'm sure you're getting enough at the moment, besides, you can bring her here into your bed I don't mind. Sleep with her every night if you like, get as much as you need but don't marry her. Peter, I'll do anything you want and will agree to anything you say. Tickle her but don't marry her."

He chuckled. "Pat, the word isn't tickle, I've grown up now and that is no longer necessary, I'm old enough to use the right word…"

"Don't you ever use that word in my presence."

"But you used it," he reminded her.

"I have tried very hard to forget that and don't need to be reminded of what you've brought me to. Your father would use it to me in bed and I hated it because it made me feel cheap and dirty. It was something he'd picked up from one of his women and that made it worse. I used it to describe your dirty deeds because I couldn't find a more fitting word at the time."

"All right, have it your way," he said lightly. "but there is more to it than simply tickling her. You're not only my mother, you're also my best friend and the only person in whom I've confided or ever will. I've shared things with you that I'll never share with another woman. I love you Patricia West, and that love is killing me. I have no right to love you the way I do because it's wrong but there is nothing I can do about that, it's too late. Pat, I'm trying to put this as clearly as I can and know you understand because we're feeling the same pain…. I must marry this girl and get out of this house. God knows I don't want to leave you and each day I'm hating myself more for what I must do to you."

"Why must you, can't you see there's no reason to marry her, you don't love her. Use her if you must but don't destroy what we have, you can have the best of both worlds, why throw it all away on a marriage without love?" she took his hands. "Peter, I gave you nineteen years of my life and now I'm asking for a little of yours. Give me five years Peter, that's not much to ask? You'll be twenty four years old and still a young man with lots of time to marry, and by then you might find the right girl. Five years Peter. It may not be that long for I could die before. Move the girl in here so you can really get to know her while you're giving me those five years, that's all I ask. You don't have to lose out on what you like and in the meantime you'd have two women looking after you. This way you'll find out if she really loves you without having to marry her. You don't want to marry her and then find you're not suited. Think about it, what I'm saying makes sense."

"I could never move her in here, she'd never understand our relationship," he said pointedly. "What do you think she'd make of me walking in and out of the bathroom while you were taking a bath, or me washing your back? What would she think of me joining you in bed on a Sunday morning? I wouldn't expect her to understand when I can hardly fathom it myself."

She looked at him with surprise. "What don't you understand?" she asked. "Tell me what you find so puzzling about our relationship?"

"Mom, you're not being honest when you ask a question like that. Something is clearly not right and I'm sure you can see it as well as I can."

"Peter, I can't see it and you'll 'have to stop being so coy and say what's on your mind. We've always been candid with each other and that has been our strength. Are you saying there is something sinister in a son washing his mother's back, or climbing into her bed on a cold winter's morning? Are you saying there is something sinful in a mother bathing her son?"

Yes, when he's nineteen years old, he was saying to himself and almost said it out loud but changed his mind. Why should he be the one to break into this unspoken taboo of a subject, and what could he hope to achieve by dragging it into the light? When she was already pretending she didn't understand his concern, implying it was normal and innocent. Opening the subject after that would only make him seem an obscene lecher who was degrading something pure. It would be worse if she wasn't pretending and honestly believed what had been brewing between them was harmless. He was not prepared to look the bad boy as she glossed it over with a thick veneer of mother's love, when he knew the truth. Like the last Sunday morning he joined her in bed, and it was neither cold nor a winter's morning. It was a bright morning at the beginning of August. He'd brought her tea and was telling her how beautiful the morning was. "Should I open the curtains?" he asked.

"What time is it?" she wanted to know. He said it was 8 o'clock.

"No it's too early, come and join me," she said and pulled back the sheet.

Without hesitation he dived into the bed beside her, fully clothed. She drew him close, almost forcing his head down to her breast and as his face got within range she lifted her right breast and put it to his lips and he did the rest, moving to the left a short time later. He was neither helpless nor an innocent victim and knew what was taking place was not some harmless game. He was an eager participant and didn't blame her then and wasn't doing so now. Then there was the way she'd embrace him with that close hip-thrusting, pelvic-locking affair that bore no relation to innocence, that would be watered down to an innocent arched hipped event in public. What kind of a man would he be if he couldn't read these signs? He kept asking himself, yet she would have him believe it was in his mind.

"Come on Peter, tell me what's on your mind, I'm waiting," she prompted. He opened his arms and fell back on the bed.

"I've thought it out and feel I may have been making a lot of noise over nothing, it could be my imagination," he shuffled the truth and hid it under his conscience.

She smiled. "I'm happy you've finally come to your senses. Peter, you are wrong. It's your overworked imagination that is dragging you into confusion, you must not try so hard to put reason to everything, for there are things in life that defies reason and understanding."

He wasn't sure what she was trying to say but had seen nothing in their relationship that had truly defied his comprehension, it was so clear, only she'd left it three years too late. Now she seems to be away on tour, acting out a play in some far off corner of her mind and couldn't be reached, completely out of touch with the realities surrounding them. He was sure that if he made love to her that moment, five minutes later she'd be putting it out of her mind, pretending it never happened. Imagination my eye, he silently exclaimed. It wasn't all in his mind the day she held him so close he couldn't help responding. The only time he'd lost control. She felt him rise turgid against her body and had expected her to pull back but she didn't. Then as he tried to back off she clung to him and with a hurt voice, accused him of rejecting her love. He didn't complain then and was not complaining now. He thrived on their embraces and had grown to love everything about her body. She was no ordinary woman, and was as attractive as she was enchanting, she was a gift from the Gods, full of a special kind of love and affection that just dripped from her body.

As he woke her each morning she'd reach out for him and he'd clamber on the bed and they'd embrace.

"Good-morning baby," she'd say, kissing him on both cheeks, then would sit up resting her back against the headboard, huge firm breasts sitting proudly on her chest. He'd been seeing them for years without really appreciating their magnificence until he met Kim. His mother was twenty seven years older but she could give the youngster lessons in beauty and charm. Kim was a dazzling beauty, in her own way, but couldn't come within a mile of his mother. She was thirty four years old when his father died and he could still recall those days and his pride as she stood outside his school with the other mothers. She was the prettiest of them all. The most blissful moments he'd known were those spent in her loving embrace. Pleasures that had not been surpassed by anything, even Kimberly has so far offered.

Drifting back he could recall great times with his young friends. Good times with their own special moments, but no matter how engrossed he'd be in those, games, the moment it was bath time his friends would be instantly abandoned. Unlike other boys who had to be called and called again, three or four times, then had to be threatened and bullied, clipped about the ears and physically dragged struggling into the house by an irate parent, who'd then batter them mercilessly before they'd submit and commit their bodies to water. He was never late, never absent and didn't have to be called for he knew his bath times. There was no greater pleasure than lying in his mother's arms, half submerged in a warm bath, his head resting on or between her breasts. He couldn't understand why that had meant so much to him and had taken on such importance in his young life. He only knew that her body represented pleasure and contentment beyond his wildest desires. Even now he still couldn't understand why it had meant so much and why he should still be having those feelings for his mother, and in spite of Kim those feeling were as intense as ever, and there was now a burning need to explore and discover her body in the same way he'd done with Kim. She was the most desirable woman he'd ever met.

Leaning against the headboard she'd drink her tea, after that they'd embrace again, kiss and say good-bye. In the evening they'd greet again with more kisses and affection. From then until bedtime she'd throw her arms about him in an embrace as the mood took her. He would stand there in her arms thinking his father was a damn fool, along with all his other inadequacies. He was the most fortunate man that ever lived but was too blind to see it, all her love and endless affection was his but he didn't bother to claim it, too busy screwing around with lesser women. He got up from the bed and took her-hands, and brought her up with him. Holding hands he looked her over in a long licentious gaze, his eyes wandering over her in open admiration. He smiled.

"Any man would be proud to have you, and most would give anything for that privilege, and pleasure. At this moment I'm wishing you weren't my mother, that I wasn't your son but a total stranger." Isn't it a crime? He was thinking. That a stranger could come in and do things to his mother he dared not do? Bashfully she lowered her head and in a voice barely audible she said. "We could pretend."

"What did you say Mom?" he asked, as though he hadn't heard.

"Oh, I said it was no good wishing or pretending.

"I know," he sanctioned. "I completely agree."

From then on it was virtually impossible to make love to Kim without thinking of his mother, and on a number of occasions found he was actively fantasizing about her, and why not? He'd ask himself. It was the closest she'd get to the real thing. Then he'd return home to hear that she had indeed received it and would be well satisfied.

Chapter 17

As the time of the wedding drew closer Peter thought about his mother's offer to move Kim into the house, and financially it made good economical sense. They hadn't got the kind of money to set themselves up with a decent place, and staying at home would give them the run of the house and two bedrooms to themselves. They would need no furniture and the whole deal would cost little more than he was paying at present. They had talked it over and she was ready to accept Kim as his wife and welcome her into the house, and for a mad moment he thought it might work, but he was soon wide awake from that dream and back in the real world.

To begin, his mother hated Kimberly with a passion. Not personally, for she'd only seen her once and didn't know her. It was simply an open resentment that had been reserved for any woman who'd dared to take her son, and the only reason she'd have that woman living in her house would be to try and break the marriage as swiftly as she could, and that would take her less than a week.

They were both in the habit of walking around naked and this freedom of undress would have to be curtailed before Kim moved in, along with some other adjustments. None of which would pose a problem for him but he couldn't see his mother conforming. Not because she couldn't but because it would be in her best interest not to, and would soon arrange such a shock for Kim, the poor girl would probably run from the house and never stop running. If she did stay around long enough to hear, and even accept his explanation, how would he cover it the next time it happened? And if they did move out together the seeds of doubts would be lodged in her mind forever.

The day she caught them in bed Kim had demanded an explanation for not trying to cover himself like any normal son caught in that situation. Instead he'd stood there shamelessly in front of his mother with his raging prick dripping wet and glistening. "What's going on with you two, and why was she slapping you around in her room? That woman wasn't behaving like your mother, more like your wife," she said. He couldn't tell her then, and he couldn't do it now.

Eventually he told Pat he would not be staying on after the wedding and as the conversation progressed he mentioned that Kim was two months pregnant, and told her the date of the wedding. She slowly drew up her legs in the chair, curling her body into a tight ball. Holding her head and groaning as though in severe pain.

She shrank away from his touch, hugging her knees and contracting her body beyond its normal size. Her face shrouded in pain and deep despair. Since meeting Kim she'd been hurt more times than all their previous years but this was the worst.

There have been times when she'd pretend not to welcome his show of affection, but was always able to see through this veil, but not this time, and could feel the chill of her misery and pain as he touched her. He could read her like an open book and didn't like what he was reading. They had been so close and had shared so much love that there were times he could feel her grief just as he'd shared her happiness. Rolled up in the chair whimpering like a frightened child, she seemed so vulnerable and helpless. This woman who'd always found an answer to their problems was now drained of ideas. She may have been buried two years later but this was the day she died and he'd felt the pain of her 'death as he'd looked on helplessly.

Through a haze of tears and enervating despair, he watched her face with concern. Why am I doing this to the woman I truly love? Why am I destroying the only woman I'm ever likely to love? Why must life be so wretchedly complicated, and why am I taking another woman in place of her. "God!" he screamed. "Why am I doing this, why?" He lifted his head toward the heavens. She looked up and saw the tears of torment and confusion rolling down his face.

"Pat, you've got to help me," he cried, voice choked up with emotion and barely coherent through spasms of sobbing. "I don't want to leave you, I don't know what I'm doing or why I'm doing it, Please help me," he sank to his knees in her open arms.

"Darling we're no good without each other, we belong together," she said, her own tears mixing with his. "You can never change that and it's best not to try for all we'll have is pain. Look what it's doing to you, and what it's doing to our love. This is what I've tried so hard to avoid, women will always do this to you, Stay with me, I'm the only woman who'll love you truly and the only one you'll ever fully understand, We belong to each other," she picked up the hem of her dressing gown and dried his eyes, and face then her own tears. She hugged him close, his face nestling against the softness of her breasts, comforting him. Rocking him gently. She opened her dressing gown, and as he latched on she nursed him as if he was still a twitching infant at her breast. Wide eyed and tearful she stared blankly across the room and back over the years to the very moment of his conception. She was sure she knew the instant his father's sperm had fused with her ovum, and she knew it was a boy. She could feel it as sure as she was sitting there holding him in her arms and he'd been hers from that moment. Not his father's, who'd practically hated children and had to be tricked into his minute contribution. No, not Philip's but hers and the God who made it all possible. Philip didn't want him, and after finding that she'd outwitted him had proceeded to make her life hell.

For the next six months he showed no sympathy for her little discomforts. Backaches, heartburn, swollen legs and feet, along with all the other complaint she'd brought to him expecting compassion, would be met with the same cold savage and inhuman response. A brusque reminder that he didn't want children and it was all her doing. "You got yourself into this don't complain to me," he'd say, and had continued using her body for sex right up to the moment she had her first twinges of labor.

Once she complained of feeling nauseous and not up to it but he got on so badly that she gave in, just to have some peace. At the time she was eight months, and as he proceeded to make her stomach even sicker he informed her he was not going to let the baby come between them. When Peter was born he'd visit her in the Heathfield Road, Maternity Hospital, and would sit at the side of her bed looking at her as 'though he wanted to climb into bed with her.

She was in the Hospital for ten days, returning home on the eleventh day, and less than five minutes after she stepped from the Ambulance into the house, he was pushing his way into her on the living-room floor, with Peter lying beside her crying his head off, not three feet from the spot he now knelt.

"I am not going to let that child come between us," he kept repeating.

I was the one that wanted a child and I got you, but how much longer will I have you? She asked herself. She kissed the top of his head. "Come on darling it's time for bed," she said, breaking his rhythm and helping him to his feet. "Tomorrow you'll feel better," she added hopefully.

For a time he just stared at her as though seeing her for the first time, then suddenly he swept her up in his arms, kissed her full on the lips, took her upstairs to her bedroom and shut the door behind them.

Peter and Kim were married on a chilly November afternoon a month later. Pat had refused to take any part in it and didn't attend, saying she had no wish to be present at her son's auction. Two weeks before the wedding he'd moved into a flat with Kim, just a ten minute walk from his mother's house. Kim had first objected to this, claiming they might just as well had moved in with his mother, but Peter was adamant and got his way.

At 6.50pm he'd left the reception, telling Kim he'd be back in ten minutes. A short time later he arrived at his mother's house and let himself in to find her sitting on the sofa in front of the TV in tears. It turned out she'd been crying since 3.pm the time of the ceremony. This she said was the real reason she didn't attend the wedding, and not because she hated Kim, or wanted to register her disapproval of their union. Her love was greater than all of this, but since the day she learnt they were to be married she'd come to hate the very idea of marriage and its outdated concept, where a woman can walk into her house and steal the man she loves, but even this could not have kept her away. It was knowing that she couldn't sit there and watch him marry without breaking down and making a fool of herself, and distracting him to the point where he'd probably leave his wife and come to her aid. "Nobody would understand our relationship," she said. Reminding him that nether his bride nor his in-laws knew her and would be quick to form their own opinion. "All my life I've gone out of my way to protect, and do the best for you, and will go on doing so until my death and beyond, as I've promised. Peter, you've damaged my heart beyond repair, moving out of this house is the deepest wound you've inflicted. Not the girl, or the marriage or the fact that your love would now be directed at someone else. All that has left me in sorrow, but nothing had cut me deeper than the day you deserted me. That day I watched you pick up your bag and walked out of this house I saw my only reason for being alive torn away from me. I can tell you now that I don't have long to live, but I have no regrets, none whatsoever. I thank God for those happy years he gave us. After all," she added philosophically. "Who said we had a divine right to infinite happiness? Some of us are destined never to know a single spark of love, yet look at what we've shared. No son, I don't have a single regret, not about you or the life we've had. I still have hopes though, hopes and dreams that have not yet been fulfilled, and may never be," she shrugged. "But who can have more than everything, and you are everything. You are all there is Peter, nothing or no one come after you. The things I never had with you I never will."

All this talk of hopelessness and death was depressing him but on this sad day he wasn't prepared to argue. She wasn't to know how much he'd dreaded the arrival of this day and how he'd hated it and what it had done to him. It should've been the day of his life, instead it turned out to be more like his mother's funeral. He couldn't remember a more horrid day in his whole life and was dying to escape it all and get back to peace and sanity and have her lift his spirit from the pit of depression. This hour with her had been the highlight of his entire day. Without it he could not have survived the reception.

When he returned Kim was livid but had met him with smiles and kisses, which quickly subsided the moment she got him alone. "Peter, haven't you got a heart, how could you walk out on me tonight of all? Our wedding reception," she spewed her disappointment and frustration. "You had me walking around like a fool trying to explain your absence with lame excuses that no one believed, and probably thought you had walked out for good. Even I wasn't sure you hadn't got a change of heart and had returned to your mother...Christ, your visit must have made her truly happy? She hates me so much that she kept away from our wedding, yet a few minutes after you put the ring on my finger you walk out and is spending our first blissful moments of marriage with her. What was so important that couldn't be left for tomorrow, and don't tell me you weren't there cause I know better."

So this is marriage, this is what it's all about? Am I truly ready for this? He thought, as he took it all without any attempt to defend his actions. He was wrong and he accepted it.

At the end of her tirade he produced a sealed envelope from his jacket pocket and handed it to her. "It's our wedding gift from my mother," he said, fully expecting her to rip the thing to pieces and throw it back at him, but to his complete astonishment she carefully opened the envelope and her face lit up. She let out a gasp of pure delight, her face ablaze with excitement and elation as she viewed the gift.

"Two thousand pounds?" she exclaimed witlessly, as though the money had zapped her good sense, and suddenly made everything right. "You have thanked her, haven't you?... Anyway I'll have to write and thank her myself."

He could not believe the speed at which her anger had mellowed, and his absence at one of the most important time of her life was quickly validated and granted her unstinting approval. She was one big smile as she came and wrapped herself around him like a bath towel, her tongue in his mouth as she held him in a tight embrace, with her hips wedged against him in a salacious apology. Whispering she was sorry for shouting at him but didn't know, and would make a real apology later, signing her promise with a delicate thrust of her hips. She stood back and looked at the check once more and attempted handing it to him but changed her mind. "No I think it'll be safer with me," she said returning it to the envelope, then folding it once she slipped it inside her bra, and that was the last he saw or heard of it. As she turned and left the room he wondered how could what he'd done be made right with money? How could she accept it when there was no reason to leave her to pick up a check that could have been collected a day earlier, or two days later. He was a little disappointed at how easily she'd prostituted her high moral ground and caved at the sight of a little money. He'd hoped her price was a little higher, and this was the first crack in her otherwise impeccable character. It was dated three days earlier. This might have told her he'd got it on the day it was signed and not as she'd assumed, that it was the reason he'd visited his mother. For three days he'd been walking around with it, trying to decide if he really wanted to take this much money from his mother.

He had planned to discuss it with Kim on the wedding and had promised himself to go along with whatever she said, but was hoping she wouldn't accept it. His mother had already given them everything they needed, including £500 toward the reception and it didn't sit right taking another load of money from her. She'd sweated blood to bring him up alone, and put that little money aside, and he should now be helping her, not taking from her. What if something should happen and she could no longer work, she'd need every penny she could find. He had argued this with her when she gave him the check but she refused to accept his argument.

"All the work I've done was for you, and every penny I've earned was with you in mind, It's all yours Peter, whether you have it now or when I die it doesn't matter."

As things turned out, the day had drifted by with them barely meeting a couple of times and his planned discussion with her had to be postponed for later, but as she disparaged his mother he decided to see what she was really made of. Her rapid retreat left him thinking his mother was right when she said. All women had something to sell, and all a man had to do was name the right price and they'd cheerfully prostitute their honesty and integrity and whatever else they felt might be standing in their way.

But she was his wife, why did her price have to be so low—Jesus, couldn't she have asked a little more? The woman he'd sold to his mother as being so different.

Kim never got around to writing that letter of thanks but it didn't matter, Pat had expected nothing better, and Peter had already said his thanks

Chapter 18

Karen was born in the Dudley Road Maternity unit, on the 15th, of May 1970, with Peter standing outside the door. Kim had requested his presence but he turned her down, saying he didn't feel he was ready for that kind of thing. Not after the things his mother had told him. Her parents and Adrianne—eight months pregnant with her third child-arrived two hours later and spent ten minutes with her.

It was after they'd left that Kim mentioned his mother, and Informed him that if she wanted to see the child she'd have to come crawling to her with an apology.

He stood back from the bed in amazement. "Apology? What apology?" he said in such a voice it attracted the attention of the Sister three beds away. "What has my mother done to you that merit an apology?" he demanded in a near whisper.

"For calling me a whore and kicking me out of her house, for hating me without reason and not granting me a chance to redeem myself."

"She didn't call you a whore," he said.

"She said I was a strumpet and that means whore, it's the same thing…well I can't see what she'd want with the daughter of a whore, can you?"

"My mother had every right to behave as she did that day."

"I thought you'd say that!" she snapped. "She had every right to beat you up in that room and send you out black and blue, bleeding from the mouth, for if you weren't man enough to stand up to her you deserved all you got. But she had no right to call me names. She didn't know a damn thing about me and I've never hurt her in any way."

"I lived in her house and knew the rules, and out of respect for her I shouldn't have taken you there. I know how painful it was to come home and find me breaking the very promise I'd made. Why shouldn't she expect a certain standard of behavior in her house? Every decent, and caring parent would. We will expect the same of Karen when she's of age, and wouldn't be pleased to walk into her bedroom and find some man stuffing her, how could you expect less from my mother?"

"Peter," she said cynically. "I don't know what pact you've signed with your mother, or what is really going on between you. She hates me for taking you away from her and that is more hate than anything that could be explained by an innocent love for her son. You two are much too close for my peace of mind, and before she sees my child she'll have to furnish me with a confession. I am your wife and I am demanding an answer to all those questions that have not yet been answered."

"It must be post-natal depression, this thing that is suddenly affecting your head. Kimberly, you're not well, you are sick of the mind." he calmly informed her.

After that their arguments grew more heated each time the subject was touched, and Peter kept touching it daily. By now Kim had forgotten about the help his mother had given them only six months earlier. Peter brought it to her attention and quietly asked how much help they'd got from her parents who now had unhindered access to the child? She accused him of wanting to sell his daughter to the highest bidder. He was mad but equally ready to compromise, and with a combination of charm and persuasion Kim was swayed, and his mother saw the baby for the first time when she was a month old. Peter would wheel her the short distance to his mother's house once a week, and continued this right up to her first birthday. Soon after that he bought a secondhand Ford Escort, and would take her on a Sunday Morning and collect her in the evening.

Patricia was never more proud of her son than at this time. He'd refused to talk about it, but she'd managed to work something out of him and knew the battle he had with Kim and his firm stand that the child would not be used as a rod to beat its, own grandmother. He'd discussed it with her and had indicated that Kim may be a little difficult when the child is born. During this time all kinds of doubts had crept into her thinking, and she wondered if her son would stand up to his wife when the time came? She had not seen Kim and had no way of assessing the kind of wife she was, or the kind of husband her son was. All she knew was what he'd told her, and that would be just what he wanted her to know, and no more. She could only see one way along a two-way Street and had no knowledge of what was coming at him from the other side. It could be that the little woman was ruling him with a heavy hand and wouldn't expect him to disclose this. Sure…he was tough and assertive, and she could vouch for this. But she'd also seen the more genteel side of him. That tranquil, almost subservient placidity which could so easily lend itself to the will of a dominant woman, who also knows how to use her charms. Thankfully, she'd made no mistakes and had taught him well. She was so proud of him.

The same could not be said by Kim, who had become so jealous of his frequent visits to his mother, and the late hour he sometimes returned that she would happily have filed for divorce sighting his mother. It seems that in spite of all she'd given him…. Love, devotion, marriage, and a beautiful daughter on whom he doted, something was still missing from their lives. There was this great cavern somewhere inside him that only his mother could fill. There was a huge chunk of his heart she couldn't reach, that almost seem to bear a big sign, that said. No entry, except for Karen and Patricia West. She felt as though she was standing on the outer fringes of her own life looking in, as if in a dream, with her will and desires relegated to mere inconsequence as she watched his mother directing his life like it was the string section of her own private Orchestra. By this she'd already taken his mother's place but was too wrapped up in her own blind jealousy, to realize she'd won the battle and had kept on fighting.

Peter saw his mother every day, but there was no longer that close loving relationship. They still embraced, but even in that close encounter it was like two strangers greeting over a barbed wire fence. Both wanting to get closer but being held at bay by an invisible barrier. He was also knocking on doors for the first time since he was eight years old, and would refuse to enter the bathroom even at her invitation, in case she was naked. She complained bitterly that his stupid wife had undone years of diligent work inside a few months, and had turned him into a suspicious, narrow minded prude, who now believes the naked body was no longer a thing of beauty, but something ugly and repulsive.

Peter wanted her as much as ever, but now he was loving her through Kim and could no longer show it. All that forbidden love he'd been saving was now being lavished on Kimberly, her proxy. He would close his eyes and think of Patricia, knowing that where ever she was, he was getting through to her. It was three years after her death before he was able to get her out of his sex life and finally laid her to rest.

As he opened the front door it was plain something had gone badly wrong and his heart started pumping with fear. The mail and other junk that had arrived during the day were still at the door.

The first thing his mother did on getting out of bed in the mornings was make a trip to the bathroom. On her way she'd look if the mail had arrived, and if her needs weren't too urgent she'd go down and collect whatever there was, and would look them over in the bathroom.

Before entering the house he could tell she'd not left her bedroom since morning, and she'd have to be seriously ill not to leave her room, or to pick up the phone and call him at work. Peter had to put his shoulder to the door to force it open. The post and a folded newspaper had jammed beneath it.

He hurriedly kicked the obstruction out of the way, slammed the door shut and raced up the stairs.

He had only ever heard of the smell of death, and wasn't sure if such a phenomenon existed, but the instant he began opening her door there was no longer any doubts in his mind and he now knew the smell of death. It was a redolence he couldn't define, but instinctively knew did not belong with the living and would've had no place in his mother's bedroom. Not the woman he knew.

He pushed the door open until it was almost flat against the wall, and stood holding it as he looked at her. She was lying on her stomach, covered by a thin cotton sheet, pulled up to just below her shoulders. His hand fell away from the door as he moved timidly toward the bed, telling himself she wasn't dead, she couldn't be, not his mother. How would he manage without her if she was dead, but she couldn't be dead she was very much alive last night when he left, and she promised they would talk again today, she couldn't die so suddenly. He could manage without Kim, or maybe Karen but not Pat.

He hung there as though trapped in a dream in which he was trying to flee from danger but couldn't move, the strangest thought came into his head, and he was bitterly regretting not making love to her. He found himself asking God to make it so she wasn't dead but in a deep sleep, and promising he'd make love to her when she wakes up. All at once he was himself again and was standing at the side of the bed looking down at her body, face turned away and partially covered by strands of long brown hair. Her left arm pinned beneath her in an awkward position.

Oh Mom, you'll be in pain with that arm when you wake, the thought went through his head.

Except for the position of her arm, and her hair, which would normally be pinned up before bed, she seemed so alive, and exactly as she would on those mornings he'd bring her tea. He wanted to wake her, to shake her gently from her sleep with the usual words. "Pat, tea," He thought how odd it was that disaster was able to concentrate the mind and heighten the senses and put things in perspective. All at once his head was full of all the things he wanted to say to her and should have said. Things he should've done and will do for her from now on, if God grants his wish, and as he fantasized he realized tears were running down his face and he couldn't think why he was crying. Suddenly he dropped to his knees and fell forward holding her ice cold body, weeping like a sick infant.

It was half an hour later before he called Kim, and in that time had managed to get her into a pair of knickers. Even in death he'd refused to let them see her like that, and would've put on her top but was defeated by her crooked left arm. What they did with her out of his sight was their business, but he would not have them gawping at her nakedness while he was standing there.

Kim was the first to arrive and found him so distressed she could not believe he was the same person. She hardly knew him and was afraid he'd have to be sedated if she didn't manage to calm him before the doctor arrived. She thought about the death of her aunt four years ago and how her mother had suffered that bereavement in near silence and hardly spoke for three day. Why dear God couldn't Peter be the same? Each person had to suffer in their own way but why was this his way. He was like a schizophrenic, being directed by unknown voices from within.

"She's not dead," he said. "Any minute now she'll wake up...she spoke before you came," he laughed fatuously.

She glanced at his mother's dead body and wanted to put him right but held back. She tried to embrace him but he struggled free and made for the other side of the bed and knelt on the floor, caressing her face with both hands, tears streaming down his face, lamenting in an heart rending groan. She gazed at him and suddenly took on his pain and began crying. The very thing she'd promised not to do. She needed to be strong, and wanted to be a rock he could lean on and not break down in tears just when he needed her most.

He looked at her and a change seem to come over him. "Don't cry," he said, touching his mother's hair. "Don't cry for her she's not dead," he quickly came back around the bed and took her in his arms. "Don't cry," he whispered softly. "No need to cry, she's gone but I am here and I love you. She said there was a better place on the other side, and promised if she went first she would come back and let me know what it's like. She will be back. Don't cry," he wiped her eyes with his fingers. "She has gone to a place where she'll make lots of friends and will never be lonely again. I hope my father is waiting for her, do you know he was the only man she ever had?" he said softly as if it was a well guarded secret.

"Yes I know, you've told me. She was a good woman."

"The best," he agreed. "the very best."

"I will try to be as good for you as she was but you've got to help me like you helped her. I can't do it without your help."

Kim had no idea what kind of help she was asking for, they were mere words, but seemed to be coming out right and in harmony with his own confused thinking.

"I will," he answered. "I will do whatever you ask for I don't ever want to lose you, or Karen."

"Peter, I love you and will be as good for you as she ever was, and that's a promise."

He broke down in tears again as his mother's body was taken from the house, but Kim had learnt that being tough only made him worse and soon he was drying her tears and comforting her.

The postmortem could find no illness that could have contributed to her death, there was no sign of fowl play, nor did she take her own life. Peter was more deeply wounded by what, in his opinion, was a piece of time wasting butchery.

He had vehemently objected to her body being carved up like a Sunday roast, and said they were wasting time and would find nothing. "Natural cause," they said. "How could death from loneliness and a broken heart be termed natural?"

The way she died was more fowl than having a knife pushed into her as she walked along the street. That way she'd have died quickly and without much pain. But for letting a woman with so much love to give, wither and die of a broken heart, made him the most gruesome murderer that ever stained the face of this earth. He felt there should be a law against such a crime and he should be in jail awaiting trial without bail, reaping the punishment for deserting her and passing that sentence of a long slow death. He had struck the death blow then sat back doing nothing for the next two years as he watched her fade like a dying ember, and couldn't claim he didn't know, for on his daily visits the subject of death would creep into her conversations. She kept talking about her life insurance and how much he was due on her death, but he had refused to discuss it and would brush such talk aside with indifference. Three weeks before she died she'd told him.

"Everything I have comes to you. I live only for you and because of you. Without you there is nothing and no one, and I now have no further reason to go on living. Since you met her your love for me has shrunk and I know that one day it'll die and I'm not waiting around to suffer that. Peter, I couldn't live without your love."

As usual he'd brushed this aside and reminded her she was only forty seven and still the prettiest and healthiest woman in the street. Now he wished he'd listened to her cries for help.

After his father had died leaving her broke and with a mountain of bills, she saw the value of making provisions for your loved ones, and it raked her to the soul at the thought of what would happen to Peter if she was to die suddenly. She immediately got in touch with Sun life Of Canada and took out a life insurance. This would mature at sixty, with a pension or yield a lump sum on death. She'd worked like a hound, saving everything she could and five years after Philip died the house was cleared of mortgage. Her life insurance had left Peter £11,000, plus her savings of £5,100, and a death gratuity from her employers of £2,250.

Peter soon got himself together and took control of things, making all the arrangements for the funeral and inviting all the guests. Kim was pleasantly amazed at his rapid transformation. No more tears or sad depressive moods, he took command and did what had to be done, frenziedly driving himself as though to evict the pain from his heart and mind.

Three day before the funeral he was so tightly wound he couldn't sleep and would lay awake all night. Then the night before the funeral he left the flat at 10pm and drove to his mother's house, returning at 7.am next morning. Kim knew it had been another night without sleep, but there was only one day to go and soon he'd sleep again, she told herself.

He had lavished his mother's final farewell with the same care and attention she'd always set aside for him and no son could have done better.

Later that day as he led the Pallbearers into the Holy Trinity Church on Dean Street Hockley, his legs seem to sag and he sank to the floor in a faint.

Kim was the first at his side, gently patting his face and calling his name as she tried to bring him round. The next instant there were a dozen people standing over him, and the Reverend Bernard Davis was urgently forcing his way through the crowd.

The man took one look at him and decided to call the Ambulance.

By this the cortege had come to an abrupt and untidy halt, with Peter's body blocking the doorway leaving the rest of the party stranded outside the church, unaware of what was causing the delay.

Kim got to her feet and looked down at her husband, then up the isle at the coffin, which by now had completed its journey, having picked up a replacement pallbearer.

The bitch don't want to go alone, the thought implanted itself in her head. She's refusing to go without him, she's taking him with her, she's killing him. She's killing my husband.

At that instant Karen tugged at her dress, and she looked down into the face of innocence and felt shame and remorse, even as another thought was abusing and corrupting her mind. She picked up the child and hugged her. "Is Daddy asleep?" the child asked.

"Daddy isn't well and have to go to the Hospital," she explained.

A path had now cleared and the rest of the party slowly filtered through as Kim sat cradling her husband head on her lap.

The proceedings was thrown into more confusion when the Ambulance arrived and Kim said she was staying with the living, and got into the vehicle with her husband. Karen began such a wailing she had to be kept out of the Church or her Grandmother's funeral would've been further delayed. The program was hurriedly shuffled and some adjustments had to be made, with Rev. Davis reading Peter's Eulogy and Kim's contribution cancelled.

His mother's body was still lying in the morgue when Kim first suggested dumping her belongings. Peter was horrified and had poured scorn on her obscene and odious prattle, but at her incessant nagging he initially agreed to think about giving them to Oxfam, or some other deserving charity. This was merely to placate her while he decided. Handing over his mother's personal things to strangers didn't excite him, and would be one hell of a battle, at best. These were things he'd helped her choose, along with others he'd bought her on birthdays, Christmas and other times. Every item evoked happy memories, and carried its own priceless value in his heart. There was no rush to shift anything. The house had Three Bedrooms and everything could be left in his mother's room until he was ready. Ideally, he'd wanted Kim to have them, but on going through her clothes the first time, he saw Kim's face light up with excitement and admiration, but when he said they were hers, her face dropped and hardened to a vindictive frown.

"I don't want them and don't bother thinking about it," she rasped. "I am not wearing your mother's clothes, have you forgotten how she resented me for loving you? How do you think she'd react if she came back and found me wearing her clothes?"

"Come back from where?" he asked.

"You are the one who said she was coming back to let you know what things are like on the other side," she retorted.

"Let's forget that for the moment," he said, "My mother is dead, she hasn't just gone out to the shop."

"And don't I know it?" she sneeringly asserted. "How else could I be here desecrating her shrine, this hallowed place I wasn't fit to grace while she was alive? I mean her spirit. Her ghost will be here in all her possessions and will be watching me like a jealous wife."

Peter shoved her imbecilic ranting aside and carried on as if she had not spoken, but her bitter words were chewing away at his heart like a corrosive substance, in spite of knowing her cries were those of help and not anger. Those acrimonious discharges were from the pain she felt, and not as it seemed, a pernicious desire to defame or denigrate. He had lost count of the times she'd cried, pouring out a frustrated desire for acceptance. Promising to do anything that would earn his mother's favor, except stop loving him. She wanted nothing more than to be accepted by his mother, and had told him it was impossible to love him without feeling some affection for his mother, they were so much alike., Even with her face screwed up in anger, she could still see the resemblance. There was so much of her in Peter. His hair, eyes and face was cloned directly from her features.

The only thing in his mother's room she cared for was the bed. Kim had fallen in love with it since the first time she saw it, and had tried to drag him into her room that day. She had wanted to make love on his mother's bed but he'd refused, and shuddered to think what she might have done had she caught them in her bed? What she'd do to them he couldn't be sure, but the fate of the bed would've been sealed by a ritual burning in the backyard. He could hardly commit a more heinous crime than bring a woman into her bed. Her bed was sacred, her shrine. A consecrated place where only the pure could enter, and only they were pure enough. Only they were hygienically sound enough to enter themselves between those sheets, and for him to take a piece of meat from the street into her bed would be sacrilegious beyond redemption.

The day after his father died she'd dragged their bed into the backyard and burnt it, because she suspected he'd taken a woman into it a week earlier, and had slept with him for the next five nights until this bed arrived.

It was much too big for the room but it was the one she wanted and nothing could stand in her way. The headboard stretched nine feet six inches along the complete width of one wall with just two inches to spare. This was upholstered in a plush ivory-colored draylon to match the carpet. The bed was of a half circular design, with its mattress sitting two inches proud of its six inch wide encircling cradle that fell in a slight concave to the floor, and was in matching pleats to the headboard. Kim loved it, and he'd thought this was the one thing on which they were in complete harmony. Five minutes later she walked back into the room and announced she was not sleeping in that bed.

"Your mother hated me…" she'd begun.

"Are you back to that hate business? My mother did not hate you," he gravely informed her.

"I'm glad to hear it, but I'm not sleeping in this bed," she said. "I'm taking no chance, she might come back and poke my eyes out one night."

"We'll discuss it," he said, trying to placate her. "We will talk about it."

How he wished they'd got to know each other, but the pain of having to accept Kim in her house might have killed her much sooner.

Peter was found to be Suffering from severe nervous exhaustion and on the verge of a nervous breakdown, and spent three days in the hospital. Within ten minutes of being discharged he was at his mother's graveside, at the Ridgeway end of Witton Cemetery, talking to her, while Kim and Karen waited in the car.

Later that day he learned that Kim had disposed of every piece of his mother's clothing and personal effects. Even the stuffed Kangaroo he bought her when he was twelve years old.

For months he'd saved his pocket money to get her that gift and she'd treasured it.

He was so angry and distraught he could've killed her at that moment, had he got the strength, and that sad episode almost put him straight back into the Hospital. He was so broken up he stood in the middle of the living-room and cried, sobbing loudly and unashamedly. More bereaved and depressed than before. Now he was also mourning the loss of his most treasured mementoes, and couldn't understand the obvious grudge she'd been carrying for his mother's bedroom. Nothing had been touched elsewhere. except the removal of her toiletry from the bathroom, and her dirty clothes from the laundry basket. This could not be the result of one unhappy encounter, there had to be a much deeper reason for her sadistic and inhuman vendetta. She had set out to wipe the house clean of all her personal effects, regardless of his feelings.

On the day he'd collected his first wage packet, he'd gone into Marks and Spencer and bought Pat two pairs of very skimpy lace-fronted white knickers.

She felt he'd walked in and in his embarrassment had picked up the first ones he liked without checking the size, for there was no other way he could have got her size so disastrously wrong when he knew her size better than his own. She inspected them closely and wondered what she would have done if they were the right size for she couldn't possibly wear them. I like my bottom covered, she told herself. And the front, what there was of it, offered even less protection. He was always looking through her catalogue and often inquired why she didn't go in for the more trendy underwear, instead of clinging to her old outdated look? So this is what he consider more fitting and up to date? He suggested she returned them, but she flatly refused, explaining that although they were too small she didn't mind keeping them. This way she would always have them to remind her of his kindness, but if they were the right size she'd have to wear them and before long they wouldn't exist. This didn't placate him and he argued that it was supposed to be a gift of real value and not a keepsake. Had he intended a memento he'd have bought a stuffed Rabbit and not items of clothing. He insisted she took them back but she dug her heels in, knowing she couldn't dare take a different style or he'd make her life hotter than hell. And she had no intention of wearing something so sparing that she'd spend her day retrieving it from the cleft of her backside each time she moved. If that wasn't torture, then it was pretty close. She would have done almost anything for him, except wear those splinters of clothing in the street.

He would have returned them but had lost his nerves about joining those women in Marks and Spencer's lingerie department for a second time. It was with the confidence and enthusiasm of ignorance that he'd faced them the first time, but the experience must have depleted his courage.

Since that day the two pairs of knickers had been placed in a draw to themselves, and that was where Kim found them on the day she cleaned out the place. This was something he'd intend keeping, thinking that maybe Karen would like to have them one day, and could have knocked every tooth from her mouth when she cynically asked… "What were your mother doing with two pairs of knickers that were much too small for her, and what part of her fat backside was she hoping to get into them?"

"Shut it!" he barked, sticking his right index finger almost up her nose. "You just shut it. You don't just have a fat backside, you also have a fat mouth to go with it. You have done enough harm to last the next four years, don't open your mouth and add to it. Don't mess with things you know nothing about, just leave it," he said disdainfully.

Chapter 19

Kim wasted no time changing things after they moved in. Within 6 months the Curtains, Carpet, and Wallpaper had gone. She was so anxious to put her own stamp on the place that she'd replaced the luxuriant carpet with one that was so cheap and trashy it had to be thrown out inside 2 years, with all the other things going much the same way. Peter watched the changes with some pain and a lot of regret, and suffered it all with a grudging acceptance that it was no longer his mother's house. Kim was now Queen of the castle, and if they were to have any kind of life together she had to be given a free hand to change those things that made her uncomfortable. To throw out those many reminders of a past from which she'd been excluded, and move in things of her choice.

The quality of those replacements was of little importance to her, they were her choice and that was all that mattered. She would remind him of the way his mother had looked at her that day, as if she was a little white maggot that had crawled from some rotting carcass straight into her son's nice clean bed. She'd felt inferior and insulted. The woman was inhuman and almost seems to forget she was also somebody's good clean daughter, that her parents loved her as much as she loved, her son. Kim felt she had no right directing her hostility at her when Peter was the one with whom she should've been angry. The house had been the most hostile place she'd ever visited, and draped, as it was, with his mother's living presence she could still feel that chilling aura. Peter didn't seem to care what she threw out until the day, about a year after they moved in, when she decided it was time for the bed to go. He had been waiting for this since the moment they moved in.

Not this bed," he shook his head.

"But we agreed we would eventually put in our own things."

"You agreed I didn't," he reminded her. "I had no problems living in this house as it was, I have lived happily with it for most of my life and could have done so indefinitely. You were the one who wanted all the changes and up to now I've given in, but not this time. The bed stays until it ceases to function as it was meant to. In fact I'd sooner throw you out than that bed," he finally said after she'd persisted.

She was now more convinced that it had some sinister meaning to him, but in spite of all this, Kim had quickly replaced his Mother and became the perfect woman and was his whole life. There was nothing about her he didn't love and admire, in much the same way he'd loved and admired his mother. He idolized everything about her. Her smile, laughter, her every mannerisms and the gentle, polite way in which she spoke, her serenity, and control, even when Karen was at her worst and would test a saint. Peter was unashamedly besotted with her and no other woman existed. He would always turn up in the bathroom the moment she did and if they weren't bathing together, he'd always be present to rub the lotion on her body, a pleasure he'd commandeered for himself.

Now he was so repulsed by her body, he'd retreat to the furthest reaches of the house when she enters the bathroom, so he wouldn't hear her calling for his assistance. He no longer wanted to see the pimple on her backside or the spot in the middle of her back she couldn't reach, or to apply lotion to her body, lingering around her inner thighs pretending he was doing an excessively good job, as he fed his craving for her body and indulged his lust. That bathroom held many happy memories, from the days of his youth to the time Michaela died, but that was all in the past. These days there were no part of her body he cared for anymore, and not just because of Daisy. There was a time he'd crawl reluctantly out of bed, then stand there looking at her nakedness beneath the sheet, thinking how wonderful it would be if he could win some money and be financially sound, so they could stay in bed all day, making love until they dropped from exhaustion. The thought of dragging himself away from her at the crack of dawn to go push Pig Iron into a stinking furnace, and to what purpose? Sometimes he'd wish he hadn't got a job so he could be home with her all day. Such thoughts were stupid and irresponsible but he didn't care. Having to walk away from Kim to throw scrap Iron around was more insane. He would curse his father rotten for fucking himself to death before his time and leaving his mother in debt. If only the bastard wasn't so cock happy he might have spent more time providing for his family. Fancy getting himself killed over a woman who was openly keeping 3 lovers with her husband? He sympathized with the wretched man, for it must have been so humiliating having to put up with these men, then to come home and find another candidate being auditioned in his bed was the final insult, the one that broke his tolerance.

Served him right, only he shouldn't have killed him, just cut off his balls so he'd live with the constant reminder how he lost them. How could any man in his right mind leave a woman like Patricia at home and climb into bed with a thing of such low morals? He'd curse Mother Nature for getting it so disastrously wrong, in handing him the finest woman she'd created, then fixing it so he barely had enough time for her.

Here he was cursing God and Mother Nature once more. This time for snatching it all back without warning, as though he'd reneged on some secret agreement. No man could've loved his wife more, he told himself, but found that statement lacking in substance and somewhat weak and hypocritical in the light of what was taking place in his own head. All at once it struck home that this could be the divine finger of providence pointing out the indigence of his love. Forcing him to accept hat he didn't truly love Kim, merely deluding himself.

They had an argument one night, and she told him he had an obscene and unnatural love for his mother, and that had drained him of any love or affection for her.

She was right, he admitted to himself. He had nothing for her and never did. Confusedly he groped around for someone to blame for his predicament but came up empty.

Like Kim, Daisy had entered his life at the right moment and was responsible for his happiness, not his disorder. Without her love and devotion he dreaded to think what he might have become. His father could not be blamed for he'd been out of it years ago, and his mother was guilty of no more than loving him. Possessive and demanding though it was at times, he had no cause to complain when he viewed the alternative. One glance down the other road she might have taken would fill his heart with gratitude for the woman she was, and his mind with despair for what he might have become. What if she hadn't loved him so much and had taken the first man who'd come along after his father died? A man who couldn't stand the sight of him and felt he was getting in the way, the kind of man that likes to beat and kick the shit out of other people's kids. A man who'd then force her to make a choice between a child she didn't care for, and a good stiff cock which she needed nightly, or there about?

He could see himself losing that contest, and from then on being kicked from one home to the next. Having the kind of childhood where the only love he may come across would be on. TV or in a book, or shoved up his rear by some opportunist Daddy. Thanks to his mother he'd known love and deep affection all his life. How could he not love her with the same soul-shattering intensity, even after death? On reflection he could see that what he'd felt for Kim was simply gratitude. He was indebted to her for saving his soul from the bowels of hell and she wasn't due the bitter rewards she was reaping, but what could he do? How could he force himself to feel something for her that wasn't within him, or give what he never had? Perhaps it would be kinder if he left her, but he'd promised his mother he'd never move out again. This was their home and it will always be, nothing can change that. The house was his intimate friend, one with whom he'd spent the happiest days of his life, and where his children would also grow up and have their happy childhood. This he'd promised himself, and his mother.

He smiled on remembering Daisy's words and her look of satisfaction as she spoke, just after they had sex that first time.

"There," she said triumphantly. "I've got that wife out of your head, next she'll be out of your life and you'll be all mine."

He'd relived that morning a thousand times, and each time he'd try to think just where their lives would be hadn't he managed it that weekend?

220

She didn't know it but that weekend was his final try. Had he failed again it would have been good-bye Daisy.

She was the best thing that ever happened to him and he loved her beyond reason, but she was rapidly destroying his self-confidence and eating away at his soul to the point where his entire day was centered on proving himself to her. Proving his worth had become paramount. He'd wake in the night with a huge erection, and before turning Kim around to let her have it he'd lay there wishing Daisy could see it. He would be taking a bath and get another rise and it would be Daisy again, wishing she was there to wrap her loins around it. He wanted so much to prove himself to her that his balls ached with the effort of trying to get the damn thing up when he was with her, and that Friday night was the worst of all.

Not long after she'd licked the last of the champagne from his body she took him into her mouth, and having failed, got to her knees and began playing with herself in front of him. He'd never known a woman like her and felt as if his heart would explode like a ruptured balloon. Next she was sitting on him, masturbating herself with his wizened member. He could feel his self-esteem, and every molecule of virility to which he'd still been clinging, creeping from his body, out through his feet and into the carpet. He felt inches tall, as a child yet to be born must feel. Not yet independent of its mother and being supported by the life giving substance of her umbilical. In much the same way she was trying to breathe life-giving sustenance into his body, and the disappointment and hopelessness on her face and in her eyes, giving a lie to every altruistic word she'd said about how little this mattered, and how happy they could be with just their love for each other. He was there but he wasn't. Just an empty shell of what was once a man, now subordinated to her mercies. Clinging to the hope that maybe she could do for him, that which he seemed no longer capable of doing for himself. No man could sink lower in his own virile mind than to submit his last hope of salvaging some vestige of manhood into the hands of the very woman he was trying to excite and impress. Lost in time and locked like a prisoner in his own mind, he begged for a miracle that would lift him from the painful jaws of humiliation. He wished he was home in bed with his wife, being the man he should be, playing the role at which he excels. He would've broken free and call a halt to both their suffering if he wasn't afraid of adding cowardice to his failings.

By the time she surrendered to his failure and stretched out exhausted on the floor, it was well after midnight. It occurred to him they were now in a new day. It was Saturday morning. Soon it would be Sunday morning then Monday. He hadn't got much time and the little he had seemed to be running away from him so rapidly. He got up and went to the bathroom, and as he crawled into bed with her he said a silent prayer to the big man.

The Phone had barely rung before Karen was on top of it. "Hello…Karen West speaking," she aired pretentiously.

"Hello Karen West, its Daisy."

"Hi Daisy," she responded happily, and Kim's face visibly tightened and her breathing quickened. She would gladly tell the woman not to call her house again if only she didn't mean so much to Karen, and the child may resent her for it. Kim listened as she babbled on about School, homework, her cousins, David in particular. Then in a very demanding tone she, asked. "Daisy, why don't you come around anymore?"

After a slight hesitation Daisy said she had been busy but would be around as soon as she could. "How is your mother?" she inquired.

"Fine, she's right here," Karen told her. "Say hello for me." She shifted the Phone and turned to her mother. "Morn, Daisy said hello."

"Hello to Daisy," Kim said dryly.

"And Mom said hello," she passed on the greeting. "So when will I see you?" the child asked. The line went silent for a long moment as Daisy fought with a question she'd already answered, but it seemed Karen was trying to tell her something and if she was alone she might have done so. "I've got an hour tomorrow, would your Mom mind if I picked you up after School and took you back to my place?"

"Mom, Daisy want to pick me up after School tomorrow can I go?"

"Ask your father, if he says you can it's alright with me."

"Dad will say yes, I know, he likes Daisy," she enthused.

So, I wasn't wrong, even this child has noticed it, she thought. The trouble is he likes her too much, but I'll castrate him with my bare hands if I find he's doing more than just liking her. "You can go if your father agrees," she repeated.

"Yes Daisy, Mom said its okay.

"But what about your father, haven't you got to ask him, I'd hate getting you into trouble."

"I'll ask Dad tonight but I know he'll say yes," she said. Daisy hung up the phone and turned to Peter. "Your Daughter wants to see me."

He pulled her down into the chair and settled her on his lap. "She's just like her father, a child with impeccable taste."

"She was delicately insistent and I feel she has something to tell me, what's going on Peter, is something wrong?"

"Not that I know of," he shrugged.

"Maybe it's all in my mind," she said lightly.

"I think you should give that overworked mind of yours a day off once in a while. That constant vigilance can't be good for you," he joked, lifted her jumper and buried his face between her breasts and pulled it back over his head. "You did say the way to your heart was through your breasts?" he mumbled.

"There is a quicker way," she giggled, and a moment later she sighed. "Peter West you're absolutely insatiable." Both fully dressed and his head still inside her jumper.

"Just trying to catch up," he said breathlessly, "trying to make up for four unproductive weeks."

In four months Peter had embezzled three weekends and was currently working on the fourth. Along with seeing her six days a week, or as often as her duties allowed, he was spending more time with her than he was with Kim. After the first weekend a pattern had developed where they'd get undressed on Friday night, and wouldn't get dressed again until Monday morning. The door and Telephone would remain unanswered throughout the weekend. Just in case someone hadn't turned up for work and they were looking for a volunteer. She'd learnt it didn't do to turn them down, it was better not to be home.

Daisy was waiting outside the house when Karen came home and they went in together, Daisy explaining she hadn't got much time and they'd have to hurry, an excuse not to spend a moment longer in the house than was necessary. Guilt, she'd learnt was a vicious emotion and it was battering the hell out of her.

Within five minutes they were out of the house and Daisy was heading for a take-away on Hagley Road. Back at the apartment she poured Karen a lemonade, put on the TV, and busied herself in the kitchen for a while, returning as Karen was putting away the last of her Hamburger.

"I could eat them all day," she swallowed hard and took a sip of lemonade. "I love Hamburgers."

"I thought you might be a little hungry having to rush out before you'd eaten," she took the chair, with Karen sitting across from her on the Sofa. "Sorry I've neglected you so badly but I have been busy, friends shouldn't neglect each other like I've been doing."

"But that's alright if you're out catching the bad people and making the streets safer for the good people, isn't it?"

"I suppose you're right Karen," she smiled pensively.

"Daddy said that's what you do-Daisy do you like Daddy?"

"Yes, I like your Father," she answered.

"He likes you too. He likes you a lot. Do you like him as much as your very good friend?"

"I don't know Karen, I've never thought about it," she stuttered.

"Could you think about it?" the child urgently inquired.

"Now Karen?"

Karen nodded silently.

What is this child doing to me? She pondered for a moment. "Karen, I haven't got that friend anymore," she said playing for time.

"So you do need a friend, don't you?"

"I thought we were friends Karen?" confusion creeping into her tone.

"We are but you need a different kind of friend. Mom has Dad, Aunt Adrianne has Uncle Keith, and you've got no one," she calmly explained.

"Looking at it like that I suppose you're right, I really do need a friend," she indulged her.

"So why not make Daddy your very best friend?"

"I don't think your mother would like that, neither your Daddy. Your mother is already his very best friend."

"But Mom wouldn't have to know, at least not yet. It would be our secret, just the three of us."

"Karen that would make me a very dishonest woman and what would your father have to say about it?" "He wouldn't mind, I know he wouldn't, he likes you."

"And what if I should agree to make your father my very best friend, what next?" her face a study in curiosity.

"After he's your best friend, could he be your boyfriend?"

"Yes he could, and what next?" she asked, her impatience tearing her apart.

"And when he's your boyfriend, it would be alright to give you a baby, wouldn't it?"

Daisy covered her surprise with a broad grin. "But I don't want a baby," The Detective stared at her quizzically.

"I know you don't but Mom does. I want you to have it for her," she innocently suggested.

"Karen, do you know what adults do to get babies?"

"They put their things together," she said brightly.

"And you want your Daddy and I to put our things together?

"Yes."

"Karen I know how much you love your mother, and that you're trying to help her but what you've got in mind would make her far more unhappy. Your mother would be sick with rage if we were to do such a thing."

"But she wouldn't know," she stressed.

"What about the baby, what would happen when your father takes home the baby?"

"But it won't matter once she has the baby, that will make everything alright," she said with childish sincerity. "Mom will get better and Dad will start loving her again."

And I could lose him forever, thought Daisy. At the same time she felt a compulsion to enlighten her on the facts of life, and point out that nothing was so simple in an adult world. There was so much she had to learn, but that was Peter's role and she wasn't going to take it on.

"That is a big decision Karen, and I'll need time to think it over," she said buying some time until she could talk to Peter.

Karen wasn't happy having to wait, for time was running out and she needed an answer. David was still stalling, even after she told him she was ready to do it naked and in broad daylight with her eyes wide open, he was still finding other excuses. Now it was to be done in bed and in a certain position, and at a certain time of the month. He was becoming so nervous and evasive, if she didn't know better she'd swear he'd never done it before.

Two days later Peter took her into the living-room and explained, what she was trying to do was not only wrong but impossible, and that he was very annoyed with her for not coming to him first. Married men are not supposed to go around making other women pregnant. Daisy was nice but he didn't like her enough for that, and even if he did he wouldn't do it.

"What you're suggesting would wound your mother deeply, and she would kill me if I walked in with the result of my adultery. No wife who loves her husband would accept that. The other thing to remember is that Daisy would not carry her baby for 9 months then give it to your mother at birth. She would have the same love for that child we had for Michaela, and could not give away her baby just as we couldn't. It just would not work and I wished you'd said it to me first."

"But I wanted it to be a surprise and was going to tell you when Daisy agreed, I know she would."

"That is the point I'm trying to make, it's up to me and I say no. Now I want no more of this from you, this is the end. Understand?"

"Yes Dad," she nodded.

"Good girl. Karen, I love you so very much, and thank you for your help, but you've done enough and must leave it to your mother and myself to do the rest." He thought over his last words and wondered what he really meant. It was almost comical. Nothing worked between them anymore, and all they had left was this interminable battle that would manifest itself in every word that passed between them.

As he rebuked the child he was wondering why? Why was he protecting Kim when she meant less than nothing to him? He could walk away and happily move in with Daisy, forgetting everything he'd left behind, except Karen. If he had to make a final choice it would be Daisy above everything. He'd turned over thoughts of leaving Kim and nothing had stirred within him, for there were nothing left inside. No feelings of compassion, duty or a single twinge of guilt. Just a heart that now belongs to Daisy May Spencer.

Chapter 20

One morning Kim breezed into the living-room and told him she'd got the answer they'd all been looking for. "Why hadn't I seen it before, it's this wretched house. It's living here that's doing it, and I can almost feel your mother's hands at my throat, slowly choking the life from my body. It was she that killed Michaela and is now doing this to me. My God I didn't think she could hate me that much for marrying you."

Peter lowered his head in despair. It seems her illness had taken a turn toward mental instability. "The dead has no power over the living, my mother died nine years ago and we've been living here since. Maybe you can tell me why, in spite of hating you so much, she didn't attack you before, and why she'd hurt Michaela, her own grandchild, whom she would've adored?"

"To get back at me for taking you away from her, the disgusting bitch wanted you all to herself."

A volt of pain shot through his body and he felt like hitting her, and would have if she wasn't all bones. "What makes you think she'd sacrifice her grandchild to hurt you? She was not that kind of person."

"Maybe while she was alive but how do you know what she's become? Don't tell me she's been in touch with you as she'd promised?" she sneered. "Is that why you've turned against me, why I'm being shunned like a leper? Have you gone back to getting your advice, and sex, from her on her nightly visits, has she told you to stay away from me and not to make love to me anymore?"

Peter stood in speechless wonder for a long time, then calmly scratched his head and looked at her. "I don't think you realize what you're saying, you're sick and need help."

"Look who's calling me sick," she ranted, "If it isn't Mr. sick himself. I expect you know all about being sick for they don't come any sicker than you Peter West, your darling Pat, pretty Patricia. You make me sick. She wasn't your mother, she was your lover before me and when we got married she became your mistress. What I don't understand is why you bothered to marry me?"

"Kim do you know what you're saying?" his voice raised.

"I know exactly what I'm saying," she hissed poisonously. "Everyday, for nearly two years, you left me to come here and visit her, but they were no ordinary visits to dear mother, and I can prove that. I also know why you wouldn't let me throw out her bed, it held too many good memories for you. How could she do it with her son then call me a whore, when she wasn't fit to clean a whore's arse?" she spat venom.

"Kim, you've gone over the top and is now in the realms of fantasy," he smiled. "Kim darling you're dreaming and reaching out for something that doesn't exist, and never have. You are out of your mind and I'll have to do something about that."

That wouldn't be such a bad idea I could move Daisy straight in. He found himself thinking and felt disgusted with himself. If I ever sink that low may I be struck down by a bolt of lightening, he swore to himself. He glared at her.

"You've thrown enough filth around and talked of proof but all I've seen is a vicious little bitch farting from the wrong end. You prove that I've been fucking my mother, or shut your big mouth." his face corrosive with anger.

"So you want to see the proof?" she said backing out of the room, "you want to see the evidence and you will," she turned out the door and he could hear her footsteps thumping as she ran up the stairs.

Peter had watched her go out the door and all at once the joke had died, and he was wondering what kind of proof she had, and how could she have proof of something that never happened? He'd always known that someone looking in from outside could easily run off with the notion there was more to their relationship, and that was just what Kim had done. She'd seen something she didn't understand and had put her own meaning to it. It never happened.…he told himself as though he too needed convincing.

She'd spent less than a minute upstairs but it seemed like hours as he waited her return, while trying to deal with a cocktail of emotion. She had something, but what? His mind was confused. One minute she couldn't return fast enough for him to clear up the stupid matter and throw her evidence back in her face. The next his guts were on fire with a feeling of helplessness and a fear of the unknown. It could be nothing but in the wrong hands could seem like a gift from the devil himself. He'd done nothing with his mother for which he felt shame or regret, but there were moments he'd prefer keeping to himself. She was only trying to get back at him and was grabbing at straws, but didn't know they were straws. Her need for revenge had affected her thinking and sent her deranged mind over the edge.

All at once the door opened and she walked in "Here," she said pushing, what looked like a black hard covered notebook at him, as she came forward, closing the gap between them.

She was calm, her anger mysteriously absent, wearing only a look of compassion or pity. No celebrating or gloating, no victorious banter. Halfway along her hand dropped to her side as if the weight of the small book had dragged it down, and her face changed to a marked penitence. Her face was like that of someone who'd made an astronomical blunder and was about to climb down in tears of apology and repentance. Looking straight into his eyes she came to within a foot of him, and in her eyes he saw the girl who had his heart in such a spin that he'd raced home to tell his mother about her. He could see the girl he had taken to his bed and had carpeted dozens of times on the floor of his friend's apartment, the girl he married, the one who loves him with a flaming passion. She had always been there and had he bothered to look he'd have seen her, instead he'd closed his eyes and had tried to deny her love and her very existence, as a way of lending respect and reason to his transgressions. Why couldn't he love her, why didn't he love her? He was asking himself when she spoke.

"Peter," she said in a tiny voice. "I have always loved you and will go on loving you, no matter what, until the day I die." She handed him a black Collins Diary, about half an inch thick and no bigger than an ordinary paperback novel. She swirled away to the chair closest to her and sat looking at him.

Staring blankly at the book in his hand, he took a couple of sideways steps and lowered himself gingerly into the other chair and slowly opened the book. Her eyes fixed on him. Appraising him with a 'mixture of sympathy and embarrassment. Like the reluctant bearer of bad news wishing she was elsewhere and some one else was delivering this devastating blow.

The diary of Mrs. Patricia West.... He read the words on the first page, his body shaking with trepidation and dread of what was to come. My darling Patricia, how could you? What we had was sacred, how could you write it down for others to find and use against me? He mused, hoping the floor would open and swallow him up, or that Kim would stop ogling him as if he was a rare specimen. Why didn't she just-just go away? So she had the proof, now what? Why was she waiting around, to gloat?

The fear was now working on his bowels like a good laxative and he wanted to go, but dared not move or Kim would have her victory. He stiffened his resolve and slowly turned the page. She saw him wince and cover his face, then seem to remember she was watching him and hurriedly composed himself. He forced a smile and turned another page. Rapidly he thumbed through the first ten pages then suddenly slammed it shut. "This is all you have, is this the evidence you made all that noise about?" he said, much relieved.

"That is your mother's diary, isn't it?"

"Yes."

"Well unless you're saying she was a liar I can't see any question about those facts."

"The little I've seen is true. However," he added, a marked bounce in his tone and manner. "I can see nothing that states, or could suggest I'd been sleeping with her."

"What you've seen is kid stuff. You weren't old enough for the real thing until page 15, try that. Or page 21, 29, 35, 42, 50, or 51."

He glowered at her. "Are you finished?"

She lifted her shoulders indifferently. "I might as well, how many numbers can you remember?"

He opened the diary and began turning the pages again.

"You'll note it's not a daily diary," she calmly informed him. "More a monthly, or an event Diary, when there was something worth recording."

"You seem to know a lot about it?"

"So I should, I've lived with it for nine years and know every word of those ninety pages by heart, and speaking of heart. Your father didn't die of a heart attack, but I expect you already knew that?"

"I did," he grudgingly uttered, as he got to page fifteen and scanned it briskly. "Exactly where on this page does it say I had sex with my mother?" his eyes carefully scanning the page.

"She didn't come right out and say it, she was too discreet for that, but she didn't need to. There is enough going on between those lines."

He wrinkled his face with disgust. "And that is your trouble, you're reading things into this diary that doesn't exist."

"Are you going to sit there and tell me those things are just good clean fun between a normal mother and her son?—Let's look at page thirty five when you were fifteen….and in the meantime I'll tell you what's there in her own words. "Peter came into the bathroom while I was taking a bath and I got him to wash my back, then the rest of me. He did a thoroughly good job and proved himself to be a man that day. Well, you know what my mind is like Peter," she said sarcastically. "I looked at a innocent statement like that and immediately read filth into it, so maybe you can tell me what she meant?"

"I did not have sex with my mother that day or any other day, and don't know what she meant," he said coldly.

She smiled knowingly. "Well maybe you can give me your version of what took place that day, and why she thought you'd suddenly become a man. Where did you wash that pleased her so much? What exactly did you do to earn those stripes Peter?" she harassed him.

He covered his face wearily. "Kim you're enjoying this, aren't you? You are really making a meal of it."

"My God Peter, you disappoint me," her face tight with emotion. "After all those years you still don't know me. Peter you're my husband and I love you. To me you're the finest man that ever lived and I don't want to bring you down form the heights I've placed you, but your mother has left a lot of questions in my mind and I have a right to some answers. Only a sick, perverted soul could get pleasure from this."

"Then why are you doing it now after living with it for all those years, why is it so important that you have answers now?"

"Because there are too many questions without answers and I must have those answers now. Not later or tomorrow, now. And if you have nothing to hide you won't mind, it's in your interest to clear your name and put the doubts out of my mind."

"How can I hope to clear your mind when it's been blocked off and stood corroding with your biased reasoning for nine years, why should I shatter your illusions by proving otherwise? Besides it wouldn't matter a damn what I said, you'd go on believing what you like."

"Oh no, you can't use that one on me," she shook her head in disgust. "You're trying to say it's all in my mind but the proof is in your hand, all you have to do is read it for yourself. Most of that diary involves you and her, and almost every entry have you doing something that is neither natural nor normal. On page fifty six you are being breast-fed at nineteen, how do you explain that? Breakfast?" she offered. "Was it time for little Peter's milky drink, was he hungry? Peter you were a nineteen year old man still sucking your mother's breast and if that isn't sick then I am. How do you explain your mother stuffing those huge tits in your mouth and you just laying back and taking it, and this was just two weeks before we met. Before reading that diary I'd always wondered why you liked my breasts so much. Jesus, you couldn't keep you mouth out of my clothes, but I'm not surprised for you were never weaned. She'd been giving you the breast from the day you were born to the day she died. No wonder you missed her so much. What a disappointment I must have been to you? From those gigantic tits your mother was carting around to my average size, then to have them shrinking even further."

"I never complained about your size, and neither did you about what we did then."

"Why should I about something I loved?" she asked. "My only complaint now is that you don't do it anymore. I wish you were on my breasts this minute. Peter I love you and none of this means anything to me. Nothing can change my love for you. Let's start again. You have not made love to me in four months and I need you, Peter I need to be loved. I know you hate me like this but I can't help the way I am."

He raised his head. "How did you come by this diary?" he growled.

"Is that all you care about, didn't you hear a word I said? Peter I love you and don't want that book corning between us. Let's put it on the fire and I promise not to mention it again. I lived with it in silence for a long time and can do it again."

He cradled the book on his lap. "That is all very generous but I'd still like to know how you came by it. I lived in this house and didn't know she kept a diary, how did you manage to get hold of it?"

"The state you were in that day I'm not surprised you didn't see it. I don't know how much of that day you can remember but I can see it so clearly. On the right side of the headboard there were four books stacked in a neat pile. I was standing right behind you when you picked up the first one and opened it, not for any special reason and I doubt if you even noticed the title. It was just another of those uncoordinated moves you made that day. Next you picked up the second book and seemed to look straight at the diary which was the next in the pile, then replaced them and walked away. It was you who drew my attention to it and I was curious about what she had to say. I picked it up and went downstairs, at first feeling like an intruder. We weren't friends and I had no right reading something so private, but I knew it would tell me something about you. Boy was I unprepared for what I found on page fifty one? That was why I came back and said I wasn't sleeping in her bed."

As she talked he turned to the page. "Ha!" he scoffed. "What's so shocking about this?" he read. "Peter joined me in bed again this morning.... Lots of kids join their parents in bed, Karen has joined us many times. What make this so distasteful?" he asked.

"If you can't see anything wrong in a 17 year old son joining his mother in bed while she's naked then it must be my filthy mind again. Forget I mentioned it and could you please forgive me? I don't know what got into me," she dripped sarcasm.

"How do you know she was naked when the diary didn't say, Is that something else you read between the lines?"

"Before we got married you wanted me to sleep in the nude and calmly mentioned that your mother always has. I was a little surprised but didn't have the nerve to ask how you knew. Over the years you've said it many times and I know it's true, so don't play smart with me unless you have something to hide. And I believe you have something to hide for you've evaded every question so far. You haven't given me a single answer I can live with. Nothing has been solved and I know as much now as before."

"I have no more to give, there is nothing to explain, it's all here," he tapped the diary. "told as it was. The diary speaks for itself, and there is nothing I can add or take from it, at least not until I've read it through. You've got the advantage of knowing exactly what it contains, I don't, but I know she could not say we had sex because we didn't. What more can I say?"

"I really wasn't expecting anything. I didn't think you'd admit to having sex with her and would probably lose my respect for you if you did. It doesn't matter what I believe. My beliefs are my own and I can live quite happily with them. What I could not live with would be your admission, or positive proof that you did have sex with your mother. That would be something I couldn't take, and not just because you had sex with another woman, but because you had the woman who gave birth to you."

Why was she lying in bed thinking about them having sex and telling herself he should be there doing it to her? Why did she resort to sleeping in his bed, and what was that about masturbation? These were some of the other questions the diary had posed but she'd dare not mention. They were much too close to the truth, a truth she couldn't live with and preferred not to know.

Kim could think what she liked for her opinions scored no points with him anymore. Their lives together was breathing its last breath and staring death in the face. She could call him whatever names came into her head, it couldn't hurt any more than being presented with the diary. He wished she hadn't got her hands on it, but he knew the truth, and that was it. He owed her nothing. How could he, and for what? Stealing his mother's private Diary and reading her filth into it? If she was due anything at all for that piece of deception it should be delivered with a clenched fist and not words of explanation or apology.

He cursed his own failure for not finding out his mother had been keeping a Diary all those years. It was his own fault it had come to this for he should have known. How did she manage to keep it from him when they shared everything? So he believed, and thought he knew her but she knew him better, and knew it had to be kept from him because he would not have permitted it, and she'd give in like so many times before.

As Kim left the room he opened the Diary again and began carefully checking the entries. There was none of that hurried scribbling she sometimes used when jotting down notes. The entries were in her best handwriting and very detailed. It began when he was a baby, and there were things about him not feeding well. She recorded his first step when he was nine months old, and his first word at ten months, his own name, "Pita". She said Philip didn't want her to go back to work until he was ready for school and she fully agreed. At six he had mumps, and at seven, chicken pox. At eight, just before his father's death, she stated. "Philip is becoming jealous of his own son, poor Peter, thinks it's something he's done wrong," Three months later she recorded his father's death as it happened and without comment.He assumed the entries would be made late at night after he'd gone to bed. As she frequently read in bed he'd think nothing of seeing her light burning if he happened to be up. Then after he met Kim she would have all the time she needed as he was out most nights. After making her entries she'd put it away so he wouldn't see it when he brought her tea in the morning. After he left home her routine would've changed, for there was no longer any need to get out of bed to hide the Diary when she could do it in the morning.

This phase dealt mostly with her sadness and loneliness after he'd left. "The crushing blow he'd delivered on the day he walked out," was how she'd put it, and the entries were more frequent now as she poured out her sadness on the pages. Stating that she only lived for his daily visits and that of her Grand daughter each Sunday.

Peter would arrive about 6.pm each evening and would have dinner with her sometimes, and they'd be together until eleven, or midnight. She recorded these visits as the highlight of her day, and being unable to wait for the end of the day so she could get home to be with him, and had now resorted to coming home by taxi so she would not lose a moment of the precious little time she had with him.

She talked of excruciating loneliness, describing those times as the blackened pits oh hell. Nights when the sickening hands of this depressive illness would drag her out of bed and send her roaming the house like a restless ghost, in search of anything that looked, smelt, or felt like Peter, some clothes or a pair of shoes he'd left behind, an empty After Shave, or Cologne bottle. Then as the white plague of solitude tightened its frosty hold she began sleeping in his bed, and found some relief in pretending he was there with her. She would try not to think of him in bed with the girl or that they were there doing dirty things. Nice dirty things he should've been home doing with her. She pleaded, coaxed, willed. Then in frustration, ordered her mind away from those thoughts, but found it was like asking her heart not to beat just for him, or not to love him so much. God!....How grossly unfair? He was her life-savings yet she couldn't draw on him, and someone who'd not put a copper Penny into the account was bleeding it dry. "Sweet Jesus why don't you take me from this pain? Let me die and rot in hell for wanting him so much, please take me, even that would be a better existence."

Her only relief would be that friendly and mysterious visitation. Since he left home it had developed a set pattern and she could almost set her watch by it. About 5.30 each evening it would creep up on her at work, like warm hands lovingly caressing her intimately, taking her breath away and leaving her heart fluttering like a million spring Butterflies. During the time he's with her, she'd be free from those thoughts that seem to trigger this feeling. Then he'd leave and within half an hour she was having another. At times she'd be awoken at two or three am, and here she describes it for the first time as a kind of masturbation of the mind. Remote and distant, but right there in her body, furtively stalking her in the dead of night like a wet dream. Around 6.am each morning she'd have another, and because they only came at times she knew Peter was with the girl, she assumed it was all being created in her mind out of her desire for him.

He turned to her final entry and found it was made on the 10th of September, and she died approximately 2.am on the morning of the 11th. The big puzzle was why did she keep a Diary, why did she feel a need to record these particular details of their lives? There was nothing about work or the people she'd met during the course of her day, yet there was so much she could have said.

She would come home and feed him all the interesting details of her day. Like that incident with the guy who {fancied her rotten} to use her own words.

He was a tall good looking man of about her age, married with three kids. Working together they got to know each other quite well, but not as well as he would've liked. Neil Gordon saw himself as the answer to a woman's every prayer and was known to be servicing a number of women on various floors…. He'd been trying, before Philip died, to get her on his team, and she would tell him how good her husband was. He was the only man for her and she couldn't think of cheating on him. She said he was twice the man he was and he couldn't hope to fill her husband's shoes.

"It wasn't his shoes I was thinking of filling," he said winking at her.

Then after her husband died he thought all her objections had been removed and dived in. Now it was invitations to the Pub, dinner, drives in the country, weekend away, and inviting himself to her home.

Pat would feed him the most intimate details of their conversations, disclosing that one day he'd come right out and asked for sex, in the most vulgar manner she'd heard. He said she had the most perfect arse and the best body in the entire Store and he'd love to fuck her from behind. Only she'd said tickle. She was so shocked and embarrassed she didn't know where to put her head, or what to do with herself, as the brute kept his eyes on her in an expectant manner, as if waiting for her answer.

From behind where? The question filtered into her head and she wanted to ask him but couldn't bring herself to speak to him. She did not believe men could be so crude and offensive to decent ladies, and wondered if there were women on whom such filth worked? After that he seemed to revel in being boorishly obscene, until he was promoted and moved to another department.

For the next six months She didn't see him and hoped he'd read her mind and was granting her wish to stay away. One day as she leaned over her desk to reach some papers she felt a hand up her dress, and before she could move some very dexterous fingers were lodged in her crotch, resting hard against her body. Disgusted, she turned sharply and the hand fell away. He stood grinning at her. "I'll do you from behind yet," he promised.

"What did you do?" Peter demanded.

"I told him off," she said quietly.

Peter was incredulous. "You told him off?—You-you didn't kick him in the balls?"

"No!" she said, shocked at his suggestion.

"Slap his face or spat on him?"

"No, I just told him off."

Peter was ravaged by a stupefying anger. "Jesus Christ, if you were my woman I'd give you the beating of your life for letting him handle your body like you were a paid whore, and allowing him to get away with it. I don't believe this," he ranted. "I can't believe you stood there and let him do it, unless you enjoyed it. Did you?" his question loaded with accusation. "Pat, did you get some kind of pleasure from being fingered, was that why you did nothing?"

"Stop it!" she screamed at him. "You've gone far enough, you're being childish and excessively rude. Neil Gordon did not finger me, he merely touched me. Do you think I'd stand there and let him do that? Peter you're insulting me with your accusations, for God sake credit me with a little more decency, you know me better than anyone alive and know I would not lend myself to that kind of thing?"…

Yes you would, you're busting out of your clothes for it, you sluttish bitch. You're no better than those women you despise….. He mused, wishing he had the nerve to tell her.

" We seem to have varying definition of fingering," she said.

"Yes, you seem to think his hand has to go inside your clothes, but I say it can be done from outside and if he touched you, then you were fingered."

"And where did you acquire this expert knowledge?" she calmly said.

"From you of-course, have you forgotten? An accomplished lover has more skill in his fingers than a brain surgeon, and can bring a woman to the boil through six layers of clothing. How could you forget that? Did he light a flame, and brought you to the boil?"

"You are neither my husband nor my lover, you're my son, start behaving like my son and less like a jealous lover. Please remember who you are and stop this insanity," she said tightly.

"I have not forgotten and you can thank heavens for that, but in my role as your servile son I'd find it impossible to take care of you, and is forced to assume the role of a lover."

"And who said I need your protection? I can do very well for myself thank you."

"And a fine job you're doing, allowing all kind of perverts free access to your most private places."

"Jesus!" she shouted. "To think I was worried women would walk all over you. God, I pity the woman who gets you. You are a patronizing, sarcastic, bugger and I'm sorry I didn't keep my mouth shut," she said with an assumed anger, while in her heart she celebrated the knowledge that he truly cared. This was the kind of reaction she hoped for, but had not expected his rabid, foaming-at-the-mouth indignation, and she couldn't be happier.

She'd noticed he'd begun to look at girls in the street and would turn to watch them as they go by. Leering at the multitude of young, nubile bodies that swarmed the City centre on those hot summer days of 1969. All at once he'd discovered girls and they seem to be everywhere. On TV, newspapers, and sauntering down their street in dresses so tight, they were gasping for breath, and the effect on her son's respiratory system was even worse.

She would sit watching him and was sure he had a radar in his head, tuned to the slightest movements outside the window for his head would jerk in that direction if there was the slightest hint of approaching footsteps. One day she found a recent edition of Penthouse neatly secreted under his mattress, and was so disgusted and offended by all the raw meat he was lusting at that she burnt it, then sat back and waited for him to say something so she could have it out with the dirty lecher.

Peter knew what she was up to and had taken his loss without griping. This left her more angry than before, having lost an opportunity to lay into him on a subject she badly wanted to air. At the same time he was hoping she would say something so he could accuse her of searching his room.

This was like so much of their life, a continuous mind game, with each out-waiting the other while the real business went on in their minds.

It was at this point she came up with the plan to test his love for her and see how much he cared. There was obviously a gap opening in his life that she wasn't filling and she had to know why. He had brought all his needs to her since childhood, so what had changed? Why wasn't he coming to her with this need? She had never hidden a thing from him, why would he need to look at such books? All he had to do was stroll into her bedroom or the bathroom and take a look at the real thing, she was there for him and he knew it.

Pat had planned a more graphic story but was glad she hadn't gone that far, for he might have struck her in his anger.

Isn't it just like a man to blame her for being assaulted, as though she'd stood with her legs apart and her knickers around one ankle waiting for the first man who came along? Men! His father was the same. One would think that with him shafting everything that came within range of his six inches he would be more considerate, but not Philip West. Some man would only have to look at her in the Street and he'd accuse her of shaking her fat backside at him. On one occasion the man was still walking toward them, and she wanted to ask how the hell he could see her backside when she wasn't wearing it in front? But didn't want to start a war right there in the Street. Men! As weak as they're stupid, and so demanding. Their women have to be the best of everything. To qualify as a wife she has to be the Perfect specimen of womanhood. Clean and respectable. Someone he can be proud of, who is a cut above the rest. Then after demanding, and getting all this you'd think he'd worship at her feet for the rest of his days? But not so. In broad daylight he'd leave the perfect woman at home, walk out into the Street and is fucking the first Dog he comes across, like the one Philip died for. Men! Always looking but they never see, so blind. The fattest, most gruesome female backside could lead them over a Cliff to their death and they'd queue up for the privilege. A woman could lead them around by the prick like a pet Labrador, so how did she manage to give birth to the only man with scruples? How did she come by the only man who would not fuck his own mother on a dark night? She cursed her husband for fucking himself into an early grave, leaving her in the prime of her life with so much love to give. She cursed her luck, for it seemed she was about to lose out again. Peter was all she had. Philip made sure of that before he died. He never had a friend, not one who was trusted in her company and not once did he bring a friend home. When they did meet in the Street he'd have very little to say and would always make some excuse about being in a hurry. Then would slip his arm around her and gently walk her away. Just so she wouldn't get too close to his friends. As if she had loose morals and legs, and couldn't be trusted around men. He took her to the Pub once but refused to take her again because he didn't like the way men were ogling her, but he was there every night. And would come home so shagged out of his mind he'd ignore her for weeks. One evening she came home and out of the blue, he met her at the door and took her straight upstairs. She could hardly contain herself and the throbbing was like nothing she'd ever known. Her heart was racing and she could feel her juices flowing. Still fully clothed he'd managed to get her breasts out and was gently licking her nipples.....God!....She couldn't remember dying but this was surely the road to heaven and she was on her way. Slowly his hand wandered down and she spread her legs, but by now she was saturated.

Suddenly he pulled his hand back as though he'd been stung, then wanted to know why she was in that state, and without bothering to hear her explanation he said she'd just fucked with someone at work, and walked out.

"What state did you expect me to, be in after starving me for months?" she called out after him. "Didn't you think I'd want it, or be ready?"

Pat followed him into the bathroom and found him washing his hands with Detergent as if he'd just put his hand in the toilet. Choked up with anger and frustration she went back to her room in tears. Later that night he apologized and although she accepted the damage had already been done.

Now his son had taken his place with the same jealous and possessive streak, dictating her life to a greater degree than his father ever did. What was she to do but accept her role and come to terms with the fact he'd be the only man in her life? And having acknowledged it, what was she to do when his attention began to drift? The man, Neil Gordon was the only element of truth in her story. There was a man by that name working in the same department, but he was at the far end of sexuality, and much closer to senility than salacity and didn't know she existed. She had no special reason for using that name, it was just another name. Pat marveled at her insane, illogical thinking. She had taken extreme measures to ensure he would believe her, and had directed the message straight to his heart. If it hadn't worked she'd have been too disappointed for words, yet she sat there castigating him for taking it to heart.

Couldn't he see the gaping holes in my story? What made him think I'd be standing there while that man's hand travelled up my thighs to my crotch, didn't he know even that much about the woman I am? Even if I'd been standing there in such a vulnerable way my legs would've come together like a steel trap at the first touch, and that person would suffer broken fingers, at least. In all this time, hadn't he learnt enough about me to know it couldn't be true? Maybe he thought his mother was above that sort of thing. But I'm a woman and if he failed to take that fact on board he has far more to learn about women than he thinks. But what could she expect from a mere man? Who, when blinded by jealousy and rage is incapable of anything rational?

Peter searched the Diary in the hope of finding something about this. He went back to page one and diligently checked that all the pages were there, nothing was missing, except that story. Why did she omit one of the most significant episodes of their lives, something that had so crucially reshaped his thoughts and brought him back to her with a much heightened interest, and affection.

He could be blind in some things but in others, he was perception itself, and had quickly grasped that she was simply crying out for his attention. He still looked at girls in the Street but was more discrete. These changes were brought about by his belief, which had been galvanized in his head, that she'd invited and encouraged that man's attention and had enjoyed it, and as he couldn't have her touting for other men's affection he quickly dug himself back under her skin. It was in the hope of learning the truth about this Tale why he so badly wanted to find something about it. Whatever she'd said he would accept as the truth, but her silence left him clinging to what he'd always believed. Nine years after her death she was still reaching out from the grave to give him lessons on the treachery of women. He had been closer to her than the clothes on his back, and still didn't know her. If he could fail with her, what chance had he of knowing any woman well enough to trust her completely? Kim was the classic case of one who couldn't be trusted. How could she claim to love him so much and keep something like this from him for so long, as if it was none of his business? It was their lives, not hers. To think she'd been reading their most tender and private moments then forming her obscene opinions, based on her own misunderstanding, only tightened his antipathy. Then she tried to make out everything was fine, nothing had changed. How big-hearted of her, very benevolent, but just a touch too damn charitable.

"Let's put it on the fire and burn it and I promise never to mention it again."

Suggesting my mother's Diary was something dirty that I should be ashamed of, to be destroyed and forgotten. Why didn't she destroy it in all those years, why didn't she put it on the fire and forget it instead of slapping me in the face with it, in a manner designed to embarrass the shit out of me, then tell me to forget it? After she'd learnt its contents by heart and could now recall every word. Who was she kidding? And why did she think he needed to forget? It could not have been made had he known about it, but could not destroy it now. No more than he could his right foot. It was a living part of his mother, and he could close his eyes and picture her sitting up in bed recording the entries. He could almost feel her presence as he held it. Where did she keep it all those years? He shook his head in acknowledgment of a more devious mind. He thought he knew every crevice and crack of the house and that nothing could be hidden from him, especially in her bedroom.

Now he understood why Kim had set out to destroy his mother's personal things, and to wipe the bedroom clean of anything they might have shared. He could now see why the bed was at the top of that list.

Chapter 21

Peter was at the top of the stairs and about to step onto the landing, when the door opened and a man came out. A handsome, dark complexioned, clean shaven man, of about his own age. Peter had seen him before but couldn't think where. He stood aside, the man nodded and went down the stairs. Peter watched him go then turned to Daisy, standing in the doorway, a strange look on her face. Suddenly she smiled. "What a nice surprise," she said pleasantly.

He sniffed ominously. "I'd like to believe that," he guided her back into the apartment and shut the door. "Who was that?" he grunted.

"Oh, he's my Partner," she said lightly.

"Partner, what partner? Why haven't you said something before? Daisy I'm in love with you, and I'm throwing my whole life at you. Don't try to fuck me around. Don't fuck me around Daisy," he stabbed home his warning with his index finger prodding her left breast.

Oh God not again, she lifted her head to the divine. Not again dear father. Please."Peter he's my partner," she leveled her head and met his gaze with sincerity. "We are a team, you've met him before, don't you remember, that first day at your house?"

"Then why was this partner such a big secret if you had nothing to hide?"

"I wanted to tell you but was afraid, and kept putting it off. I didn't want you involved in my work in any way and didn't want any of them to know about you, not while you're still at home with your wife. They can be a very bitchy lot and this is the kind of thing that makes good gossip."

"That doesn't explain what you were doing here at one o'clock with him when you said you'd not be home until four. Try me with that one Daisy," he stood waiting.

"Are you saying I've got something going with Andy, my partner?"

"What am I to think when you distinctly said you'd not be home until just after four and I turn up and find you with a man?"

"So what are you doing here at this time when you should be at work, checking up on me?" she said tersely. His heart vibrated like a Jackhammer and the blood rushed to his face. "I came to sniff at your stinking knickers," he snarled. "Then rob the fucking place before leaving. Have you any objections?"

"Peter you're being silly...."

"Have you any objections?" His voice raised in turpitude.

"No."

"Then don't you ask me what I'm doing here, I have a right to be here whenever I like. You gave me that right when you handed me this key to your door. Daisy, don't you ever ask me what I'm doing here again, or I'll shove your key..." he stopped, bit hard into his bottom lip and hung there glaring at her. "I'm glad you didn't finish that threat," she said calmly. "It sounded nasty, and painful. ooh, that could bring tears to my eyes. Jesus; I love you even when you're angry."

"I'm not sure I like you when you're being deceptive."

"Pete, you're not being deceived, I've told you the truth, but do you know this is the first time you've come here and not kissed me?"

"Are you trying to change the subject?"

"Oh, stop fussing and kiss me, you're like an old woman," she kissed him. "And you kiss like an old woman."

"What does he mean to you...what was he doing here?" his tone frosty.

"Andy is work, nothing more. That is the reason he was here, to discuss some changes in today's routine."

"Daisy, what were you afraid of, why didn't you say something about' him before?"

She sighed heavily."It has to do with the guy I was with three years ago. He suddenly got it into his head I was having an affair with my Partner.

Frank and I had been together a year and things were going well. All at once this docile quiet man became an absolute animal.

When we met he knew what I did, and that a woman always worked with a man, and had accepted this completely. Then suddenly, and without reason he started accusing me of having an affair with my Partner. The man was happily married with four kids and was the perfect gentleman. He never once made a play for me. I soon found out that Frank was following us around at nights, and I tried talking to him but it did no good. Next he met Dave's wife in the Street and told her I was screwing her husband. The woman didn't know what to believe and was so upset she came to see me demanding the truth. Dave had told her Frank was lying but she wasn't convinced. Fortunately we've always got on well, I'd been to their house a number of times and had met at social gatherings. She trusted me and I was able to put her mind at ease," she forced a smile. "At this point I was thinking about moving out, but might not have gone through with it, then one night he hit me and the following day I moved out. A colleague had agreed to put me up until I got a place. Next he began throwing it around that I was a lesbian, and had left him for another woman. Her boyfriend began asking questions, and doubts and aggravation took over their lives. All this time Frank wouldn't leave me alone, on or off duty and the whole thing was becoming nasty. I was warned to clean up my act or else. It was then I noticed he was showing signs of mental illness. Two weeks later he was fired from his job with Birmingham City Council, for gross misconduct. The exact reason was not disclosed at the time, but I later learned he'd sexually assaulted one of the Secretaries. Ten days later as we drove along Bordesley Green East he stepped out from behind a parked Car—I don't think he was trying to kill himself. He probably wanted to talk to me, but his mind wasn't right," she paused, and took a deep breath and exhaled painfully. "Peter I'm not ashamed to say I went to pieces. Until you've seen the brains of someone you love scattered over the Road you have every right to think you're tough. The car was travelling at about forty mph. when it struck him, he went into the air, fell on the bonnet and bounced off into the Road. His skull had' split open and everything that should've been inside was outside and lying next to him on the Road. I was off work for a month, lost two stones and my hair fell out. Not all of it but in patches. Some parts were as long as it is now but in about four places I was completely bald. Peter I was a mess, and did think about leaving the force but was talked out of it. After my month leave I was put back in uniform and given a desk job. Peter, I wanted to tell you about Andy, but when I thought of Frank it scared me senseless, and when you started swearing my stomach hit the floor."

Silently he worked her to the Sofa and they sat down, he held her hands. "Daisy I'm sorry about all that, and that I had to rake it up again, I know how much it must hurt…"

"No it doesn't anymore," she said brightly. "That thing you've been giving me has killed the pain, I can't feel a thing anymore. All I feel is you, how can you believe…" she hesitated. "Peter, the man is full of himself and thinks he can have any woman he wants."

"Does that include you?"

"Most of all," she said with some amusement. "He's been trying it on for some time and shows no signs of giving in, but I can handle him and don't want you, even thinking of him, he's no trouble to me. Andy don't stand a chance in hell, you're the only man I want… I would've preferred him not seeing you," she added thoughtfully. "He knows who you are and has already put it all together."

"I don't care about him."

"I do. The next time we have an argument he'll throw it back at me and he won't care who is listening."

"Hey," he patted her thigh. "Let's get off this subject. How much time have we got?"

"An hour," she answered after checking the time.

"Well let's get on with it, I have to make you pregnant."

She laughed. "God, Peter, isn't that Daughter of yours something? What a mind, she's amazing, and would be surprised the things we've been putting together. I spoke to her yesterday. "Daddy thinks it's a bad idea and I'll have to forget it," she said sadly.

She grudgingly climbed from his lap thirty minutes later and hurriedly got dressed.

Peter sat watching, her red French knickers were on the sofa beside him.

"I have to go, aren't you getting dressed?" she asked.

"Not just yet," he answered, smiling mysteriously.

She darted into the bathroom and he heard the tap running. She came out a moment later. "There," she said. "I've just had one of your thirty-seconds-wash." She came to the Sofa, picked up her knickers and climbed into them and headed back to the bedroom.

He watched her coming back towards him, unable to take his eyes off her. Thinking how lucky he was. How privileged to have this fine woman. She was his woman, every tiny piece of her, whenever he wanted her, she'd told him so. One night as they lay in bed she'd taken his hand and placed it firmly between her legs. "It's all yours," she whispered. "No other man will ever touch it while you're alive, it's yours alone."

She got to where he sat slouched on the Sofa. Her black handbag on long straps slung over her left shoulder. She leaned forward, left hand resting on the back of the Sofa, supporting her weight as she kissed him, his limp manhood in her right hand. She got to her knees and kissed him again. He rose with her and followed toward the door. She turned. "You are not corning with me to the door in that state, you stay right where you are," she said firmly. "And another thing, mister West, you're going to be very disappointed." His face contracted into one huge question mark. "You'll have to sniff your underpants, I don't keep dirty knickers, they are washed as I take them off."

"I wouldn't have it any other way," he said as she went out the door. "As pretty as you are I wouldn't touch you with a long stick if you weren't clean. That thing is much too close to the other place for my peace of mind," he dropped himself back on the Sofa, eyes closed as he tried to take stock of their lives, but Andy was the first thought in his head. Andy was the last person on earth he wanted to think about, but the man had walked straight into his head, grabbed a seat, demanding to be heard, then began filling his head with questions about Daisy.

Suddenly the man was laughing at him, rocking back and forth in a gut-splitting uncontrolled laughter. You fool, he spoke. Who do you think she is? Just another pussy, and I've yet to meet one I couldn't have. Once in my Car, and right where you're sitting now, not ten minutes before you came up the stairs. Great pussy, and a natural Blonde. Believe me, they're not many of those about.

Peter sprang to his feet. "Fuck off Andy," he shouted. "Piss off and leave me alone. Daisy is the' best woman I've known. An exceptional lady and you'll never plant doubts in my mind."

He went to the bathroom, filled the basin and washed himself, then picked up her washcloth from the side of the bath to dry himself and could smell her all over it as though she was right there in his arms. It was neither offensive nor sweet and synthetic, just a redolence that was naturally hers. A rich vibrant womanly smell, the essence of lovemaking and eroticism. A fragrance you don't get until you've worked her into a sweat of orgasms and all her assumed smells have taken flight, leaving the real woman oozing from every delicious Pore. An essence that's as natural as woman herself. He had breathed it in, and drawn it deep into his Lungs so often, and had failed to record it before now. It took a moment like this to do it. This was Daisy, the real Daisy. Not the powdered and perfumed version that went out the door earlier, but the one he climbs off on a Sunday morning after a good Saturday night. He brought the cloth to his nose and drew her deep into his lungs, before drying himself.

Back in the living-room he picked up his clothes from the floor and began dressing, but Andy was crawling back into his head. Where were they at that moment, and what were they doing? "Get stuffed Andy, you're not messing up my head," he said as though the man was standing next to him.

A minute later he went to his car and picked up two Sainsbury's shopping bags and brought them back into the apartment. The contents of one bag he packed away in the Fridge and the other he left on the floor, and by 2.30pm he was back at work and at his job.

At six o'clock he was back in the Apartment, and five minutes after nine he opened the door as she was about to put her key in the lock. He stood in the doorway, a tea-towel draped over his left Forearm. He gave a low servile bow, genuflecting slightly. "Will madam be taking a bath before Dinner, or shall I serve it now?" he asked.

For an instant she was caught off guard and couldn't quite make out what was taking place. He'd promised to Phone at 9.30, she wasn't expecting him. What Dinner? She was about to ask but a quick glance through the arch into the dining area answered that question.

The table, lit by candles was set for two, complete with a floral display of wild Daisies and Carnations, with a bottle of Bollinger Special, being chilled in a bucket.

"Oh Peter," she wrapped her arms around him and fastened her lips to his, her tongue probing his mouth. "Madam had better take a bath before," she said breathlessly. "cause she isn't gonna have the time later. You are an Angel Peter, you know how to get into my heart and stay there. Darling I'll be loving you forever—but what's all this for, It's not my birthday?" she asked.

"For no other reason but that I love you."

"And I love you, Peter Philip West. Come, let's both take a bath," she took his hand.

"Why not? I believe I've earned it," he fell into step with her.

After the bath she slipped into a gold figure-hugging evening dress. Nothing else, just the dress and a pair of gold high heel shoes, and was escorted to the table.

The starter of Prawn and Cucumber Salad was already on the table, and as she settled herself Peter cracked the Champagne and poured it.

"To you Daisy, the second, most gorgeous lady I've had to dinner." She made a face. "And who was the first?" she said with a frown.

"Mrs. Patricia West," he proudly proclaimed, "my mother." Her face brightened with a delightful smile. "Such a lovely complement to pay your mother, that is nice, and I'd like to propose a toast to you Sir. To the nicest, sweetest man in the world, to a brilliant cook, to the man I love," she opened her serviette and draped it across her lap. Peter sat sipping his Champagne, staring at her in open admiration, his face a mask of pride and ecstasy.

Like a bewitched soul, he watched her put a single Prawn in her mouth, and his breath quickened. This moment alone was worth the effort. Nothing turned him on stronger than watching a woman eat. Not when she sits on the Sofa wearing tired overworked clothes, wolfing down a

Sandwich and assaulting a Mug of tea. That engenders nothing, except the urge to get as far away from her as he can, but to hit him hard in the groin she has to be dressed in her fineries and sitting in front of him. The sight of a woman delicately feeding herself tiny morsels drives him wild, leaving him rampant.

"Hmmm, Peter, this is delicious," she gushed.

"The lady is far more delectable and I'd rather have her than all this, and I can barely wait, but I'm glad you approve."

"Why wait?" she said licking her lips and grinning suggestively. "Darling I'm ready for anything you are, and we wouldn't have to leave the table."

"Daisy, you are a demon and you make it difficult to say no, but I'll wait, I can't take you from your dinner."

"Who said I'd stop eating?"

"Jesus, you can't be serious?"

"Try me and see Peter," she offered.

"You mean you'd sit there and carry on eating while I'm having sex with you?"

"Precisely, a little appetizer, something to hold you until later." He sat with a bewildered grin across his face, itching to call her bluff.

She looked at him. "Why do all this for me?" her tone rapidly changing to one of disbelief.

"Because I'd love to take you to the best Restaurant and show you off to the world but sadly I can't, and have to bring the Restaurant here."

"I'm glad we can't. Peter I would not enjoy going out to Clubs or Restaurants, or any such place. You are all I want, and when I do get the chance to be with you I don't want others coming between us, and refuse to share the rare and very precious moments we have. You are a part of my life I share with no one. I want you to myself. If you had taken me by golden Carriage to the Ritz and turn me lose among Royalty I wouldn't enjoy that any more than this night with you. I can't begin to express my happiness and how good I feel tonight. No man has ever been more thoughtful, more loving and you make me feel special."

"You are someone special. Very special, and I want to bring a mountain of happiness into your life. I love your smile and your laughter and just want to bask in your happiness. You did something for me that I'll never forget, and will always be in your debt and eternally grateful," he lowered his head shyly.

"Look at me Peter. Come on I want to see your eyes when I speak to you. "

He picked up his head slowly.

"That's better, now tell me what you're talking about," she sipped her Champagne, keeping her eyes on him, the questioning frown still on her face.

He reached across and topped up her glass.

"Oh, forgive me for being so thick I know what you mean," she quickly said. "But it wasn't my doing, you did it all by yourself."

"What about your patience and understanding, your kindness, and inexhaustible faith in me, at a time when even my confidence showed signs of crumbling? Had you been a different person I'd have walked away from you within a week from sheer embarrassment. You lifted my spirit from the pit of depression I stumbled into that first night, and kept me afloat right up to that very moment when I finally made it."

"Peter you don't throw out a Rolls Royce because it's got a flat Tire, and if I was so dumb that I couldn't recognize what I had in you from the start, then I would certainly not deserve you. You think I'd stand around scratching my tail while the best man I've known walk out of my life? Whatever it took to keep you I'd have done it gladly. I was doing it for myself, I wanted you."

"No more than I did," he said.

"At the time I couldn't be sure," she said, "You could've been just out for some quick excitement and the fact it wasn't working had me thinking you might not bother."

"And there I was thinking the same thing about you. I thought you were just another randy Detective out for some quick stick."

"Just as well, cause I didn't get it."

"You'll never know how happy I was that wonderful Saturday morning when it finally worked," he smiled broadly. "Not so much for myself but for you. For four miserable weeks I watched you frustratingly working your arse off to bring me to life, and the harder you tried, the worse I'd feel. I wanted to do it for you, not for my pleasures, I didn't deserve any, but you did. I will never forget that moment when I looked in your eyes and saw a different woman, complete happiness and contentment. I am a very lucky man and keep reminding myself so I'll never take you for granted." he noticed she'd finished. "I'll take your plate."

"Not until you're finished, you've not touched yours," she said.

"And I don't think I will. Just some of the main course, maybe."

"Why aren't you eating?"

"If I don't eat my dinner when I get home tonight I'll never get to sleep. "You don't make love to me anymore, now you don't eat from me. Are you eating at the same place you're having sex Peter? Well, I hope you're not having them both from the same dirty vessel," and she'd go on all night."

"Here," she said, "you can take my plate, and put your starter in the Fridge I'll have it tomorrow, I can't have you losing sleep over a little thing like that."

A little later he returned with two plates and placed the first one in front of her. Curried Lobster, Sprouts, and new Potatoes. "A little thing I created just for you," he smilingly said, took his seat and again he sat looking at her.

"It looks delicious," she said.

"What did Andy have to say?" he inquired.

"I would rather not talk about work when I'm with you," she said stiffly.

"I understand but 1 would still like to know what he said, I am involved."

"Who said you were?"

"You did."

"I didn't."

"You said your loud-mouth Partner would be asking questions about me. Did he ask about me?"

"He did," she answered curtly, then dried up and carried on eating.

"What did he want to know?"

"Darling please, you're spoiling our Dinner I don't want to talk about him," she said firmly.

"All right, alright!" his irritation quickly rose. "We won't talk about it, let's pretend it's not happening." "Darling I'll tell you all about it but not tonight, I promise."

"I said it was alright!" he bristled.

From then on he adopted an icy politeness as he answered her questions without adding to the conversation.

"Don't do this to me, please. Peter, you can't let that shit-hole frig this beautiful evening," she spat angrily.

He was shocked. "Jesus Christ, what kind of words are you using at the table? You talk about him frigging the evening but you've just fucked it with all that shit you've spat over the food. I know you like to talk dirty, but do you have to do it over Dinner?"

This can't be, she told herself. We are fighting on the happiest night of my life. She emptied her glass and grinned at him. "Darling, what time did you start cooking?" her tone sweetened.

"Six o'clock," he said. Adding that he was planning to start earlier but she was home.

"Which was a stroke of luck, for you wouldn't have known about my change of shift," she offered with a smile of pure pleasure.

"It wouldn't have mattered."

"But you couldn't do all this in your lunch hour?"

"Not difficult, an hour is all I need for a Seafood dinner. I'd get things ready then call you about five to turn on the Oven, and we'd dine about six."

"It's a lovely meal and a wonderful surprise. Thanks Darling."

The frosty air had melted by the time the dishes were being cleared and their warmth had returned, with kisses flowing freely.

She offered to help him wash the dishes.

"Not in that dress, you could get it soiled."

She suggested putting on an apron.

"Not over that dress, it wasn't made to be covered with an Apron, and would be sacrilegious, almost gruesome." He handed her another bottle of Champagne with two clean glasses. "Take a seat," he pointed her toward the living-room. "Be with you in less than a minute, if I can stay away from your succulent body that long." He ran his hand gently over her bottom and patted her on her way.

As he placed the dishes in the sink Andy was back inside his head and he couldn't shift the man from his thoughts. What the fuck is going on between them, and why won't she talk about it? What did he say to upset her so much, that the mere mention of his name brought her close to convulsions, and had her swearing like a cheap whore with a sore crotch? He came into the living-room and went to the Record rack and picked out a Marvin Gaye LP, and put it on. "Shall we?" he requested with a polite bow.

She smilingly got to her feet and came into his arms, gently rotating her hips against him, feet bolted to the floor, with just their bodies moving against each other. Peter began talking to her through Marvin Gaye's words.

"What's going on? What's going on? Talk to me, so we can see what's going on."

"Darling don't you ever give up?" she whispered.

"And I'm glad you got the message," he said. "We have to talk."

"I love you very much and want you to myself, I'm not sharing this night with him. He mucked up my day and I'm damned if I'll let him screw my night as well. Don't you understand, I want to be alone with you tonight?"

"And we are alone."

"We are not alone. There is someone up there in your head and I want him out of our lives tonight."

"The quickest way is to talk him out of my head."

"Peter, I don't want to talk about him, I want to get drunk on Champagne and make love with you all night."

"But I haven't got all night."

"All right, whatever little time you have for me then!" she exploded. He stopped moving, astonished at her outburst. Her arms tightened and she thrusted her body apologetically against him.

"Was that a complaint I heard Daisy, are you saying I don't 'spend enough time with you?"

"Forgive me," she said, "It's the Champagne that's gone to my head."

"You can't blame the Champagne for speaking your mind, it had nothing to do with it. Daisy, for me to get any closer to you I'd have to be, either a Cyst on your Tits, or the hair on your crotch. I'm here six days a week, how much more do you expect from me?"

She kissed him. "Peter, I'm not complaining, but you see what that man has done to me? It's only frustration and I was wrong to take it out on you. Will you forgive me?"

He nodded. "I'd forgive almost anything when you hold your body against me like this."

"Friends?"

"No.... lovers," he corrected.

"And that too," she wriggled out of his arms, and went into the bedroom, returning a moment later wearing just a smile. "You took care of the main course, now I'll see to the desert."

"But we've had desert, your favorite."

"I was thinking about your favorite," she said. "And it's my turn to serve you."

He got home at 1.30am to find Kim sitting up in the living-room waiting for him. She looked pointedly at the clock. "This is a fine time for a married man to be coming home to his wife and daughter. You'll note I didn't say family, for it seems we are no longer a family," she said with a poisonous tone in her voice.

He dismissed the frosty greeting and sat down. "I expect you've eaten wherever you're coming from?"

"No I've not eaten," he said politely.

"I'll get your Dinner," she got up and went into the kitchen.

Peter wondered what state it would be in, for she'd probably been keeping it warm since six o'clock. She appeared less than a minute later with his dinner on a tray, and to his utter amazement it wasn't burnt, or dried out but steaming hot, and as fresh as if it had just been cooked.

She lowered the volume on the TV and left the one eyed monster flickering silently in the corner. "What's happened to us?" she asked. "What will become of us Peter? You're leaving me to fight this battle alone and it isn't fair. I'm being treated as if I was that...door. A block of wood without feelings, something you push aside and walk away. I play no part in your life except as cook and maid. I clean the house, wash your clothes, and look after your daughter, nothing else. Come to think of it

I'm not even a good maid, for men have been known to have sex with their maids. Where is the love you had for me, what has become of all those kind words of love you once had for me? Can't you share some of those words with me, as an acknowledgment that I'm alive and that you think I'm human? I won't ask for deeds Peter, just words, a smile to say, Kimberly, you do exist and I once loved you,. I know you don't want me anymore, and if I could live without you I'd have moved out of your house, and your life months ago. Peter, you're all I have, without you I don't exist and wouldn't want to." She walked across the floor on her knees to where he sat and inquired if he was finished.

He nodded, and she took the tray from his lap and placed it on the floor. "Please Peter, come back into my life I need you."

He sat looking down at her, but unable to hear for his mind was back in Daisy's Apartment, wondering what Andy had said to her that had made her so mad?

"Love me again," she pleaded with him. "Make love with me tonight, please. I know you don't want to but do it for me, in the name of that love you once had for me. Make me a woman again. Let's go up to bed now," she begged.

He stared into her eyes then at her body, but could see nothing in her wizened frame of the woman he once thought he loved. She was seven stones three pounds of shrunken skin, wrapped over some indiscriminately place bones, with a mass of radiant red hair, the one thing that had not changed. He felt a mixture of compassion and regret, motivated by a love that should've been hers. It was unfortunate that such a truly wonderful person had blundered into his life, at a time when he was so vulnerable, he'd have loved a Viper in his subconscious search for the recipient of his Mother's love. She didn't deserve to be used in this dehumanizing manner, and was much too good for him. He wished it had been someone else. He had used and all but destroyed one of the best women he'd known, and brought her to her knees at his feet begging for sex. Not love, but raw, stinking sex. He struggled to keep the tears of shame from his eyes, and felt like sinking to his knees, confessing it all to her and begging her forgiveness. He thought about his Mother's death and how she'd stood by him, literally holding his hands and drying his tears through those difficult moments, and as she continued to stab his conscience with her poignant words his heart melted and he relented.

"Okay, but not upstairs. Right here, and with your clothes on," he obligingly offered.

Jesus, she thought, remembering the days when he would insist on removing every stitch so he could drink of her beauty with his eyes, and of her breasts with his lips.

Then as she knelt there ruminating on days long gone, he unzipped his trousers, and picked her up like a rag doll and brought her to his lap.

Deftly, he slipped a finger inside her knickers and pulled it aside and began entering her. Then placing a hand under her bottom he dragged her hard onto him, and her mouth fell open in a gasp of discomfort as he entered her for the first time in over four months. No kisses, caresses, no tenderness, no love. Just a straight fuck. She'd requested making love, but it seems she had been asking too much of him and a fuck was all he had to spare. She lifted her blouse and offered him her breasts, and saw him wince as though in revulsion, then leaned back in the chair out of range. Eyes closed with his hands clasped behind his head. Detached and indifferent, his thoughts back in Daisy's bed as he tried to put her face and body in Kim's place.

He made no further movement. Nothing that would indicate he was alive to what was taking place. It was as if she'd crept up on him in a deep sleep and began ravishing him.

She sat working him for all she was worth, and felt duty-bound, thinking if he wasn't getting any pleasure he might become even more disgruntled and call it off. She felt it was her duty to bring him into the act. She owed it to herself and her womanhood. If she could not bring him back to life and arouse his interest, then his passion, then she'd truly lost it, along with any hope of ever getting him back. She looked at him then at herself, and a wave of sadness washed her at the sight of what they'd become. Fully clothed, she had been reduced to snatching something that should've been hers as a right and not granted through pity after she'd been reduced to crawling on her knees. And now to be ignored as if she didn't exist was the most hurtful move of all. He would've been more alert had it been a fly sitting on the end of his Prick, at least he'd make some attempt to shoo it away. That said how much he thought of her.

In spite of all this she couldn't bring herself to despise him and was loving him at that very moment as much as she ever did. He was the only man she'd known and the only one she wanted. Suddenly there was a spark of life, a well known jerk of his loins, and an instant later his eyes popped open like a ghostly corpse returning to life.

For fifteen minutes he'd played dead but could hold out no longer. She knew his game but was way ahead of him. He was hoping she would've been so demoralized by his apathy that she'd satisfy herself and shamefully crawl away to die in some corner, but he was wrong. She'd sooner drop dead from exhaustion than give him a reason to gloat.

That first gasp she'd let out as he tried to displace her womb was more ecstasy than pain, but he didn't know that. Neither was he aware of the second, or third. God! His mind must have been a thousand miles away for him not to have felt her contracting? she thought.

However, she was determined to suppress them so he wouldn't get it into his head he'd done something for her, and call time. She had no intention of leaving him standing proud, as if to say, you didn't even touch me. You did nothing for me.

She had a much better plan, which at that moment was rapidly coming together with his heightened breathing and his low, breathy erotic groan. His hips were now getting into the act. Slowly at first, but was soon throwing her around in a wild and frenzied gyration.

With their eyes locked, he brought himself forward, and lifted her Blouse and fastened his lips hungrily to her breast. Drawing it into his mouth and rapidly moving to the next and giving that the same attention. This was the man she knew and could recite his moves like a much loved Poem. Any second now he'd clamp his teeth to her nipple and erupt like a Volcano.

Maybe he'd started out with the intention of doing the skinny bitch a good turn, but she was about to do the same for him. Suddenly his teeth locked and an instant later he went into this wild convulsion, accompanied by another low breathless groan. She still can't understand how he manage to control himself and not take off her nipple or do her serious harm. Kim sat with a broad smile on her face, pleased with her performance and could feel him rapidly shrinking inside her.

Then as though she was a huge toy he held her by the waist, picked her up and stood her on the floor. He slowly stashed his limp equipment, adjusted himself on the chair and zipped up his Trousers.

"What was all that about?" she asked, her tone laced with sarcasm. "I begged for that on my knees and thought you were doing it for me, but all you did was satisfy yourself and shut the door in my face. Is it because you're no longer the man you were, why you don't make love to me anymore? If that is the case then I don't blame you for you'd only leave me more frustrated than you found me, and I can do without that."

"What are you talking about?" he sneered. "Who are you trying to fool?"

"You're the one fooling yourself Peter. You've known what I'm like since the first time we made love, and you know how I react at my moment of excitement and you know I haven't."

He laughed. "Kim I don't know how you managed to keep it quiet but you did it to try and make a fool of me."

"Wha—why would I want to do that, and how did you expect me to get something you didn't give? You didn't move a muscle until it was time for your fun, and who did that for you, who created that excitement for you? What have you done for me, the one who really needed it?"

"So what are you trying to say Kim?"

"That you're not the man you were, and you're good at making promises that you can't keep," she said bitterly.

Peter knew he was being had but there was nothing he could do. His virility had been impugned and this was as disconcerting as failing with Daisy. How dare the little shrimp make out he could no longer fuck her properly?

"Tonight Kim," he said grinning. "Tonight I'll take care of your needs."

"Not another empty promise, I hope?"

"No, you won't be left frustrated this time, I promise."

At 8.30 that morning Daisy turned over and picked up the Phone. She dialed and waited. "Could I speak to Peter West, please?" she said to the woman at the other end. "Who's speaking?" the woman asked. "His wife," she answered,

Peter came on and they spoke for a minute. She hung up, went to the bathroom, took a wash and went back to bed.

Peter went to the changing room and took a quick Shower. At 9.am he was in her Apartment and heading straight for the bedroom, got undressed and climbed in with her.

She explained that by the time she got to the Station Andy had already passed it around that she was sleeping with a married man.

She asked him about it and he claimed it was a joke. She got mad, they had a quarrel and he called her names. Said she hadn't got a heart, and had taken the woman's husband while she mourned the loss of her Baby.

"Peter, I could not believe the things he was saying and I'm a little concerned for you."

"For me, but why?"

"He is jealous of you, sick with it, and it came pouring out yesterday. There is no telling what he might do, the Police are not above using the job to settle private scores, and I can't claim to be any different. I used my job to get back into your house, and get close to you....Peter, I didn't want you involved in any of this. He talked as if I was his woman and was giving away something that he had a right to, you should've heard him."

"I wouldn't want to," he sniffed disdainfully. "He's not human, how can you continue working with him?"

"I don't intend to, there are a number of things I can do and would like to discuss them with you..."

"Later," he said. "We'll discuss them later." He buried his face between her Breasts. "I must get back to work," he murmured.

About a month after Kim had presented him with the Diary he dreamt his Mother was standing at the side of his bed wagging a finger at him. This was something he seem to remember his father doing when he was not pleased with his behavior. He wouldn't speak but simply shake his head and that warning index finger. He couldn't remember his Mother ever using that gesture, so why was she doing it now? He had tried speaking to her but couldn't get the words out, and as he tried to find his voice she went to the door and walked out. The next thing he remembered was Kim waking him, to say he'd been talking in his sleep. Anxiously, he inquired how much she'd heard, and was relieved to hear it was an incoherent ramble she couldn't make out.

He breathed a sigh of quiet relief. What would she think of him, telling his Mother how much he still loved her, and was still waiting on her to keep her promise and get back to him.

She'd promised that death could not rob him of her love, and if the dead had any powers she would be back to watch over him and continue taking care of him, and he'd agreed to do the same if his time came first. Why hadn't she come back to see him before, and why did she leave without speaking to him? Was it a dream, or was she really there? It had to be a dream, but it was so real. Like the times he'd over slept and she'd come to his room to wake him.

He would feel someone touching him and would wake to find her standing over him in smiling admiration. Then she'd speak. She never woke him with her voice, always her hands. Could it be she was trying to wake him before speaking?

For the rest of that night he lay there thinking about her and remembering he hadn't visited her Grave in ten days, and promising he'd come by later. At lunchtime, if he could.

That Friday turned out to be the most disastrous day he'd known. Even things that couldn't go wrong suddenly did, and the men sat around all day drinking Tea and playing Cards as the fitters and Staff struggled to get the antiquated machinery back in working order.

At 5.15 he joined the men and headed for the Showers…. A row of twenty six open cubicles, backed on to each other in two rows of thirteen. Twenty men, blacked up with soot and burnt Casting sand from head to toes. The whites as Black as the blacks, and the blacks, blacker than the night before last.

This area consists of two communal changing rooms, at opposite ends of the showers. The men would enter the clean changing room at the start of the day and get undressed, then walk past the showers and into the other changing room. Get into their working clothes and leave through that exit, and at the end of the day would make the same journey in reverse. At the entrance to the showers they would be handed a clean towel and a bar of soap, provided by the company.

On the day Peter first arrived he saw how much nudity was involved and saw young newcomers, like himself, bashfully trying to cover and hide themselves, and only succeeding in attracting attention, he thanked his Mother for putting that pride in him, and an open acceptance of the naked body.

He soon realized that men were really big boys at heart, and the same games that were played in the School toilets when he was twelve, were being repeated here. Grown men would wander around, laughingly checking, scrutinizing and noting the size of other men's parts, and openly commenting on their findings.

"Pick it up Bill, the fucking thing is hanging in my way I can't get by...Or, fuck me, you must be a community worker? You have to be, that Prick is so worn down I can barely see it...Or Jesus, my wife would love to get her hands on that...Don't let me catch you near my house with that thing or I'll shoot you."

This was done with such lighthearted banter that only the most sensitive could be offended.

Peter stood there letting the warm spray dissolve the tension of this bitch-of-a-day, his mind on Daisy's body, distantly aware he was standing proud, but thought nothing of it. Peter opened his eyes to find three guys staring at him.... suddenly one exclaimed... "Fuck me Peter," But before he could continue, Peter said, "No thank you, my wife is a fine woman, she'll do for me," They walked away laughing.

Chapter 22

Peter slipped on his Overcoat picked up his Briefcase and went out the gates with a feeling of elation, the day had finally ended and he was alive. At 6.pm he was standing at his mother's grave, with the cold May wind drifting across the vast open space, hitting him from behind as he talked to her. "Pat I've got something to say that I've shared with no one else because I wanted you to be the first to know. You said I wasn't in love with Kim and you were right, you knew it from the first moment and said I was making a mistake, but I didn't listen. I look back and can see what I had been doing all those years. I took everything she had and threw them out like garbage, then replaced them with your qualities. I gave her your eyes, face, body breasts, your mannerisms and temperament, and even had her washing herself twice a day the way you did. She ceased to exist from the moment we met, and in my mind had taken on your identity. I married her and she became Mrs. Patricia West. For the first five years I didn't make love to Kim, it was you. Your body that lay beneath me and your nipples I was biting into. Once again I was at your breast being fed your sweet milk of life. Pat I loved you then and I love you now, and wanted to love her as I loved you, and kept telling myself I did, but I don't have to kid myself any longer. I have found true love at last. Mom I'm in love with the finest woman alive. This time I'm in love with a woman for herself and not trying to make her into your image. What I want to say is that I'm leaving Kim. I'm not in love with her and it isn't fair to keep her hanging on, neither is it fair to Daisy. I can't bear to be away from her….

Spending my nights with someone I don't love, while she waits alone in bed, needing me as much as I need her. In June it will be a year since Michaela died, and I'm only waiting for that to pass, I want to be with Kim at that time, but will be moving out at the end of July. Yes Mom I will be moving out," he repeated. "I do remember my promise but it's only fair. She should be getting my love but I have none to give, so she'll have the thing I love most, our house. She deserves more but I have no more. The house and my savings are all I have. £8,000 of my own with what you left, totaling over £30,000 in the bank. Kim has her own account, £2,000, of her own savings, plus the money you gave us as wedding gift. I plan to give her another £8,000 and will continue paying the bills, don't you think that's fair? I'll see that they never go short of anything.

I love Karen and would like to have her with me but Kim would die if I took her," he pulled a white handkerchief from his hip pocket and blew his nose then dabbed his eyes. He snuffled. "I'm not crying it's just the wind that's making my eyes water," he said as tears filled his eyes and ran down his face. "Pat, why couldn't I love her? Why couldn't I have loved her for herself, the remarkable lady she is, and not as a watered down version of you? She is a good woman with so much love to give….God, why couldn't I love her. Why couldn't I share my love between my mother and my wife, why did I have to destroy one in order to love the other? She was entitled to more than I gave and I hope she finds it. I'll visit her often to see they're okay and that no man takes advantage of her. I wish I'd loved her but it's too late, my heart is no longer mine to give." He looked at his watch. "Mom it's 6.30 I've got to move, I'm seeing Daisy tonight. I know you'd love her Pat. I'm sure you would."

Chapter 23

On the Sunday evening he was sitting alone watching TV when his mother appeared, and this time it was no dream. He wanted to speak, to call her name. Patricia, Mom, to ask how she was, anything to let her know he could see her, but as in the dream he couldn't speak, his mouth was opened but he couldn't get the words out.

The soul, ghost, spirit, or something of his dead mother was right there next to him and he wasn't afraid, instead he felt safe, she was back as promised. At the same time he was sick with frustration at having waited nine years for this moment only to lose his speech.

His eyes followed her as she moved around the room. Not walking through walls and furniture as ghosts are supposed to, but carefully picking her way around each item like a living person, Except she touched nothing. Not even her feet touched the floor as she glided around as if floating on a thick cushion of air. She came to a stop directly in front of him, blocking out the TV. "Don't be afraid Peter you know I'd never hurt you, I'm here to help as I've promised," she said in her usual soft voice.

But if she's a Ghost why can't I see through her? he was thinking.

"I'm not a ghost, just an aberration of your making. My visual form exist only in your mind. One of the conditions placed on my return is that you will not be allowed to speak to me, but I've been granted the ability to read your thoughts and will answer all your questions."

I haven't waited all these years to hear I can't speak to you.

"I know how you feel but we have no choice," she explained. "I have been granted three days with you, and each time I appear like this your voice will fail you, but only when you try to speak to me. If there are others in the room you will still be able to speak to them as normal. The other thing is, you are not allowed to touch me. You must not try to touch me, if you touch me I'll be recalled instantly and there will be no hope of my ever returning. Death changes everything Peter. In life I was yours completely, to do as you desired, but at death all that's changed and I have new masters. You don't own me anymore and they feel you have no right to touch me, those are the rules. For three days I'll be here to direct and guide you, point you in the right direction, and it seems I couldn't chose a better time. From what I'm picking up your life is in a rotten state," she frowned.

I don't mean to sound ungrateful, but after all the plans we made before you died, why has it taken you so long to come back? Then you say I can't touch, I don't own you, and worst of all I can't speak to you. Is there anything else I can't do? Heaven forbid, I wouldn't want to break the rules through ignorance. "You can't call me Pat my new name is Zelda."

Zelda? He shot to his feet, and she zipped across the room like a flash of lightening.

What kind of name is that?

She hovered against the wall close to the fireplace watching him prancing around the room.

I don't own you, I can't touch you, I can't speak to you. Your name is Zelda. I just got up to stretch my legs and you flew across the room as if I was the ghost. Are you sure you're my mother?

There was the ring of her familiar laughter, but not with the usual zest, it was somehow cold and unreal.

"I understand how you feel son and don't blame you for thinking I'd deserted you, I would think the same. Because we both thought when someone died they'd raise after three days and as a ghost would have infinite powers to kill or cure, and the freedom to go where they liked and scare who they didn't like. That my son is all a silly myth," she said. "We have no powers and can do nothing, compared to the living. I had more powers while alive than I do now. Everything I possessed died with me, all my commitments, everything came to an abrupt end, except my love for you. Love is the one thing that doesn't change."

How can you say you have no powers when you can walk without touching the ground, read my mind, and look into the future. What do you call power?

"I wish it was all that simple," she sighed. "If it was, your life would've been perfect, I'd have seen to that. Peter it is much more complicated, let me unravel the mysteries of death for you," she offered. Peter took his seat and she drifted back to the place in front of him.

"We live in a Quadrant on this same plain, and is neither up nor down. We live right here among you, controlling a space and time that is out of your reach and beyond your consciousness and comprehension. A space and time that is far advance of the living being. Like all the Deserts of the world that man has been forced to leave as creation intended, because his abilities does not extend to harnessing their hostility. Just the same you have a vast Desert right here among you that does not exist in your knowledge. Like all the discoveries you've not yet made, and those you'll never make. We live among you in that vast nonexistence of your being, yet we are as distant as the far side of the moon. You can never reach us but we can reach you. We live in that space between your time and movement, and is governed by strict laws that must be obeyed, and we adhere to them because we have no choice.

Unlike your world where you could arm yourself with any weapon you choose, then go out and kill as many as you like, we can't. Apart from the fact we are dead and can't die again, we can't hurt each other and we can't hurt the living. You are sacred. We can help you but only when we are granted the ability, and we are never given the ability to harm you. If we could harm the living then there would hardly be anyone left alive today. Think of all the people that have gone to their graves nurturing grudges and in some cases open hostility, and hate for some wrong. Think of all those people who've been murdered, wouldn't they've come back to seek revenge, if not personally, then at least to inform the Police.

In truth you don't know where we are, we don't know where you are, and cannot reach you until we've granted the powers to do so. Until then we're like a flock of sheep, servile and obedient. With my visiting rights came my limited powers, which will be revoked immediately I return. I would've loved to come sooner but I had no say in the matter, it is a privilege that has to be earned and no one get's it as a right, and many has been turned down. We have no mind or a will of our own, we are totally without self-determination and couldn't function independently for a minute. Before the breath of life left my body there was a deliverer standing over me, waiting to transport me to Quadrant Z. Without him I would've been stranded in your dimension, spending the rest of eternity wandering through this house and when it cease to be, the land on which it stood, or any subsequent building that might be erected on this site. I would haunt this house until I was forcibly evicted, or as you say, exorcised. Not because I wanted to but because I'd be a lost soul. A deliverer can deal with numerous deaths at the same time, because it's a spiritual presence, he can be in more than one place at the same time. He is told about sudden, and accidental deaths ten minutes before they occur, and long term illness and suicide a month in advance. If I wasn't met at death I would be like a baby deserted at birth and left to fend for itself. Occasionally the system fails and the departing spirit is left to wander aimlessly and become fair game for evil beings who possesses the power and has the desire to use that lost soul to their own evil ends. We are born at death, and are as new born and have to be cared for, and like a baby is at the mercy of our real, or adoptive parents.

If the deliverer is not present to take control of that soul then it's lost forever. A soul cannot be accepted a moment after death. Half a second after death is too late, because at the point of death the soul will drift toward the nearest and most dominant force and the deliverer has to be that force. A soul left in limbo for a mere fraction of a second could well have been sniped by an evil force standing around the body at the time of death.

They might not have been compromised but that's a risk Quadrant z. cannot take. An impure soul entering our Dimension could cause havoc among souls without a will of their own. It is fortunate that most people who sees, or thinks they have seen a ghost quickly turns and run the other way. Sadly there are a few people around whose sole quest is to find and get hold of these wandering souls and inflict their will…"

But if you have no powers what good are you to these people?

"Those left behind has powers, and are still able to use their bodies. Once we've been transported we lose all link with our bodies and for us it no longer exist."

But you've got your body it does exist.

"We have no status, No color or creed, just equality. We cannot identify individuals we knew in life and therefore have no relatives, we are one."

I'm looking at your body and can recognize you, why can't you identify each other?

"Peter, I'm here without visual form and what you're seeing has been projected by your own mind. All I did was let you feel my presence and your mind provided the image. The picture of me you're seeing is the one furnished by your memory of me. I can't see myself for I have no form except inside your head, and from your mind I can see you've got me in that black dress. The devil's woman," she smiled.

He buried his face in his hands. I don't understand where I got the ability to do what you claim.

"It does not require any special abilities, you see me because you want to. Kim could walk into this room right now and she wouldn't see me. You are the only one who'll see me while I'm here. Now that you know how I got here, we can begin to deal with why I'm here. First I'll deal with you, Kim, and Karen, then the outsider."

What outsider, her name is Daisy and I told you about her on Friday.

"And you think you're going to marry her, well you can put that out of your head, you're already married, and don't bother reminding me, I know what I said all those years ago, but that was a mistake. I was wrong about her and have to admit it. I thought no woman could love you as I did, but Kim loves you more" She is the only woman who can bring you true happiness. Don't leave her, you'd be making a big mistake and would spend the rest of your life regretting it. You've began to destroy her love and one day she'll have nothing left for you but pity and contempt, then she'll leave you in much the same way I did. Don't doubt my words I can see it all and you don't have much time. She's dying. Peter you're killing her. What she has only you can cure, she needs your love and will get well again when you start loving her. I know you don't love her and I know why you married her, but you must learn to love her. Only your love can save her. Don't let it happen a second time, you can't leave another woman who loves you to die alone, of loneliness and a broken heart. You can't go through life doing that, or you'll pay a terrible price in the end. Peter, you're not dealing with one life, think of Karen and what you'd be doing to her. She still feels responsible and you ignoring her mother doesn't help her guilt. At this moment she's sitting on David's bed trying to persuade him to make her pregnant, to replace the Baby she thinks her mother can't have. The boy don't want to do it and has been putting her off, but soon he'll give in. Don't sit there telling yourself she's only ten, she'll be eleven in six days and he will make her pregnant, you have to do something."

I'll kill him.

"That won't do, it isn't David's fault, she takes after her Grandmother, it runs in the family, but she's much better at handling her men than I was," she chuckled. She stared at him thoughtfully. "And I know you're planning to confront her but don't, that will only make her more obstinate. She'll think David told you and turn to someone else. That will only make the problem worse. Let me tell you what to do…The minute you get them back into this house tonight, get them together and tell Karen you'll be trying for another baby. Kim will be shocked but will be too excited to argue. This will stop Karen in her tracks, there is no other way. Don't confront them or you'll be sorry, it'll blow up in your face. You must make your move tonight, tomorrow will be too late…"

And what about later when she sees that her mother isn't pregnant?

"Kim will become pregnant, I can see it," she said, her face alive with an overwhelming glee. "She will get pregnant this year. Forget the operation, they don't always work as they should and fortunately this one has gone wrong. Your wife is fertile, do your duty and leave the rest to nature. Forget that woman, you may seem happy now but it won't last your future is with Kim, and your new family. Michaela's death started it but you can end it. Peter, you're holding the key to happiness, don't break it in the door on your way out, thinking you'll not be coming back. What you may think is infinite will only last a few months, and by then Kim and Karen will be out of your reach in a safe place you can no longer hurt them. Peter, I can see Kim taking her own life and that of you daughter." she issued her grim warning. He fidgeted uneasily as she seemed to be shelving his questions. He hit her again with the same thoughts and sat waiting.

"Peter, don't you care about the life of your wife and child, is that woman all you can think about at this time? Jesus, the older you get the more you behave like your father, he got killed over a sour crotch and you are ready to sacrifice your family for another bit of unclean meat.... And I don't know the answer to those questions you're asking, I'm forbidden to deal with such things."

But you said Kim will get pregnant, why can't you tell me if Daisy and I will marry and if we'll have children, it's almost the same thing.

"It is not the same thing, she's an outsider and does not belong in this family. I'm restricted to family matters, but I'll try to get those, answers," she drifted toward the door.

Where are you going?

"To seek the answers to your questions."

When will you return?

"When I'm ready to speak with you again. I have been sent to this house and have to remain within these wall until I leave. I will present myself to you when I'm ready to speak with you, at all other times I'll be with you but you'll not see me."

Twisting around in the chair his eyes followed her to the door. He got up, but the instant his eyes left her she vanished, and his voice was back.

"You are making a mistake," he said loudly. "Just as you were wrong about Kim you're wrong about Daisy, and you'll have to meet her to understand…Pat, I know you can still hear me. As you cannot leave the house I'll bring her here so you can meet her. I'll get her to come and see Karen tomorrow," he suggested.

She was back and standing just inside the door with a poisonous look on her face. "Don't you feel shame or disgust using your innocent child to aid your depravity? How can you look her in the eyes and say you love her?"

But that is the only way you can meet her. "I don't want to meet her and don't you ever bring her back to this house," she said and was gone.

"Jesus!" he exclaimed, throwing out his hands in despair. "Don't mothers ever change, not even after death? We had the same argument about Kim in this same room, now she's back nine years after her death making the same stupid assumptions that I'm wrong and she's right. You are not the only one who can look into the future Miss Zelda," he raged. "I can do it too and can see good days ahead for Daisy and myself. Marriage and children and there is nothing you can do about it, so put that in your future and leave it there. I wish you hadn't come back cause you're no good to me, all you've brought is pain and sadness. You're not here to help me or you'd have come when we needed you. Where were you when Michaela was dying, why didn't you come to me then? Instead you hid away in your Quadrant Z. as though your Grand daughter's death had nothing to do with you, deserting us through the misery and pain. Now you're back at the moment I found love and happiness, trying to confuse me and make my life hell again. Why don't you leave me alone and go back to hell where you belong? You're not my mother you couldn't be, she loved me and I loved her, you can get out of my life and' stay out, don't bother showing yourself again. I managed without your help for years and don't need it now. I have made good provisions for my wife and daughter and they'll be well cared for and will want for nothing..."

Except a husband for Kim and a Father for Karen and the love you will have stolen from them, she said to herself.

He dropped himself dejectedly into the chair, wondering if she heard him, hoping she hadn't.

Ten minutes later he was driving as though in a dream, along Great Hampton Row heading for Gun maker's Walk to collect his family, and a minute after he arrived he took David aside and threatened him. "I know what you're planning," he said, taking the boy by surprise. "I know what's going on inside your filthy head, but she's your cousin and only ten years old so put it out of your head... David, if you so much as let that

Prick rise in your pants near her, I'll rip it off so close to your body you won't know whether you're a boy or a girl. Get it?" he snarled.

"I haven't touched her Uncle Peter, and I wasn't going to," the boy calmly said.

Peter smiled. "Good lad," he patted him on the back. "I've always said you were a very astute and intelligent lad."

Don't confront him, she said, what does she know? I don't know how they handle things on her Quadrant but this is Quadrant Lozells, the kind of neighborhood where they only understand one language. You have to let them know if it gets in your way you'll chop the fucking thing off. That is what they understand round here. You pussyfoot around and they'll fuck your daughter then do it to you, that's for sure.

As he drove slowly home he was busy planning his next move, but the ten minute drive wouldn't give him enough time to work things out. His plan had to be ready for its first trial by the time he got home, so he bought the time by taking a fifty minute detour. Kim soon noticed they were going away from home and looked about her anxiously. "Where are we going Peter?" she said, when they were on the Walsall Road, heading for the Scott Arm Junction in Great Barr.

He grinned suspiciously. "Can't a man take his wife and daughter for a pleasant drive on a Sunday evening?"

She turned, her face wrinkled in surprise and a hand covering her open mouth, as she scanned him with mock concern, wondering if he was alright? He hadn't said a kind word to her in months. "You okay Peter?" she questioned. "Where are you planning to dump us, somewhere far so we can't find our way back?"

He headed through the lights and she saw the sign saying M.6 Motorway. "Oh, you're thinking of pushing us out along the Motorway and out of your life for good?"

"'He glanced at Karen in the mirror. The child's body tremulous with suppressed laughter, hands covering her mouth. "What's wrong with your mother?" he asked. He turned to Kim. "Why can't you sit back and enjoy the ride like Karen, see how happy she is?"

The car was silent as he drove into Walsall and browsed the town for awhile then headed out again, all the time his mind ticking over feverishly.

So you want me to do my duty, he reflected his Mother's request. You want me to make her pregnant. Peter wasn't sure how she expected him to go about that task, but she was there waiting, and he was planning a return she could think about on Quadrant Z. and remember for all times.

She wants me to blow up your Balloon girl, he glanced at her bare thighs, flattened against the seat and spreading deceptively wider than their true dimension. Her short blue skirt riding way above her knees, tightly hugging her thighs. She wasn't at all bad. She had proven herself on that Tuesday night. After she'd ridden him like a Donkey and made a fool of him, then the Jackass within him had to go and promise her a better performance. He never dreamt so much sex could ooze from mere skin and bones. She was fighting a battle royal to win back his affection, and if she was up against anyone but Daisy, his money would be on her to win by a length. He smiled to himself, thinking....

"To what do we owe this pleasure?" she interrupted his thoughts.

He looked at her then quickly fixed his gaze back on the Road. "Kimmy, don't be so skeptical," he said jovially.

She forced a laugh. "You've never called me that before. In all the years I've known you it's either been Kim, or Kimberly. Now you've called me a strange name for the first time and is asking me not to be suspicious?"

"I only thought it was time we got together and did something as a family."

She turned to Karen. "Isn't that nice of your Father?"

"Don't knock it Mom, he's trying," she said.

"I should've known you'd be on his side," she said with an exaggerated frown.

Soon his mind was back to the business and picking up his thoughts. It was strange how he could make her into anyone when it suited him. She was like a lump of clay in his hands. Or something without form that could be molded into whatever size, shape, or color his sexual desires demand.

First she was his Mother, then Daisy. And sandwiched between them she'd been a thousand others. Whores, dirty Vulgar bitches he'd come across in the street. Movie stars, the woman two doors down with the big arse and tits to match. He couldn't remember her being Kimberly, and he doubt if she ever was. Once again he was fitting her with a new mask, and crowning her, little Miss Sexy thighs, the randiest bag of bones this side of the grave. He couldn't believe his own thoughts as he rehearsed his act and began to savor the moment he'd gently squeeze himself into her.

Well, it was the only way he knew to make her pregnant, but what his Mother didn't know was that she was reaching for the Sun. Kim's tubes were so tightly knotted her periods had to make an appointment to get out. Shit, he hadn't thought of that. What if she's menstruating? That could throw the show right off his stage. She wouldn't be clean until after his Mother left. He had to know before he could advance his plans and there was only one way to find out.

"Kim, what dress is the doll wearing?" he said.

"What?" she questioned.

"You heard me."

"I wasn't sure my hearing hadn't gone wrong. Boy, you are just bursting out of yourself with surprises today."

"Answer the question and stop dancing me around," he said dryly.

"She's been in green for three-days," she said in a tiny voice, not wanting Karen to hear, wondering if she understood.

In Perry Barr he stopped at a Wine shop and bought three bottles of sparkling wine and a bottle of Brandy. Not quite the same classy vintage he habitually shares with Daisy, but then Kim was only his wife.

Karen wanted Crisps, Peanuts, and surprise, surprise, a bottle of Babycham.

He looked hard at her, but his frosty stare soon thawed into a smile.

"Why not? You'll be eleven in a few days, we'll pretend it's your birthday." He got into the car and placed the bottles at Kim's feet. Something was cooking and she could smell it. Peter loved playing tricks in bed with Champagne…So this wasn't the authentic stuff, but who cared, it was the thought that mattered, and right now her heart was throbbing for his thoughts were in the right place. What have I done to earn this? Shut up you idiot, you're his wife and it's your right, like taking his name and wearing his Ring, It's not a prize to be presented when you've been a good girl, or at his convenience to bury his stiff. Your body is not a graveyard.

Nice words, but who the hell are you? What part of me are you, and where were you all those months he never touched me, why didn't I hear from you? Why didn't you come around and give me your support? If you are my pride, shame, or self-respect, then go away, I don't want you standing in my way tonight. You are not welcomed in my bedroom tonight and you will not be admitted. I'm going to be the most vulgar and obscene bitch he's ever fucked and nothing is going to stand in my way, you come back tomorrow I may need you then.

As they got home he went to the cabinet and picked out two long-stemmed glasses. He turned to Karen. "Your Mother and I are going up to the bedroom and we don't want to be disturbed."

Kim's face rapidly turned scarlet and she had an overwhelming urge to kick him for embarrassing her in front of the child, but that rash impulsive notion quickly passed into a philosophical acceptance. Why kick the Goose as she was squatting to produce that rare golden moment?

He went on. "Did you have a wash before you went out?"

"No Dad," she shook her head.

Jesus, what's with this man and washing? Kim thought. If he hadn't watched me doing it before we went out he'd be sending me off to the bathroom as well...But I did have a Pee, wonder if he'll notice? The thought amused her.

"Karen what did your Mother tell you about washing before you leave this house, you go up to the bathroom this minute and take a wash then you can have your drink," he looked at his watch. "It's now 9.30 and we want you in bed by 10.15, understood?"

"Yes Daddy."

"Good girl."

Holding the glasses in his right hand he embraced the child with his left arm, hugging her close to his body. "Good night," he kissed her on the top of her head. Then almost like a Father taking his little girl for a walk he took Kim's hand and led out the door.

The following morning as he got to the bathroom his Mother

appeared. "You filthy disgusting, degenerate swine, how could you do those things to your wife?" she spewed her distaste.

Good morning Mother. Peter thoughtfully filled his toothbrush and started brushing his teeth, grinning happily to himself.

She moved closer. He looked at her. You're getting dangerously close, aren't you afraid we touch?

"Go on and touch me, please Peter, touch me. It would be one way out of your sick debauchery."

He stepped back, trying to keep away from her. The show had only just began and he didn't want to lose her, besides, there were important questions she'd not yet answered.

My darling Patricia, he chuckled. If you didn't like what was going on you could've left the room. It's the second time you've walked in on me with Kim, haven't you got the decency to leave the room when you see me making love to my wife?

"What love? There was no love, that poor girl, I felt ashamed for her, and that I'd given birth to you." What are you talking about, you were there watching, did you hear her complain? Or see disgust on her face, or object to what we did? Did you see any chains binding her?

"No but I saw a wretched and pathetic girl who was ready to hang by her teeth from the light fitting to please you."

Hmm, I thought she did at one point, must try that tonight.

"Peter, you used her disgracefully."

You are the one who demanded I made love to her. Peter she's dying for your love, make her pregnant and things will be fine again. Isn't that what you wanted, or do you know another way to make her pregnant?

"I didn't ask for that sick performance. You used her to shock me. To hurt me, and you didn't care what you did to her in achieving that. I couldn't believe you were the same person who had so much love in this house. You grew up in that room."

If you don't care to see me doing my duty then stay out of my room tonight.

"Please Peter, for the love we once shared, spare me the humiliation."

All you have to do is stay out of my room.

"I can't. I cannot leave the room. I came back to you and my time must be spent with you while you're in the house. The minute you come in I'm with you until you go out. I have to be by your side. You knew I was there, you couldn't see me but you knew it. Then I showed myself, thinking it would alter your behavior but that made things worse. Well I've had my show and if you attempt a repeat, I'm leaving and you'll be on your own. I came back to help you and it would be a mistake to think you don't need my help. I told you how to handle that thing with David and Karen but you didn't listen and had to do it your way. Well I hope you're proud of yourself, because you've blown the whole thing wide open and its after-shock is about to hit you. I'm just glad I won't be here to see it." She followed him to the front door and watched him go, Daisy, still locked into his thoughts.

"What has that woman done to my Son that he can't get his mind off her?" She tracked him until he was out of range and he was still thinking about her. He didn't even have the common decency to think of his wife while he was abusing her, then he had the gall to tell me he was making love to his wife. She came back upstairs, went into Karen's room and stood looking at her as she slept. Something she frequently did when Peter was a child.

He was just about Karen's age twenty years ago, and had become the man of the house. She smiled at the thought of his impudence. He wanted so much to be a man and was ready to do whatever he had to prove it and drove her out of the bath.

Karen stirred and opened her eyes, and a minute later got out of bed, stood in front of the mirror lifted her nightdress and began a diligent scrutiny of her body. First her chest, by gently stroking the areas around her nipples, then pinching the nipples and pulling them. Next it was her pubic region. She flashed a disappointed frown.

"When will they grow?" she asked despondently. "I'm almost eleven, when will anything grow? Am I going to be a freak, the only flat-chested, hairless teenager in my class? I'll be ashamed to show my body in the changing room. David said it would start growing when I got to eleven, but he didn't say which would be first. I hope my breasts grow first." she pulled off the nightdress and stood naked, smiling with her reflection.

"Never mind what David said," Pat spoke to herself. "And you can put those dirty thoughts out of your head right now little girl. You're ten years old and shouldn't be thinking that tripe. You've got your whole life ahead of you and there'll be enough time for boys, besides David is your cousin."

All at once a high-pitched squeal shattered the calm, and Pat appeared in Kim's room to find her joyfully bouncing on the bed, wearing only a pair of red knickers with her breasts flopping about.

She felt compassion and some responsibility for what her son was doing to her. The wretched girl was so starved of love, she was ready to adopt whatever he threw at her and call it affection. Karen appeared in the doorway wearing her dressing gown, staring at her mother with much confusion. The times she'd told her off for jumping on the Bed and here she was doing it.

"I'm happy because Daddy is falling in love with me again," she said, trying to justify her actions. The child grinned. "Does that mean things are going to be alright now?"

"I hope so," she stopped bouncing and beckoned her with open arms. They met at the side of the bed and embraced. I sincerely hope so darling," Kim crossed her fingers for luck.

"Does that mean you don't miss Michaela anymore?" she asked.

"We will never stop missing her, never. Neither will I ever forgive myself for blaming you that day. It was thoughtless and inhuman. I couldn't see your pain or how you were hurting, just my own selfish loss, please forgive me."

"Mom, I don't blame you for that, at the time I thought it was my fault."

"How do you feel now?"

"I'm very sad she died and I still miss her, but I know it wasn't my fault, Daisy explained everything." That damn woman again, am I ever going to be rid of her? Kim thought.

"Mom, why did you burn her?"

"Cremate darling. We Cremated her, your Daddy and I have plans to be Cremated when we die and decided to do the same for Michaela."

"What plans have you got for me?"

"We've made no plans for you darling, we'd like you to decide that for yourself. That is your choice."

"Well I don't want to be Cremated, I don't think I like that. What else can I have?"

"You don't have much of a choice, there is really only one other way. To be buried like your Grandmother, you still visit her grave."

"Then I want to be buried so you and Daddy can visit me every week."

"Okay Miss West, I'll make a note of your request. One burial and a visit every week....And it's time to go and get ready or you'll be late for School, off you go," she patted her on her bottom.

Pat was pleased to see that love wasn't completely dead, and more than a spark still lived in this house. That touching little scene had made her very happy.

At eleven o'clock that morning Peter was on the phone cancelling a date he had with Daisy that evening. He gave no reason, just that he couldn't make it. The first time he'd broken a date with her.

She said she'd be doing a peculiar shift on Tuesday and wouldn't be home before 9.pm, but would be off on Wednesday and would be home all day.

He promised he'd call on Tuesday, and would see her after work on Wednesday. For the past eight days he'd wanted to discuss things with her but had been putting them off because of doubts, and the wisdom of sharing his plans with her at this early stage. There were so many questions that had to be answered. Where would they live? Her place was fine for the purpose it served. A great place to visit and bed down for the occasional sex junket, but it was a single woman's apartment. A month ago he'd kidded himself he could live anywhere with her, and it didn't matter how cramped they were, being together was the business, but now he was finding major flaws with that kind of myopic thinking, and not because their relationship was sagging. The trouble wasn't even the size of her apartment, for she'd be out like a bullet if he suggested a bigger place. It was just that he'd started guilt pains about leaving Kim and wanted to let her down gently, by not moving straight in with another woman. Having a place of his own would mean he could move freely in either direction without the restrictions he now faced. Moving in with Daisy would be diving straight into the constraints of another kind of marriage, and he'd now be making excuses to her if he felt like, innocently spending the night in his own home with his family. Then there was his mother's words rattling around in his head.

"If you leave her she'll take her life and that of your daughter."

He had no love for her but she was a part of him. She was all the parts that was good and kind, loving and unselfishly giving. She was his conscience and his soul and the Mother of his child, on whom he doted. He felt a divine right to follow his heart up that Road to true love, but had no desire to trample Kim's love for him, or any crumb of happiness that may spill from Daisy's overflowing Cup. It was Daisy who'd made their lovemaking Possible, and bearable. There were nights when he'd lay in bed thinking about Daisy and the thought of not having her in his life would scare the hell out of him, and the craziest notions would go through his head.

What if he should turn up one day and find her in bed with Andy or someone else? He would visualize himself standing there looking at them. Trying to think what he'd do, but would be lost for an answer and have wondered about that.

That night as he sat looking at her across the dining table, removing her dress with his eyes and drinking in her delicious body, he was telling himself.... Daisy May Spencer, if you ever use that body against me I would hurt you real bad. Another man climbing your enchanting frame?.... Daisy May, I'd probably wind up in Jail for you.

Next he'd try to predict her reactions. Would she go soft and tearful pleading forgiveness and promises of eternal faithfulness? Or would she be the tough, hard-arsed strumpet, and lay there, unashamedly throwing abuse at him? Would she admonish him for bad timing, for walking into her Apartment unannounced and disturbing her? Ordering him to leave her key on the table and get out of her life?....This was another reason for having a place of his own. She was less likely to turn him out in the middle of the night when she knew he had a choice of two homes. No, when they eventually move in together, it would be she moving in with him, and not him with her.

He decided not to say anything to her until he'd found an apartment.

That evening as he walked in the door his mother was waiting. "I hope you're proud of what you've done to that girl, she's so confused she can't tell depravity from love."

Yes mother I've had a nice day, he thought sarcastically.

She followed him into the living-room and watched him greeting Kim and Karen, then back out the door and up the stairs.

In the bedroom he heeled off his shoes and slipped out of his Jacket. He looked at her. Mom, are you going to stand there staring at me while I change?

She laughed. "The day I brought you into this house your Father raped me on the floor in the living-room. You were lying there screaming your lungs out but he wouldn't, let me pick you up. It was as if you were feeling the pain with me, for you never made a sound until he started pushing into me. I felt each of those six stitches as they popped. When he was finished I was bleeding and in pain, but all I cared about was your pain. I looked at you and saw you needed changing and brought you to this room and put you on the bed, and as I changed you I looked at your little thing and wondered if it would grow to cause women the kind of pain I was feeling, but wasn't to know the kind of pain it would cause me.

After changing, and getting you off to sleep I called Dr. Grant, and while we were alone I told him of my fears that as soon as he patched me up Philip would do it again.

"Let him try," he said, then called Philip into the room. "Look at what you've done your wife, is that how you express your love and gratitude for the child she's just given you?" He took him into the front bedroom and I heard him giving Philip a sound warning. "I'm going to patch her up and if you touch her before I tell you it's safe you'll have me to deal with. She must be allowed to heal.

Philip caused me lots of pain over the years, but nothing as savage as the day I walked in and found you in bed with Kim. It was mine and there you were giving it away to someone else. Peter I wanted you and you knew it, it couldn't be made any clearer without physically taking you and I didn't want to do that. I couldn't live with myself if I had made you do it. I wanted you to make the move in your own time, when you were ready. I died of wanting you, of thinking about you and her in bed. I died when I finally realized I was never going to have you and saw no reason to go on living."

How did you die, how did you manage it?

"I willed myself to die. It took a week and I'd began to wonder if it was really possible. Peter, it's hard to understand when you're alive and have so much to live for and life is buzzing all around you. What you have to understand is that I was already dead. I died long before the breath left my body. I was walking around but everything inside me was dead."

Mom I never stopped loving you, why did you think I was here every day? I wanted you as much as that night on your Birthday, but as I got older I knew it was wrong and couldn't do it, even so, if you had taken me I'd have done it gladly. God, I wish I could put my arms around you Mom. How, I'd love to hold you.

"That is the point I was trying to make Son, I don't want to hold you. I love you as much as ever, but feel nothing for you in that way and your body no longer means pleasure. I watched you flashing it about Last night and all I felt was shame and disgust. Every sexual urge I had for you died with me and my soul has been washed clean. You go right on and change your clothes, don't worry about me."

What about those answers you promised?

"I can't help you any further, I'm forbidden any dealings with such things. It delves too deeply in the future. All can say is that you won't find true happiness with her, because she wasn't meant for you. Your happiness is with Kim…"

I know about Kim, you've been telling me about the rosy future we are destined to have since you arrived. I've had enough of that, now I want to know about the woman I love. Tell me about us, Daisy and me.

"Daisy and I," she corrected him.

Say it how you like, but just say it. Tell me you could be wrong like you were with Kim, tell me you're not sure and I'll accept that.

"Peter, I am sure. There is no Daisy and you. There is Peter and Kimberly as far as I'm allowed to see, but there is no Peter and Daisy beyond what you now share. Your best days with her are gone."

Kim and I could never be happy. Any feeling of love I might have had for her died on the day she gave me your Diary and accused me of having sex with you.

"That Diary was meant for your eyes only, and I thought you'd be the one to find it. I'm sorry for the trouble it's caused. That was my mistake and I'll put it right before I leave. I will remove that barrier from your path to happiness."

At precisely midnight on Tuesday he saw her leave the bedroom and he followed her down the stairs firing questions at her. At the foot of the stairs she turned. "Darling my time is up I've just been recalled."

But it's not yet three days, he protested.

"It would be nice if I could stay longer but I have no say in the matter. I love you Peter and always will." And I love you Patricia West.

"I must not say good-bye or I'll never see you again, in our world Good-bye is the end…"

Can't you stay one more night?

She shook her head. "Until we meet again darling," she said then vanished.

He stared at the spot he last saw her with tears in his eyes…. The words…."Don't leave Kim," ringing in his ears.

Just as it was the first time, he was thinking of all the things he'd wanted to say to her, and should've said, but once again it was too late.

He sat in the living-room collecting his thoughts for over an hour, then went up to Bed and woke Kim. She turned over and wrapped her arms around him.

Chapter 24

On the Friday evening Karen gave David a call. He took the Phone into the hall and told her the deal was off. "I want nothing more to do with your silly games, and I would advise you to forget it," he said coldly.

"You said you'd do it when I became eleven and today is my Birthday, you can't change your mind. I believed you. David I trusted you and you lied to me." She began crying. You've got to do it, you promised. I'm now eleven," she went on.

Unknown to her, Peter had arranged a surprise party that night and had invited some of her friends, Adrianne and her family, and a few of the neighbors and their children.

By the time she'd finished with him David was dreading the party and the prospect of meeting his irate cousin. Then there was that threat from her father. He began searching for excuses, telling his Mother he wasn't feeling well, and didn't think he could make Karen's Party.

She pointed out that he was Karen's favorite, how she worshipped, and was almost in love with him. "Look at the time, it's almost 6.pm you can't disappoint her at this late stage, you'll ruin her Party."

"I have a stomach ache," he said, screwing up 'his face as if in pain. "Mom I can't go."

His mother's face changed and she spoke harshly. "David you will go to that Party if I have to get you there on a stretcher and with a Doctor in attendance. You understand?" She said then suddenly remembered something. "David who were you talking with on the Phone?"

He hesitated at first, then told her it was Karen.

"So that's it, you had a fight, why were you so angry, and why were you shouting at Karen?"

"Nothing," he said.

"Good, in that case you have no reason for not going."

David Arrived at 8.pm, and for the first fifteen minutes Karen pretended he wasn't there, ignoring him as she brushed him aside with indifference, then when she was forced to offer him a drink, she pushed it at him, spilling some of it over his trousers, then called him a rotten swine and walked away.

David kept a brave smile on his face, but inside he was shaking with fear. The game was up and he was out, but how would he make her understand? Tomorrow, he told himself. I'll come over and talk to her while Uncle Peter is at work...But he might be home, he doesn't always go to work on a Saturday. Could he talk to her tonight? He wondered. No, he decided, not with her father watching him like a hungry vulture.

Was this a sample of what he'd have to go through for the rest of his life with women? She was only eleven but already had begun to issue all the adult subterfuge he'd seen in his mother. As he was thinking about this she came by and deliberately trod on his foot. "Get your foot out of my way pig," she spat.

David erupted in a loud synthetic laughter. He put his empty glass on the Dining Table, went out the room and up the stairs. Karen saw her chance to have it out with him and followed him into the Bathroom. Trembling like a leaf with fear, he tried to eject her but she wouldn't budge. And when he decided to leave she threatened to scream if he walked out on her.

"Please yourself," he said, and pulled the door open.

She screamed.

Peter was already on his way up the stairs to investigate, he quickly got to the bathroom and grabbed David.

"Dad he hasn't done anything," Karen interceded.

"Then why did you scream?"

"It was a joke, we were playing a game."

"A joke? a game?" He echoed, angrily lashing out and slapping her face.... Releasing David he came at her as she coward behind her arms to protect her face. He seized her arm. "This is all your doing, and if it wasn't your Birthday I'd take a belt to you. What you're playing is no game. Eleven year old girls do not go chasing boys around to make them pregnant, and I want no more of this from you. And this time I mean it. Karen I'm not fooling around with you any longer."

She nodded.

"Do you understand, this is the end?" his fury hitting her like another slap in the face.

"Yes Dad," she answered. Her head lowered dejectedly.

"What was all that about?" said Kim.

Peter turned to see David's parents and his sister Bonnie, standing at the door, all looking for an answer to the same question.

"David, what's going on?" His mother asked.

"I don't know," he shrugged, lifting his hands in a gesture of innocence. "Excuse me," he politely said and squeezed by his parents out the door.

A hurried conference was called in Kim's bedroom, with the four adults and Karen. David sat downstairs insisting he knew nothing and refusing to take part.

This was the cue Karen needed to keep her mouth shut. Peter tried threats but she knew they were mere words, and there was nothing he could do. This was the first he'd lifted his hand to her in anger, and she knew he was bitterly regretting it even as he stood there promising more of the same.

He obviously knew everything, but how did he find out? It wasn't David and she was ready to bet her life on it. Well, let him tell them what he knows, then he'd have to tell how he knew.

Peter had begun to explain but without Karen's help he was forced to shut up, or make a bigger fool of himself. He couldn't explain how he got the information when both kids denied all knowledge of it. As Kim and Adrianne threw questions at him, Keith sat drinking Beer from a bottle, totally indifferent.

Peter had worked himself into a corner from which his only escape was surrender. "Alright, let's forget it," he suggested. "I made a mistake, we'll forget the whole thing."

"Just like that?" Kim voiced her displeasure.

He glared at her and she quickly backed down. "Let's forget it," she offered wistfully.

About the time Karen was being grilled Daisy had called and someone said Karen wasn't available. The following night she called again and Kim picked up the phone. "Are you sure it's Karen you want?" Kim asked.

"I don't know what you mean," Daisy quickly countered.

"You must think I'm a damn fool, don't you? Not bright enough for the clever Detective. Well let me tell you something Daisy, or...."

"I don't have to listen to this...."

"Oh yes you do," Kimberly shouted. "You will shut your mouth and listen, and if you dare cut me off I'll go to your superiors and tell them you're sleeping with my Husband. If you know what's good for you you'll shut your lying mouth and listen..."

"You can take it where you like but I will not stand here and be abused by you. Don't you threaten me, I'm not afraid of you or what you think you know...Now, If you care to change that tone and talk to me in a civil manner I might be prepared to listen."

"You think you're pretty tough, don't you? You swung your half-naked arse into my house and walk off with my Husband and I have to be civil to you? The reason you got away with it is because in the past he would not have wiped his arse on something like you and I trusted him."

"I have no idea what you're talking about, there is nothing between your Husband and myself and you can't prove otherwise."

"So you want proof?"

"I don't care for your damn proof, you can stick it where you like. I have not taken your husband," Daisy insisted.

"You're insulting me by making out I'm a fool, but I want you to understand that the only reason I'm talking to you and not your boss, is because I don't want to hurt you. I have nothing against you except a Husband, and I'd rather fight you for his affection with just the equipment God gave me, because when we get right down to it I'm more woman than you'll ever be. Your big Breasts, your oversized backside, and whatever else you've got that's too big for you, don't scare me. I'm already inside him and he can't get rid of me…"

"Are you finished?" Daisy calmly inquired.

"No I'm not…" Kim barked.

"Yes you are, you've said enough and it's time you listened to the truth…"

"Truth you said. Call yourself a Detective? Don't make me puke. You wouldn't know the truth if it bit you in the groin, and I hope he bites off both your nipples…"

"You are obviously having trouble holding on to your Husband, but before you start blaming every woman who crosses his path, look to yourself. Ask yourself why, and look at your own equipment before you start criticizing others. Look for those failings within yourself. I don't know what you think you are, but don't kid yourself into believing that you've got it, because you haven't. Just remember that the woman who can take your Husband has got to be a better woman than you…"

"And you're that woman?"

"Darling I've just told you, I've not got your Husband," she said lightly.

"Daisy, you're a fucking liar…"

"Really, does your daughter know you use such words?"

"You leave my Daughter out of it and don't call this number again, or try to see her. It's disgusting the way you've used her but that's finished now, and there will be no more excuses to call here. And if you tell my Husband about this conversation you'll be in trouble."

"Who do you think you're talking to you silly bitch," she was saying as Kim hung up. Daisy slammed down the phone in anger. "Shit! What the hell went wrong, and how did she find out?"

After careful assessment she decided that Kim didn't know a damn thing and was only guessing. Just the same she'd have to keep away from Karen and keep her mouth shut, while she think of an excuses for not getting in touch with Karen. It wasn't a question of, if Peter would notice, it was simply how soon? What would she do when he dialed the number and handed her the Phone? Faint, Heart attack, sudden Fit, or death?

It wasn't that she was afraid of telling Peter, but it seemed that was just what Kim wanted. That way she would get the proof she was looking for. If he knew she'd warned her to stay away from Karen he'd raise the roof with her head, and for that reason she couldn't tell him. It seemed Kim had all the good cards. She could indeed, go to her Boss, or failing that could start trouble with her in the Street. It wouldn't take many of those to land her in hot water. She grinned. "That would be one way of getting rid of my Partner."

On Wednesday night they had looked at all the avenues she could take to shake off her troublesome Partner, and Peter had a particular likeness for a 9 to 5 job.

This meant their lives would not be jerked around by sudden shift changes that destroyed well made plans, and throw their lives into a tangled rumpus. It was becoming inordinately difficult to have a sane love affair. He couldn't always be there, then when he could, she'd be working. Then a couple of times when fate did conspire to their meeting she'd be wrapped up tighter than a Mummy's armpit.

This way they could get together without any forward planning and could have every weekend together, except for her monthly considerations, which had began to annoy her.

She'd tried to ignore this at first, but it kept creeping in between them like a pernicious flow of lava from an erupting volcano, until one evening she could take it no longer and met him head on.

She had suddenly began two hours before he was due and had thought about calling him at work to let him know what he was up against, but decided not to indulge him any further. It had gone far enough. He didn't love her company at such times and was decidedly uneasy. Uncomfortable, and would handle her lower body as if she was unclean, that's if he bothered to touch her below the waist.

Peter would normally enter the apartment and take her in his arms, and within three minute his hands would've completed its grand tour of her body, stopping in all the little interesting places. Because of this, he hated her wearing Jeans, or any kind of trousers and she had willingly met with his desires, for it was also in her interest.

Peter was a very tactile man and she adored his touch. However, during her periods she'd be lucky if he stroked her bottom, regardless what she was, or wasn't wearing.

Their weekends had to be planned so as not to coincide with this dreaded period for he'd also voice his objections to sleeping with her. Daisy hated this, knowing that what they had wasn't just a sexual thing, it was consummate love, and not just a burning lust. They loved each other's company. The lighthearted chat, and the heavy involved debates about life and Children, and the funny anecdotes about her work. They would sit for hours with Peter splitting his sides with laughter as she related these tales. They shared a Thousand things that didn't involve sex. Yet the moment her periods arrived he'd lose the ability to share and the relationship would gravitate into something cheap and Whorish. He could not see the pain he was dealing her.

Peter was the most loving and thoughtful man she'd known, but he could also be very insensitive and dogmatic. He had laid down the rules from the start and had never wavered... He detested Periods and dirty genitals. She knew the rules and was expected to respect them regardless.

The hygiene thing was no problem for she'd always been an exceedingly tidy lady, but to keep him sweet she'd began washing so often she was in danger of getting waterlogged. This hand taken care of that thorn in his side and he no longer had reservations about her body. On this score they were the best of friends and he praised her incessantly. As for the other matter there was nothing she could do about that, short of a complete Hysterectomy. Yet he seem to feel he was within his rights to shun her, because as it were, she knew the rules and was flaunting them, as if she had to power to stop the flow but was doing it to annoy him, therefore should be punished.

The irony was, she didn't like the damn thing herself and wasn't expecting him to be in love with it. She wasn't asking him to have a touching affair with the thing, just to acknowledge that it was a normal part of her womanhood, and that it didn't make her unclean or render her untouchable. She was the same woman, with all but a tiny zone restriction.

This was a very private thing that should've been kept under wraps and not unduly highlighted, and she saw no need to discuss or debate it. But his attitude seem designed to remind her she was less than human and should be handled with gloves.

She could remember the time she couldn't wait for the dawn of a new day to see if this symbol of womanhood had arrived in the night. Between the age of eleven and thirteen she was like an anxious child waiting for a Christmas gift that was being perpetually postponed each year, and seemed no closer as time passed. At twelve she was convinced that would be the year, for it was then that those two prominent lumps had appeared on her chest. Her sister had said the two changes would come together, but this was not to be her year for the big league, and was to be kept waiting for another year.

Then one day, shortly before her 13th Birthday it appeared as she walked home from school. Her first thought was, perspiration, but couldn't understand why she should be sweating in that area on what was a very cool day. So it had to be Christmas at last.

She couldn't wait to get home and began running. Once inside the house she lifted her dress, and it was the most beautiful sight she'd ever behold. A bright scarlet veneer, pasted to the insides of her upper thighs by her running action.

For the next hour she kept it to herself and did nothing as she savored the feel of her arrival into womanhood.

At fourteen she hated the bloody nuisance of a thing so much she felt it had been inflicted on women as natures curse for some dastardly deed the female sex had perpetrated at the very beginning of time. But what could woman have done that was so bad to reap the full wrath of Mother Nature's most evil intent? To this day she still hates her periods with an inhuman passion, but had learned to live with it, and if he was to live with her he also had to learn to accept, and live with it, but he wasn't even trying.

Odd as it may sound, it was Peter who'd taught her to love and fully appreciate her body. She'd always felt her nose was too wide. Her eyes were too close, and too big, her backside too fat and her calf too muscular, and thought she looked a little like an Owl. When she first told him he laughed out loud. "You're perfection," he said. "Your face, body or legs cannot be improved. Daisy you are perfection itself. I love you as you are and wouldn't change a thing."

He was inside the apartment two minutes when he made the discovery and she watched him shrink with distaste.

"Don't you make that face at me Peter West, I'm a normal human lady and not something dirty and detestable," she defended her injured pride. "Why didn't you tell me?" he demanded bitterly.

"I don't see why I should when you can easily find out for yourself."

"I hate finding out for myself, and have told you…."

"Peter I have never dragged you down to the floor, or off to the bedroom for sex when I'm in this condition. I know you don't like it and wouldn't do it, and have always told you in advance. But I no longer see the need to warn you from three miles away as if I was carrying a nasty, contagious disease."

"Daisy you're making a silly fuss over nothing by trying to fix something that has been working perfectly for nine months."

"It hasn't been working," she shook her head. "It has been shelved and allowed to collect dust. So much dust that you were unable to see it, and because you couldn't see it you assumed it was no longer there.

All I've done is dust off your paranoia and brought it back to your attention."

He balked at her suggestion that he was not quite right upstairs, and the argument developed into a full blown row. A parody of one he had with Kim just after they got married.

"I know what this is all about," he informed her. "You want me to Fuck you while you're seeing your periods…"

"No I don't," she said calmly. "But what if I did Peter? Would that be such a bad thing? Are you in love with me four weeks out of every month, or just three? And what am I supposed to do for that week when you don't give a shit what happens to me, go on the street, is that it?"

"I wonder which of us isn't right in the head. Where did you get the notion I didn't care for you one week out of four? Are you just saying the first thing that comes into your head, or are you thinking before you flap your mouth?" he said, then suddenly seem to get bored with the silly fight and just dried up. He stood, arms folded, staring blankly at her as she raged on about him needing help to fix his problem. "Of all the men I could've had I had to fall for a head-case. If you can't love me full time don't bother," she stormed off to the Bedroom.

Peter had barely sat down and closed his eyes when the door swung open and she came back into the room and stood over him. "My God, you don't even' love me enough to have a good fight with me, even there you're holding out on me."

He caught her arm and pulled her, struggling, into the chair with him. "You talk too much," he kissed her. The only way he knew to shut her up when she got going.

She tore away from the kiss, breathing heavily. "Aren't you living a little dangerously, letting me sit on your lap in my state, what if I bleed all over you?" her tone defiant.

"Daisy, you're really looking for a fight, aren't you?"

"Peter, you're wrong," she breathed softly. "Darling I'm looking for love, not a war, and if I'm fighting it's only for your love, your affection."

Chapter 25

Peter was only a week into his search for an Apartment, but was already becoming disillusioned. He'd viewed five Apartments. Three were simply glorified rubbish tips, and were in a part of Aston, even stray Dogs were afraid to roam the Street at nights and would run around in packs during the days. The fourth was a comfortable one Bedroom job in a block on Grants Street Highgate. This had a full-time Warden, a communal Car Park, and private Garage parking at extra cost. He was merely indulging himself by viewing this one, for although he could afford it he really wanted two Bedrooms. The fifth was much closer to his needs. This was a two Bedroom job with Garage, on Grove Road, Winson Green, conveniently situated between his house and Daisy's place. Five minutes drive in either direction. This was also a better place to live, work-wise, and would save about two miles per day in travel.

The ground floor was occupied by the family who owned the place and this was the problem. As he climbed the stairs that first time he could hear the' sound of Sewing Machines going at full flow in the Apartment below, and when he got to the living-room the place hummed with the constant drone of a thriving industrial premises. By the time he'd got to the window and saw the bundles of half-finished garments being loaded in a Van his decision was already made.

That night as he sat with Karen on the Sofa watching TV, with Kim seated on the floor across the room, it came to him. There was no need to move out, it was so simple and couldn't fail.

All he had to do was discuss a trial separation with Kim. Pointing out he didn't want to leave her, but needed time to think and get his head together and he had two choices. To move out of the house, or out of the Bedroom. Karen could be moved into Michaela's Room and he'd move back into his old room. He couldn't pretend she'd like it and sit quietly while he moved out of her bed, but faced with the other choice she would almost certainly go for this. And once it was settled he could come and go as he liked, with a license in his pocket to commit adultery. He could sleep with Daisy any time he liked and there wasn't a thing Kim could do about it. This would carry a price, but one he could afford and would gladly pay. To keep her happy he'd have to resume sex with her on a regular basis, which would also highlight the advantages to her. It couldn't fail, she would go for it with open arms, legs, and every other part of her, in an effort to bring him back into her bed.

This way he'd be in no hurry to leave home and there wouldn't be the risk of him moving out, only to find things didn't work out with Daisy, as his Mother so vehemently insisted. Whether he agreed or not he was obliged to heed her words. She was no charlatan, he told himself.

He was elated, and with childish exuberance he hugged Karen and kissed her on the side of her mouth.

She looked at him in mild surprise, and glanced at her Mother.

Kim smiled, happy in the knowledge their love was so rich for she was the only remaining link between them. She loved the child as much as he did, and Karen loved them both with equal fervor, and had never taken sides.

A bolt of shame shot through her as she recalled thinking, just before Michaela died, that his love for Karen might not be the innocent Father and Daughter thing he made out, and felt sick at the thought.

"What was all that about?" · she asked, trying to push the stupid thought from her head.

"Can't a happy man embrace and kiss his Daughter?"

Never mind his Daughter, what about his wife.... "Of course, but what suddenly made you so happy?" she said, thinking that the last time she saw him in this mood was three weeks ago, when he took her off to Bed with a sparkle. And the scintillating sex that lasted three nights.

Foolishly she'd believed things were getting back to normal, but since that Tuesday night he'd returned to covering with separate Sheet, so he wouldn't touch her. Could he? She wondered, be once again in the mood for love? "Peter, would you like a drink?" she decided to strike while the man was hot, with a little fawning.

"Yes please, tea or Coffee, whatever you're making."

"I'll make whatever you want," she said, smiling prettily.

"In that case, could I have some Horlicks please?"

"Horlicks it is," she asked if Karen would like one and she nodded. "Yes please."

A minute later she called Karen into the Kitchen, then came back into the living-room and knelt at Peter's feet, hands lightly placed on his thighs. "Can we go to bed early tonight?" she asked.

His face warmed to her suggestion. Maybe she was learning to read his mind? "Sure," he said, sounding as if the question wasn't necessary.

She smiled and briskly got to her feet. "I'll make your drink."

"Karen will make it," he said.

"No I want to make this one,'" she rubbed her hands with glee. "Then I'll go up to the Bathroom for five minutes and you can come up when you've finished your drink."

A week later he revealed his plans to her and she was allowed no discussions, or any chance to voice her opinions. The decision had been made and the edict issued. All objections and counter arguments were brushed aside with threats of him moving out. They needed a trial separation to sort themselves out and that's how it was. The master had spoken and there was no more to be said.

He hated doing this to her for she didn't warrant being trodden on in this manner, he told himself once again, and when she began crying he almost called it off to save her further pain. But as he'd learned with his mother, it didn't pay to be soft. Regardless how badly he was hurting inside, he had to project that hard exterior. Hit hard. discredit and disarm her counter moves before they were made, destroy her ability to fight back. Take the fight out of her by whatever means possible. Give her a single sentence and she'd build it into a winning argument before he got his mouth open again, taking over the conversation and mesmerizing him with words. One of woman's finest abilities. He was yet to meet a woman he could defeat with simple words and was forced to use foul means to get his way.

Kim could've chopped off her tongue for dropping herself into this stinking quagmire with that brave speech. It seem the woman was now calling her bluff and she couldn't do a damn thing about it. If only she'd kept her mouth shut it might not have come to this. What was the point of making threats she had no intention of backing up? It was about now that she should be walking onto C.I.D. Headquarters and tipping the scales in her favor, but she couldn't do it. She was not the type.

Two days later Karen was moved out and Peter moved in, but it was all in his mind, for not a single item was moved into the room, and the bed had remained stripped of its sheets as Karen left it.

Peter celebrated his first night of freedom by sleeping with Daisy, and going straight to work the next morning. That evening he was back with her. They took a bath and was in bed by 7 o'clock. He got home at 10.30pm, and climbed straight into bed with Kim.

For the next three weeks he never once went near his room as he drifted conveniently between the two women. One night with Kim and two with Daisy. Two nights with Kim, and three with Daisy.

At the end of the third week Kim moved Karen back into the room and it was another five days before he knew she was back. But it didn't matter now, he had no further use for the room, it had served its purpose.

After putting it all together and adding the sum total, Kim wondered what complaints did she really have? Yes, he was sleeping with the woman and there wasn't a neighbor within shouting distance who didn't know it. Even Karen knew her so-called friend was sleeping with her father.

"She is a rotten Swine," she told her Mother. "and if she comes back to this House I'll kick her."

Peering through the long darkness and deep heartache, Kim could see a light that no one else could. In four weeks Peter had slept with her fifteen nights, and had made love to her each night, sometimes twice. This was their most consistent period of lovemaking since the night their Daughter died. And she wasn't just talking about a release of sexual energies and frustrations, as most of their recent encounters had become.

This was lovemaking with a heavy emphasis on love. The kind of love they shared before the tragedy, together with a multitude of new tricks he'd obviously picked up from Daisy, which had revolutionized their sex life, and he was almost back to the time when he couldn't leave her body alone.

He would get home at eleven o'clock and she could tell he'd come straight form Daisy's bed, but she was always ready and willing, and was quick to adopt everyone of Daisy's tricks. It was now an open battle and it helped to know just what weapons the opposition were using.

Things were not rosy and she wasn't trying to pretend they were. Her husband was running a full time affair, and regardless of any improvements that brought to their live it was still tearing her heart apart. She could sit at home and blame Daisy for taking her husband but that wouldn't be the truth. Daisy didn't bring about the changes in him. It was because he'd changed why someone like Daisy was able to move in. She had lost count of all the gorgeous creatures Peter had thrown at him throughout their Marriage and not once did he stray. That was the reason it was so difficult to accept he was having an affair with this one. Sure, she was a pretty Blonde with a good body but she was nothing special, and two days before Michaela's death he would not have wiped his Prick on her best dress. Peter didn't look at other women, they had nothing he couldn't get from her in abundance, served up the way he liked it.

"You're all the woman I need," was a song he'd sing to her daily and would confirm with deeds of love. Then suddenly things changed.

In those early dark days, friends would come bearing sympathy for their bereavement and would point out that she still had a Daughter, and a loving and loyal Husband who would stand by her. All they could see was that he was always home, and to them that spelt love and loyalty. They could see no further than the closed Bedroom door and could not see the man who turned his back on her each night, pretending she didn't exist, and that was only when he came to bed. Most nights he'd fall asleep in the living-room, catching four or five hours sleep before coming to bed, more of a token than any real need to share the bed with her. In their eyes he was the perfect Husband. They couldn't see him avoiding her as they moved around the house in their daily routine.

For ten months they were completely blind, but ran around making out they could see. Now suddenly they think they can see but they are just as blind as before.

"Leave him, don't stand for it. Kick him out. Put something in his food. Don't let him into your bed, you're a bloody fool to keep giving him sex. Get an injunction."

What the devil is an injunction? she'd asked herself. "File for divorce. Find the bitch and scratch her eyes out. Take a knife to his privates. Take a knife to her and see that she never take another man."

It came in torrents from well meaning people who could not see Peter Putting his arms around her in the kitchen. Patting her behind or tweaking her nipples as they met in the hall. Putting his hand up her dress or just smiling with her. They couldn't see any of this because

they were standing too far back, and would've had no meaning to them anyway.

Adrianne was among the most vociferous of her many advisors. Adrianne, who'd spent most of her married life cheating on her husband was now advising her on fidelity. It would've been laughable if it wasn't so perverse.

"I think you should leave him Kim, he's not right in the head," she'd said. I knew he was cracking up from that incident on Karen's Birthday. Didn't I say something was wrong? Fancy accusing his Daughter of something like that? The man is off his head and you should both get out before it's too late. You can stay with us," she offered.

Kim didn't have the heart to inquire just where they'd stay. They had seven people sharing three Bedrooms and she was offering to put them up. Kim found the whole thing very strange and couldn't understand why she'd suddenly turned against Peter. He was her favorite person, she was besotted with him and he was never wrong. Had he been a different person she'd have been worried sick about an affair.

Adrianne had no idea how Peter really felt about her, for he took great care not to offend her. However, she had read this as some kind of invitation and would push her little rear at him constantly. There could only be one reason for turning against him now, and that was jealousy. Her sister was eating her heart out with jealousy. Peter had dared to reject her in favor of another woman, cheating her of some divine right to his affection. As her twin sister she felt it was her place to take up the slack in their marriage. Kim laughed. Sister, you're just a cheap, white-livered-strumpet, and you couldn't keep your knickers in place if your life depended on it.

Only a year earlier Keith almost put her in the Hospital when he learned she'd brought one of her old Boyfriends into the House. They were inside about ten minutes and she swore they had done nothing, but Kim knows better. Five minutes standing behind a door is all Adrianne needs in an emergency, and such times all she need is penetration. Just to feel the man inside her, and she'd walk away happy and fulfilled. Kim knew of a dozen such instances that her sister had shared with her. This was the woman who was now throwing advise around as though she'd never bent, or broken a single marriage vow in her life.

Chapter 26

It was about a week after the party before Karen and David met again. She ran into his arms and embraced him, and thanked him for what he'd done, or as he puts it. What he hadn't done.

"Don't mention it," he said magnanimously. "That was private, between you and I. Sorry I made your Father look a liar but couldn't help that."

"He can take care of himself," she said. Then added thoughtfully "I wonder how he knew? He was very secretive, like he was trying to protect someone."

"Did it hurt when he hit you?"

"Not really."

"Well it should have, you deserved it, why did you scream, you silly girl?"

"Thank you David Turner," she said frostily. "That's the thanks I get for saving you from a beating."

He grinned. "I'd swap both my sisters for you, and I'd have gladly taken that beating for you. That's how highly I think of you my dear cousin. Now, how about this pregnancy, are we still in business?"

She lowered her head in embarrassment. "My parents are much happier now and there is no need for that anymore," she lowered her voice. "Sometimes I hear them in bed with Mom making funny noises."

"Maybe he's choking her," he joked.

"In that case she'd be dead by now...No,' they're doing something else, I have a good idea what it is."

Karen had much more than a good idea for she'd seen them doing it and knew exactly what they were doing. She'd also learnt that David had outwitted her but was too embarrassed to take it up with him and had let it pass. He was a rotten swine, but still the nicest Boy she knew. He could have taken advantage of her, instead he'd used every trick he could find to protect her.

She stood naked in front of the Mirror inspecting her chest for signs of those budding mammary, turning sideways to check her profile. She stood in silent thought for a time then said. "You know, I think I'll still let David do it. Yes I will let David do it," she paused delicately and thought for another long moment. "When I'm fifteen he'll be nineteen, and a lot more experienced. I want him to be the first and I won't let another boy touch me. David can be trusted... David Turner we've got a date for the 15th of May 1985. My 15th Birthday, I've chosen the gift," she giggled. "This time you will not get away from me David. When I'm fifteen you won't stand a chance," she released her nipples and arched her back, then stood looking with satisfaction at her little behind. That end of my body is shaping up quite nicely, she told herself.

She thought about Bonnie and wondered if she'd look like her when she was fifteen. Bonnie was thirteen but looked sixteen. Her Breasts were perfectly formed, she had a tiny waist and hips that reminded her of Daisy. At fifteen she wants to be like Bonnie, and at twenty, like Daisy. She was a rotten swine but she was still the prettiest.

One night as Peter and Daisy was about to turn in the phone rang and Daisy picked it up. "Could I speak to my Dad please?" said Karen coldly.

"Hello Karen," Daisy said, putting on her best voice.

"Could I speak to my Dad," she repeated impatiently.

"Aren't we friends anymore?"

"No we're not," Karen answered churlishly

By this Daisy had told Peter Karen wanted to speak to him. He ran his fingers through his hair in despair and after a thoughtful moment he nodded.

"Why aren't we friends anymore?" Daisy asked.

"You know why, and I just want to speak to my Dad."

"Okay your father is right here. Good night Karen."

"Good-bye!"

"That hurts more than a kick in the guts," she remarked as she handed him the Phone.

He covered the Phone and embraced her. "Don't worry about it, things will work out right, you'll see."

After speaking to him for a minute, she said. "Dad, I don't hate Daisy."

"Why don't you tell her yourself, it would make her very happy," he suggested.

"Why should I make her happy?" the child retorted. "Is she making Mom happy?"

"What was that, trouble?" Daisy inquired at the end. "She only wanted a chat," he said. "She wanted to talk for a while, nothing important."

It was this call that planted the first seeds of doubts in his mind. Uncertainties about the life he was leading, and questions about responsibilities. Karen had called for an innocent chat and to say she loved him. She wanted to talk with him and he wasn't there. She had to call him at another woman's house. It was all wrong. I was quick to throw stones at my Father's grave for what he'd done, but at least he had the decency to die before I was old enough to witness it. What am I doing to this child I claim to love so much? How would I like it if a man had done that to my Mother?

Adrianne was still advising Kim when her own troubles arrived and she was caught without a single constructive thought. Kim was busy in the Kitchen when the Phone rang and Karen answered it. She came into the Kitchen and told her Mother Aunt Adrianne wanted her. Less than five minutes later she had changed and was leaving a message for Peter to pick her up at Adrianne's house. Some minutes later Kim turned up to find her Sister, Keith, and Bonnie upstairs in the Bedroom.

Earlier, Bonnie had told her Father she was Pregnant, he'd told her Mother, who immediately packed her things and ordered her out of the House.

"If she's woman enough to open her legs and get herself into that state she can find a place of her own." Was what Kim heard as she came into the room and couldn't contain her disgust. "What is wrong with you Adrianne, are you crazy, are you completely out of your mind? She is thirteen years old." She turned on Kim. "I don't need you to remind me of her age, she's my Daughter…And what are you doing here anyway?"

"Keith called me and I'm glad he did. I have a duty here, I'm family."

"Well I don't know why he bothered we don't need your help. She's going out and that is final."

Kim erupted in a corrosive anger. "You cretinous bitch, all these years I thought you had some intelligence but you're totally devoid of even common sense. Where will she go when you put her out on the Street?" Kim slung her handbag on the bed and it bounced off and fell to the floor in the corner. Bonnie quickly retrieved it and put it on the Bed.

Adrianne turned her head and looked at Kim, a raging flame in her Grey eyes. "You can piss your Knickers until it runs down your legs if you like. I don't give a shit what you think. This hasn't got a damn thing to do with you, Sister. It's between me and my Daughter."

"That's what you think. You try and put her out of this house and It'll be between you and me," Kim warned.

"You're only making noise Kim, there isn't a thing you can do about it."

"Try me," Kim challenged her. "Don't forget who used to beat the pants off you."

"Oh yes, and what you think Keith would be doing?"

"He'd be sitting there and keeping out of it….That's another thing," she turned on him. "Are you going to sit there and do nothing while she dumps your Daughter in the Street?"

"What can I do?" he shrugged.

"Jesus Christ!" Kim said in disbelief. "What a pathetic excuse for a man you've turned out to be. It seems you can only stand up to be counted when you think she might be giving away your prized crotch. If you had the slightest inkling she was lifting her skirt for another man you'd beat her senseless, but you're ready to sit there warming your backside while she throw your Daughter into the Street like rotting garbage."

Keith sat looking blankly across the room as if he hadn't heard a word, and Kim suddenly last all respect for him. If he could sit there and let her talk to him like that, in front of his wife and Daughter without retaliating, then he was of no worth as a man.

"I would like to talk to my Sister alone," she ushered them out of the room. At the door she told him. "Don't come back no matter what you hear. She's, going to see sense if I have to beat it into her."

Back in the room Kim had calmed. "Before we start fighting let's exhaust the alternatives. Abortion. Have you thought about that?"

"It's too late she's nearly five months."

"Do you know the Father?"

"Norman Gibbs, her best friend's brother."

"He must like this kind of thing. Didn't he make a fifteen year old pregnant some time back and his parents had to pay for an abortion?"

"He's twenty and should've learned his lesson. He should be put in Jail for this," said Adrianne bitterly.

"You can forget that," Kim advised. "Think of your Daughter and what you'd be putting her through." "What about me?" she asked, denuded of compassion. "Did she think of what she was putting me through? ... Kim I had such high hopes for that girl, she's the prettiest thing is the entire neighborhood and I had such high hopes for her."

"But this doesn't change that. When it's over she can go back to School and pick up where she left off and be whatever she wants to."

"That's just it," Adrianne postured. "I know what she wants to do and she's not going to do it in this house. Kim I don't want her here, she can't stay."

"Adrianne, you've surprised me. You were the last person I expected to take this holier-than-thou attitude. How many men, and boys did you have by the time you were thirteen?... Ten, twelve, or was it nearer fifteen?"

"What's that got to do with this, I didn't get pregnant until I was fourteen and I married the Father of my child," she said haughtily.

"Don't give me that crap, you think I don't know you got pregnant at twelve and Mom hushed it up and got you a quiet abortion?"

Adrianne gazed at her in stunned disbelief but said nothing as, Kim went on to read out her history. "Every Boy within a mile had fucked you by the age of thirteen. There were so many you couldn't tell which one made you pregnant, and you have the nerve to sit there and pass judgment. The girl is a saint, compared to you at that age. Just remember, I know where your garbage are buried and might just decide to dig them up."

"Kim, you're full of shit," said Adrianne. "You won't do a damn thing, we both know it. And here is something more to put with what you already know."….she hesitated…."Keith is not Bonny's Father." Kim's mouth dropped open and she stood staring foolishly at her sister.

"She has been a thorn in the side of his neck for years but there was nothing he could do about it until the stupid bitch got herself pregnant."

"So it was true?" Kim said. "He said the child wasn't his before you got married but no one believed him."

Adrianne shrugged. "Keith had doubts from the start but I managed to convince him she was his, but he kept saying he wasn't a fool and knew the truth. Then came the accident when she was five…"

"That time she was knocked off her Bike, I remember."

"Well, to cut a long story, they had to cross-match her in Hospital and it came out she was a different Blood group from both of us. He had his proof at last."

"Who is her Father, or don't you know?" Kim said somewhat indelicately.

Adrianne silently chewed on the question for a time then slowly a frown of uncertainty unfurled. "Could be anyone of three," she said evenly. "Roy Collins, John Mendicot, or Steven Graham. Personally, I'd go for Roy, she has everything for him. His face, eyes…"

"Good God Adrianne, how can you be so callous?"

"You shouldn't be surprised, I got it from Dad. For years he went around saying I wasn't his Daughter. How do you think I felt? I needed his love just as you did, but he didn't care if I got killed by a Bus. Kim, do you know how much I longed for that man's embrace? For him to take me in his arms as he did with you. At ten years old, I asked him why he didn't love me, and you know what he said? You know what that bastard said to me? "Because you're someone else's mistake and I have to be living with it." I didn't know what he meant then, only that it was meant to hurt me, and it did. One week later I had sex for the first time. In fact it was rape, but I didn't know it then. I got so sick of watching dad with his arms around you and all over you that I asked this boy to embrace me. He was fourteen, and lived in Windsor Road just around the corner. We had agreed to meet in the Passage at the side of our House that evening. When I got there he was waiting and we did embrace. He stood holding me close to his body for about five minutes and it felt good. Then his hands were all over me and that felt even better. Next he was pulling down my pants and telling me it was all a part of the game. Well, without going into the dirty details, he raped me and did other things. Kim, the most sickening thing of all was that I liked it. And since then have not stopped searching for love. A man offers me something that looks like love and I grab it with both legs and don't bother to question it. You didn't have to you were the pretty one whose shit didn't smell, where that man was concerned. He didn't even attend my Wedding. I asked him to give me away and he broke out in loud laughter. "Not to my worst fucking enemy." He said then spent the day in the Pub drinking himself sick and betting his friends the Marriage wouldn't last a month. Then I had to watch him sniveling and crying like a sick child at your Wedding."

"Adrianne, I know you had a bad deal and I felt the pain with you..."

"God, that's nice to know," she said with a stabbing sarcasm. "I only wished I'd felt some of your happiness with you."

"Be that as it may," Kim returned philosophically. "Why are you now rejecting your Daughter? This is worse than what Dad did.

"Nothing could be worse than..." Her voice tailed off and her lips quivered. "Kim I don't want her to go, she's my Daughter and I love her," her eyes rapidly filling with tears. "Keith threatened to leave me if I don't get rid of her..."

"But it was he who called me, why?"

"Because he's a bloody coward and is only trying to cover his arse and make me look the villain. Kim, I know what you must think of me and I couldn't blame you, but you should know how I feel. You've just lost your Husband to another woman and I don't want to lose mine because of Bonnie. I have to go with Keith."

"Does she know he's not her Father?"

"No, and you're the only other person who knows."

"Adrianne you've made the wrong decision and is kicking out the wrong person. The poor child now has neither Father nor Mother."

"There is something else," she said reluctantly. "Some months ago the stinking bastard tried to...Well...she fought him off and bit his hand," she blurted in one breath. "He slapped her around and she came to me crying. Kim I'm ashamed of myself for doing nothing about it. I comforted her and showered her with love but I didn't do a damn thing about him. He swore she made it up but I knew he was lying. She had the marks on her thighs and her breasts were sore where he'd grabbed her. I should've given him hell but was afraid if I'd worked him into a corner he'd kick her out, but I was wrong. He didn't even have the guts to do it himself."

A thought flashed through Kim's mind. "Are you sure it wasn't Keith who made her pregnant?" she said in a near whisper.

"I'm positive!" she exclaimed. "Bonnie wouldn't lie to me. She said he hadn't bothered her since, and I notice he barely speaks to her."

"That's it!" Kim glared at her. "You get the rest of her things together she's coming with me."

"You mean that Kim?" she asked, her voice exploding with vibrations of joy. "Stop asking asinine questions and get her things together," Kim said, her anger spewing from every word.

"Kim, you'll never regret this, and it won't cost you a penny. I'll pay for her clothes and her keep."

"You can keep your money we're not impoverished."

"Are you sure Peter won't mind?" Adrianne asked, slightly concerned.

"Let me put it this way," Kim said, her head held high with pride. "If he does mind then he's not the man I think he is and I'll pack my things and leave. Peter is one of the most outstanding men God has created, regardless what everyone thinks." Kimberly called Bonnie into the room and explained she'd be corning to live with them until she has the Baby.

The sudden incandescent smile that lit her face was more gratitude than Kim felt she'd earned and brought tears to her eyes.

Karen sat with a frozen smile of incredulity as her Mother related the story. Overwhelmed by the way things were miraculously coming together. Even with all her careful planning she could not have arranged anything so agreeable to everyone concerned. When the Baby is born Bonnie will have to go back to school and her mother would have the Baby. And of course she was no longer spreading that yarn about Babies corning from Heaven but was spelling it out for the first time.

Peter smiled to himself and wondered how his Mother could've got it so wrong? She'd obviously seen someone pregnant in the House, but her Crystal Ball must have needed cleaning at the time and she confused Bonnie with Kim. He almost laughed out loud, thinking about it.

She wasn't infallible, which meant she could also be off target about Daisy, and they did have a life together after all.

After a long discussion they agreed Norman Gibbs should be told Bonnie was carrying his child, if only to give the child its Father's name. Peter called his House and his Mother answered the Phone and put him on. Peter explained it was a private matter that couldn't be discussed on the Phone, and could he drop in one day that week.

"I know what it's about and I'll be there on Wednesday at 8.pm," he said in a hushed tone.

The other thing that concerned Kim was the kind of influence Bonnie would have on Karen. She was a very dominant personality, with a full measure of her mother's indiscrete, and immodest habits. Kim hoped she'd shed some of her unpleasant tendencies, now she didn't have to compete with the boys for everything.

Here there would be no rivalry for food, clothes, bed, or love and affection. The two girls would be treated equally. Kim hoped she'd warm to this and quickly lose her rough edges.

Chapter 27

David's concern ran a lot deeper than Kim's, and if he could've stopped Bonnie being thrown in with Karen he would. He could see this precious Gem of a child being corrupted by his vulgar and odious Sister. For the best part of a year he'd been telling himself she'd wind up with a fat stomach and he couldn't be more disappointed the silly girl had proved him right. There was no satisfaction in her unfortunate plight. She was his Sister and he couldn't wish that on her, but he could see it coming, why couldn't she? She knew so much about everything. Mostly things that did not concern her, yet she knew nothing about guarding her most private possession. He could kill her.

One Evening he turned up while they were watching TV, said he wanted a chat with her and they went up to her room.

David came straight to the point. "Don't make any trouble in this house Bonnie, I'm asking you, Please," he said softly. "Don't do to Karen what you've done to May. Aunt Kim has kindly taken you in, don't repay her kindness by messing up her home," he beseeched.

She threw her head back in a broad rebellious laugh. "What is it to you?" she spat coldly. "Who do you think you are, coming here to lecture me? Your reign is over, King David. You have no say in this House. The days when Mom and Dad would sit there and let you insult me and I dare not open my mouth are gone forever, cause I'm never coming back. I got out of your way, now you get out of mine, and don't come here telling me how to behave. If I behaved like a Pig at home it was because I lived like a pig and was treated like one. Now things have changed, can't you see?" she smiled, spreading her arms demonstratively. "My own Room, Furniture. My own bed, and Aunt Kim has promised to buy me a TV. Do you think I'd open my big mouth and lose all this?" her eyes wide with amusement. "Come on David, I thought they said you were the bright one?"

David was confounded. "I don't know what to make of you Bonnie. You seem almost glad to be pregnant, as though you'd planned it all."

"That is another silly remark David. Even if I'd been sure of all this it still wouldn't be worth a pregnancy. Getting in this state wasn't my choice…"

"You chose to have sex without protection, it was your choice."

"It's not as simple as you think," her face suddenly drooped into sadness. She swallowed hard. "Over the next few months I hope we become friends. All we ever did was fight and I want to change all that. There are things I want to tell you, things I must share with someone, and a big Brother would be the best person."

He was intrigued, and tried to coax it out of he her but she wouldn't be drawn.

The chat with Norman Gibbs left Kim more confused than before. He'd arrived ten minutes early and was eager to have the matter cleared up. Swearing on his Parents life he didn't have sex with Bonnie.

They'd met in the Street a few times and he'd chatted her. She'd always sold an image of sexuality, making out she had lots and was ready to give, but in fact was the exact opposite, a fraud. She wasn't interested in Boys and cared even less about sex. There were at least a dozen guys of varying age who were after her. All conned by her act, but there wasn't one who could say he had sex with her.

About four months earlier they'd met in the Newtown Row Shopping Centre, and as they talked she invited herself to his House. He should've questioned it at the time, and knew he should. It was 11 am on a Monday morning and she should've been in School, and not sauntering around the shops in tight Skirt and Sweater. He knew she was thirteen but that morning she looked seventeen and he wasn't going to question this rare gift. This was a girl for whom most guys would've walked into Hell and picked an argument with the Devil if she'd suggested it. Here was his chance, his parents were at work so he happily agreed. They walked along laughing and talking about what they'd do at his house. She said she was only coming to see his paintings, and he joked that he'd not got any Paintings, just a big wooden carving that he was sure she'd like.

They came out the Shopping centre and walked along Newtown, past the Swimming Baths and crossed the Road at the lights. Went up Selston Rd, and turned right on Cambourne Close.

Throughout the five minutes walk she was relaxed and knew precisely what she was getting into. To his surprise, she wouldn't let him near her once they got into the house. She had two cups of Tea and a Glass of Coke and left an hour later, without him even kissing her. A month later he heard the whisper that she was pregnant and he was responsible. It was then he knew the reason she'd invited herself to his house. Somebody she can't name, had made her pregnant and she used him.

After he left Kim turned to Peter. "That boy wasn't lying, he told the truth. Bonnie is the liar," she said.

"I don't know what to believe," Peter ran his fingers through his hair. "Why would she lie?"

"Just as he said. The father is someone she can't name, but she doesn't need to, I already know who it is." Kim told him the entire story, exactly as she got it from Adrianne, including her suspicions.

Chapter 28

Peter sat on the floor, his back against the wall. The two girls were upstairs watching TV, the new pattern since bonnie settled in. Kim was taking a bath. He glanced idly around the room reflecting the moment his Mother had appeared. Looking at the state of his life at that moment and assessing what profit he'd shown from her visit. It was unfortunate but her visit had severed some of that close bond they'd shared and he no longer felt that close to her. She'd fed him some happiness but had also left him a basket of gloom. And here he was enjoying the happiest period of his life. Nothing he'd shared with her or Kimberly could compare with what he now enjoyed. This is the way to live. Everything that passed before had been reduced to the mundane, a boring journey into experience and maturity, a journey into success.

Couldn't his mother, with her window on the future see this, or didn't it really exist, and he was merely living a dream, to be rudely awoken and brought to his senses? It felt like a dream, too good to be real, too fine women falling over themselves in a bid to win his favors. Each complimenting the other in her own special way, filling a separate place in his life without duplicating or trespassing on the other's ability. Like the two halves of a Tennis ball, coming together in perfect symmetry and bounce, they were as one. There were no perfect women, but he felt closer to perfection than he'd dared desire.

Kim had also began gaining weight. It was almost imperceptible, but couldn't escape his attention. Her body was programmed and finely tuned to exclude all excesses, and she wasn't packing an ounce she didn't need. For years he'd been telling himself he knew her, and if he did then who was this woman? This person, who though grudgingly, and with much reluctance had accepted his gross indiscretions, and in return was serving up a fullness of love he didn't deserve.

Kim was unashamedly, fighting a war of attrition with an adversary she couldn't see but whose presence was constantly with her. Peter would bring her into the house daily. On his clothes, hair, hands, and worst of all on his breath. He would kiss her and she could smell, and almost taste, the woman's private parts, and would instantly want to be sick. How she avoided throwing up all over him at such times, couldn't be credited to her constitution, but simply the conditioning of her mind not to acknowledge the woman's existence.

It was now two months since he'd embarked on his double life and she'd not uttered a word to him about the woman. There were times when she wanted to send him straight to the Bathroom to scrub himself with disinfectant before touching her, but never did. She just stood there and drank in the woman's flavors, then would go to the Bathroom and wash herself. In two months she'd collected enough blonde hairs to fashion a full size Wig.

The day he'd exploded that bomb under her she'd felt as if her Bloodstream had dried to a trickle, and her body was collapsing in on itself. As though he'd just beaten her heart to death with a stick and had stepped on it as he walked away.

For the next two days she couldn't hold a rational or coherent thought and couldn't stop crying.

She'd watched Karen's things being moved from the room and decided something had to be done, she had to stop crying and start fighting. Kim fixed herself a strong drink in a long Glass with two cubes of ice, and took both the drink and her problem into the living-room and quietly dealt with them accordingly.

Finally it was whittled down to two choices. Give him Love, or give him pain. She chose Love.

She was the wife, and had his name and his Daughter, along with a deep and endless love for the man, which was the very thing he'd turned against her and was now holding at her throat like a Scythe. Threatening to cut her down if she struggled, but she had a surprise for him and had no intention of struggling. Neither was she about to surrender to some trashy blonde, not after battling with his Mother for all those years. If she was of no value to him as a wife, then as a mistress, she had to be worth ten times the other woman.

Daisy had the same congenital flaw as most, (other-women) they want him to themselves and ultimately want to be his wife. Well she can sit there and play wife if she like. Her desires are so strong and burns with such fervor, that without realizing it she'd started to assume the role of a wife and less of a lover.

At the start she only wants one night a week with him, next she wants two, and once she gets that she goes for three. At the same time she's become unhappy with the places he's been taking her, and would like a holiday, and what is he doing about leaving his wife? How long does he expect her to wait? She's now rushing pass thirty and wants to have Children before it's too late. What about the cupboard he'd promised to fit in the Kitchen, it's been sitting on the floor for two months mow? How about mending the fuse for the Vacuum Cleaner, the place hasn't been cleaned for the past three weeks. And all the time she's nagging the Prick off him without realizing it, and he's thinking of the woman he's left at home for all this. shit!...He doesn't need this. She has him doing all the things he refuse to do at home, and all the time he's doing them he's hating himself for what he's rapidly becoming, a damp Crotch-cloth, instead of a rampant Stud.

Their sex life has also gone off the boil, because the sight of her wearing old distressed Cardigans, and worn out, ill fitting pants around the place is turning him off quicker than an ice cold shower, and he has began looking homewards to the lady who never complains and has given him nothing but love. No jealousy or anger. No displeasure about the time he's spending away from home, or holding out on his carnal pleasures. No nagging. Just a great lady who's always ready and willing whenever he is. A lady with time on her side and can afford to wait for the other woman to burn herself out.

"I may not be much of a wife," Kim told herself. "But my God, I'm going to be one hell of a mistress. You are going to be thrashed with your own weapons, Miss Fat Police Woman. I now know all your little tricks in bed and I've learnt them well. Peter may not care much about me but he loved his Mother and he'll never leave her House.

Kimberly knew all the tricks and wasn't above getting Karen to call him just before he climbed into bed with his woman, to say how much she loved him and wished he was home.

Kim looked through her underwear and was amazed how badly they fitted, and that she hadn't noticed it before. It's been like this since she lost weight but hadn't bothered, and of course it didn't matter for Peter was never around to see her. He would get out of her way when she started undressing, or bury his head under the sheet. No, this wouldn't do. She looked at herself in the Mirror and had to laugh. She was like a toddler in an oversized nappy.

Three days later she went into Nationwide Anglia and drew £600. She bought Bonnie a 14 inch Color TV, went into Rackhams and bought a Ice Bucket. Over at Lewis's she bought six bottles of Moet and Chandon Imperial. Down the Road at Marks and Spencer she spent £150 on the most scintillating underwear she could find, and another £100 on some well fitting, inexpensive outfits.

That evening the kids had their dinner early and got out the way. She took a long bath, he liked his women clean, and slipped into a little black dress she'd bought for the occasion. Recalling the excitement in his voice when he talked about his Mother's 42nd Birthday.

When he got home and saw the table set for two with Champagne on ice he almost died of embarrassment, and nearly choked to death on his first sip. She got up and came to him, rubbed his back and inquired if he was alright.

He slipped his arm around her tiny waist. Yes just my conscience, it got lodged in my throat, he said to himself. He looked up at her and said thanks, then stood up and kissed her.

Kim began visiting the Hairdresser once a week, and would no longer drag herself around the house in a Dressing Gown, but would be wearing something nice when he comes home.

The house was becoming a home once again and the sound of laughter more prevalent.

Bonnie had quickly become a friend to everyone and fitted in as though she'd always been there, and her Rapier-sharp tongue had been sheathed. Her spirit was not broken. Far from it, and she was nobody's footstool, but now she would argue her point with less bluster and more respect, and got on with Karen like they were long lost Sisters, just as Kim had hoped.

Kim was prepared to accept whatever time Peter had to offer, and after he'd slept out the first night she decided, the next night he was home she would go to his bed and not wait on him to visit hers, but he had the same idea and was in her bed before she could get to his.

At no time had he wished for someone like Daisy, and here he was wondering, and dreading the thought of life without her. While at the same time he was having feelings for Kim he thought had died with Michaela. He would sit at work thinking about her, wanting her, impatiently rushing home so he could take her to bed and be singed by the flames of her love. She didn't possess Daisy's worldly experience or abilities but was eager to learn and had soaked up everything. Adopting, and adding her own ingenious variations, until Daisy had nothing left to teach her. She'd become the perfect woman. The loving wife who washed his clothes, cooked his food, clean the house, and looked after the children. The lover he comes home to each evening, and the Whore in Bed. Whatever time he got home she'd have a smile for him. There was never a face on her, so he had no dread of coming home. It ripped her soul to shreds, but she had to suppress pain, jealousy, and excruciating heartache in her fight to win him back, and it was rapidly coming right.

He was back home because it was happier than the other place, and Daisy no longer had anything to offer he couldn't get at home. She had attacked his conscience by design and had indulged him unashamedly. "I'm full-time," she told herself. "I have all day and night to be a woman and have to think of nothing else." She didn't have to go out to work, and they were never short of money. Her health was no longer an issue. So what other concern did she have, except to win back her Husband?

It was sudden nostalgia that drove Peter to pick up his Mother's Diary for a gentle stroll through the past, and for a brief moment had wondered if he had the right book. But there wasn't another like it, and it was in the place he'd kept it. He briskly thumbed through the entire book and every page was blank, wiped clean as if the Diary had never been used. He remembered his mother saying something about correcting her mistake before leaving, and he suddenly felt relieved that the thing no longer existed. As long as it did there was the risk of someone else getting hold of it. What if Karen saw it and began asking questions? Where would he keep it so Daisy wouldn't get her hands on it? She was nothing like Kim, who was trusting and inordinately gullible. Kim would believe until she had reason to doubt, and wasn't in the habit of going through his things or searching his pockets.

Daisy was trained to be suspicious, and would doubt until she had good reason to believe. She wouldn't come right out and question him, but he'd see it in her eyes. She was trained to observe and missed nothing....One day he turned up at her Apartment with a faint smudge of lipstick on his Lips. It was the result of a minute peck on dropping Kim at the Supermarket.

She opened the door and stared at him a short time, then reached into his trousers pocket and took out his handkerchief. She drew it lightly across his lips and held it in front of him. "Is this your wife's or someone you ran into on the way over?" she said in a perfect May West impersonation.

The Diary had begun to worry him but he couldn't destroy it. Not his mother's words, they were too much a part of his own life. Now that she had taken care of it he felt no loss. It was hers, she'd taken it, and that was the end of it.

But Kim knew it s contents, he thought, but realized his mother would never have left the job half done. He went to Kim with the story, but she'd lost all trace of it from her memory.

"What Diary? I gave you no Diary," she scanned his face dolefully, eyes critically narrowed. "Peter what are you talking about? We were there together all the time and I didn't find a Diary."

He laughed. "Isn't it amazing, it must have been a dream."

"It was a dream, and a very vivid one," she said.

He later found he was able to look through the Diary and read each entry as though it was still there on the page in bold print. It had been meant for him and she'd ensured no one would again discover it's contents and use their love against him.

Peter had talked about moving in with Daisy and eventually getting married, but Daisy now saw this as just hollow talk and was getting restless. She had done what he'd suggested and made the move to administration, and now worked a straight 9 to 5 with weekends off. But he no longer spent the entire weekend locked away with her, and would leave her bed about midday on Saturday and head home. Between 8 pm and midnight, he'd see to Kimberly's needs, then get dressed and be at Daisy's for 12.30am. Probably taking her out to a Club for a few hours, depending how she felt. Most nights she just wanted to bed down with a bottle of Champagne.

On Sunday they'd rise about 2pm. He'd have a light lunch with her and get home for 3 or 3.30, and would spend Sunday night at home. This didn't sit too well with Daisy and she complained bitterly about being short-changed. She couldn't understand why he had to be running back home to a woman he didn't love or care for, when they didn't share the same bed or had sex anymore. She now had every weekend free but he wasn't there with her. This duty suited him perfectly, and would allow them time for each other. No more turning up to find she'd left him a note.

"Sorry Darling, had to work. These crooks have no conscience and are a very thoughtless bunch. Keep the good stuff warm for me, and put the cold stuff on ice, I'll need a full measure of both when I get back. Don't you dare leave I'll see you at nine."

She would invariably return to find a note scribbled on the back of hers saying he couldn't wait.

All of a sudden Kim started putting on weight and in one week she'd gained five pounds. "Are you sure you're not pregnant?" Peter inquired.

"Have you forgotten I've been sterilized? And besides, I'm seeing a period at the moment," she made a face.

"Are you sure?" he quizzed her.

"Would you like to check for yourself?" she smilingly offered.

"No thanks, I'll take you word for it."

"Why this sudden preoccupation with pregnancy, I'm only putting back the weight I lost. Our lives are getting back to normal and my body is responding. Soon I'll be back to the shape you fell in love with."

Every pound she added brought them closer and was another nail in Daisy's coffin. One evening Kim overheard him telling Daisy he couldn't see her that evening because he was working late, then he took Kim straight off to bed with a bottle of Bollinger. No man could have a better mistress than his own wife, he told himself. She was on the verge of winning the biggest battle of her life with sheer patience and fortitude. No fights or accusations. She could look back with pride and dignity. There were no severed limbs or bloodstained walls or Carpet littering the path behind. Not one angry, or even slightly naughty word had passed between them since the day he brought it into the open. Except the ones he used as they made love.

One Saturday morning after an exceptionally passionate night of lovemaking, she felt sick and ran to the bathroom, sank to her knees and emptied her stomach in the bowl. "Kim you're pregnant." she heard his excited pronouncement behind her. "I said you were," he gushed like an agitated bottle of Champagne.

What is he talking about? she wondered, unable to respond as the food continued to desert her stomach. My last period ended four days ago.

"Kim you're expecting, my mother said…. " he quickly caught himself. "My mother said it could happen. That you could be pregnant and still have a period. She was right, you are pregnant." Kim will become pregnant. He ran his mother's words through his head. I love you Patricia West…I love you. I don't know how you did it but thanks.

Kim got up and washed her face and mouth, he handed her the Towel. "Don't do this to yourself," she said, reproaching him. "Darling, you're trying to live an impossible dream, one that will never come true. I have been sterilized and is still having normal periods. Those are facts that cannot be shoved aside and I don't care what your mother said."

He scoffed. "Why are you having morning sickness if you're not expecting? You had it with Karen and Michaela and is having it again, why?"

"Peter I'm not having Morning sickness," she smiled. "It's that thing you had pushed up to my stomach for most of the night that did it. That was last night's dinner you just forced out of me."

He put his arms around her, their laughter reverberating around the bathroom.

Peter was happy to let the debate slide into conviviality for the moment, he was too elated to argue the matter any further. His mother had said so and he needed no further confirmation. Everything she'd predicted had come true.

Daisy was hanging by a slender thread and he could barely understand it himself. This was something he'd refused to believe a month ago.

Daisy was such a warm, vibrant person. He'd be sitting quietly watching TV and she'd saunter out the Bathroom dripping wet, toss him a towel and sit on his lap, soaking him to the skin as he dried her body. He loved every little thing about her and can't understand what could have brought about his rapid change, and was sure his mother had a hand in it. This was none of his doing, he did not go off her. Just as she'd wiped Kim's memory clean, she was also cleaning up his act with Daisy.

To humor him Kim had agreed to see the doctor that Monday Morning. The Blood drained from her face when he announced she was about twelve weeks and could be carrying twins. She burst into tears and threw her arms around to Doctor.

"Wait a minute," he said laughingly. "There is the man you should be hugging, I'm not responsible."

"How did you know?" she asked as they drove home.

"It was a lucky guess," he said modestly.

"Peter, you weren't guessing you knew. You said it for the first time ten weeks ago and kept repeating it, how did you know?"

"It was a combination of wishful thinking and a feeling in my bones."

"Some bones," she said cynically. "Peter I'm happy but I wonder if we dare? Things have a habit of going wrong just when we think they're perfect."

"Come on snap out of it,," he patted her knee lightly. "Let's move ahead and stop looking back. Someone is looking out for us and I feel we've got it right this time. I don't know why Michaela died but there has to be a reason for her death, if only to show us we shouldn't take life, or each other for granted. Her death took us into hell and spat us out again. This time around I know we're stronger and will be ready for whatever lies ahead."

Daisy was looking at a Pair of shoes in British Home Stores when someone bumped into her. She turned and was struck speechless. Kim wore a huge grin that became a laugh, and she then waddled off with Karen in toe.

"Peter, could you tell me how a woman you've not slept with for nearly a year gets to be pregnant?" Daisy inquired.

He scratched his head.

"Peter, she's your wife and I couldn't tell you not to fuck her, it wasn't my place. You're the one who told me you weren't. You lied to me without reason. There was no need to give me all that shit about moving out of her bedroom, you might have been out of her room, but you weren't out of her crotch."

"Daisy, you're being unreasonable…"

"I'm unreasonable? Why, because I expected you to keep your promise to me? You said you'd leave her, and while you had me believing that, you were planning to start another family, and had the operation reversed."

"I have not been planning to start a family and Kim didn't have an operation, and what the fuck you complaining about?" he suddenly got angry. "Everything has its price. How do you think I managed to get out and sleep with you, I had to keep her happy…."

"So it's my fault? … You fucked her to pay for the times you spent with me? Next you'll be telling me how much you hated it, but did it just for me, and when were you planning to let me know she was pregnant? She looks about six Months and it would seem I'm the only one who didn't know. What hurts most is that you've deceived me, not that she's pregnant, she's your wife and if you can't make her Pregnant, then who can? I just think you should've had the decency to share your plans with me, after all, I am a part of those plans, or am I?" Peter quickly got bored with the conversation and lapsed into silence.

Chapter 29

Kim was six months when Bonnie had her baby, a boy weighing in at a little over seven pounds. Kim and Peter were at her bedside when her parents arrived and discretely got out the way. Her father kept peering at the Baby but said nothing. Not a single word. Not even hello. Adrianne did all the talking, rattling on about everything and nothing in particular.

Bonnie just listened, occasionally glancing at her father, who refused to meet her eyes.

Slowly Adrianne got around to talking about the baby. She said he was her Grandson and was proud of him. How it wasn't right for her first Grandchild to be living with someone else. They were family, but it still wasn't right, and wanted her to come home.

At one time Bonnie would've laughed in their faces, but she was now a lady. She smiled sweetly. "You are joking, aren't you?" she asked.

"We mean it," her mother answered.

"Where would we sleep?" she said quietly. "Are we coming back to share a bed with May?"

"We'll get a Cot for the baby," her father offered.

"Thank you both, but you should've thought of that before you threw me out. I'm not coming back. Uncle Peter is putting on an extension and the Baby will have his own room."

"You are thirteen years old and we can make you come home," the wimp asserted himself.

"Yes I was thirteen and pregnant when you kicked me out and it didn't bother you, and by the way. I was fourteen two weeks ago, thanks for the card. Happy Birthday to me. That's how much you care about me. You can forget about me ever coming back, and if you think you can force me, you're wrong," she looked straight at her father. "You'd better not try anything or I'll have plenty to say. Know what I mean Dad?"

"What do you mean by that?" her mother asked.

"You ask him," she lifted her head in his direction. "Ask him….My father," she snarled, almost forgetting she was a lady.

Kim had decided not to say anything to Bonnie before the Birth, but the day she came home from Hospital Kim pounced, demanding the truth.

Bonnie explained how she'd sold an image of sexual experience when she was in fact a virgin and clinging to her prize with both hands. Her father, like everyone else, had bought her act and tried to rape her. After beating her up, he didn't bother with her for a time, until one day they were alone in the house and he brought a drink up to her room. She hadn't asked for one, but he brought this glass of coke and handed it to her. He said he was going out and would be back in three hours. She couldn't understand why he was telling her this. However, she did hear him go down the stairs and slam the front door.

She took a sip of the drink and thought it tasted funny but told herself it must be diet. After finishing the drink she felt tired and lie back on the bed. The next thing she remembered was May waking her two hours later. She felt a strange discomfort and a burning sensation she'd never felt before. She went to the bathroom to look at herself in the mirror, and noticed her knickers were back to front. She knew then that he'd drugged her and had pretended to leave the house, then raped her and went out, just to be sure he wasn't in the house when she came round.

Bonnie wanted to tell her mother but she wasn't much help the time before, and she couldn't prove it. She would not accept such a flimsy story and would tell her. Go wash yourself and forget it. An hour later her father came home and she told him she knew he'd drugged, and raped her.

"Prove it," he said then laughed.

"Aunt Kim, I didn't know what to do and there was no one I could tell, but was sure he'd raped me, and couldn't get it out of my head that he could make me pregnant. I remembered seeing something on TV about the Police checking an empty glass for traces of drugs. I told him I still had the glass and was taking it to the police. I came home the next day to find the room had been searched, and knew he had done it. He had raped me and was trying to destroy evidence that didn't exist. When I realized I was pregnant with my father's child I wanted to kill myself, and almost did, but as time passed I began to accept it and decided to have the baby. After seeing what losing a child had done to you there was no way I was having an abortion. I waited until was nearly five months, because I heard they couldn't do an abortion that late. Then told him I was carrying his child. He went white and almost fainted. He went upstairs and told Mom she had to get me out or he was going. Pointing out that with her reputation she'd never get another man. She broke down in tears begging him to let me stay. He hit her. "Get the bitch out or I'm going," he shouted.

All of a sudden Peter no longer needed Daisy, she was just a sexual adventure. The sex was still electric but he'd lost that addictive craving for her body and her company. This wasn't helped by a pervasive discontent which had become a part of her. He could no longer please her and the laughter had vanished from their lives. He was frequently searching for excuses not to visit her, and when they did meet he was restless and uneasy, while she kept telling him she still loved him and would wait for him. Then would contradict herself with numerous inquires about his plans when the baby comes, and how long after that would she have to wait? Not unreasonable questions for one who'd put her life on hold for him, but unknown to her the deal was off. It was just that when the time came to tell her his spine suddenly sagged he couldn't get it out, and had made some off-handed promise to sort it out when the baby was born.

Daisy wasn't one of these blind, subservient women who believed anything, but this was the role she'd willingly adopted at his feet, and would swallow the most unpalatable excuses. Twice a week he'd see her for sex, and to renew old promises and feed her new ones.

She said there was no point in being home in bed every night if she had to be alone, and was resuming her old duties with a new partner. Assuring him that when he needed her she'd be there, even if it meant leaving the force. If she thought this would upset him she was wrong, it gave him an excuse not to see her.

Seven days later when he turned up pretending to be upset, she apologized, then took him into the bedroom and undressed him. He still couldn't resist her, and stood wondering how long it would be before he found the strength to say no to her?

She was wearing blue-green eye shadow. The first time he'd seen any trace of make up on her face. All she'd ever used was Estee Lauder Cream Cleanser, and Swiss Performance Cream, and of course a pale pink lipstick.

"Why the change of image?" he asked.

"It goes with the changing times," she said. "You're changing and I have to try and hold your interest, and add a little mystique to my fading beauty."

He shook his head. "Your beauty hasn't diminished since the day we met."

"Something has gone missing and if it isn't from my side, then it's yours. What's happened to us Peter? What has gone wrong? If we are through I'd rather you come out and tell me, than have me hanging on to promises you can't honor. You owe me that much." she said with a flourish of defiance. This quickly frittered away into a smile of an odd pedigree, a kind of obsequious acceptance. "It's ironic, but I'm so in love with you that I fear I'll go on being your mistress whatever happens." She looked at the time. "Seven thirty, it's time for work," she said, kissed him and got out of bed. She didn't go to the bathroom but climbed straight into a clean pair of white, satin knickers. One of a set of twelve he'd bought her. Next, she delicately squirmed into a pair of sheer, black tights. "Darling I'm taking you to work with me tonight," she smilingly informed him. "And when I get home in the morning I'm going straight back to bed with you. These days I have to take you anyway I can, when I can."

Two hours later she was dead. Daisy and her new partner were caught in a hot pursuit along Bristol Road South, the car skidded, left the road and hit a tree. They died instantly.

The following Monday Peter and Karen attended her funeral service, held at Saint Martins in the Bullring. As they stood for the first hymn he heard Karen snuffling and looked at her, she was crying. He put his arms around her. "I know how you feel," he said softly. "I loved her too." He thought of his mother's words. "We cannot harm the living," and wondered if she'd found a way to break the rules. Someone or something had plucked Daisy from his life, but why should I complain? he asked himself, and once again counted his blessings.

Bonnie's baby was christened, David James Turner. Kim thought about telling her the truth about her father, but decided not to, at least not yet. Not until she'd spoken to her mother.

When Kim told Adrianne that Keith was the baby's father she impatiently retorted. "I already know that. Keith has told me."

"And what are you doing about it?" Kim wanted to know, trying hard to repress her distaste.

"Nothing," she grunted irritably. "It's all over, finished. "The little slut gave herself to him and he took it. I'm not happy with what he did but I blame her just as much."

Kim was surprised. "Oh, so you don't know the truth, well it's time you did. Your daughter didn't give herself to him, he drugged, and raped her. It may also interest you to know she was a virgin."

Adrianne sat staring blankly at her. "Can you prove any of that?" she said brutally.

"Can you prove his version is the truth?" Kim asked her.

"No, but that is the one I choose to believe," she snapped.

A cold look came into Kim's eyes. "Adrianne," she said quietly. "Do you know I believe Dad was right all along, and you're a fucking mistake. You don't belong to the human race and you never will," Kim spat and rolled out through the door like a barrel.

She later felt ashamed of herself and regretted her behavior. She knew better and should've held her composure. Losing her head only took her down to Adrianne's level and it solved nothing. The woman was a strange breed, who seemed to derive some kind of perverse satisfaction from being insulted and abused, verbally and physically, preferably at the same time. But it really didn't matter, as long as something nasty was being thrown at her, and there couldn't be anything nastier, and more depraved than Keith Turner. He was a stinking degenerate and they were well suited to each other. It was the children she pitied.

A month later Kim had twins. A boy, seven pounds ten, and ten minutes later, a little Girl seven pounds exact. Peter Philip West Jr. and Patricia Serena West.

The house was suddenly filled with screaming babies, and builders knocking the soul out of the place, to extend the kitchen and dining room, adding two bedrooms and an extra bathroom. The noise, dust and dirt were everywhere, but throughout the three and a half months it lasted Kim never complained. By this Bonnie had returned to school and Kim had three babies to care for. None of whom could sleep properly during the day because of the noise, but their cries were sweet music to Kim's ears. A rich symphony of love and thanks to God. At the end of each day she would be so tired that she'd go straight to bed the moment Peter got home and had dinner.

Since the day he knew she was pregnant he'd been nurturing thoughts of having a vasectomy. It was reasonable to assume Kim would need protection and they were no longer happy with the pill. Kim didn't push him either way and was ready to go along with whatever he decided. He made up his mind one night as he sat watching TV. He picked up a bottle of champagne and two glasses. It was 10.30 when he got to the bedroom and Kim was still awake.

As she sheathed him in rubber, she smiled. "Peter I think I'm going to miss this. Over the past month I've acquired a taste for rubber. Do you think I've become perverted?"

He chuckled. "Not nearly as perverted as I'd like," the rhythms of laughter in his voice.

"Some things I don't mind and will most definitely adopt, but I draw the line at opening the front door naked." They laughed.

The End

Lightning Source UK Ltd.
Milton Keynes UK
25 September 2009

144180UK00001B/201/P